Shadow War

by
Charles Lee Lesher

Combined Edition 2092

"Where knowledge ends, religion begins."

Benjamin Disraeli (1804-1881)

Republic of Luna

The Republic of Luna is humanities first extraterrestrial nation. Science and a humanistic society mark it as a target for the powerful Islamic Brotherhood, a global empire with billions of believers. Luna is a world created by pioneers whose only religion is the humane treatment of one another in their common struggle to survive the ultimate hostile environment, space. The heroes that conquered the moon must now defend it.

Shadow War combines *Evolution's Child - Earthman, Evolution's Child - Lunarian, Evolution's Child - Thread*, and *Science of the Republic* into one huge Print Edition.

File Compilation: 2016

Print ISBN 978-1-938586-09-5

Revised Edition

Book 1: Evolution's Child - Earthman

Book 2: Evolution's Child - Lunarian

Book 3: Evolution's Child - Thread

Science of the Republic

Preamble

In a century filled with strife, the dogs of war are gathering once more. By late 2092, climate change and war have devastated the planet. Even thinned by bloodshed, famine, and disease, Earth's population exceeds 10 billion. Food and water are in short supply, refugee's number in the hundreds of millions and lawlessness abounds. Humanity is in turmoil.

Religious zealots exploit this despair, claiming it's God's punishment for man's misdeeds. Within the North American Federation, Christian theocracy displaced democracy, plunging once proud America into a Dark Age. On the other side of the planet, the Islamic Brotherhood controls a third of the world from Indonesia, across Asia and the Middle East and well onto the African continent, India the only holdout. China, the leading space faring nation on Earth, allies with the Brotherhood providing them with science and technology for a price. Only within the European Union is there still a semblance of individual freedom. The nations of the world align along sectarian lines as global violence escalates.

In sharp contrast, the Republic of Luna is a technocratic society where information flows freely and nothing is secret, a place governed by humanism and the laws of science. Out of necessity, life on an airless world burrows deep underground and to stay alive, Lunarians unlock nature's deepest secrets, gaining mastery over the genetic foundations of life itself. In doing so, they become the first true extraterrestrials.

From Washington to Rome to Mecca, when Earth's theists learn of the Lunarians meddling in human genetics, they denounce them as abominations. Prince Ahmed Mohammed Al Zarqowi, Caliph of the Islamic Brotherhood, believes he can hide behind this turmoil to attack Luna with impunity and create humanity's first multi-planet empire. To the Caliph this is simply the next step in a plan to bring an unbelieving world under Islamic Law. He unleashes forces intent on destroying the Republic before it's a half-century-old.

The Players

Quan Kiai

- » Captain Kitajima Osaka
- » Master Sergeant Susan Hackling
- » Doctor Howard Grady
- » Lieutenant Tempel Dugan
- » Lieutenant Tatiana Tushar
- » Sergeant Consuela Navarro
- » Sergeant John Kipper
- » S.I.T. Angel Lopez
- » S.I.T. Samantha Odegaard
- » Officer Lei Cheung
- » Officer Brice Guyart
- » Officer Marcel Piqualow
- » Officer Karl Svensson
- » Officer Corazon Montano
- » Officer Karyl Stormberg
- » Officer Zoey Tanaka
- » Officer Alonzo Tushar

Lunarians

- ❋ Analyst Lazarus Sheffield
- ❋ Captain Lindsey Marquest
- ❋ Pilot Nell Goddard
- ❋ Councilor Abigail O'Neil Dugan
- ❋ Security Chief Corso Dugan
- ❋ Officer Cristobal Calatrava
- ❋ Magi

Islamic Brotherhood

- ☾ Mohammed Basayev
- ☾ Imam Nassah Bakr
- ☾ Commander Ghafour
- ☾ Major General Abdel Salam Arif
- ☾ Minister Hasin bin Aunker
- ☾ Captain Mustafa Malik
- ☾ Havildar Anwar Jafa
- ☾ Dalal

Minor Players

- ☼ Isaac Crenshaw
- ☼ Constance Haig
- ☼ Tara Dugan
- ☼ Mallory Higgins
- ☼ Lee Chin
- ☼ Justine Harman
- ☼ Nicole Dugan
- ☼ Elizabeth Dugan
- ☼ Krystin Dugan
- ☼ Skylor Dugan
- ☼ Jordan Dugan
- ☼ Jamie Dugan
- ☼ Ben Dugan
- ☼ Zachary Taylor
- ☼ Yang Lee
- ☼ Chen Zhi
- ☼ Odessa Simpson
- ☼ Zechariah Hargrove

The earth, the air, the land and the water are not an inheritance from our fore fathers but on loan from our children. So we have to hand over to them at least as it was handed over to us.

Mahatma Gandhi (1969 - 1948)

Book 1: Evolution's Child – Earthman

"My earlier views of the unsoundness of the Christian scheme of salvation and the human origin of the scriptures have become clearer and stronger with advancing years, and I see no reason for thinking I shall ever change them."

Abraham Lincoln *in a letter to Judge J.S. Wakefield, 1862*

North American Federation

*"It is always better to have no ideas than false ones;
to believe nothing, than to believe what is wrong."*

Thomas Jefferson (1757-1820)

The semi is full of lettuce, radishes, and onions on their way to market. The driver doesn't think twice about barreling through the green light at full speed. He never sees the white sedan, hitting it square in the side.

With a terrible sound of rending metal and breaking glass, the impact obliterates the little car, sending it spinning wildly across the intersection to wrap around a metal pole.

Lazarus sprints towards the wreckage but no matter how fast he runs, he can't make any headway. The smashed car bursts into flames. He throws up his hands protecting his face from the intensity. No one

could survive the inferno.

"Rachel," Lazarus cries out. A child screams. Lazarus falls to his knees, tears streaming down his face.

"You can't help them now," a man's voice said from somewhere behind him. "God have mercy on their souls."

ЯL

The woman entered the bedroom. "Lazarus... Wake up."

The man in the bed groaned and pulled the sheet over his head. "Rise and shine." The voice pulled him out of his nightmare but cannot purge it from his mind. The horror of it sticks with him.

"Lazarus, you're sweating. Are you ill?" The voice almost sounds like Rachel but it's not. Rachel's been gone two years yet the pain of her death has never dimmed thanks in part to this damn machine.

He moved into Hayden's Crossing right after his wife and little girl died in a horrific traffic accident. He never even had to pack. The Regional Director of Homeland Security, his boss, John Dempsey, ordered everything moved even before informing Lazarus of the tragedy. The director was thoughtful that way and Lazarus appreciated the personal attention at the time. He never had to go back inside the house that he and Rachel had shared with Courtney.

The surrogate arrived a few weeks later. The director had volunteered Lazarus for a study to determine if using surrogates could alleviate a person's grief. Lazarus couldn't believe it when they first introduced it to him, a machine that looked like Rachel. It smiled, laughed, and agreed with him on everything. It may look like Rachel, but it wasn't.

The study doctors insisted that he treat her just as he had treated Rachel, including sex. They even had a pastor come and talk to him. The man of god assured Lazarus that having sex with a machine did not constitute fornication and he spoke for the church.

Still, Lazarus resisted for several weeks but finally succumbed after dinner one night. Two bottles of wine, good food and a massage wore him down. After all, the surrogate did look and feel like Rachel. It was easy and he was human. He learned fast that the surrogate couldn't refuse him anything.

Lazarus throws off the sweat-soaked sheets and sits up pushing his unruly mass of hair out of his eyes. "I'm fine," he said evenly. It wouldn't be good to attract any undue attention on this of all days.

"Good, because today we are going on a vacation. Vacations are fun," the surrogate said cheerfully.

"How would you know?" He couldn't resist baiting it.

The machine looks at him for a moment, smiles and said, "I must have read it somewhere." She smiles even broader. "We are going to have so much fun." The machine claps her hands in front of her face like a little girl anticipating a new doll. It was something Rachel had done on occasion and it sent a jolt through Lazarus.

Lazarus gathers himself before responding, "You're right. We're going to have a great time."

Director Dempsey insisted Lazarus take the surrogate on his vacation. Lazarus tried to convince him that he needed a break from it but no one argues with the director for long.

Lazarus stands and moves past the surrogate pulling the heavy drapes aside letting in the early morning light. He'll miss the view from his ninth floor apartment. Directly below is manicured grass and concrete with Tempe Town Lake along one side. A tall wrought iron fence surrounds the complex. Opposite the lake, a road cuts into the hillside past a large sports stadium southeast of the apartments. The huge structure was a remnant of a bygone age and falling apart. It was the unobstructed view of the Superstitions due east that he enjoyed most. This morning, towering dark clouds beautifully backlit by the rising sun hang heavy over the mountains.

He turns away and goes to the kitchen, the surrogate following a few steps behind. Pouring a steaming cup of black coffee, he heads for the shower.

"Fix me toast with orange marmalade and a small glass of juice."

"Yes Lazarus," the machine watches him leave.

He and Rachel had dreamed up the Athens vacation two years ago. They had wanted to wait until Courtney was old enough to appreciate it. That dream ended on a dark Scottsdale intersection, a single lapse of judgment snuffing out their lives in an instant.

A few months after the accident, Lazarus considered canceling the vacation, and went as far as to broach the subject with a representative from the agency. The man had politely informed him that his travel arrangements were nonrefundable. It was all in the contract.

Just as well. The truth is, planning this trip was the last big thing he and Rachel had done together and fortunately, he couldn't work up the enthusiasm to fight them. It was easy to let things ride.

Emerging from the bath, Lazarus begins to dress. "Turn on *Good Morning Lord.*"

"Yes Lazarus," the surrogate didn't need the remote.

"...and read with me at First Corinthians 11:14.... *Doth not even nature itself teach you, that if a man have long hair, it is a shame unto Him?* Can it be any plainer than that? God doesn't want men to have long hair. It shames Him. Pray with me and support my bill with your votes and together we shall right this ungodliness."

As one of the leading fundamentalists within the Reformation Party, South Carolina Senator Elijah Hanley is a vocal advocate for a more literal interpretation of the bible. This morning he's on the Federation's most popular early show.

Senator Hanley is a short pudgy man, mostly bald with a ghost of white hair around three sides of his head and a neatly trimmed beard. He glows with the energy and vitality of a man much younger. The Senator is wearing his usual white shirt, black tie, and black greatcoat.

He chuckles when reporters call him Modern Moses, but never corrects them.

"I tell you my brothers and sisters, the increase in violence in our cities, the crop failures all across the Midwest, rising sea levels and hurricanes pounding our shores, are all signs of **His** displeasure. We are falling away from **God** and must find our way back before it's **too late**." The Senator waves a fat index finger at the camera.

Screw you Senator. I will keep my hair. Lazarus also keeps his true feelings to himself. He shoves a stray strand back behind his ear.

Lazarus has planned for weeks what to take. In his bag are his bible and a well-worn copy of Robert Heinlein's *Time Enough for Love*, the only thing he has that belonged to his father. So far, the 120-year-old novel has escaped the Morality Commission's black list, but it's only a matter of time. Tucked into Heinlein's novel are several photos and a packet of aging longhand letters, fading ink on brittle paper.

Munching on a piece of toast, he adds a hygiene kit, a new Achilles soccer cap, his hair brush, and an antiquated VR headset, the only device he could get approved by Homeland Security to take out of country. He doesn't bother packing clothing, preferring to buy new instead of lugging the old around.

The man that followed Senator Hanley on the show is a pencil necked geek wearing a buttoned down blue business suit at least two sizes too large and a bright orange tie. His beak-like nose overshadows a lipless mouth, thin mustache, and receding chin. Narrow eyes dart about restlessly under greasy black hair.

"The North American Federation don't need to get involved with the length of hair of its citizens." His shrill voice grates on Lazarus. "For too long, we have stood by and watched our freedoms slip away, one little bit after another until they're practically gone. We don't need the government making laws about how long our hair should be. Some things are better left up to individu..."

The Earthnet mediator interrupts the smarmy little man. "Thank you Professor Gladstone and thank you Senator Hanley for taking your valuable time this morning to join us in the No Spin Zone, the only place you get all the truth and nothing but the truth, so help me God... I now invite all of you to do your patriotic duty and cast your vote. This is, as always, an unofficial poll, but rest assured, Washington is listening."

Lazarus laughs, a strange mirthless sound, devoid of joy. The surrogate joins in.

"What are you laughing at?" Lazarus asks.

"I'm laughing with you," the surrogate said cheerfully.

Lazarus uses the remote to cast his vote. He looks around the apartment one last time. How superficial his life had become. There's nothing here he gave a damn about.

"Call us a cab."

"Yes Lazarus," the surrogate said sweetly and follows him out the door.

They are alone on the elevator ride down. It's early for the residents of Hayden's Crossing. They're still in bed or having breakfast. Walking across the lobby, Lazarus waves impatiently as the attendant opens and holds the door for them.

"Have a great day, Mr. Sheffield. Rachel..."

"Henry, I've asked you not to do that." Lazarus shoots a hard glance his way. He wants to scream *'that's not Rachel,'* but instead said, "I'm fully capable of opening the door myself."

"I don't mind, Mr. Sheffield," the man smiles pleasantly. That too is part of his job.

Arizona in late October is beautiful. Even though the sun is well above the horizon, the chill is still in the air when Lazarus emerges. Outside is a courtyard surrounded by more tall buildings identical to his. The main drive encircles a small pond with a single jet of water rising a few meters straight up. The circle drive has a canopied stop in front of each building.

Lazarus is oblivious to the splendor as he walks to the cab.

The side of the vehicle has a sketch of an empty cross on top of Calvary hill with the words **Christian Cab Company** below. Lazarus hears the car unlock as they approach. The rear door on their side swings open and Lazarus climbs in. The surrogate follows.

"Where to?" the cabbie asks over his shoulder.

"Gateway Airport, Global Airlines," Lazarus replies settling back on the worn bench seat. The cab is neat and clean but at least ten years old, a lifetime for a vehicle in its occupation.

"Shouldn't be much traffic this early in the morning…" The cabbie said and proceeds to tell him all about rush hour and the horror he endures every day. Lazarus tunes him out, staring at the passing city without hearing a word the man said, lost in his own thoughts.

They navigate out of the neighborhood and onto a six lane surface street. This is an older section of the city, many of the buildings need paint and the roadway is full of potholes. Lazarus watches the shabby shops and fading strip malls go by and his stomach knots up. *Am I doing the right thing?* He takes a deep breath and runs his hand through his hair like a comb. It's his only choice.

He misses Rachel. This damned machine at his side has done nothing to ease the pain of her death. In fact, it made it much harder. Every time he looks at it, it reminds him of her, the real Rachel. It's an open wound that's been festering for almost two years.

God Damn. He misses Rachel. When he closes his eyes, he can feel her presence. His heart aches even as his destination instills a sense of adventure. Did the Pilgrims feel this way boarding leaky wooden ships and setting sail across the Atlantic, or settlers packing everything they owned into Conestoga wagons and heading west?

"Friday and Saturday's the best, taking home all those drunks whose cars won't start…," the cabbie said.

The cab enters the onramp and accelerates towards Interstate 10. The whine of the electric motor rises in pitch as it comes up to speed. Early morning traffic is light. They are almost alone on the wide ribbon of asphalt. Maintenance crews have the inner lanes segregated using concrete barriers. Trucks and other vehicles share the freeway in near perfect silence.

"You couldn't pay me to trade in my cab on one of those new models…" the cabbie drones on.

Now the scenery flashes by. Lazarus can only get fleeting glimpses of the structures and signage along the industrial corridor between Phoenix and Tucson. Lazarus runs his hand through his hair, pushing it back in place. *Relax, I can pull this off.*

The surrogate reaches out to hold his hand. "What's wrong Lazarus?"

He looks at her, "Oh… you know about me and flying. We don't mix very well."

"Fear of flying?" the cabbie injects. "Let me tell you. You would never get me in one of those machines. No sir. I'm stayin' right here on Mother Earth…"

It's a short trip to the airport. Located at the intersection of Interstate 8 and 10, Gateway International Airport is the Southwest's regional hub and services over a hundred million citizens yearly. Hypnotized by the city flashing by, and with thoughts of Rachel and his little princess filling his head, Lazarus doesn't notice when the cab cuts back across the lanes of traffic and climbs the airport's entrance overpass. He finds himself swinging in a great arc above I-10's sixteen lanes of traffic. Below him, the freeway is a ribbon threading through an endless city as far as he can see. He has a momentary pang, hearing his daughter ask sweetly, *"Daddy, are we up?"*

Descending from the heights of the overpass, the cab eases into traffic. The first checkpoint comes and goes unobtrusively, its MRI scanners poking into every nook and cranny looking for anything out of the ordinary. Comparing the results to the millions of previous scans, it finds nothing of significance.

"Never been outside Arizona myself..." the cabbie keeps talking.

As the vehicle passes through the open spaces surrounding Gateway's main terminal, Lazarus can see arriving planes in the crisp morning sky appearing almost motionless. The road tunnels below all three east-west runways. To his left, a huge Airbus Maximus lumbers through the sky in slow motion, touching down just as his cab dips into the shadowy passage below the runway. By the time they emerge, the giant plane is gone. The road curves away from the tunnel bringing into view the bone-white terminal and the silhouettes of planes clustered around its gates.

"Idiot politicians talkin 'bout puttin' in a second airport..."

The pride of Arizona, the terminal's main construction is an enormous structure that fills the horizon as the cab approaches. It reminds Lazarus of a giant circus tent that drapes and swoops over huge metal supports hundreds of meters tall, each topped with an radiant Christian cross that's visible for many kilometers. The building itself is shaped in a giant cross and when the sun is just right, it can be seen from space.

"Too much vote'n if you ask me..." the cabbie never stops talking.

The main thoroughfare drops incoming travelers along a concrete and glass canyon running through the heart of the airport. The outside lanes on both sides are for unloading passengers, the inner lanes for through traffic. The cab stops a short distance from Global Airline's main entrance.

The cabbie twists about to look at Lazarus, "Total is ninety-six thirty-five. It's already been deducted," the cabbie said when Lazarus reaches into his pocket.

Lazarus gives the man a fifty, "God-be-with-you."

The man beams, "God-be-with-you, and a pleasant journey." It's the best tip he's had in over a year.

Clutching his bag, Lazarus steps out and looks around, half expecting airport security to be waiting. Around him, a steady succession of vehicles squeezes into curb side openings as soon as they become available. As one pulls out, a new one takes its place in a tightly choreographed dance of disembarkation. Farther down, busses disgorge their passengers. The drop-off area seems tiny in the vastness under the canopy.

Lazarus moves through the crowd with the surrogate staying close beside him. They stop in front of a large information screen. Lazarus scans the display until he finds Global Airlines Flight 119. It's on time in Gate 4B. *So far, so good.*

Turning abruptly, Lazarus nearly collides with an old couple. They had stopped behind him to read the screen. Both are wearing typical Federation attire, the man's dressed in a black suit, white shirt and dark tie. His wife's in a plain brown dress that covers her from chin to ankles, her faded red scarf the only real color.

"Forgive me. I need to look where I'm going," Lazarus addresses the man as is proper.

No one notices the exchange. Most people prefer to keep to themselves, their eyes never wandering far from what's right in front of them, wishing nothing more than to remain an indiscriminate particle amidst the homogeneity of humanity. Bright clothing is almost completely absent and the women all wear scarves covering their heads.

Putting his arm around his wife, the man said, "No harm done. God be with you, brother." The old woman smiles at Lazarus and ignores the surrogate. Her dark eyes are full of life putting the lie to the wrinkles surrounding them. She must have been beautiful once.

Lazarus returns the smile. Looking back at the man he said, "And with you, brother," he moves around the couple and heads for the screening area, the surrogate keeping pace.

Federation security personnel in cobalt blue uniforms are the only people within sight wearing Earthnet communication devices. They look like dark sunglasses. Decades earlier, during the Great Revival in '62, pious politicians enacted laws under the Freedom of Information Act forbidding all unauthorized access to Earthnet and giving themselves control of the manufacture, distribution and usage of the devices that provided it. Possessing an unlicensed Earthnet portal became a felony and every good American knows breaking the law's a sin. Consequently, the travelers sharing the terminal with him are barefaced and introverted, avoiding each other and the armed men among them.

He picks the shortest of the lines feeding into airport security. Like his fellow citizens, Lazarus avoids eye contact with the nearby guards. The line moves quickly. He cut the time tight on purpose but that's not what makes him run his fingers through his hair, time after time. He isn't exactly afraid of flying. Flying just makes him jumpy, that's all. Running his hands through his thick hair charges his courage like a capacitor sucking up voltage, a habit he picked up years earlier. Most times, he doesn't even know he's doing it.

The security scanners are contained in tunnels that each passenger must pass through to go deeper into the airport. Upon entering, the bioID embedded in his left hand provides Lazarus Sheffield's complete personal history to the DHS database. Comparing this data with his prerecorded and approved travel plans verifies his current activity. Meanwhile, powerful olfactory sensors identify and categorize substances on him and his clothes down to parts per million, and a bank of MRI scanners sweeps over him many times looking for anything unusual inside his body or belongings. Finding nothing out of the ordinary, he receives authorization to enter the terminal. The entire security process is complete by the halfway point in the tunnel. If DHS lifted his authorization, armed police will be waiting at the far end.

The sides of the tunnel glow with a tranquil green, specially designed by DuPont to calm a troubled psyche. Lazarus walks slowly down its length, convinced this is where his journey ends. Sweat beads up on his forehead. He swipes at it with his sleeve. The automated tracking and surveillance system recognizes his body's nervous signals but attributes them to his documented phobia of flying, something he's counting on. Upon emerging, he moves forward with his fellow travelers.

Just when he thinks he's made it past the checkpoint, a heavyset security guard steps in Lazarus's path, taking him by the arm saying, "Sir, please come with me." He motions to the surrogate, "You too, come with me."

Shock and dismay flash through Lazarus, "Is there a problem officer?" He asked as the guard pulls him away from the stream of passengers, a few of whom glance fearfully at the enfolding scene. Lazarus finds himself staring at the thick black mustache beneath the dark lens of the guard's visor.

Suddenly, a vice clamps around his other arm. He utters a startled yelp. The two guards hustle Lazarus into a waiting area. The surrogate follows smiling pleasantly. The second officer points at a row of chairs lined up against a wall and orders gruffly, "Sit."

Lazarus obeys and the surrogate sits beside him still smiling.

Something's gone terribly wrong. He runs his fingers through his hair. He must maintain a clear head.

He stares at the officer's twitching mustache. The man's talking rapidly with someone online. Nodding, the officer abruptly turns and walks towards Lazarus.

Lazarus convinces himself in those few seconds that he's about to be arrested. Everything he knows about reeducation flashes through his mind.

"Thank you for your cooperation, Mr. Sheffield. It's standard procedure to check the travel permits of any Homeland Security officer leaving the Federation. I hope we didn't delay you too much." The guard's words say one thing but his body language another.

Confused but relieved, Lazarus manages to stammer, "No, not at all." The guard escorts them to the exit and returns his bag.

Lazarus glances back. The guard stands at the checkpoint staring after them as they disappear into the cavernous terminal.

Bewildered but elated, Lazarus follows the signs down several flights of stairs before finding the subway that will take them out to Terminal 4. He stands and waits patiently for the next train, the smiling surrogate at his side. The crowd is so thick by the time the train arrives they have no choice but to move with it as it surges aboard. Neither Lazarus nor the surrogate manages to get a seat. He stands clutching a cold stainless steel rail, his bag slung over his shoulder. The surrogate just stands there.

The acceleration's smooth and almost unnoticeable. Infomercials flash by on the walls outside the cars windows. One is selling a Hawaiian time-share and another is pitching the spiritual insight of Reverend Gausault's newest book, *When Angels Speak.* The passenger's move forward in anticipation as the train comes to a stop. The doors are not fully open when the first traveler squeezes out followed closely by the horde. Lazarus has lived with crowds his entire life and deals with it stoically. He knows nothing else.

While walking up the stairs back to the surface, he can't stop thinking about the incident at the checkpoint. Why did they let him go? The authorities don't move until they're sure they have a person dead to rights. Then they move quickly and decisively.

He's lived under the Federation's eye his whole life but this felt different. *Am I bait?* DHS agents could be following him to identify his contacts, waiting for him to lead them to others before arresting them all. Much more likely but it still didn't make sense. Why alert him by stopping him at security?

He shudders, feeling like the mouse in a game of cat and mouse, a sentiment shared by most Federation citizens at one time or another. *As far as I know, the vacation story's intact.*

The stairs lead up to a large circular room. Around its periphery are a number of airline gates. Gate 4B is bustling with activity as Lazarus and his surrogate approach.

Thirty minutes. He couldn't have timed it better.

He spots a small Old-Mex style citizen's lounge among the terminal's coffee shops and eateries. No telling when he'll have this chance again. "I need a drink…" Lazarus said to the surrogate. "It's good for my nerves." He heads for the cantina.

Inside, men sit on barstools and around the tables. A middle-aged brunette with bored eyes tends the bar. She's appropriately dressed in a formless turtleneck sweater and a scarf. Stepping up to an open section, Lazarus waits for her to acknowledge him and said, "Jack's Hard Cider, three fingers, straight up."

She nods, sets a shot glass on the counter, snatches a black labeled bottle from under the bar, and pours. Sliding it across, she said, "thirty-two-fifty."

Lazarus shakes his head, marveling at the cost of things in the airport, and peels off a hundred. "Bring me a refill in ten minutes and keep the change."

"Ten minutes," the woman said. That was quite a wad of bills. What else can she sell him? As johns go, this one doesn't look bad. She has a cot setup in one of the maintenance closets downstairs to supplement her income on occasion.

Picking up the drink, Lazarus walks over and sits at a table overlooking the terminal. The surrogate comes in and joins him. Bringing the small glass under his nose, he looks across the rim at the surrogate, "To our vacation."

She beams back at him, looking beautiful. "To our vacation." she repeats.

Taking a generous sip, he holds the fluid in his mouth, anticipating the coming fire. It burns all the way down, going off like a bomb at the bottom. He leans back letting the harsh elixir relax him from the inside out.

Several flights arrive at the various gates, disgorging their passengers and collecting more. DHS guards are evident everywhere. There are two at each gate and more walking the floor. No one looks, much less speaks to them. A child squeals loudly and runs from his mother, coming too close to a guard. Reaching out, the guard picks up the boy by the back of his shirt and holds him. Fear replaces glee and all's quiet once more.

The brunette sets his second drink on the table and picks up the empty. She stares at the surrogate wondering when this smiling bitch showed up. All thoughts of getting some extra cash slip away. "Is there anything else I can do for you?"

Lazarus glances up, "No, I'm fine."

"God-be-with-you," she said in the monotony of endless repetition.

"And-with-you," Lazarus replies. He notices something unusual about the man walking past in the terminal. He thinks back and tries to remember where he had seen him, realizing the man has passed at least twice before. Once means nothing, twice understandable, but three times starts the warning bells ringing in his head.

As inconspicuously as he can, Lazarus studies the man, medium build, short brown hair, and clothes that merge him into the surrounding crowd. If he were any more nondescript, he would be invisible. His luggage, pulled along behind him, is virtually identical to hundreds of others. He makes a beeline for the information panel, stopping and looking intently up at it, his back to the cantina. Turning abruptly, the man walks towards Lazarus.

Picking up his drink, Lazarus takes a sip, letting action cover his nervousness. With as little concern as he can muster, Lazarus casually focuses directly on the man. For an instant, their eyes meet and Lazarus is certain that the man is shadowing him. He's seen it done plenty of times and knows the routine almost as well as this field agent, but therein lies the heart of the matter. Lazarus has never actually been to the field. His participation as a DHS Senior Analyst was always early in the process identifying the target or later after the suspect was in custody. He finds it much different to be the target. His heart pounds in his ears.

Instead of arresting Lazarus, the man walks right past him and enters the dim interior of the bar. Now he's behind them. Resisting the temptation to turn, Lazarus pushes his hair back in place and takes a deep breath. He looks around the terminal floor. Field agents are never alone. Teams consist of at least two agents.

With relief, Lazarus hears the announced arrival of Flight 119. He gulps the dregs of the second shot and uses his peripheral vision to check on the man at the bar. Slinging his bag over his shoulder, Lazarus and the surrogate leave. He must stay cool and play the part of a man and his surrogate going on vacation. They walk side by side across the terminal.

If he's right and not just letting his imagination run amok, the normal procedure would be to watch and wait for the quarry to show their hand. Obtaining court evidence is simply a matter of time. Eventually, everyone who has something to hide gives it up. Just keep watching.

On the way to his gate, Lazarus pops a couple of mints designed to mask the smell of cider. A quick glance back at the lounge did not reveal any sign of the agent, but that doesn't make him feel any better.

They end up close to the front of the line. The giant Airbus Maximus is in plain view outside, distinctive with its double row of windows. Double-decker walkways extend out from the terminal servicing both the upper and lower decks of the Airbus. A seemingly endless stream of people exits the colossal aircraft. The big planes can deliver over eight hundred people anywhere on the globe and this one arrived fully loaded.

The disembarkation process is orderly and the flow of humanity finally dwindles and stops. An attendant steps forward and directs the people in the front of his line to proceed to the checkpoint. Again, Lazarus is sure this was as far as he's going to get.

"Please move forward. We have a lot of people to get aboard." The attendant looks bored as she walks up and down the line urging compliance. Some ignore her but most do as asked.

When Lazarus reaches the checkpoint, he passes his left hand over the reader. His seat number and name flash onto the screen.

"Good morning, Mr. and Mrs. Sheffield." The young flight attendant sees his unease. "Is something wrong?" She asked.

"No, nothing's wrong. I don't like flying, that's all. Not to worry. I fly often and it's always this way." Lazarus tried to disarm her concern with a smile.

"Just the same, I'll keep my eye on you," she said.

Lazarus finds their row and shimmies down until he comes to his seat. The surrogate follows and sits beside him, still smiling. A man, his wife, and their child are beyond his and a young man in a business suit takes the seat on the far side of the surrogate. Lazarus buckles the lap belt and lays his head back, listening.

From somewhere behind him a woman complains, "How can this machine possibly get off the ground with this many people. It don't seem natural."

"This is just the top level. There are five hundred more seats below us," a man drawls in response.

"Dear Lord, don't tell me that," she shrieks.

"Calm yourself woman. Put yourself in God's hands and everything'll be just fine," is the man's stern response.

Finally, after everyone's settled, the plane lurches forward. A powerful tug tows them all the way to the takeoff staging area before detaching. In spite of his phobia, Lazarus wishes he had a window seat, but that would be out of character.

Lazarus grips the arms of his seat as the giant plane lumbers down the long runway. He endures the takeoff and the steep climb to altitude. The ride is smooth up here, and quiet. He lays his head back and to his surprise, dozes off.

He awakes as the plane is landing. Athens International Airport is even more crowded than Gateway. Tens of thousands of people share the space under its enormous roof at any given time, day or night. Over a billion tourists pass through this single complex every year and it seems to him that most of them are still here.

As Lazarus and the surrogate move past an information board, he lets his eyes run down the list, careful not to give away what he's really looking for. He finds it. The next flight to Heaven's Gate is on time.

Looking around, he locks eyes with the man from the bar who turns away and disappears into the crowd. Lazarus is stunned. "Come on," he said to the surrogate. "I've got to use the facilities."

Stretching as far as he can see is what appears at first glance to be an ancient market, the facades of shops and stores line both sides in a capitalistic imitation of a 600 BCE Greek city street but much wider. This is the world famous Athena's Marketplace, a tourist trap of mammoth proportions.

The buildings have an ancient look, as if they truly have been here a long time. Tables loaded with merchandise are in front of each establishment and surrounded by shoppers. Down the center of the mall, thousands of people move in both directions. The web of struts and rafters holding up the roof diminishes the affect. Modern signs in several languages hang from the rafters, pointing the way to other gates, ground transport, and luggage carousels, a reminder that this is an airport and not just another mall.

The last big weekend of the fall season sweeps Lazarus along like flotsam on a river of humanity. The predominantly Asian horde paws through the merchandise packed along its banks, gleefully haggling with the locals to get the best price. To his left several small electric trams ease their way through the crowd, their bells dinging warnings for people to clear a path. A thousand different sounds assault his senses.

Lazarus discreetly looks for the agent but fails. The throng is just too thick. Carried along by the crowd, Lazarus spots the entrance to his gate. He keeps going for another hundred meters then stops outside a public bathroom.

"Wait here," he tells the surrogate.

"Yes Lazarus."

Outside the bathroom is a traffic jam. Lazarus moves into this scrum. Once inside, he catches the eye of a young man among a group of young men standing over by the sinks. He gives him a subtle wink and head motion towards the stalls in the back. The youth looks Lazarus over and nods. Without a word, he comes over to stand next to Lazarus. They wait their turn.

Lazarus is first. When a stall comes open, he enters, shuts the door and locks it. Ignoring the smell, he removes his backpack and hangs it from the hook on the inside of the door. Bending down, he slips off his shoes being very careful not to step in the puddles on the floor. In place of socks, he's wearing soft-soled slippers of a style currently popular in Europe with the younger generation. He instantly loses almost eight centimeters of height. His blue jeans are next, exposing a pair of baggy shorts underneath. He transfers his cash money from his pants pocket to the shorts. Unzipping his red jacket, he slips it off revealing a dark blue t-shirt underneath.

Reaching inside his bag, he puts the copy of Heinlein's *Time Enough for Love* into his pocket and removes the hat and headset. He stuffs his shoes, jeans and jacket in beside the bible then hides the backpack behind the toilet.

He hears the toilet flush next door and someone new enter the stall. Lazarus taps his foot under the divider separating the two stalls. A second later, a large bath towel appears on the floor and someone whispers from under the panel. "Com'a mate. We dun got all day."

Lazarus lies down on the towel and slips under the panel with help from the youth. Standing up, Lazarus smiles and shakes his head. He holds up a small roll of bills.

"This will be the easiest three hundred Euros you have ever made. All I want you to do is walk out of here with me like we are together. Make it a good show and there will be another three hundred when we are back in the mall."

The young man stares at Lazarus for a moment, smiles and winks, then reaches out and takes the roll of money. "Whateve' U speak gove'na'. U da boss."

Lazarus puts his hat on backwards before sliding his thirty-year-old headset over it. State-of-the-art when it was new, its low tech is precisely why it's so popular with young Europeans. The lack of advanced features give the wearer a certain amount of anonymity by their very absence, not to mention it completely obscures the top two thirds of his face behind a dark shield. Unlike a modern visor which lazes directly into the wearers eyes, the image Lazarus sees is projected on the inside of the shield.

Lazarus takes several sections from the roll of toilet paper and stuffs it into his mouth. Chewing carefully, he works the paper into a long narrow blob that fits behind his lower lip extending out into his cheeks, breaking up his jaw line, making it difficult for the facial recognition software to identify him. The youth nods approvingly.

They exit the stall, arm in arm. The guy is all over Lazarus, making good on his deal. The two merge with those leaving the bathroom. Outside the exit, they pass within a few meters of the man from the bar. Lazarus doesn't trust himself to look at where he left the surrogate. She might see through his disguise.

Seconds later, they're in the market's main corridor, surrounded by people. In less than a minute, he's changed his height, posture, clothing, hidden his hair and most of his face behind a mask, and added a companion. Lazarus came up with this plan from watching countless

DHS training vids describing in detail the tricks of a terrorist, then added a few twists of his own. He slips another roll of money into the prostitute's hand.

The young man bats his long eyelashes at Lazarus, "Gracias. I hope you get away with whatever you're doing," he said in English with a Latin accent. He speaks a dozen languages including the pigeon talk used in his profession.

Lazarus hugs the lad, whispering in his ear, "Thanks. You might want to be someplace else for a while." The youth nods and they part ways.

Navigating the river of people, Lazarus spots what he's looking for. It's a large statue of the Greek goddess Athena. Armed with spear and shield, she's standing on a column in front of a temple. The goddess is serenely beautiful, gazing forever at the horizon.

Wide steps invite tourists to enter the Temple's inner sanctuary. Hidden speakers play classical Greek music. Outside the entrance, women dressed alluringly in revealing white robes call out to the people as they pass, enticing them to enter the Temple of Athena where they will find only the finest quality of merchandise.

Moving up the stairs, the nearest siren assures Lazarus that he will not be sorry. He stares at the young women, unaccustomed to such bawdy displays of nudity. Upon entering the shop, he glances at the time. If his calculations are correct, the employees of Athena's Temple should be finishing their break soon. He moves through the store picking out shoes, shirt, a pair of pants, and a small overnight bag, blending in perfectly with the tourists that frequent Athens.

He lays his items on the counter. From a rack close by, he picks out a pair of dark sunglasses, a cheap imitation of a Federation visor. He adds them to his pile. The touch panel pops up with the price and a voice informs him, "That will be three-hundred-fifty-one Euros."

"I want to talk to the manager," Lazarus states, knowing he must haggle or risk drawing unwanted attention.

"Certainly. One moment please," the voice answers.

Tourists, most of them Asian, far outnumber store employees who are easy to spot by their flowing Greek robes exposing one tit or the other. He sees several people who might be Federation agents but no one stands out. He must assume his deception has worked.

"Sir, may I help you?"

Lazarus turns and looks down at the bored little woman standing behind the counter. She's wearing a white robe with her left tit exposed and a gold belt drawn tightly about her narrow waist.

"Yes, I hope so. I want to purchase these items but the price seems excessive to me. I think two-hundred-fifty Euros is a fair price," Lazarus states.

"For you it would be, but for me, the Temple would lose money. We cannot stay in business long if I do that," she's clearly bored with a conversation she's had uncountable times.

"You won't stay in business if you don't sell your merchandise either. What about three-hundred even? I think I can stretch that far," Lazarus is acutely aware he's wearing baggy shorts, slippers, and a headset that hides his face like some EU teenager.

The woman knows Lazarus is not what he seems. He's obviously involved in some self-conceived fantasy, not the first to do that. After all, whatever happens in Athens, stays in Athens. "Very well… three-hundred plus tax totals three-hundred-forty-one Euros." She enters the sale before Lazarus can blink. When he still hesitates she adds, "The Union gets its cut. There's nothing I can do about that."

Lazarus shrugs and doles out three-hundred-fifty Euros while the woman puts his items in a bag. "So why is the Goddess of War the mall symbol?"

Amusement flickers across her face. "Athena is not only the Goddess of War and the patron deity of Athens but also the Goddess of weaving, pottery, and crafts."

Picking up a brightly colored cigarette lighter from a countertop basket, He asked, "Then this must fall into crafts?"

"No, that's a fire maker. It falls under the war category," the woman answers.

"Oh," he replies unsure if she's serious. He replaces the lighter and continues, "I'd like to change. Is your dressing room in the back?"

She points, "The door on the left. Someone's using it but they shouldn't be long."

"Thank you," Lazarus accepts his change, picks up the bag and walks deeper into the store. To his right is a second door, obviously not the dressing room. Lazarus busies himself by looking at racks of garments. Minutes later, the person in the dressing room exits and still he waits, feigning interest in a rather frilly shirt. Finally, it happens. Two employees emerge from the second door, laughing about something as they return to work. With his heart racing, Lazarus slips through the open door without even touching it, making sure it clicks shut behind him. This part had worried him greatly and now it was past.

He's in a warehouse. To his right is a paper-strewn desk, a computer touch screen peeking out from the mess. Boxes and racks of clothing fill the rest of the room. Near the large rollup door is a big pile of discarded packing and shipping material. Lazarus breathes a sigh of relief that no one's in sight.

The employee bathroom is a storage closet equipped with a toilet and sink. Lazarus uses his forefinger to clean his mouth of paper. Next, he removes the headset, strips and puts on his new clothing, tucking in the shirt and lacing up the shoes. Using another paper towel, he folds it carefully and wets it in the sink before inserting it into his left upper cheek. A second towel mirrors the first, blurring the outline of his high cheekbones, giving his face a round full appearance. The water soaked paper should escape notice in the MRI scans he will encounter, at least for a while.

He transfers everything he wants to keep into the new overnighter. Everything else goes into the empty shopping bag, which he hides among the boxes destined for recycle. Slinging the new bag over his shoulder, he completes his second changeover.

Lazarus unlatches the loading dock's rollup door and pulls upward. The rattling shatters the quiet. He looks over his shoulder at the mall door uneasily, half expecting someone to walk in.

Perched precariously on a narrow ledge a meter above the pavement, Lazarus pulls the door back down. Outside the massive building, he can see trucks backed up to various loading docks. Here and there, people and machinery move about keeping Athena's Marketplace stocked with goods.

Lazarus jumps off the ledge and begins walking along the backside of the mall.

Oil and tire rubber stain the concrete in front of each dock. Avoiding the worst of the mess, Lazarus moves as fast as he dares, passing under several of the giant rigs, their drivers too busy to take notice. Finally, he decides he's come far enough. Approaching the next trailer, he cautiously peeks into the gap between it and the storage room beyond.

A man and a woman are working inside unloading the delivery. Lazarus listens for a few minutes, keeping well out of sight. The woman is recording the items using a handheld scanner as the man expertly wheels them off the truck. On each trip, the pile grows in the center of her floor. Lazarus can't understand what they're saying, but it's obvious the two know each other.

He leans against the wall until it becomes quiet inside. Waiting patiently for several more minutes, Lazarus pokes his head into the room. Seeing nothing, he hoists himself up and moves behind the newly stacked boxes. Only then does he hear them. From behind the door to his left comes the unmistakable sound of two human beings in the throes of passion, the woman being particularly enthusiastic. Seems they know each other pretty well.

Lazarus walks down a short hallway, stopping to listen at the door. He concentrates, categorizing what he hears. This is another crucial moment where something unexpected can ruin everything. He doesn't know what's on the other side. Taking a deep breath, he squares his shoulders, opens the door, and moves through as if he belongs.

It's a gift shop. The shopper closest to the door has her back to him and the only person that notices him looks up but turns away. Lazarus walks through the store doing his best to look like just another tourist. No one pays him the slightest heed.

Lazarus picks up a miniature Parthenon as it would have looked in 400 BCE and marvels at the detail in the piece of colored plastic. Putting it back, he casually meanders his way back into the crowded mall. A few minutes later, Lazarus passes the restroom where he had made his first change of clothing. He spots the agent talking to a woman, slight with dark hair and pastel clothing, her features unremarkable, a perfect match for the man. Lazarus memorizes their faces as best he can.

As he watches, the woman shrugs and the man swears in frustration, unheard from this distance but intense. He grins, thinking about the trouble they'll be in when they finally admit they lost him. He's counting on them delaying until they're sure he's gone. Just thirty minutes more is all he needs. In the Federation, they would scan for his bioID to pinpoint his location. That's not possible in Athens where human rights have placed restrictions on the government's right to know where you are at all times.

Moments later, Lazarus is beyond sight of the agents. Athena's Marketplace was built almost thirty years ago and is considered one of the great wonders of the modern world. In a land of ancient learning and humanity's first democracy, this is but a hollow reminder of what once was. He pities the travelers who fly into Athens and never make it beyond this tourist trap. Lazarus shakes his head with regret when he realizes he's one.

He takes the corridor leading to his gate. Lazarus goes directly to the ticket console and places his left hand on the pad.

The image on the screen looks like someone's grandmother, kind, compassionate, and wise. Caring brown eyes and welcoming smile draws him in.

"Greetings, Mr. Sheffield. My name is Margaret. How may I assist you this morning?" She has perfect inflection and looks human in every way but she's not. AI's have been doing this type of work for many years and most people don't even realize they're talking to one, but Lazarus knows.

"I want to purchase a round trip ticket to Heaven's Gate, outbound on Frontier Flight 701 and returning in three days on Flight 1205."

"I'm sorry sir, but Flight 701 is full. May I offer you some alternatives?"

"No. I'm invoking DHS591 Section 9, Paragraph 34B of the International War on Terror. Use account number 119186722." His voice rings hollow and fraudulent in his own ears.

"Very well, please hold…" A mountain stream replaces grandma, its sights and sounds intended to be soothing.

As the seconds drag on, he stares blankly at the screen without seeing it. Lazarus succumbs to the temptation to worry about things he has no control over. His position within DHS authorizes him to make the purchase, and the number is for an offshore account that should not attract attention until he's well away. There should be just enough in it to cover the ticket and the penalty for bumping someone off a flight, unless DHS has frozen the account. Sweat trickles down his back and he wipes damp hands on his pants. At that moment, his plans seem foolish and transparent. From somewhere deep within grows the conviction that this will never work. Each second an eternity, he runs his fingers through his hair and stares at the screen.

Abruptly the AI reappears and said, "I have debited your account eight-thousand-four-hundred-fifty-eight Euros. Is there anything else I can do for you?"

AI's aren't curious. They run their programs and if he stays within certain parameters, nothing will happen. So far, Lazarus has only done what agents of the Federation, the European Union, China, and even the Islamic Brotherhood have been doing for decades. By the time anyone notices, he'll be gone.

"No," he said hoarsely, "That'll be all," not bothering to make nice. What would be the point? It's just a program.

With his boarding pass secured, he goes to the waiting area. The newly arrived Stratoliner empties quickly in comparison to the Airbus. Lazarus notes the strained faces and laborious movements as they pass just a few meters away. It must be the sudden immersion back into high gravity.

As his line begins to move, he avoids any thought he's going to make it. Nothing could jinx him faster than overconfidence. Running his hand through his hair for the hundredth time, he keeps a tight rein on his emotions, managing a weak smile for the young flight attendant at the boarding checkpoint. He's come too far to blow it at this late stage. *I'm going on a vacation, something to enjoy, not dread.*

As the line advances, he hears an angry voice back at the checkpoint, "What do you mean, my seat's been taken?"

"I'm sorry sir. There's another flight this evening and I'm sure you can get on it."

"Why can't I take this one? Fifteen minutes ago, I had a seat and now I don't? What gives?" The man asks irritably.

Lazarus glances back, sincerely hoping his little maneuver will not cause too much trouble. Besides, it's not as if he had a choice. The man is still arguing as he moves out of earshot.

It's a short walk down the tunnel to the Stratoliner. All he's leaving with is an out-of-print novel and an out-of-date headset. *I came into this world with nothing and I'm leaving it the same way.* At least he's not naked. He allows himself a smile.

Lazarus runs his fingers through his hair and walks right by the flight attendant, wiping away sweat from his upper lip with the back of his hand as he shuffles past. She thinks nothing of it, accustomed to people being nervous boarding her flights. After all, they're on their way to space, many for the first time. Lazarus finds his seat and stows his meager belongings.

Leaning down as though looking for something beneath his seat, Lazarus pulls the paper out of his cheeks, stuffing the soggy mass into a hollow. Straightening, he buckles in, fumbling with the unfamiliar four-point harness. He runs his hand through his hair dividing his attention between observing the activity outside his window and watching the stream of people entering the Stratoliner.

Near the end of the procession, Lazarus is stunned. No. It can't be. It was the surrogate. In total shock, he watched the woman nod pleasantly to the flight attendant and turn towards him. There was nowhere to run, nowhere to hide, but the closer she came, the more he realized, that's not the surrogate. Removing his sunglasses, he stared incredulously at the face under the bright blue scarf. It's Rachel's. A little older but it's Rachel.

She moves purposefully down the aisle, glancing at row markers, flashing her bright smile and quick wit along the way. Her movements, her smile, her connection with others, it's Rachel. She reached up and swept her long hair back in place sending memories cascading through long abandoned regions of his brain.

The thumping in his chest thundered in his ears. Lazarus can't take his eyes off her. The coal black hair held in check by a bright blue scarf, the tilt of her head, her radiant smile, it's Rachel and the closer she gets, the more surreal it becomes. Lazarus stares, his mind swirling in a million different directions as memories of his beloved wife overwhelm his senses. His vision narrows until all he can see is her, the chatter inside the Stratoliner recedes to the bottom of a well.

The woman stopped at his row, and looked down at Lazarus with a puzzled expression, "I believe this is my seat."

The spell shatters. Lazarus gasps and turns away, his senses reeling as they snap back to reality. Clearly, the lady is very attractive but she's definitely not Rachel. How could he think even for a moment that she was?

"Please forgive me. I thought you were someone else," Lazarus stammered.

"No worry... I rather like having that affect on a man." She flashed her smile at him.

It was an image Lazarus would never forget.

Heaven's Gate

*"All our science, measured against reality, is
primitive and childlike - and yet it is all we have."*

Albert Einstein (1879-1955)

The woman settles into her seat and said "Lindsey Marquest."
Lazarus hesitates, "Lazarus."

"Just Lazarus?"

"Lazarus Sheffield."

"Well Lazarus Sheffield, looks like we have a full plane today." She
looks him over. Square jaw… high cheekbones… long hair pushed
behind his ears… bushy eyebrows overshadowing intense blue eyes.
Not bad looking in a rugged sort of way. He was wearing a wedding

band on his finger and a Christian cross hung around his neck on a gold chain. The man reeked of tension verging on fear, and for that single fleeting moment, a deep sadness had flashed across his face.

"I believe you're right," Lazarus said, licking dry lips. They taste of paper. He watches her adjust the four-point harness around her tits.

Lindsey can sense his interest and puts on a good show. Glancing up, she catches him staring and smiles.

Lazarus grins weakly in return and looks away. When the hull door finally shuts, his worry shifts from the Federation catching him to what lies ahead.

With a lurch, the Stratoliner moves away from the terminal. On cue, the flight attendants spring into action, running through the obligatory safety presentation, pointing out the exit ports, flotation devices, and emergency beacons. Lazarus doesn't pay much attention. It only makes him more nervous to think about useless escape plans while streaking through the sky at seven kilometers per second.

Lazarus wipes sweat from his brow with the back of his hand and wills himself to relax. Lindsey smiles encouragingly.

The powerful tug pulls the Stratoliner in line with the other aircraft waiting for takeoff, shepherding it in time and space towards a very specific launch window. The tug releases it at the far end of a long ribbon of concrete and immediately the pitch of the hydrogen turbojets increase. The spaceplane picks up speed.

Acceleration pushes Lazarus deep into the padded seat and he feels the rotation as the nose rises. Seconds after liftoff, the wheels tuck away with a thud. A rivulet of sweat runs down his cheek.

Lazarus grips both armrests, knuckles turning white, his head hard back against the headrest. He hates heights. His knees grow weak just climbing a ladder, yet his eyes remain locked on the scene enfolding out his window.

Lazarus concentrates on the view, not his perspective, using the incredible detail to control his fear. Athens stretches out before him under the late autumn sun, its roads and structures partially hidden beneath the green canopy of an urban forest. Rising sea levels have blurred the coastline. When dikes and levees proved ineffective, people abandoned many of the world's coastal cities but Athens is relatively unscathed. Along the shore, rooftops stick out of the water. Other buildings are completely submerged. Yet, the majority of the city remains high and dry.

As the spaceplane banks into its trajectory, he catches a fleeting glimpse in the distance of the Acropolis and the Parthenon, influential architecture from the dawn of civilization.

As the avenues and buildings disappear into minutia, the world below becomes a mottled swatch of color bordered by the blue of the Mediterranean along one side and the many shades of browns and greens of the Greek peninsula on the other. The ship shudders and Lazarus feels the brief sensation of weightlessness as the hydrogen turbojets give way to the magnetoplasma thrusters.

Mountain climbers reaching the summit of Mount Everest, almost nine kilometers above sea level, can see the curvature of Earth's limb. It's so slight many think it's an optical illusion. Lazarus watches spellbound as the curvature becomes more and more pronounced.

As Mother Earth dwindles, the first bright pinpricks of stars appear. A sudden pitch change startles Lazarus and marks passage of the sound barrier. Later, a gradual fade to near silence as the outside air pressure drops to zero. Only the low throb of the ships thrusters remain.

Earth's mountains and seas dwindle to a mosaic of browns, greens and blues, and cloud systems become great white smears across the vast landscape. The higher he goes, the more fragile the atmosphere shrouding Mother Earth appears and strange as it seems, the less he fears.

Eight minutes into the flight, a chime softly rings out, "Welcome to space, everyone. We just exceeded one hundred kilometers."

Lazarus feels like cheering but holds his tongue.

The acceleration continues. The long sleek spacecraft keeps its nose pointed up long after the blue-sky morphs into the diamond-studded black-velvet of space.

Twelve minutes into the flight, Mother Earth is a giant globe spread out below him, only partially seen from his window. The sun is behind him and out of view. Before him, the intense points of light from a hundred thousand stars burn brightly, more stars than Lazarus has ever seen on even the clearest desert night.

"Your first time?" his neighbor asks.

Lazarus reluctantly turns away from the window. Lindsey smiles as their eyes meet and his reluctance fades.

"I don't like flying," Lazarus returns the smile. A bead of sweat rolls off his forehead and into an eye causing him to blink and rub.

"There's really nothing to be afraid of. Statistics show space travel is far safer than any ground transport," she replies.

Still shaking his head, "I'm not afraid, just aware. In an automobile, if you have a flat tire or the motor shorts out, you call roadside service. You can't do that out here."

"How far are you going?"

"Heaven's Gate… and you?" Lazarus said.

"Aldrin Station"

"Republic of Luna," Lazarus blurts. "Are you a citizen?"

"Yes," Lindsey nods.

"What do you do?" He asked.

"Up until yesterday afternoon, I worked as an engineer for MetCal, but not anymore."

In an instant, the last whisper of sound disappears and freefall begins. Lazarus feels as if he were falling. As far back as he can remember Lazarus has had serious nightmares about falling. As a child, they terrified him. As he grew older, he came to terms with the dreams but they still haunt him.

Lazarus grips the arms of his seat until his knuckles turn white. His inner ear delivers one message, his eyes another. It feels like his head is getting larger and his sense of time warps. A few seconds later, nausea threatens to bring up the liquor and his breakfast. He grabs an airsickness bag and prepares for the worst.

Lindsey raises her arm, signaling the attendant that her neighbor needs some extra help.

Lazarus accepts the pill offered by the pretty attendant floating above the aisle. He bites down on the nipple of the juice bottle and uselessly tips it back just as he would have done back on Mother Earth. Realizing his mistake, he squeezes the bottle.

The chime sounds again as one of the attendants prepares to address the passengers, "My name is Lee Fong, Sarah is the pretty one. We will be your flight attendants today. On behalf of Frontier Flight 701, let me welcome aboard everyone. We are currently on schedule to dock with Heaven's Gate in 42 minutes, weather permitting." He chuckles at his own joke. "Seriously folks, if Heaven's Gate isn't in your travel plans, you need to let one of us know immediately. We will be glad to help you into a parachute and shove you back out the door."

Lindsey keeps a wary eye on Lazarus, not wanting a surprise if he pukes.

"For those of you staying, we will periodically make orbital corrections, that is, we will turn on the thrusters now and then as we make adjustments on our way to Heaven's Gate. We'll warn you when this is going to happen by turning on the Fasten Seat Belt sign and sounding the acceleration alarm." He demonstrates by blinking the sign a few times and giving the acceleration klaxon a short burst. "Please immediately return to your seats and fasten your seatbelt. Take your time, you'll have about a minute." Lee Fong chuckles again.

"Connecting flight information can be obtained using Frontier Spaceline magazine located in the seat back in front of you or at www. frontier.spaceline.org. Thanks again for selecting Frontier Spaceline, your gateway to the stars."

While the pretty flight attendant, Sarah, is serving refreshments, Lee Fong demonstrates his freefall prowess by soaring from one end of the cabin to the other, snagging a headrest, flipping over and landing smoothly on the forward bulkhead. He receives a mixed reaction from his passengers. A few laugh and applaud, some smile, most simply ignore him.

The little pill works wonders. Lazarus is famished. He turns to the fruit juice and the package of cashews. The juice mixes pleasantly with the rich oiliness of the nuts and lingers on his tongue long after he swallows, savory and delicious.

"I'm not going to eat these. Would you like them?" Lindsey offers.

Lazarus looks into her riveting gray eyes. "Yes, thank you. They're very good."

"Freefall affects taste buds, usually in a good way," Lindsey said, pleased the handsome young man has accepted her hospitality.

"That seems to be the only good thing about freefall." Lazarus shakes his head, eating another nut.

"Oh, believe me, there are loads of fun things to do in freefall," Lindsey said with a wistful grin, staring straight ahead, ignoring Lazarus when he stares inquisitively at her.

"That sounds like the voice of experience," Lazarus comments. When it becomes obvious she's not going to elaborate he continues, "Have you spent a lot of time in freefall?"

"Enough," she replies, "I worked the Hyundai Shipyards for a while." Hyundai Shipyards is an enormous manufacturing facility located at Lagrange Four.

Smart and beautiful. Lazarus is feeling a little out of his league. "I'm a desk jockey. Not very exciting, I'm afraid."

Raising her eyebrows Lindsey said, "Excitement is a human response that has only a weak dependence on physical surroundings. You would be surprised at how many boring people are in unusual and romantic occupations and how many exciting people do the most mundane things." She leans over conspiratorially, her breath hot on his cheek, "My first husband was a taxi cab driver. By far the most exciting man I've ever known."

Lazarus is stunned when she actually winks at him. He can't help smiling, feeling a little more at ease with this beautiful and unusual woman. Her openness and self-confidence is magnetic and those eyes...

"There must be something about being a desk jockey which excites you," she's the very picture of innocence, mouth puckered, head tilted. "Come on, tell me what it is," she insists intimately, pulling the truth out of him.

The religiously correct answer involved God and duty but staring into those gray orbs only centimeters away, he realized this woman was not asking for a recital of the slogans and sound bites that dominate Federation politics.

"You don't mess around, do you?" Lazarus asks.

Her dimples become even more pronounced. "I'm a Lunarian."

He's reluctant to provide any real information, even to so charming an inquisitor. "Well... I guess I just like tilting at windmills." He settles for a vague half-truth, a trick his father had taught him at an early age and one that has worked well throughout his career.

Lindsey laughs and lets him win this minor skirmish, "Oh, a modern day Don Quixote. Or perhaps you are just doing God's work?" Nodding at the cross floating on its chain outside his shirt.

"Perhaps. With God, one never knows," he said removing the chain from his neck and putting them in his pocket.

"What kind of a desk jockey can commandeer a seat on an

international flight?" She watched him intently. The dilation of his eyes and sudden increase in breathing signals she'd hit a nerve. "Mr. Hamlin should be sitting in your seat."

"He's your friend?" Lazarus blurts out, caught off guard yet again by this remarkable woman.

"Friend? No, not really. He's a MetCal employee I worked with on occasion. What you did will cost him money, but don't worry, MetCal pays well. He can afford it," Lindsey states, making Lazarus squirm. "So tell me, what kind of desk jockey can requisition a seat on a Stratoliner at a moment's notice?"

Lazarus bows his head and ignores her question, "I'm sincerely sorry for that. Perhaps you can give me his address and I can send compensation later?"

She shakes her head, "Stop changing the subject and answer the question…" When she realized the man was not going to respond, "Then at least tell me why you're in such a hurry to get to Heaven's Gate?"

Lazarus weighs his options and for some inexplicable reason, tells her the truth, "Actually, Heaven's Gate is not my final destination. I want to go on to Luna."

Lindsey rewards him by hooking her arm under his and pressing her left tit firmly against him. Casually, she lays her other hand on his wrist where she can monitor his pulse. "See, that wasn't so bad… any particular place? Luna contains well over a million citizens," she said, measuring and probing for the slightest sign of falsehood.

"Aldrin Station," Lazarus replies, the only Lunarian city he could think of at that moment. It's an instant decision that will prove to have far-reaching consequences.

"What are you running from?" Lindsey asks, not giving him time to come up with a better story.

"No, it's nothing like that," Lazarus denies much too quickly, "This is strictly a vacation. I simply want to see an underground city with my own eyes and this is the only way I'll ever do it. Homeland Security would never grant my request for a Luna visa."

The best lies have some truth in them but Lindsey lets it drop for now. Looking down at Lazarus's wedding band, "Is your wife going to meet you at Aldrin Station?" She asked. Once again, sweeping changes in his polygraphic indicators tell her she's hit another nerve.

Lazarus sits stiffly, staring straight ahead, wondering how the conversation had gotten here, of all places. He turns back to Lindsey before speaking. "My wife died two years ago," he said twisting at the wedding band, "I wear this just to keep all the women at bay." He grins weakly at his own halfhearted attempt at humor.

"I'm so sorry…" Lindsey said softly. Putting two and two together, she declares, "You thought I was her. When I boarded the plane, you thought I was your wife."

Startled, Lazarus stammers, "Only for a moment." This woman is driving him nuts.

The Earthman actually told her the truth, Lindsey noted. "You must have loved her very much."

Lazarus slides the ring off and stares at it for a moment "Yes, I did," he puts it in the pocket with the cross.

The silence extends uncomfortably long, "You're going to love Aldrin Station," she said.

Lazarus gratefully accepted her change of subject. "What's the Republic of Luna like? I've seen every National Geographic vid, played net games, and read everything I could get my hands on."

The Federation discourages its citizens from reading and by the time the censors finish with a NatGeo vid, it's of little value, depicting Lunarian cities as dark subterranean caverns deprived of sunlight and stripped of humanity, the implication of hell never far from the surface. Without exception, the games are even worse, designed to vilify Lunarians. They are terrible sources of knowledge for anyone seeking truth.

Lindsey shakes her head, "Then you know nothing. Lunarian cities are bubbles of air carved from solid rock containing life in all its diversity. There are forests and meadows complete right down to the bacteria in the soil. Luna is a place of light and life that is diametrically opposite to what the Federation would have you believe."

"What's it like to live in the Republic? We hear so many reports of violence. Do you live in fear?" Lazarus asks.

"To be sure, we are threatened by an enemy not willing to negotiate, but I do **not** live in fear." She frowns and shakes her head, "Over the last decade, necessity has made the Republic of Luna an armed camp with everyone contributing to the common defense, just as Israel has done the last hundred-fifty years and for pretty much the same reasons. It seems there are many who hate us."

"Do not count me among that number. I'm looking forward to my stay on Luna."

The acceleration klaxon blares, sending passengers scurrying back to their seats.

Located in a near perfect circular orbit just over 1600 kilometers above sea level and in the Earth-Luna plane, Heaven's Gate serves mainly as a passenger transfer point. Most outbound cargo rendezvous with freighters in much lower orbits and transfer payloads across the vacuum of space without the need of elaborate orbital structures. Going the other way, earthbound shipments are packaged within heat shields, decelerated by an orbital mass-driver before plunging through the atmosphere in well-established drop zones. Humans, on the other hand, pass through Heaven's Gate, coming and going.

Supporting only a small permanent population, Heaven's Gate contains a hotel and several restaurants in addition to harboring spaceline support personnel. Tourists come here to enjoy freefall and it's somewhat of a honeymoon status symbol. For many Earthmen, this is as far into space as they will ever get.

Lindsey retrieves the Frontier Spaceline magazine from its pocket on the back of the seat in front of them. The magazine is a thin flexible touch screen with a wide variety of flight information available through it. Lindsey accesses a live view of the station as the Stratoliner draws near.

Together, they watch the station grow from a bright spot on the screen into a dull metallic tubular shape hanging motionless in the void of space. From the Stratoliner's direction of approach, the structure appears at an angle. The end facing them is a shallow dome with its edges melding smoothly into the sides of the cylinder making Heaven's Gate look like an over-pressurized aluminum can on the verge of bursting. Stubby appendages protrude from the body of the station at various points like nails driven partway into a log. Antenna and power receptors sprout here and there.

A sense of scale eludes Lazarus until he realizes another Stratoliner is docked to Heaven's Gate, held fast by one of the stubby extensions. It looks like a child's toy airplane, dwarfed by the bulk of the station.

Another quite different spacecraft comes into view during approach. It doesn't have the aerodynamic outlines of an atmospheric craft. It's an open framework of beams and girders enclosing a thick disk. Instead of minimizing the frontal area, this vehicle maximizes it.

"I believe that's our ride," Lindsey said. "The front part is the Lander and the tanks and other stuff is the TLM or TransLunar Module. It will thrust all the way to Luna."

The station grows on the screen. At the last possible moment, the thrusters vibrate to life, bringing the ship almost to a stop in relation to the station. Much more slowly, the sleek atmospheric craft closes with the orbiting station. Outside the window, the stars rotate as the spacecraft positions itself for docking. On the screen, multiple external cameras seamlessly maintain the view of the station.

When Heaven's Gate fills the screen, one of the extensions reaches out and closes around the fuselage of the spaceplane. Lazarus feels a bump and the sound of metal against metal as the electromagnetic grapplers find their place. A whirring vibration fills the cabin as the mechanical safeties screw down, signaling the end of the docking maneuver. The Stratoliner is now physically part of the station.

A soft chime sounds, "Welcome to Heaven's Gate. Please be patient for just a few more minutes while the crew checks everything. We wouldn't want to open the door to vacuum."

Most of the passengers unbuckle, retrieve their luggage, and start moving towards the exit. Many are clumsy, bumping and jostling each other, chuckling at their own inexperience, excited to be here. It's easy to pick out the veterans, they move with grace and skill.

Lindsey puts her hand on his arm stopping Lazarus from unbuckling, "Might as well relax, could be awhile. The first time I was here, they had us waiting for over an hour. Besides, our connecting shuttle isn't scheduled for departure for three hours," Lindsey informs Lazarus. "There's a nice java shop inside. Do you feel up to joining me for a cup?" Lindsey asks smiling.

Lazarus has a fleeting moment of suspicion that evaporates with one look in her gray eyes. "I don't know about the coffee but I would be happy to join you," he said, returning her smile, thrilled that she wants him to stick around.

"Good," she said enthusiastically.

"I need to get my ticket for the shuttle first. Perhaps you could spare the time to accompany me?" Lazarus asks hopefully.

Lindsey laughs, "There isn't a ticket counter or agent. The only way to get a ticket is through Luna Central. You do have a visor, don't you?"

"Yes, of course... in my bag," Lazarus said.

Lindsey unbuckles and floats into the aisle. Hooking her toe under a loop, she opens the overhead and takes down her bag first, and then what must be Lazarus's. She hands it to him and buckles back into her seat.

Lindsey stifles a giggle when he pulls out his antiquated headset. State of the art several decades ago, it still works but just barely. She takes out a visor from her bag and slides it on. It molds itself into her ear channels, and fits snugly across her face completely covering her eyes. This is the first time she's worn her visor since arriving on Mother Earth over six weeks earlier. For her, putting on the visor means she's home.

She tries to link with Lazarus but the old headset is not equipped to handle modern protocols. "Go to lunacentral.rol," she directs him. She watches as his hands flail about.

"Got it," he said triumphantly.

The blurry image of an AI appears before him and asks politely, "How may I be of assistance?"

"List the availability of passage on the next Lunar Shuttle," Lindsey said.

The information appears within their VR as a seating chart.

"You're lucky. There are still seats available…" she selects two together next to a window designating one as hers and the other as being purchased. "Go on. This is where you pay for your passage," Lindsey tells him.

Lazarus nods and with a few jerky hand motions, downloads his financial information into the site.

"I'm sorry Mr. Sheffield, but passage is denied," the AI said.

Lazarus is stunned.

When he remains silent, Lindsey asks, "Why?"

"Federation authorities have indicted him on multiple counts of Earthnet security breach, lying to a police official, and failure to obtain the proper visas. They have requested his return on the next available flight."

Lazarus is horrified. Without knowing what to say, he silently runs his fingers through his hair.

Lindsey seizes the opportunity. "Under the Lunarian constitution, Lazarus can stake claim to Freedom of Movement. He is not a violent criminal and has the right to go where he pleases." She knows what the AI's response will be.

"To do so he must reject his Federation citizenship and apply for Lunarian. Do you, Ms. Marquest, sponsor him in this?"

Lindsey sits back and looks intently at Lazarus. His peculiar headset makes it impossible for her to see the upper half of his face but she knows she has him right where she wants him. "So... what do you think? You want to become a Lunarian?"

Lazarus struggles to control the emotional roller coaster of the last few seconds. In planning his departure, he didn't let himself dwell on the things he had no control over. Being brutally honest, he never believed he would get this far. His comrades in the Department of Homeland Security are just too good at their jobs. When imagining what kind of people he would meet along the way, never in his wildest dreams did it occur to him that a beautiful woman would magically appear to help him.

He wonders briefly why she's doing this, but frankly, he doesn't care.

"You would sponsor me?" Lazarus asks, hardly daring to breathe. "You don't even know me."

"You're running from the Federation. What else do I need to know?" Almost flippantly, Lindsey continues, "It's not that big of a deal for me. On the other hand, for you this is huge. Do you even know what you'll be expected to do?"

"I must pass a test and a physical," Lazarus croaks, his voice harsh with barely contained emotion.

"It's much more important that you never lie to me or any other Lunarian ever again. Can you do that?"

He thinks for a moment and said, "I don't know but I can try."

"That's good. You learn fast. You must also find a freehold that will take you in. Would you accept Dakota hospitality until you decide?" She asked.

There are times in a person's life where a single decision, contemplated for only an instant, completely changes the path of their lives. "Yes, of course, I would be honored." Lazarus said not daring to believe what is happening.

"It's settled then." Lindsey chuckles, "You didn't fool me for a second with that vacation story. I suspect the Federation would skin you alive if they got their hands on you. It only makes sense if you're running… emigrating. With Lunarian citizenship, you may return someday and visit your family. Without it you're dead meat," Lindsey ties the knot firmly about his neck. Addressing the AI she said, "Yes, I will sponsor Mr. Lazarus Sheffield in his application for Lunarian citizenship."

"Your sponsorship has been recorded and Mr. Sheffield has been granted provisional Lunarian citizenship. His passage to Aldrin Station is secure. The shuttle will depart in three hours and fourteen minutes."

Lazarus can hardly believe it. He never imagined it could be this easy or painless. It seems all he had to do was ask. He begins to understand one of the basic tenets of a free society, that it cannot withhold its freedoms from anyone, even those wishing to harm it.

"Lindsey, I can't thank you enough. I will never be able to repay your kindness." His emotions are raw and stressed to the breaking point.

"Like I said, it's no big deal, really. You're the one that will bust your ass getting up to speed. Have you ever been in a vacsuit?"

Lazarus shakes his head, "No, but I have extensive training time in environmental contamination suits and they're similar."

Lindsey chuckles. What desk jockey needs training in environmental contamination suits? "That's debatable but the fact remains, you will need to be qualified in the Lunarian version before you can even take a walk on the surface."

"Oh yes, certainly." Lazarus would agree to just about anything at that moment. Nothing was going to stand in the way of Lunarian citizenship.

With a clank, the Stratoliner's door disengages and swings open. "Be sure to collect all personal items before leaving. Watch your elbows and knees during disembarkation. Do not leave your luggage unsecured while in the station." The message softly repeats, over and over, with a few seconds pause in between.

Lazarus removes and returns his headset to his bag, maneuvers out of the seat, and joins Lindsey in the aisle without mishap, something he hardly notices in the magnitude of the moment. Smiling her congratulations, Lindsey gracefully propels herself towards the exit, leaving Lazarus to admire her behind. To his credit, Lazarus only ricochets once.

He does his best to keep up with Lindsey but finds he's the last to leave. Beyond the Stratoliner's open door stretches a long tubular corridor, its far end clogged with departing passengers. Lazarus manages to keep to the center, more or less, reaching out to brush the walls as he traverses the tunnel.

His mind races and he can't rid himself of the feeling that this is a dream and he will awaken only to find himself alone in his luxury apartment, stuck in a job that no longer holds value, in a culture that makes him hide his true beliefs and live a lie.

Already he's come further than he had dared hope was possible. After all, he's entering Heaven's Gate. Never has a name been more apropos. Moreover, thanks to Lindsey, he will be on his way to Luna in a few hours with the very real possibility of citizenship. He quells the surge of euphoria by reminding himself that provincial status is not full citizenship.

The other passengers are long gone by the time Lazarus emerges from the tunnel. He's in a small sunken alcove, its depth maybe three times his height and its breadth not much bigger than that of the airlock. Netting similar to the climbing rigs found on an old three-mast sailing ship extends out of the alcove and into the station. As most recent arrivals from Mother Earth will do, he orients himself alongside the net. Movement overhead catches his eye.

"Thank you for flying Frontier," the young woman said as he clears the airlock, interrupting his thoughts. Floating effortlessly within easy reach of the net, she's holding out an odd dumbbell shaped item for Lazarus to take.

Seeing his confusion she explains, "This is a Personal Maneuvering Unit or PMU. It will help you get around while you're here." It's something everyone learns about in the mandatory classes that all tourists must take. She glances over at the waiting Lindsey.

"It's an aerosol. Use it when you can't reach something to push against," Lindsey explains turning so he can see the PMU clipped to her belt. "Everyone gets one, not just the shortimers. They would have talked about them in orientation if you had taken it."

"Great," he said clipping the PMU onto his belt. In the process, he releases his bag, which promptly spins away.

"Sir," the attendant exclaims as she retrieves the errant luggage.

Without realizing what he had done, Lazarus is now floating in midair. When the attendant returns his bag, she gives him a slow spin. Reaching out he can't quite touch the net as it passes by repeatedly. Stretching out his leg doesn't bring him any closer. He realizes he has no way to move forward or back, or stop spinning. Just centimeters from the net, he's stuck. He watches helplessly as the world leisurely turns around him.

Lazarus can see them both grinning at him and realizes that she's testing him. Fine. He retrieves the PMU from his belt.

"Think about the physics of what you're doing," the attendant instructs him. "Remember, force equals mass times acceleration. You are just another satellite obeying the same laws as every other body in orbit," she struggles to keep her amusement in check. It happens all too often that people show up with inadequate training, skipping or daydreaming through the classes. Even after only a few months on Heaven's Gate, she can recall more than one Federation visitor who after messing up, prayed for God to save them.

"Why not just grab me?" Lazarus asks irritably, losing his good humor and getting a little peeved at the smirking young lady. He's not in the habit of being the butt of a joke. Worse yet, he can feel the first twinges of space sickness returning.

"That won't help you when you do it again. Everyone goes through this at some point. You would be surprised at how many do it in the first few minutes," she said openly smiling, giving up any pretense that this was not entertaining.

Lazarus ignores the churning of his stomach and concentrates on the PMU. The hourglass shaped device has a small nozzle at one end and padding at the other. In between is a comfortable hand grip with a power dial in easy reach of his thumb. Figuring to curtail his next screw-up, he turns the dial to its lowest setting.

"You trigger the PMU by squeezing," the attendant volunteers.

Glancing out, Lazarus catches Lindsey grinning wickedly. He dredges up the mechanics of motion he studied years ago. For every action, there is an equal but opposite reaction. Referencing the nets, he gauges his plane of rotation as best he can. Extending his arm straight out in that plane, he squeezes. The PMU hisses and he flexes his arm muscles against its force. His rotation slows considerably. A few more seconds proves too long and actually starts him rotating in the opposite direction. He flips the PMU over and gives it another very short burst, coming to a stop, more or less.

"Hey, this isn't so hard," Lazarus proudly exclaims until he looks over at the attendant and sees that he has stopped upside down in relation to her.

She couldn't care less about his orientation. She has lived in Heaven's Gate long enough that she doesn't think about her environment in terms of up and down, recognizing people no matter which way their heads are pointing.

She smiles at Lazarus, "Very good, sir. You'll do fine with a little more practice." Speaking to Lindsey on her way out of the alcove, "Maybe you can stick with him while he's here?" she suggests with a knowing look.

"Maybe," Lindsey said with a grin, "Come on, Mr. Sheffield. Let's go get that coffee."

Still thinking about physics, Lazarus places the PMU against his side just under his rib cage. He squeezes a couple seconds, pleased when he moves, without much rotation, towards the webbing. Grabbing the net with his free hand, he pulls himself towards Lindsey. It reminds him of scuba diving off the coast of Mexico.

"This gadget might actually be fun," he said, returning it to his belt. The two float along within reach of the webbing.

With disconcerting suddenness, they emerge from the confines of the small alcove to openness beyond his wildest imagination. Fear grips him. He's falling into the abyss. In danger of fainting, he gropes for the net, clutching the nearest thing to solid he can find. A whimper escapes his lips.

Lindsey's at his side, "Are you okay?" She asked, real concern etched across her face.

Lazarus focuses on the webbing and by strength of will, begins to regain composure. "Yes, I'm fine," he said gripping the net with both hands, concentrating on its fine weave. "Just give me a minute. I wasn't ready for... this." He manages to bring his fear under control.

Glancing at Lindsey, "You did that on purpose," he accuses her.

Nodding, "You're right. I wanted to see how you handle yourself."

"How'd I do?"

Lindsey shrugs, "At least you didn't pass out." She likes the resilience he demonstrated. It shows courage.

The video in the online magazine did not do Heaven's Gate justice. The station is a huge cylinder with one end dominated by the sun and the other capped like a gigantic tin can. Like a crazy inside out planet, the interior buildings extend inward from the walls. Many buildings are covered in vid projections, sometimes working together to form a single enormous picture, other times they are a chaotic tangle of independent images.

Webbing, similar to what he and Lindsey are using, stretches across the space at strategic locations and at different angles but never intruding far into the central open space. More webs stretch from one end of the station to the other, also staying close to the buildings.

The entire center of the massive cylinder is clear air where hundreds upon hundreds of people are flying using wings in every color, shape and size ranging from the length of an arm to four or five times that. Some are made of fabric, others with artificial feathers, and still more are plastic. Some are utilitarian strap on wings while others are full costumes incorporating a theme. Birds, dragons, insects and even pterodactyls populate the space.

The flyers seem to be everywhere, soaring with joyous abandonment. The large eagle-like wings are the fastest. About ten of them in tight formation are on an oval path the length of the station, their speed astounding and the ability to swoop into a turn thrilling to watch. Lazarus can hear their wings stroke the air as they pass just a few meters away.

Many use small maneuverable wings and dart about like a hummingbird. They fold against the body to reduce drag when not being flapped. Out in the center, a group using these wings is playing a game, twisting and cavorting around a huge ball. All the flyers wear visors of one style or another without exception.

The ambience reminds Lazarus of a bustling ice rink or a busy Colorado ski resort. People come here to play and have brought every gadget and device they could dream up to help them do it. Humanity has finally found a way to fly and is enjoying every minute.

"Is that the sun?" Lazarus asks indicating the brightness at the far end. It lights up the interior of the space station like a giant floodlight.

"Mirrors reflect sunlight into the station. That end is actually pointing away from the sun," she said.

"Incredible. This is better than Las Vegas." Lazarus exclaims in amazement.

She removes her visor and slides it into her pocket careful to fasten the Velcro restraining strap. Lindsey reaches out and pulls him to her, holding him tight with one arm around his waist. He drops his arm about her shoulders just as she weaves her leg past his crotch and hooks her toes on his ankle. She pushes off.

"Relax and let me pilot." Lindsey said. "The first thing we need to do is get you a real visor. That thing you call a headset runs on vacuum tubes, doesn't it?" She asked not expecting an answer. "We can get you a visor over there."

"Do you think I need one?"

"Yes Lazarus, you need one," Lindsey replies. "And that's not all you need."

Lindsey's boldness draws him to her like a fly to honey. Yet, he's sailing in unfamiliar waters and fearing he may be misinterpreting her signals. He would never be so bold as to make sexual advances. Sexual solicitation is a serious offense within the Federation.

"OK, lead the way," Lazarus said.

She grabs the webbing and swings them like a monkey on a branch, sending them soaring across free space towards the shop.

Lazarus shuts his eyes, briefly feeling his stomach churn but maintains control. Lindsey swings her free leg making them rotate with just enough angular velocity to be facing backward when they hit the webbing.

She giggles as he gropes for a handhold. "Relax," she repeats, using the rebound to swing them through the circular front door.

Inside is a world of gadgets. On one wall are wings of every shape and size, hovering in mid air are racks filled with merchandise, another wall is one large vid screen.

"Greetings. Can I help you find something," a disembodied female voice asks.

"Greetings. Yes, we need a visor. Nothing elaborate, just something solid for a new emigrant." Lindsey said.

The lights flicker and dance around a nearby rack. "We keep an assortment of visors here," the velvety voice said.

"Thank you…" Lindsey guides Lazarus to the rack before releasing her hold on him. Looking over the selection, she picks up a silver and black model. "Here, try this on." She hands it to him.

Lazarus takes the device and fits it over his eyes, maneuvering the flexible earpieces deep into his ear canals. At first, it felt all wrong, putting pressure at the most peculiar places. Then it seemed to relax and get better.

"The Razors come with a free fitting," the voice observes.

"Of course. How much?" Lindsey asks.

"Our basic Model CS130 is $2149.99," the silken voice said. "We can also provide you with a CS190 for $8949.99 or a CS160 for $5749.99. Both the CS160 and CS190 cover the standard spectrum. The CS190 uses the latest Archstone interface."

"Let's go with the CS160," Lindsey said.

Lazarus is stunned. That's a huge chunk of his cash.

"Charge it to my account," Lindsey said.

"No." Lazarus blurts, "I can pay for it myself," he said a little more calmly. He pulls his money out of his pocket.

"Put that away. You don't pay until the mods are complete."

"Are you sure I need a visor?" Lazarus asks again.

"Trust me on this, you do," she replies.

The modifications take less than a minute, not even enough time to look around. His new visor emerges from the depths of the display case. He puts it on. The visor molds itself to his face enclosing his eyes completely, creating a perfect blindfold, and the audio inserts fit comfortably into his ear canals blocking all sound. Yet, Lazarus can still see and hear, only now it's filtered through the visor.

"How does it feel?" She asks.

"Fine," Lazarus said. He's not thinking about the clarity of the image or the comfort of the fit. He's oblivious to the technology he uses so casually, clueless about the sophisticated visual sensors providing live video of his surrounding directly onto his retina.

He is however, aware of the young woman standing next to him.

"Oh." He turns awkwardly to face her. "Who are you?"

"My name's Helen. I'll be serving you today." It's the owner of the velvety voice. She has regular features, a head devoid of hair, and clothes pleasantly fashioned for comfort and utility. The woman is totally non-threatening and helpful, the perfect combination for a salesperson.

Lindsey smiles and puts on her visor, "That's better. You're one step closer to becoming Lunarian."

Lazarus retrieves his change from the dispenser and looks at Lindsey. "Didn't you just put your visor on?" He asked.

She chuckles, "I did. The reason you don't see it is that internal sensors pick up my facial expressions and broadcasts this information to other visors, including yours. Your visor simply overlays your live feed with my transmission, effectively making my visor disappear. There isn't any magic here, just a simple set of graphic calculations."

Lazarus swallows hard, "This is better than anything available in the

Federation."

"Better than anything on Mother Earth," Lindsey corrects him, "even the Chinese."

"It's not perfect, though. I can still see your visor when you move your head around."

"That's done on purpose. It lets you know who's wearing visors and who isn't." Lindsey turns her head side to side causing a ghostly outline of her visor to fade in and out. "Don't worry, in a few days you won't even notice. Right now, it's much more important for you to become familiar with using the virtual control panel. If you'll allow me, I'll link to your visor and demonstrate."

"By all means, show me," he said.

Lindsey chuckles, "This is demo mode," she said. "It duplicates my visor settings in yours."

Looking down, he sees Lindsey's hands where his should be. In the virtual world, she's taken control of his visor. She gives him a moment.

"Ok, the first thing to learn is how to turn the control panel on and off. Observe."

Lazarus watches as she rolls her hand counterclockwise in a graceful twisting action. Suddenly, a ring of pictographic icons appears about his waist, flat as if lying on a table. She repeats the movement and the icons vanish. "Now you try it," she said.

Lazarus emulates her motion and the icons reappear.

"The icons you use most frequently are arrayed to your front. All you need to do is look at one and move your hand down. Subtle hand movements will do. No need to go swinging wildly about," she grins. "Or you can touch the icon if you want. That works too... The pictograph of the satellite is your Earthnet portal. Right beside that are the search engine, visor settings and link monitor icons."

"What's a link monitor?" Lazarus asks.

"It shows you how many citizens are linked to your visor."

"It's a number, two. Does that mean there are two other people linked to my visor right now?" Lazarus asks without understanding.

"Sort of... It's you and me. Look, there are over two hundred icons and we have a long flight ahead of us. Let's study the ones you find interesting then." Lindsey suggests.

"Great idea," Lazarus said. "This part is similar to what I've used on Earthnet. I should be able to catch on quickly." What he does not elaborate upon is the clarity of the graphics or their response speed. Far superior to anything in the Federation.

Lindsey files that away with the other information. Very few Federation citizens have access to Earthnet.

"Let's go then," she takes his arm and wraps her left leg inside his right leg pressing her hip against his crotch. She skillfully pushed off, sending them soaring gracefully across the shop and through the entrance portal.

If he would notice, the interior of the station looks different now. The most obvious is he no longer sees any of the visors on the people around him and now when he takes the time to look at them, the advertisements strewn across the interior of Heaven's Gate are more distinct, their sounds clearer, and their colors sharper. In the same way, distances shrink. He can now make out the eagle flyers even at the far end of the station, but only if he stares for a few seconds. The fact is, he's already forgotten he's wearing a visor, so perfectly does it meld to his eyes and ears while supplying him with a flawless reproduction of his physical surroundings. However, exploring this marvelous device will come later. Right now, all he can think about is Lindsey.

"I will never in a hundred years be able to repay your kindness," Lazarus said hoarsely, intensely aware of her tit pressing against his arm and her hip wedged against his bulging crotch.

"You don't owe me anything. I did what any Lunarian would have done. I helped someone who needed help," she said, her leg expertly putting pressure in the most delightful places.

"Do you know what you're doing to me?" Lazarus asks softly, losing the fight against millions of years of evolution.

Batting long eyelashes, she purrs, "Oh… I have a pretty good idea." She did indeed.

Lazarus looks outward at the people flying, trying and failing to use them as objects of distraction.

Pointing at Heaven's Crib, "I stayed there my first time, had some time to kill waiting for my ride." Looking impishly at Lazarus, "That's when I joined the club."

"Joined what club?" Lazarus asks hoarsely, his brain frying under her administrations. He has problems focusing on her words.

"Freefall sex. There's nothing like it on Mother Earth." Lindsey smiles, her gray eyes limpid pools of sexual attraction inviting him to dive in. "Why do you think this place is so popular? It's not the food." Everything about her drove him crazy, her low husky voice, her hot breath on his cheek, her hotter body pressing against his.

He pushes back. Sexual energy from the hard spike between his legs surges through him, pounding his brain like a hurricane lashing the Florida coastline. He can stand it no longer. Lazarus pulls Lindsey into a full embrace, his lips engulfing hers. Her arms encircle his neck and her legs clamp down around his waist, focusing even more pressure on all the right places. His blood boils, matched perfectly by the furnace burning inside of Lindsey.

From somewhere in the vastness of Heaven's Gate a voice calls out, "Get a room."

Lindsey reaches out and grabs the webbing, expertly swinging them towards the Crib's front entrance without even breaking the kiss. She'll take enthusiasm over experience any day.

ЯL

The Data Acquisition and Control Center (DACC) of the FBS Yorktown is a dimly lit cocoon nestled deep inside the battlestation. Exposed braces march down its length like ribs inside a giant whale. Mounted within the braces are sixteen high-G couches containing the bridge crew.

Lieutenant Gilmore is tracking a spacecraft just leaving low earth orbit (LEO). He retrieves its information and runs a preliminary check on its registered flight plan. "Sir, I have an outbound freighter, Evolution's Child, Republic registration. Request permission to interrogate," he said to the watch commander.

"Proceed Lieutenant," Admiral DyGoon replies. The admiral thrives on bridge duty. It keeps him in touch with the inner workings of his battlestation and her place within the fleet.

"Yes Sir."

The lieutenant initiates an encrypted command that cascades through a constellation of seven Forward Observation SATellites, none bigger than a briefcase. The FOSAT closest to the freighter sends a powerful MRI beam sweeping over the spacecraft, the equivalent of a sonar ping in Mother Earth's oceans. The returns are collected and transmitted back to the battlestation then compared with a vast storehouse of other scans, looking for any abnormalities in the data. The entire exercise requires less than thirty seconds.

"Nothing unusual, admiral. Standard heavy-lift freighter, cargo is mining equipment and foodstuffs. Destination is Cullman Outpost, Luna. Only the pilot aboard, no passengers."

The admiral asks, "Where, pray tell, is Cullman?"

The lieutenant does a quick search, "A small mining settlement outside Herschel crater, at the northern edge of the Four Craters Region."

"Very well, Lieutenant, carry on."

The admiral's much more interested in finding the Houris, the Brotherhood's newest battlestation. They have been playing a game of cat and mouse for over a week, each battlestation trying to maneuver her FOSATs to find and maintain track on the other. Freighters half an orbit away don't merit more than a few seconds of the admiral's valuable time.

Evolution's Child continues on to Luna uninterrupted.

Lunar Transit

*"Religion belonged to the infancy of the human race;
it had been a necessary stage in the transition from
childhood to maturity. It had promoted ethical values
which were essential to society. Now that humanity has
come of age, however, it should be left behind."*

Sigmund Freud (1856-1939)

They're early. Human and robotic handlers are still loading supplies onto the shuttle as they approach. Lindsey has Lazarus in the now familiar lovers lock. Neither appears willing to disengage any time soon. Not that he wants her too. In fact, he can't remember the last time he felt so good. Lazarus vows to be worthy of this amazing woman. For the first time in his life, he feels truly free, like a hawk riding desert thermals a thousand meters above the desert.

Even though Lazarus had managed to keep up with Lindsey, it would take months before he could come close to matching her skill in freefall. He remembers her face, framed by coal black hair, hanging over him. Her legs wrapped tightly around him, breasts rippling with every move, gray eyes boring into his as she brought them to a simultaneous climax. He grins. Who knew that sex could be so good?

Lindsey glances at him, "If you keep that up, people will think you're a sex addict."

"Maybe I am," Lazarus said, his smile fading. He can't avoid feeling guilty about making love outside of marriage, an echo of endless lessons that sex is something dirty performed in the dark of night for the sole purpose of procreation and is a sin in any other circumstance. Certainly not just for fun. Sex is a sacred duty within a marriage. Making it cheap entertainment perverts it. At least, that's what the Church and his mother hammered into Lazarus.

Lindsey maneuvers them towards an apparent hole in the skin of the station. Several people float out as they come to a stop. "Are you ready?"

Lazarus nods and Lindsey guides them headfirst into the hole. They emerge outside the hull of Heaven's Gate. Lazarus grits his teeth. Running his free hand through his thick hair, he concentrates on the shuttle a few meters away. It's easier to maintain rather than regain control and being prepared for the experience certainly helped. More likely, it's because Lindsey's there and he would rather die than look weak in front of her.

The shuttle rests at the end of one of the stations many appendages. It's an ugly conglomerated tangle of components. Small free-flying robots scurry about the vessel completing final inspection and detaching lines.

He shifts his gaze to the incredible beauty of the stars framing the shuttle. Even the dimmer ones shine true in uncounted millions. At his back, the immense curving expanse of Heaven's Gate seems so tiny when compared to the vastness of the cosmos.

"You handled that nicely," Lindsey said, impressed with the mental toughness and tenacity she senses within him.

"Thanks... The stars are magnificent." he hasn't yet realized his visor is bringing everything more sharply into focus. Lazarus reaches out, banging his hand into the invisible material of the portal. "What's this?"

"Duraglass, a fully-transparent non-reflective ceramic."

"This would be considered magic by our ancestors," he said.

"It's more likely they would mutter some unintelligible mumbo jumbo and start a new religion. Our ancestors were very inventive when explaining things outside their knowledge."

Lazarus finds her criticism strangely disturbing, "Yes, I suppose you're right. I'm just not used to hearing religion ridiculed."

She looks sharply at him, "I'm not ridiculing the need for ignorant savages to believe in gods, but I am ridiculing modern humans for believing in those same gods in the face of real answers."

"I didn't say I don't agree with you. It will take a little time for me to adjust to things being discussed so..... freely," he said.

It didn't take long for you to set aside the Federation's sexual code of ethics... but she doesn't say that. Instead, she said, "Lunarian society is quite different from the Federation... Are you sure you want to go through with it? There's still time to go back."

Lazarus swallows. "I can't go back. There's nothing for me back there."

"Well then, you better prepare for some rather radical changes in your life." She pulls at his arm, "Listen to me."

They embrace and she wraps her legs and arms around him bringing her face right up to his.

"When things pile up on you I want you to remember you can always come to me... We might even talk once in a while," she purrs seductively, rubbing the tip of her nose on his.

Holding Lindsey so close, feeling her heartbeat next to his, Lazarus doesn't feel alone for the first time in years. He grins. "Did you know that the ancient Greeks believed the Milky Way was actually milk spilled from the tits of the Greek god Hera? The story goes that Zeus, the king of the gods, tricked Hera into nursing Heracles whom she didn't like. Discovering who she was suckling, she pulled him from her tit but a spurt of milk escaped and formed the smear across the sky that we call the Milky Way."

Lindsey chuckles, "In fact, I have heard the story, but where did you learn of it?"

Before he can answer, a lazy drawl interrupts their conversation. "That's gotta be most godforsaken ship ever bolted together. A Winnebago with a thruster up its tailpipe."

Lazarus and Lindsey break their embrace and turn. It's an old man dressed conservatively in a dark gray jumpsuit open at the neck. Close-cropped white hair forms a fringe around his gleaming baldness. A bushy white mustache hangs in a sweeping arch below his nose almost hiding his upper lip and extending down past his chin. With leathery skin covered in wrinkles, he's without doubt, the oldest individual Lazarus has seen since leaving Athens. Despite his obvious age, there's no missing the lively twinkle in his eye. This old man loves life.

"I hesitate to ask what a Winnebago is, but I assure you, this ship is well designed for what she does. There's not one unneeded kilo in her design." Lindsey said with a smile, "Where you see a collection of hardware, I see the fruit of many hours of dedicated labor. There's beauty in simplicity."

"Humph," the old man snorts, "Is that what you engineering types call the KISS principle? Keep It Simple Stupid? Yes….Well… Nothin' beats first class, if you ask me."

"Maybe the shuttle is a little crowded but we'll be comfortable.

Besides," Lindsey continues, "unless you're some big corporate weenie with keys to the company yacht, this is the only way to get to Aldrin Station. Why waste your breath on something you can't change?"

Huffing like an old male lion on the plains of Serengeti, the old man chuckles dryly, "Darlin' I' been do 'in that my whole life... but you're right, why waste energy. It's a freighter and we're the freight... Name is Isaac Crenshaw but you folks can call me Izzy," he said nodding in the customary Lunarian greeting.

"Lindsey Marquest," she said with a nod in return.

"Lazarus Sheffield," he extends his hand. By necessity, handshakes are different in freefall where one simply grasps, squeezes and releases, without actually shaking the other persons hand. That is, if it's done at all.

The wrinkles on the old man's forehead deepen but he accepts the gesture. Lazarus immediately starts to pump, sending them all into motion.

"Whoa." Isaac exclaims.

Lindsey laughs.

"Sorry," Lazarus mutters with embarrassment.

"It's alright. No harm done. So where you folks headed?" Izzy asks. "Don't tell me, let me guess, y'all are emigrating?"

"I'm going home," Lindsey said.

"A citizen. How about you?" Izzy asks Lazarus.

Lazarus feels Lindsey hug him tighter, waiting for him to respond, but in his world, a person does not willingly reveal truth to anyone, let alone strangers. He hesitates, shrugs and said, "I'm waiting to see how the story ends."

"Ain't we all?" Izzy laughs. "What 'bout you sugar, what freehold stakes claim on you?" Izzy asks bluntly, not bothered in the least that these two are not a couple, even though they certainly act like one. Maybe they just didn't realize it yet. It happens.

"Dakota," she replies, finding the old gentleman charming.

"Fine freehold… solid traditions…" Izzy said nodding approvingly. His eyes gleam mischievously, "Y'all ain't gonna believe this but Abby and I go way back." A chuckle erupts from deep in his belly and his eyes glaze over. The old man laughs again, "Hell, who'd forget ol' Izzy?"

The flight announcement sounds, "Passengers are now free to board Trans World Flight L95 bound for Aldrin Station, Luna." The three of them float up and out of the observation portal and head for the gate. They join the gathering throng entering the boarding tunnel. MRI scanners sweep over them, identifying who they are and where they're going, looking for anything out of the ordinary or out of place.

At the end of the tunnel awaits a rather petite flight attendant, "Welcome aboard," she said hovering just outside the shuttle's airlock door. She's wearing a Trans World fight uniform consisting of loose grey slacks and a white blouse with TWS monogrammed across the left pocket. Her brown hair is cut short in what Lazarus concludes is the popular style. After glancing down at something only she can see, she looks back up at Lazarus and smiles, "Mr. Sheffield, you're in 29A. To your right and six rows down. It's the window seat." Looking at Lindsey she adds, "Miss Marquest, you're in 29B, right next to Mr. Sheffield."

Looking around the shuttle Lazarus feels he's entering the proverbial padded cell, only much larger. The seats are in rows like spokes in a wheel and the ceiling is high and roomy.

Lindsey expertly maneuvers them through the shuttle looking for row twenty-nine. She playfully pushes Lazarus into his window seat.

Izzy takes the seat next to Lindsey and a middle-aged woman the seat next to him.

His window faces Heaven's Gate and thus, doesn't afford much of a view but Lazarus can see the portal they had been in a few minutes before, packed with people waiting to see the shuttle depart.

The outer airlock closes with a thump. A moment later the inner door swings shut with a clunk and the male attendant screws down the safeties.

"Good day everyone, on behalf of your crew, let me welcome you aboard Trans World Flight L95. Your attendants on this flight will be Alan and my name is Susan. We will be departing shortly so if your destination isn't Aldrin Station, Luna, now's the time to speak up. We will begin serving as soon as we're underway."

The acceleration klaxon sounds off, followed by a soft whirring that fills the cabin. A clank and a sharp sideways jolt rocks the shuttle as the station releases it, supplying a little push in the process. Lazarus looks out his window and is amazed to see how far the shuttle has already separated from Heaven's Gate. Even as he watches, the station grows smaller. Very gently, almost imperceptibly, the shuttle rotates.

A minute after separation, acceleration pushes Lazarus down into his padded seat. It builds until it reaches one-sixth Earth normal and holds steady. A low throbbing accompanies the acceleration. Lazarus is not sure if he's hearing it or feeling it in the seat of his pants.

"Nice to have a little weight back," Lazarus said with relief.

"You telling me you didn't like freefall?" Lindsey asks lifting her eyebrows inquisitively.

"It has its moments," Lazarus said grinning. "Where's the pilot on one of these?"

"There's no human pilot on a shuttle." Lindsey said.

"Folks don't pilot out here. A computer runs the show and we're just 'long for the ride," Izzy adds.

"So there's no one onboard who can fly?" Lazarus asks looking past Lindsey at the old man. His weathered face looks like it would be more at home on an Arizona ranch than a shuttle on its way to the moon.

"That's a big affirmative. All we have are two flight attendants. A pilot would be dead weight, one more payin' customer left behind." The old man rasps. "Besides, if somethin' went haywire, we'd just sit tight and wait for Luna Control to send a rescue party."

"I would appreciate it if you didn't discuss all the things that could go wrong," said the woman on Izzy's far side.

"Yes ma'am. I'm Izzy Crenshaw and these two love birds are Lindsey and Lazarus."

The woman shakes hands with Izzy, then leans forward to see past him, "Marcy Stephens. Pleased to meet everyone," she said. Marcy looks to be in her mid sixties with a round face and dark eyes. Her collar-length brown hair is fashioned in a serviceable square cut contained under a fine fishnet. Conservatively dressed, Marcy is out of place aboard the shuttle, like a fish out of water.

"I don't mean to be trouble," Marcy continues in an apologetic tone. "It's just that I've never done this before and it makes me bloody nervous to think about what's just outside that window. Better I not think about it."

"What you don't know can kill you out here," Lindsey smiles at Marcy.

"Oh dear," Marcy exclaims in a panic. "I told Christopher I shouldn't come but that boy never listens to me."

"Easy lass." Izzy reaches out and takes Marcy's hand, "Where exactly you goin? Is Christopher your son?"

Marcy shakes her head, "Grandson. He talked me into coming to see him. Said I'll love it. Well, I don't love it." Her lower lip trembles ever so slightly.

"Have you been in an airplane?" Izzy asks her.

"Yes, many times. So don't try telling me it's the same 'cause it's not. There's air outside of airplanes and I can see the ground."

"You're right, space is different," Izzy said rethinking his approach. Is this your first time in space?"

"Oh my yes. I was raised on Ford Farm. Ever here if it? It's a beautiful 14th century farmhouse about eight kilometers east of Plymouth in southwest England. I don't know about all this high technology. I tried to tell him I was too old but he wouldn't hear of it… This last summer was bloody horrible... Lost everything and had nowhere else to go… The farm had been in my family for generations… It's all gone now, under water."

"Tell me about it," Marcy likes to talk and Izzy likes to listen.

Lazarus and Lindsey snuggle ignoring the subdued chatter around them. Lazarus wonders how many fellow travelers would choose to remain at Heaven's Gate if they knew what he knew. He had to admit, he only has suspicions, nothing truly solid. In his line of work, you seldom get solid verifiable facts.

His years in DHS have stripped him of youthful enthusiasm and the belief he was on the side of good. He loves his country but hates what it's become. The greed, the lies, the hypocrisy, and the intolerance made it impossible for him to trust anyone. The final straw was his superiors choosing not to warn the Lunarians of impending disaster, a selfish decision that promises dire consequences for millions of people, perhaps the entire world. His polygraphic indicators reflect the weight of his burden.

"I see the smile's gone," Lindsey said.

He squeezes her hand affectionately. "Please forgive me Lindsey. I was just thinking of the sorry state of affairs back in the Federation."

"Which sorry state is bothering you?" She asked.

Lazarus looks into Lindsey's gray eyes and bows his head breaking eye contact, a frown furrowing his brow.

"What is it?" Lindsey asks again. "Come on, spill it. What's on your mind?"

Lazarus has a brief moment of panic. He's not ready to start talking about the Brotherhood. He searches his mind for something else to say.

"Throughout my life it was pounded into me that sex outside of marriage was a major sin. On my church wall behind the pulpit is a number of biblical passages including one from Matthew 15. *For out of the heart proceed evil thoughts, murders, adulteries, fornications, thefts, false witness, and blasphemies. These are the things which defile a man.* The punishment is death."

"To equate murder with sex is ridiculous," Lindsey said. "Do you think someone deserves to die for having consensual sex?"

"No, of course not..." Looking up in confusion, he hesitantly asks, "Why?" and can go no further.

Lindsey knows instinctively the unspoken details contained in that most-complicated one word question. "Because you needed it," she said. "Are you sorry?" She asked, watching intently for any sign of regret or deceit.

The question hits him like an electric shock. Lazarus looks into her eyes and squeezes her hand almost to the point of hurting her, "Oh my, no. I don't know how but... You hit the nail on the head Lindsey. I needed to break the mold and you did that. I feel hope for the first time in ages. No. What you have given me is much more than just sex."

"Easy tiger. Things are a little different on Luna. Lunarians don't have the same sexual mores as the Federation. Sex is something that brings us together, not something that divides us." Sensing confusion within Lazarus, she adds hastily, "Don't get me wrong. The manner in which a Lunarian conducts their sexual activities is critical but realistically, there's only one rule. As long as everyone concerned is in agreement, then pretty much anything goes."

"Reverend McCarthy claims the Lunarians condone rape, child sex, and incest. Is he right?" Lazarus asks.

Lindsey knows exactly what Lazarus is referring. During this last stay on Mother Earth, she had witnessed a growing animosity within the European Union directed at the Lunarians and fed by government propaganda. Made to look like factual documentaries, they exaggerate the cultural differences and minimize the similarities. Some are subtle, others blatant. The worst of the vids utterly vilify the Lunarians, making them out to be Satan worshipers who have orgies every night. The worst of the worst are the twenty-eight McCarthy videos containing the biggest lies, exaggerated and repeated to the point of absurdity. What's more revealing, Lindsey never heard anyone make a serious rebuttal or challenge the weak evidence put forth. The vids had deeply disturbed Lindsey at the time, a feeling that refuses to subside.

"Rape means at least one party was forced against their will to have sex and child sex means at least one partner was too young to make an informed decision. Either situation could result in the General Council voting for expurgation. What the good reverend calls incest is the fact that Lunarians don't hide sex from their children or fill them with lies. We believe knowledge is the key to making good choices in one's life, not ignorance." Lindsey explains.

Seeing doubt on his face, she changes tack, "Look, Reverend McCarthy is the worst kind of liar, using just enough fact to hook his listeners into believing something hideously wrong. None of his self-described documentaries reflects reality. They're designed to control and manipulate you, not educate you. No Lazarus, completely the opposite is true. If a Lunarian commits rape, the person raped, as well as their family, friends and associates, decides the punishment of the person who did the raping, up to and including expurgation. The laws are really quite simple, letting the people most intimately involved have the most say. The only hard and fast laws in the Republic define how officials collect, analyze and preserve evidence. Everything else is flexible, decided by citizens on a case-by-case basis in open council. Literally any action taken by one party that causes harm to another is subject to adjudication before the General Council." Lindsey said.

"What's expurgation?" he stumbles over the unfamiliar term.

"It's the total wiping of a person's memory. This penalty is only for the most heinous crimes. It's seldom used."

"So someone could get… expurgated… for stealing? That seems a little harsh." Lazarus said.

"Does it?" Lindsey said, "Expurgation requires a supermajority. If that many fellow citizens think you need a total head job, then just maybe you're not a very nice person."

"What about homosexuality? Others besides McCarthy speak of the promiscuousness of the Lunarians," Lazarus points out. "Leviticus 20 verse 13; If *a man also lie with mankind, as he lieth with a woman, both of them have committed an abomination: they shall surely be put to death; their blood shall be upon them.*"

"Again I ask you, do you think someone deserves to die for having sex?" Lindsey asks.

"Well… no…"

"Then how about for blasphemy or speaking ill of the Church?" she presses. "Does someone deserve to die for disbelieving the ridiculous superstitions underlying Christianity?"

"Ah… no…"

"Then you must tell me how a man raised in the heart of the Federation can be so reasonable. I thought they would have ripped out any semblance of logic from you long ago?"

Lazarus sighs and lays his head back. "They tried. I studied the bible every day from kindergarten through college along with everyone else. When I was a kid, I studied the creation story of Adam and Eve, Noah and the Flood, Moses and the Passover and many others. The more I learned, the more confused I became and my teachers didn't help. They didn't like answering questions, not the hard ones anyway. When they bothered at all, their answers were vague and when I pushed for better ones, they kicked my butt."

"Go on," Lindsey encourages him.

"In third grade, I kept asking why God put the tree of knowledge in the middle of the Garden of Eden, told them to not eat its fruit, then left. Was God laying a trap or trying to trick them? Granted, I disrupted the classroom insisting on a reasonable answer, but I really wanted to know. Didn't God realize they would head straight for it once He told them not to? It's what I'd have done. That incident landed me a month's detention…" Lazarus sighs, "Later that same year I asked the schools spiritual advisor why God killed so many innocent people during the Passover. Why didn't God cut out the middleman and just appear before the Egyptian Pharaoh instead of killing the oldest sibling in every family that didn't smear lambs blood on their front door? … And why did God make it rain frogs? None of it made any sense. I was positive that an all-powerful God could have made it perfectly clear to the Pharaoh what He wanted without the need for the ten Egyptian plagues or anybody dying. Well… they didn't see it that way."

"I'll bet they didn't," Lindsey smiles.

"That earned me a trip to the Headpastor's office. Mom and dad had to come to the school. Mom didn't say a word during the entire meeting. She just sat there and stared at me. Total guilt trip. Dad was pissed from the moment he walked through the door. Later I learned the school board fined him a day's wages. They suspended me for a week, gave me another month in detention and two hundred hours of community service under the direct supervision of Pastor Marsh, the history instructor at my school. Needless to say, I learned my lesson…"

"That doesn't explain how you know Greek mythology." Lindsey remembers his story about the Milky Way.

"My real education began that evening when my dad came home from work. The first lesson was all about the mechanics of deception. He told me not to openly question the authority of the Church but to simply say the right things and go through the motions. When he thought I was ready, dad showed me a secret hide-a-way in the floor of the tool shed and explained its use. It wasn't elaborate, nothing but a few loose floor boards with a shoebox space below, but through it passed treasure more precious than gold… Books."

"Books?"

"Yes, but not just any books, outlawed books. If I were caught with them… well, let's just say I'd be in serious trouble."

"So your father put books in this hole?" Lindsey asks incredulously. She can sense he's telling her the truth, but it's so bizarre.

"It wasn't him personally." Lazarus shakes his head, "All I know for sure is a different set of books would appear within days after I finished the last."

"How would they, whoever they are, know when you were done? Or what books should be next?" She asked in wonder.

"I left questions, sometimes several pages of questions. The books that answered them were never far behind, a few weeks at most. I read constantly. Some I even read twice. It was the single most precious gift Thomas Oliver Sheffield ever gave me, and it continued long after he was gone. I never did find out who exchanged the books. Better I not know if caught."

Thomas Oliver Sheffield is his father, a name she can check on later. For now, Lindsey wants to know more about his unusual education, "What authors can you remember?" She asked.

"Oh let's see… There was Twain, Stevenson, Paine, Ingersoll, Plato, Kafka, Bruno, Thoreau, Melville, Darwin, Einstein, Aristotle, Homer, Defoe, Keats, Mann, Steinbeck, Hemingway, Rand, Dickens, Vonnegut, Woolf, Orwell, Jefferson, Faulkner, Fitzgerald, Shakespeare, Asimov, Hawking, Shelly, Lee, Kipling, Sinclair, Machiavelli, Odegaard, Poe, Rousseau, Johanson, Sagan, Wells, and my father's favorite fiction author, Robert Heinlein. There were more, many more, too many to count. In each new set of books was always at least one textbook. I studied astronomy, physics, biology, human psychology and of course, religion. These gave me answers to questions I didn't even know existed before reading them. The more I learned the more I realized just how much there is to know."

"Remarkable." Lindsey said, "Tell me more about your father."

Lazarus sits quietly for almost a minute, "He died when I was ten," he finally said, "KIA... killed in action. I really don't know any more. Believe me, I've tried to find out. Nothing in the official records reveal anything about his mission or his death other than a posthumous medal, Hero of the State. Everything else was marked Top Secret and I didn't need to know."

Another piece of useful information, "I'm sorry for your loss. It must have been hard. Do you have any other family?"

"Two brothers and a sister. I'm the oldest. My mother lives in Portland... After dad died, I shared the gift of books with them. Even though I was cautious, it wasn't enough. When I was a senior in high school, my youngest brother Elijah rebelled against a particularly harsh pastor. He compounded his mistake by quoting a passage out of the Diary of Anne Frank. The school authorities pressed him for two days straight to tell them where he had learned of it. He finally convinced them he had read it on a new not-yet-restricted netsite. Dad wasn't there to stop them, so the school sent Elijah to a camp outside Albuquerque. He came back a total zombie. He couldn't put a sentence together, or play, or even climb a tree... The worst part... his inner fire was gone, totally extinguished. In its place, a child-like zeal for spouting religious platitudes, all his curiosity had been smothered under the oppressive hand of state sponsored truth..." Lazarus said bitterly. "I never again talked with my brother about the secret place or books. For me, Elijah died that day, driving home a very harsh lesson. Never get caught, and I never was."

Lindsey shivers. His tone chills her to the bone. Three decades earlier, she had gotten out just before the Federation became a full-fledged theocracy. What must it have been like to grow up in such a repressive state? She hopes never to find out. "Do you have any kids?"

she can sense him tighten up.

He pauses, "Had… I was married to a wonderful woman I met in college. We had a daughter… they were killed in a traffic accident two years ago..." his voice trails off.

Lindsey squeezes his hand, "I'm so sorry…" Changing the subject She asked, "So tell me, what happened to make you run?"

Lazarus pushes his hair back and wipes away the sweat from his upper lip.

"Relax… I know you must have a very good reason for emigrating. Tell me what it is, beginning with what you did for the Federation." When he still hesitates she continues, "After all, you're going to tell somebody sometime. Do you want it to sound like a first time presentation with no practice at all?"

Lazarus frowns, "I don't feel comfortable discussing this in public."

Lindsey shakes her head, "It's different here. Public and private have different meanings than you're accustomed too."

His frown deepens, "Yes, of course…" but he remains silent.

"Look, you're watched wherever you go in the Federation, right?"

"Sure," he replies thinking of his apartment, work, and social life.

"The Lunarian system is about the same only the data is available to everyone, not just government officials keeping tabs on you, or corporations trying to sell you something. The flow of information goes both ways. The Law of Full Disclosure gives every citizen access to all things public, including all individual, corporate, and governmental dealings. Only agreements made in public are valid under the law. Total visibility. Secrets are not only impolite, they're against the Law. The only exception is when the Republic or someone's life is in jeopardy and even then, it's permissible to maintain secrecy for only a short time. As soon as the crisis is over, all records must again be made public."

"The Law, as I understand it, seems to put everything in public domain, every discussion, every meeting, even conversations between friend's falls into the public domain. Then what is privacy to a Lunarian?" He asked.

"It has the same definition here as it does in the Federation. Privacy is simply the courtesy extended from one citizen to another to leave each other alone, to mind your own business. For instance, our fellow passengers have granted us privacy. Any one of them at any time has the right to watch us, listen to our conversation, and even join in if they are so inclined. But they don't because they have given us privacy…"

"…but this is public transportation," he interrupts.

"When are we not in public?" she retorts. "When we are at work? No. On the street? No. At home? Maybe, but only if you are a hermit totally disconnected from the rest of civilization. Privacy is the state of being apart from others and as such, is more about an individual's pursuit of happiness than a separate constitutional right. Personal privacy suffered a quick death over a century ago in the opening rounds of the Age of Information."

"Not true. Privacy is tightly guarded within the NAF."

"The sheer number of Federation privacy laws is astounding, but it's not your privacy they're protecting. It's the right of State and Corporate organizations to collect facts about you but reveal nothing of themselves to you. Don't you realize you invite corruption when the flow of information is one-way? Those in power use that power to stay in power."

Lazarus feels a sharp pang of guilt. He knows firsthand the power of the federal government, having personally compiled electronic evidence that convicted forty-three men and a woman of information theft. These were the real hard-core offenders, hackers who illegally accessed financial, medical, and corporate data without permission, passing it on to the highest bidder. Now she's telling him this information is openly available to anyone on Luna?

"But shouldn't a company be able to reap the rewards of internal research without fear of competitors riding their shirttails for free?" He asked.

"That's not a privacy issue. That's patent infringement and the Law provides protection for their investment. Again, it's to everyone's advantage if all records are public, everything from raw research to the final marketing plans. How can a company have a right to produce something if they cannot show a logical progression of knowledge? How can a pharmaceutical lab create a finished formula without a history of research and testing? How can a widget maker market a new widget without having records of the designs progression? There must be a litany of meetings, computer data, partnership agreements, and impromptu hallway discussions showing they actually did the work. Because everything is accessible, even a bad solicitor can easily prove who stole the widget design by simply viewing the act of stealing. How can anyone sustain any criminal activity if their every move is public knowledge?"

"I have a lot to learn," Lazarus said.

"More than you know lover..." he blushes and she smiles, a gentle reminder of their relationship. "Now that you understand there can be no secrets, tell me why you're here..." she purrs, her breath hot on his cheek.

He doesn't feel threatened. It's as if he has known her much longer than just a few hours. Sex has a way of doing that. Yet, it seems traitorous to be telling Lindsey any of the things that concern him most. Long years of training are hard to throw off, even with such a beautiful inquisitor as Lindsey.

Through his visor, Lindsey monitors his polygraphic indicators better than an old-fashioned lie detector. It relays heart rate, sweat production, eye movement, and many other observations, making it physically impossible for him to lie. Whatever it is that he thinks he knows, he considers it important enough to turn his back on everything familiar and embrace the unknown, this much she's certain of.

"Ok, let's begin by you telling me your occupational details."

He still hesitates, "I'm a programmer." Lying by omission is still lying.

Lindsey looks intently into his eyes, just a few centimeters from her own, "And?" She watches the last wall crumble.

He sighs and runs his hand across his hair. The lifelong liar realizes he must finally speak the truth and nothing but the truth, "I'm a Senior Analyst for the Department of Homeland Security. My job was to gather and analyze data from a wide assortment of sources and incorporate it into presentations the Director uses to brief the President and the Joint Chiefs."

Well, this is indeed interesting. "What kind of data?" Lindsey asks.

"Pretty much anything pertaining to the War on Terror," Lazarus replies.

"War on Terror. **Bah.** The Federation illegally kidnaps foreign citizens and imprisons them for years without trials. They torture and abuse their own people. They reeducate any who dare disagree. To me, that's a War on Sanity." Lindsey said.

"That may be true but if I ever talked that way, I would not only lose my job, I would wake up in a reeducation program myself. Director Dempsey doesn't mess around," Lazarus said.

"My point exactly. So… you're a Senior Analyst working for Director Dempsey. Doesn't that make you an agent?" She asked.

"Not really. I'm more of a technician. I specialize in interviewing suspects and covert data mining. I'm part of a team working towards determining who, what, when, and where the next attack will come from."

The Lunarians have known about this group for some time, but Lazarus is the first defection from its inner circle. In fact, he's the highest-ranking NAF defector in twenty years. Lazarus will answer many questions, a process that has only just begun.

Something substantial must have rattled his cage hard to make him take this drastic step. Now, she's beyond curious. Lindsey snuggles up to him, squeezing his arm, willing him to lock eyes with her, "So tell me, what have you discovered that is worth turning your back on everything?"

Sighing, he runs his fingers through his thick hair before continuing, "Something big is happening within the Brotherhood. People have been falling off the radar until nobody's left. I've never seen this level of participation before."

"What do you mean, falling off the radar?" She asked.

"Homeland tracks thousands of individuals connected with radical fundamentalism within the Brotherhood. We scrutinize their communications, their employment, bank records, who they meet, netsites they use, that sort of thing. Sometimes we had our guys follow them around and even become friendly."

Lindsey nods and motions for him to go on.

"Three months ago these individuals began disappearing without a trace. One day they were there, the next gone. No more network traffic, no more bank expenditures, their apartments empty, their jobs abandoned. They're just gone. Vanished."

"Who are these people? What do they do?"

"They're virtually all male, between the ages of eighteen and forty, and members of at least one fundamentalist splinter group. All of them have received military training at some point. We believe they are the soldiers who will carry out whatever the Minister is up to." Deeply concerned Lazarus continues, "The few thousand we know about is only the tip of the iceberg. It could mean as many as a million men are involved."

"Wait, go back. Who is the Minister?"

"DHS tracks all the upper echelon in the Brotherhood including the important military figures. Most of these remain accounted for but there are a few notable exceptions. In particular, the Defense Minister, Hasin bin Aunker and Major General Abdel Salam Arif are both missing. They are considered high risk and extremely dangerous in the West."

"Go on," she can sense he's not finished.

Lazarus sighs and continues, "It's also a general belief among Homeland agents that the Brotherhood has completed a nuclear program which produced an unknown number of weapons. We haven't the faintest idea where they are, or how many."

"Well… you are just full of good news, aren't you?" Lindsey said. "It doesn't sound like a terrorist attack to me, more like an invasion."

"I totally agree. We picked up indicators the target was off world. Hyundai Shipyard is building the Brotherhood's space fleet and Taurus Colony controls the Brotherhood's electricity. That leaves the Republic. Since the Federation has interests throughout Luna, I managed to convince Director Dempsey to inform the President of my concerns. I thought for sure President John Paul would tell the Lunarians. I was wrong. The prevailing attitude is to stay out of it. Don't get involved…"

"… but they are involved." Lazarus argues with himself, "and not in a good way. Federation media constantly portray Lunarians as villains and monsters. It's not terrorist's people fear anymore. It's Lunarians."

"Relax, don't get yourself all worked up." Lindsey nods in agreement, "But you're right. Even in Europe, I was surprised at the hostility when people found out I was from Luna. I'm glad to be leaving."

"It's just like Hitler's Jewish propaganda leading up to the Second World War." Lazarus said angrily. "Criticize. Demonize. Neutralize."

"I said relax. It doesn't do any good to stress out. How exactly did you plan to tell the Lunarians of this wonderful news?"

"I thought I might speak to a Councilor."

"So you're just going to cold call a Councilor?" she smiles at the hubris of his plan. It just might work.

"Why not?" he replies. "Actually, I never thought I would get this far… I left this part of the plan to ad hoc. Perhaps I should start with the local police department. I just need five minutes with the right person, someone who knows someone, who knows someone. I don't mind going through channels."

"What makes you think the Lunarians will listen?"

Returning her gaze steadily, Lazarus said, "Someone will listen. They must."

She leans back pondering her options. If she helps Lazarus and he turns out to be a quack, she would be embarrassed and possibly labeled unreliable by some. However, if he has information about an imminent attack on the Republic then many Lunarian lives are at stake. Her pride is worth the risk.

"Do you know of Abby Dugan?" She asked.

"Yes, of course," Lazarus said. "She's Luna's most famous Lunarian." What he didn't say was that DHS considers Abigail Dugan a hothead and troublemaker.

"I can't promise anything but I may be able to get you your five minutes. Corso Dugan is her son and he's also Aldrin Station's Security Chief," Lindsey said.

Lazarus is astonished, "You can do this?"

Smiling she said, "Don't look so surprised. I'm a Dakota citizen and have the right to ask. The worst that can happen is they say no."

Something in the way she said it makes Lazarus realize the risk she's taking. "No, Lindsey… The worst is a Lunarian city incinerated by a nuclear bomb… In any case, it looks like I owe you again. Thank you."

"No promises Lazarus. Abby may be too busy to see you herself… For now, settle back and take a nap or go online. I will rejoin you in a few minutes. No matter what, we still have a long flight ahead of us and I plan on sleeping as much as possible."

"I couldn't sleep right now."

"Then read a book," she turns to face front.

"Good idea," Lazarus settles into his seat.

ЯL

Lindsey relishes using her visor again. It's been too long. She routes a call and almost immediately, the seat in front of her disappears. In its place materializes the stately image of Luna's AI. Wisps of gray highlight her dark hair and her broad smile welcomes Lindsey home. The woman radiates acceptance.

"Greetings, Lindsey. It's so good to see you." she said warmly.

Lindsey smiles back, "Greetings, Magi, how are you?"

"I'm fine. Did you enjoy your time on Mother Earth?" The lag as the signal travels to Luna and back is barely noticeable.

"Some, but I'm glad it's over. I'm ready to come home," Lindsey said and Magi nods knowingly, "Is it possible to speak with Abby or Corso right now?"

"Corso is unavailable but I can check with Abby," Magi said. "It may take a few minutes," she smiles and disappears.

Lindsey nods and accesses the Republic's main database. One of Luna's national treasures and an essential component of the Law of Full Disclosure, the Public Records database is dispersed throughout the Republic on a vast array of Zettaspheres.

The size of a grain of rice, Zettaspheres are data storage devices with enormous capacity (zettabyte = 10^{21} bytes). A single Zettasphere can contain all of humanity's written works thousands of times over, store a century's worth of audio/video from a security sensor, or record a person's life as viewed through a visor.

Within these tiny data storage devices resides not only the accumulated knowledge of the human race, but also the historical record of its recent past. For the last half-century, the Lunarians have archived into Public Records every digital recording of any kind. They didn't delete anything. Any citizen can access Public Records to determine what really happened. Everything is recorded somewhere, but you need Magi in order to find anything within the enormous database.

Lindsey occupies herself with catching up on the Republic while she waits. For the last six weeks, she's been getting the news filtered by Earthnet commentators who have only the vaguest notion of Lunarian society. They typically oversimplify the underlying issues if they bother to present them at all. Media hacks carefully screen news items and show only those they can twist into support for their agenda. The interpretations of these snippets are rarely accurate and never questioned by the citizens who view them. This black journalism has become known as foxing a story after an early cable news network called Fox News who perfected the technique almost a century before. Truth has very little to do with power.

For almost a decade, the bombings on Luna have made the news. Graphic images of violence attracts users which sells net time and that's the name of the game. The major networks relish showing the hell suffered by the Lunarians, replaying the bloodiest scenes repeatedly.

Lindsey's shocked by the escalation of violence while she's been gone. She sucks in a breath when she finds the vid of an incident in Hell's Kitchen almost two weeks earlier. A bomb had exploded in a mall killing three, wounding twenty–two. She'd eaten there many times. One of the dead is a young man barely out of puberty and the son of a colleague. The Brotherhood adamantly denied any responsibility and offered compensation to the victims' families who flatly rejected the blood money.

The news vid freezes and shrinks to an icon, replaced by Magi. "Excuse me Lindsey but Abby is ready to see you."

Abigail Dugan takes Magi's place. Abby has her blond hair pulled back in a ponytail. She smiles at Lindsey.

"Greetings Lindsey."

"Greetings Abby."

"How was Mother Earth?" Abby asks.

"Worrisome, I'm afraid. Let's just say I'm looking forward to home and don't intend to leave again for a very long time, but that's not why I called. I met someone on my trip back I believe you should meet. A runner named Lazarus Sheffield. He's a Senior Analyst for the Department of Homeland Security and a member of the Directors inner staff, no less. He claims to know about the Brotherhood's nuclear program and the disappearance of Hasin bin Aunker and Abdel Salam Arif, among others," Lindsey said.

The names got Abby's attention, "Does he know where they are?"

"No, I don't believe so. He said at least four thousand have vanished with them, but it could be as many as a hundred thousand. He wants to talk with a Councilor."

"Why's he running?" Abby asks.

"Mainly because the Federation refused to warn us. Quite admirable, actually. Beyond that, I think you should meet with him because he offers a unique insight into the political situation within the NAF. Worth your time."

Abby raises her eyebrows looking intently at the younger woman for a moment. "OK, I'll meet with him but he's your responsibility."

"My responsibility? You mean until we get to Aldrin Station, right?" Lindsey asks.

"You're the one who's sponsoring him, therefore, you're his mentor. It's highly unusual for the NAF to let such a high-ranking official get away. I want to keep a tight rein on the situation. That means you must stay close to him." Abby pauses, peering intently at Lindsey, "From the look of things back on Heaven's Gate, it seems to me you're already half way there."

Lindsey doesn't even bat an eye, realizing that Abby is reviewing the public data available from Heaven's Gate even while talking with her. "It's traditional to get laid your first time in freefall. Besides, it's not every day I meet such an adorable virgin."

"Um… He reminds me of Robert Pattinson," Abby said.

"Robert Pattinson?"

"Pattinson was a teen heartthrob from my youth… Never mind. I don't expect you to know the name."

"I'm scheduled at the clinic on arrival so someone will need to hold his hand for a few hours," Lindsey said.

"I'll send someone to meet you."

"Who?" Lindsey asks.

Abby shakes her head, "Don't know yet. I'll make it a surprise. I know how much you like surprises." She nods and vanishes.

ЯL

While Lindsey was busy making her call, Lazarus explores the net with his new visor. He starts by requesting a general background check on Lindsey.

Lazarus creates a summary using a familiar program. …born in Oxford, England on Monday morning at 9:05, October 12, 2043… She's forty-nine years old? He would have guessed thirty at most.

Grandmother was the technician who first measured Type 3 superconductivity… Mother was a history professor at a community college when Lindsey was growing up… Mother died of unspecified causes… Father still alive and resides in a retirement community outside London… Her only brother, Harley Marquest, killed in 2062 while serving in the Royal Marines somewhere in the Middle East.

She relinquished her citizenship in June 2062 and immigrated to the Republic of Luna… Received a Bachelor of Science in Mechanical Engineering from the University of New London in 2067 and followed that up with a PhD in Materials Processing from the Albert Einstein

Institute of Technology in 2070… Joined Metcal soon after graduation and stayed with them for twenty-one years. Long list of places, responsibilities and accomplishments attributed to her while with Metcal, all of them off-planet. Wait. What's this? Captain, Lincoln County Police Department, Metro Division?

His gut knots up. She had not mentioned being a police officer. It's ironic that his first instinct is to fear, considering his only job since completing college was with DHS.

Lazarus continues reading the summary, noting that all of her accomplishments are engineering in nature. Near the bottom, he scrolls through a list of articles and professional papers she has written over the years. There is only one general enough for him to try reading. Lindsey had written it for Science Weekly, an EU network magazine devoted to promoting science education among the general population. He touches its icon.

"Please select how you would like it read," Magi said.

"No… that won't be necessary. I will read it for myself," he replies.

"Very well"

How Superconductivity Changed the World appears and he starts reading.

ЯL

Lindsey waits until he's finished reading, "I've completed my call."

Lazarus sweeps the document from his virtual desktop and turns to face her, "What did you find out? Will she meet with me?"

"Abby will have someone waiting for us at Aldrin Station when we arrive. Let's take it one-step at a time, ok? If there's one thing I've learned, it's not to push too hard, especially Abby."

"Whatever you say, Captain Lindsey," Lazarus said looking intently into her gray eyes. "I thought you told me you're an engineer."

She returns his stare, "I am, but I'm also a captain in the reserve.

What's the problem?"

"No problem. I just don't understand how you can be both?"

"Most able-bodied citizens are also members of their local police reserve and are expected to serve eight weeks out of the year. After you're a citizen, you can join." Lindsey glances at his polygraphic indicators.

"It's mandatory?" He asked.

"No, but why would you not want to participate in your own defense?" She hopes she hasn't made a mistake taking on this project. For all her skills at detecting lies and deception, she cannot see into a man's heart.

"Don't get me wrong, I want to participate. Where I'm from, the government discourages a person from taking an active part in society. They entertain and distract with a wide assortment of venues, church, movies, sports, and politics are the biggies. The less interest people have, the easier it is to keep them in the herd, so to speak. It doesn't matter if they vote and most don't bother. The Reformation Party hasn't lost an election in my lifetime. Do the math. Those in control will not allow anyone to upset the status quo." He shakes his head, "No, far from it, I'm looking forward to being a part of something that I can respect. If joining the reserve is expected, then I will gladly do it."

"Let's just say participation is encouraged. No one is forced to do anything." Lindsey stretches, enjoying the feeling of Luna gravity after so long. "Before I go to sleep there's one more thing."

"What's that?"

"Let me stress once again that you must always be honest and open… with every Lunarian, not just me. Lying is never an option. You've admitted being very good at hiding your true feeling and beliefs, and I can understand why... but you cannot allow that part of your former life to continue. If you hope to meet Abby, don't even think about lying or stretching the truth. That would be disastrous to your chances of citizenship. Lunarians despise the dishonesty of secrets and respect a person for being true to themselves and the world around them."

"To thine own self be true," Lazarus said. "And it must follow, as the night the day, thou cannot be false to any man."

"Hamlet, Act 1, Scene 3," Lindsey said completely caught off guard. "Why am I surprised you know Shakespeare?"

"That's the first time I've dared utter those words. It feels... incredible." he looks at Lindsey and a cloud of worry flashes across his face, "Are there subjects I should avoid?"

She shakes her head, "Freedom doesn't tell you what subjects are permissible. Lunarians will discuss anything at anytime with anyone. Feel free to run your mouth, but let me warn you right now, Lunarians are not shy about expressing their opinions on religion, or the Federation, or the Islamic Brotherhood, or anything else." Lindsey said emphatically. "So, if you think I've been hard on you, let me tell you... you haven't seen anything. You had better be prepared to defend whatever positions you take with facts and not opinions."

"I look forward to it," Lazarus said eagerly.

"I'm sure we all will benefit from your insight, but for now, just stop sticking your hand out. That's bad manners on Luna. You see... the majority of Lunarians have this thing about touching. So until you get a feel for how it works, don't touch anyone unless they offer first. OK?"

"I understand they don't like to shake hands, but you're saying avoid all touching?"

"That's exactly what I'm saying, just until you get to know someone, or they give you permission. Lunarians do so much vid conferencing it's become traditional to avoid all physical contact. For the same reason, it's considered bad manners to remove your visor during meetings." Lindsey pauses and adds, "There will be many things you will not understand at first. Just give it time and keep an open mind. Most of them will make sense eventually."

Lazarus smiles, "If other Lunarians have even a fraction of your kindness, than the Republic of Luna will be a paradise."

Lindsey kisses him gently, "Flattery will get you everywhere."

ЯL

This is round trip one-thousand-thirty-nine for Evolution's Child, christened by her first captain twenty years ago. The ship isn't much to look at. Born in the vacuum of space, it will never feel an atmosphere.

Hyundai Shipyards had just completed a refit that included four new magnetoplasma thrusters. They raise the freighter's payload capacity to almost a million kilos. It seems a crime to have less than thirty thousand aboard for the engines shakedown voyage.

Above the engine section is a large pressurized disk containing over five hundred cubic meters of living space. Known as the pilothouse, it's literally the pilot's house.

Above the pilothouse is the cargo bay. It's almost empty with only a few crates secured by ratchet straps.

Evolution's Child is built rugged, both locomotive and boxcar of the late 21st century, able to pickup and deliver cargo from LEO to the surface of the moon and back. Six massive shock-absorber landing-legs surround the engine compartment and extend up past the roof of the pilothouse, each at an angle avoiding the thruster's exhaust.

Pilot Nell Goddard initiates the link with Luna Central, "This is Evolution's Child. Standby for burn in one minute."

The image of a uniformed police officer appears before her. It's the first time she's seen a police officer working LC. Something's amiss. Nevertheless, she keeps her questions to herself.

The two-second round trip is just long enough to notice but not long enough to be a real nuisance, "Roger, Evolution's Child. You are go for trans-lunar burn. We show you at orbital insertion in T-minus seventy-two hours."

"Roger that, Evolution's Child out," Nell breaks contact. The uniformed controller vanishes, "Emcee, you are free to initiate the burn," she informs the autopilot. Emcee is a primitive AI, but always does what she can to make her pilots life easier.

"You got it Nell," Emcee said.

With a subtle flick of her wrist, Nell takes the movie off pause and settles back. The image grows until it fills her visor, immersing her in one of the Harrison Ford oldies. Nell is a film buff, common for those who sail the vast distances of space. She's looking forward on this trip to viewing the latest additions to her collection, the remixed conversions of some of her favorite flat screen classics.

After years piloting this route, Nell is a veteran spacer. Her mind tunes out the acceleration klaxon and handles the three Gs stoically. Only after the burn is complete does she turn away from the movie to check her position.

Right between the white lines. Nell turns back to Harrison.

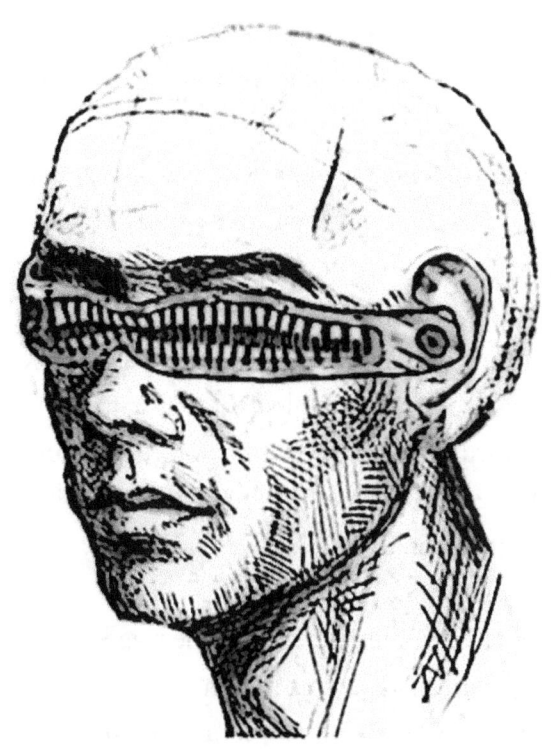

Quan Kiai

*"When I do good, I feel good; when I do
bad, I feel bad. That's my religion."*

Abraham Lincoln (1809-1865)

It's Halloween and Club Rio's packed. Three times as long as it is wide, the room is without corners or angles to mar its smoothness. A vid of the universe plays across its domed ceiling in exquisite detail giving the crowd below the illusion of moving through the cosmos at enormous speed. It lights the room with dim flickering luminance that is constantly in motion. Around the periphery, brighter stationary pools of light silhouette the bar and highlight the public entrances at each end. Looking down at the center of the room, the stage is a raised dais that pulses and ripples with every color of the rainbow. The room is alive with people.

On stage, a four-man band in garish skin-tight orange and purple jumpsuits belts out their version of a heavy metal classic. The bands singer leaps high into the air as he wails, twisting and cavorting in Luna's gravity.

The guitarists are both playing Duraglass Gibsons. Only the titanium strings are visible when silent, but with the slightest strum, the body of the instrument infuses with color, running up and down the spectrum in cadence with the music. Sound and vision merge, sometimes harsh and violent, other times smooth and subtle, depending on the musician's slightest whim.

At the geometric center of the stage, the drummer hovers high above the guitarists, his drums floating in a great arc about him. They too pulse with color at each impact, complimenting the guitars with a driving beat of sight and sound.

Around the stage, dancers undulate in total unison like a kelp forest in high seas, their heads tilted back and arms reaching for the ceiling. They fill the dance floor and push out among the tables. The haunting echo of the drums pull the dancers into the music's spell, their closely packed bodies swaying in rhythm.

Above them, the domed display is constantly changing, taking them all on a wild ride, passing galaxies like sand flowing through an hourglass, sweeping past one gigantic swirl only to plunge headlong into the billions of stars contained in the next. The vid slows as it soars past an enormous black hole at the heart of a spiral galaxy, its event horizon defined by thousands of stars torn asunder in a gigantic whirlpool of destruction and creation.

Light marks the clubs main entrances, one at each end. The polished stone bar follows the curve of the wall along its perimeter broken only by the two doors. All along the bar, it's standing room only. A lucky few sit on barstools while most stand, crowding up to the bar. Glass shelves behind the bar display an assortment of alcoholic beverages, more than half from Mother Earth. A single shot of authentic Black Label whisky imported from Tennessee or Smirnoff vodka from Moscow will cost a miner a half days pay.

Behind a row of room dividers, several low-G snooker tables are the center of attention. Laughter and the sharp crack of ball-to-ball contact occasionally penetrate the music.

Tables and booths make up the majority of the club's main floor. They're packed with the young and not so young of Aldrin Station. The overhead projection casts a flickering light over intimate conversations deciding the nights sleeping arrangements or some juicy bit of gossip, a human close-order-drill evolved over many generations.

Without exception, everyone in the room is wearing visors. Although Lunarian visors come in many shapes and sizes, most of these are standard Razors, a silver and gold bar that extends from ear to ear with vertical segments along its length. Regardless of the model, visors have one unifying feature, they all have sensors that pick up the wearers underlying facial expression and broadcast this information to other visors thereby rendering themselves invisible.

In the midst of the merriment, a server skillfully weaves through the crowd. She's showing a lot of skin in a tight fawn-colored costume with a large white fluff-ball attached at the base of her spine above a shapely set of butt checks. On her head is a pair of rabbit ears and she's wearing an old-fashioned bow tie.

Arriving with a smile, the server places the full tray on the table and leans down, showing the tab and more than a little cleavage to the young man sitting closest to the end.

"Outstanding costume Sue," Tempel smiles at her. Their visors make it possible to hold a conversation over the music.

"Thanks," Sue replies, "I'm a Playboy Bunny."

"I don't know what that is," Tempel said, "but I like it." He glances at the total and passes his left hand across the scanner embedded in the ticket.

"Where's your costume? You guys are not getting with the program," Sue scolds. Many in the club are wearing standard issue off duty police uniforms including everyone at this table. The only difference is the small blue shield over their heart.

"We decided to come here at the last minute," Sam said reaching for a piece of deep fried soymeat from the tray, getting sauce all over her fingers. Tempel and Samantha have known each other for all of their young lives and their families go all the way back to the founding of Aldrin Station. For twenty years, they have shared classrooms and teachers, friends and family, they even wear each other's clothing on occasion.

"All of Luna is celebrating Tempel's birthday. Didn't you know?" Sam said licking her fingers.

"You don't say. And I thought it was Halloween or something." Turning back to Tempel, she smiles. "How old are you?"

Tempel grins wickedly and said, "Old enough."

"He's twenty," Sam replies for Tempel.

"Twenty is a good age, but so is forty-eight. Let me know if you need anything else." Sue winks and eases back into the crowd, bunny tail swishing in time with the beat.

Their booth is one of many in the nightclub. Its raised position gives them an excellent view of the dancers and stage.

Around them, off-duty officers sip their beverage of choice and unwind. Men and women alike have short-cropped hair or no hair at all and most are over two meters in height.

Brice and Odessa are down at the far end trying to tickle each other's tonsils with their tongues. Oblivious to everything except each other, Odessa is running her hand inside his shirt. Next to her, Marcel is earnestly talking with Consuela, who is doing her best to look interested but not succeeding. Beyond them, Kipper leans forward snagging two beers, handing one to Karyl before taking a swig of his. He makes a big production of laying his arm across the back of the seat behind her before snuggling close. Corazon and Tatiana have their heads together in deep conversation, the newly arrived food and drink ignored for the moment. Tatiana's twin brother Alonzo is exchanging smiles with a dark haired shortimer several booths over.

Sam leans against Tempel, firmly pressing a tit into his arm. "Happy Birthday," Her lips brush his ear, her breath smells of barbeque. Tempel playfully licks a smear of sauce from the corner of her mouth.

Alonzo slips out of their booth, heading for the dark haired girl. Sam nudges Tempel and nods towards Alonzo.

"Lover boy's at it again," she said playfully. Her warm breath caresses his cheek.

The girl smiles as Alonzo approaches. He leans over and said something causing her to laugh. She slides over making room.

Tempel grins, taking another pull off his beer and nuzzles Sam's ear, "Who is she?"

"A shortimer working out at Far Point. Tatiana has met her. Don't know her name." She ends the conversation with a kiss.

When used by a Lunarian, shortimer is a rather derogatory term referring to the people sent up from Mother Earth for a month or a year. Most shortimers tend to keep to themselves but there isn't any law against them being here on a Saturday night but it's unusual.

Tempel's intensely aware of Sam's supple body pressed tightly against his. Time slips by.

The two men enter the club by the east entrance. Their clothing marks them as shortimers.

"Excuse me, weapons must be checked in at the bar," the clubs doorman calls out.

The men ignore the command and continue to walk deeper into the room. The volume near the entrance is not much louder than elevator music. Unless they're deaf, they heard.

The doorman signals for help and several bouncers armed only with non-lethal tasers converge on the men before they can get far. "Stop immediately…" Mac addresses them from behind, his hand resting on the butt of his stunner. "You must check your weapons or leave." Several bartenders pause, resting their hands on more firepower stashed under the bar.

"We will be here only a short time," growls the older man.

"That's fine but you will still need to check your weapons."

The younger of the two has continued to look about inside the club and has fixated on the dance floor. He leans over and whispers something in an unknown language to his companion who said with a single syllable grunt.

Turning away from the bouncers, the older man walks to the bar. Sliding his sidearm out of its holster, he lays it on the countertop.

"Left hand please," a female bartender said. "We need to establish ownership."

He stares intently at the woman before placing his left hand on the bar beside his weapon.

She ignores him. "Mustafa Malik, welcome to Club Rio. You can pick this up on your way out. Can I get you a drink, compliments of the house?" She stares back at him.

Without responding, Malik turns away, motioning for his companion to take his place.

The younger man does not attempt to hide his contempt, pulling his weapon from its holster in a show of quick-draw prowess. The bartender steps back and reaches for her stunner.

Malik growls, "Anwar."

The young man laughs, flips his weapon end for end, and lays it on the surface of the bar. With exaggerated slowness, he splays his left hand next to it, palm down.

The bartender, clearly not amused by the maneuver, nevertheless, does her job, "Anwar Jafa, welcome to Club Rio," she said stiffly as the sidearm disappears under the bar. "You can pick it up on your way out. The first drink's on the house."

"Later," Jafa replies. He flashes white teeth, turns, and follows Malik deeper into the nightclub. It was just as Malik foretold. The sound near the entrance is not very loud, but as they penetrate the infidel's lair, the volume soars upward dramatically until it overwhelms any chance to talk normally. Jafa steels himself against its power. *Allah be praised, this is not music.*

ЯL

A few minutes later, feeling safe within Club Rio, distracted by each other and the alcohol, no one at the table sees the fight start. The bands sudden silence causes Tempel and Sam to break their kiss. Out on the dance floor, people scramble to give the combatants room.

Alonzo is flat on his back, his visor hanging from one ear, with a stranger sitting on his chest slamming his head repeatedly against the stone floor. The dark-haired girl is just beyond them, excitement twisting her pretty face.

No one among the onlooking Lunarians know what the fight is about, but even so, many of them are starting to press forward demanding loudly that the attack stop.

Tempel doesn't wait. In a flash, he's out of the booth and heading for the dance floor. Moving with speed and power, the young Lunarian launches himself and plants his shoulder into the side of the man attacking Alonzo. The impact sends them rolling in a tangle across the floor. By the time they stop, Tempel has the man in a death grip, one twist and he could separate his spinal column between the 4th and 5th cervical vertebra.

The man struggles but soon realizes he's in big trouble. He gasps trying vainly to hold his own even as his face turns crimson.

Just as suddenly as it started, the club bouncers put a stop to the fracas. "Tempel. Let him go," Mac said laying his hand on the young warrior's shoulder.

Surprised by how quickly he became willing to kill, Tempel relaxes his hold and rises to his feet.

The shortimer gasps as the blood surges into his brain, rubbing his neck and only beginning to feel the oncoming headache.

"What's going on?" Mac demands.

Tempel shrugs and growls, "Ask him," without taking his eyes off the shortimer.

Instead, Mac turns to the older man and said, "Malik, you have worn out your welcome. Gather up your comrade and leave."

Malik looks strangely pleased as he observes the group spread out behind Tempel. Sam and Tatiana are kneeling beside Alonzo who is telling them he's fine, to stop babying him, all the while blood continues to flow from a nasty cut on the back of his head. Young Jafa stands glaring at Tempel.

"Cheryl, give these gentleman back their guns... empty," Mac said. "Then I will walk you to the door."

Malik couldn't care less that they are ejecting him from Club Rio and when Jafa starts to speak, he raises his hand stopping him. "Anwar, see to Dalal while I retrieve our weapons." He walks to the bar where

Cheryl has placed the two empty guns. He slides one into his holster. Returning, he hands the other to Jafa. "Peace be upon you," he bows, then leads them out the way they had come. The girl follows a few steps behind, her head down.

Once well out of Club Rio, Jafa turns to Malik, "*The one they call Tempel must be one of them. Only Djinn could do that to me.*" He speaks in the ancient Aramaic dialect of Nabataean, a language seldom heard since the seventh century. They are reasonably sure the infidels have not translated it but they are cautious, speaking seldom and even then, using special code phrases to increase the confusion.

"*Indeed,*" he motions for the girl to walk beside him. "*Tell me Dalal, what have you learned?*"

"*I agree with Jafa. The man I danced with is Djinn and the one who attacked Jafa is a leader. The others I am not sure but I believe they are Djinn as well.*" In Islam, Djinn is an evil supernatural creature. According to the Qur'an, God created Djinn out of 'smokeless fire' and created man out of clay.

The fear has evaporated from the young woman but subservience remains. She knows dancing with the infidel pushed the boundaries even for an undercover operative, but it was all for Allah. "*They call themselves Quan Kiai,*" she said.

"*Quan Kiai...*" Malik mused. "*Allah may yet smile upon us...*" He has heard mention of special police units but never anything concrete, just disturbing rumors of advanced technology. As Malik mulls this over, they emerge onto Brooklyn Mall's North Courtyard and are once again among the infidels.

"Come, let us stop and have a cup of fine Lunarian coffee," Malik said in English. He changes direction leading them towards a small cafe. An ad hoc plan is forming. He switches back to Aramaic, "*Let us see what Allah has in store for us.*"

They approach *La Bruschetta*, an old-world style sidewalk café.

Set in a stone façade, a heavy wooden beam spans the door and both windows, the cafés name prominent upon it. An old-fashioned menu displays in the left window, an arrangement of nuts, cheese and chocolate is in the other. Two replica oil lamps grace the stonework, one on each side of the entrance. A bright red awning tops everything.

Outside the front door, rough-hewn cobblestones and a series of planters define the extent the sidewalk café intrudes on the main plaza. Small round tables with matching red tablecloths are scattered across the patio. A small pot overflowing with live flowers adorns the center of each table. More oil lamps glimmer atop metal posts adding to the old-world ambiance of the café.

Malik selects a chair that puts his back against the wall with a clear view of the courtyard.

Magi makes note of the exchange, placing the conversation in its entirety into a growing database in an effort to decipher this new language. Without a proper cross reference, she stands little chance.

Mac glances at Tempel after the three shortimers have left, "That was some tackle. Where did you learn that?"

"Captain Osaka," he replies, still shaking off the adrenal effects of the encounter.

Mac chuckles, "I should've known."

Tempel kneels beside Alonzo. Tatiana has managed to stop the blood using a bar towel but Alonzo still looks in bad shape. He had suffered several hard blows.

"How you doing?" He asked his friend.

"Never better," Alonzo said. Reaching for Tempel's arm, "Give me a hand," and begins pulling himself up.

"I don't think that's such a good idea…" Tatiana said even as the young man stands, holding the towel against his head. Others see for the first time the extent of blood that has soaked the back of his shirt and stained the floor beneath him.

Mac frowns and orders "Lay back down Alonzo… Emergency Response, report immediately to Club Rio."

Despite his repeated assurance that he's fine and a steadfast refusal to lie down, they finally persuade the young warrior to sit. Quan Kiai gathers around him.

A club patron steps forward to offer assistance. She's an off duty ER medico. "Let me take a peek at that," the woman said as she moves around behind Alonzo. Looking under the bloody towel, "The bleeding's stopped but you will need a surgeon to close it properly." She moves back around, pulling down his cheeks, gazing into his eyes, "You're suffering from a mild concussion. If you take it easy, you should be fine."

"So… was she worth it?" Corazon asks after reviewing the start of the fight as recorded from Alonzo's visor.

Alonzo glares at him.

"I can't believe you let a pretty shortimer set you up for a sucker punch." Corazon grins at Alonzo then shrugs. "Facts are facts."

"On the up side, at least she was pretty. Most of them look like they shaved their ass and walk backward," Brice chuckles at his own crude joke.

Upon receiving a call, Consuela turns away and heads towards the nearby exit. Only Marcel notices.

Tempel listens to the banter and watches a cleanup disk scurry across the dance floor collecting the blood and other biomaterials. Before it's finished, the band starts playing again and things begin returning to normal. Would it have been the same if Alonzo had died? Tempel pushes these dark thoughts aside. "It's been a long day. After Alonzo is taken care of, I'm going to catch a bite, then get some sleep."

"Mind if I join you?" Sam purrs.

Tempel grins and nods knowing he wouldn't get much sleep.

"Not me. I want to party." Brice declares, "SuperNovA has a new game I want to check out. Who's with me?" Brice looks around the group. SuperNovA is nightclub that's glitz and bright lights instead of hard rock and star light.

Turning to Tatiana, Corazon asks, "What about you?"

"I think I will go with Alonzo then hook up with Karl. I'll see you tomorrow at roll call," she said, shutting the door on anything more. She and Karl have become hot items recently, cutting down on the time spent with other friends.

"Tell that big Swede he's the luckiest man alive," Corazon said with a grin. He's not surprised. He turns back to Brice and said, "I'm in." Corazon never lets one rejection spoil his entire night and SuperNovA is one of his favorite hotspots. He never sleeps alone.

Brice snuggles up to Odessa, "An hour or so at the tables, then my place?"

She grins and nods. "Sure, why not. I love kicking your ass right before I kiss it and make it all better," she coos.

Kipper and Karyl both shake their heads when Brice looks at them, "Sorry, something has come up that needs tending." Karyl grins mischievously, tightening her hold on Kipper.

"I'll tag along," Marcel said, suddenly wanting to get shit-faced drunk.

"Great." Brice exclaims and asks Tempel, "Why not eat at Lucifer's Diner? You and Sam can walk with us on our way to SuperNovA."

Tempel looks at Sam and shrugs.

"Sure, why not," Sam imitates Odessa perfectly.

The arrival of ER interrupts them. Without any fanfare, the medicos walk the injured man out to the waiting ambulance, Tatiana at his side. They already know the story and the extent of his injuries and waste no time in getting him on his way to the hospital. By morning, he will be good as new without even a scar to show for his carelessness.

ЯL

Emerging from Steinway Avenue, the group starts across the North Courtyard. Two teen girls are sitting on the edge of the fountain dangling their feet in its water. Other young people move about the courtyard, laughing and enjoying each other's company. Only the three shortimers sitting at the café pay them any attention.

Swinging wide of the tall three-level fountain, they make a beeline for the eatery on the other side of the square. It has a striking holographic sign on its roof just above the entrance featuring a red devil complete with horns and a forked tail. Every so often, he points towards the sign with his pitchfork, *Lucifer's Diner, Fine Dining with a Flare.* The apparition turns to look down upon those passing by, eyes flaring briefly as he flashes a fang-filled smile. Then it turns back, stabbing once more at the message. The basic sequence repeats for every citizen, but never twice in the exact same way.

Tempel and Sam walk towards the diner's entrance and Brice, Odessa, Marcel and Corazon wave and continue, disappearing into the mall beyond.

The interior of the diner is long and narrow with a counter on one side and a row of booths on the other. The booths are next to windows that look out upon the courtyard. Beyond the counter is the kitchen. The booths and stools are bright red imitation-leather upholstery. Everything else is chrome.

"Greetings Sam, Tempel. What can I get for you?" The man behind the counter asks as they come in.

Sliding onto a stool, Tempel replies without bothering to look at a menu, "Greetings Lou, chili and a beer and don't be stingy with the onions."

The man smiles, Tempel always orders chili and a beer. "You got it. And for you, Sam?"

"The same," she replies. The aroma of fresh corn bread wafts from the kitchen. "And a slice of corn bread."

Lou smiles and nods, turns and calls out, "Lucy, two chilies hold the peppers, extra onions and corn bread." He picks up a tall glass and places it at an angle beneath the tap before pulling back on the slender handle. Beer slides in smoothly, building up a fine head. He sits it down and repeats the process, placing the two beers in front of his customers. Reaching under the counter he adds a squirt bottle filled with honey and a platter of butter. Nothing beats fresh baked corn bread smothered in butter and honey.

Behind them, beyond the windows of the diner and across the courtyard, the three shortimers pay their tab and leave the sidewalk café, heading directly towards the diner.

"Tempel, Sam, you have company coming in from across the courtyard. The same people that attacked Alonzo." Magi said. "I have notified the closest police patrol but they will not arrive in time. I have told Brice, Odessa, Corazon and Marcel to return at best speed."

Tempel links to the diner's outside sensors and watch the three shortimers come across the courtyard. He follows Sam to the door, "Keep that chili hot, Lou. We'll be right back."

Outside the diner, Tempel steps away from Sam giving them both a clear field of fire.

As the two shortimers draw near, they too separate putting a few meters between them. Jafa, the younger of the two, locks on Tempel, hate for this particular infidel boiling to the surface. Malik confronts Sam.

Tempel senses the arrival of Odessa, Brice, Marcel, and Corazon but keeps his focus on the man across from him, the one who wants to kill him.

"We got your back." Brice said scanning the courtyard.

"Prepare to meet Allah." Jafa exclaims.

"If it's death you seek, you came to the right place," Tempel growls back.

Jafa's anger grows until he cannot contain himself a moment longer. He draws and dies an instant later. He never had a chance.

The sharp crack of Tempel's laser burning its way through air and flesh echoes harshly across the courtyard. None of them will forget the smell.

A split second after Tempel fires, Malik throws his hands up and backs away.

The girl rushes over throwing herself on the fallen man. "Jafa." She wails. "Jafa." Looking up at Tempel, she screams. "*Murderer.*"

"Murderer." Malik repeats. He's looking down the business end of Sam's pistol so he's very careful not to let his hand get near his own. However, he has what he needs. He would have preferred that Jafa kill the infidel but this will serve just as well.

"The vid will verify that he drew first and I defended myself," Tempel said. It's shaping up to be a long night but not in the way he had imagined.

ЯL

The locker-room is loud and boisterous as LCPD prepares for shift change. Steam roils out of the empty showers and the sound of hundreds of lockers closing signal it's time for roll call. Quan Kiai is but a small portion of this organized mayhem.

Men and women dressed in Lunarian Police uniforms exit the room and move up the ramp. The bright blue patch on Tempel's right shoulder further identifies him as a member of Lincoln County's 22nd Metro Division, and the clenched fist puts him in Quan Kiai platoon. Named by its founder, Captain Kitajima Osaka, Quan is a Chinese martial arts term meaning, "*fist*", and Kiai is Japanese meaning, "*fighting spirit*."

Emerging onto the parade grounds, Tempel falls in line with his squad and starts counting heads. It's the job of the Senior Lieutenant to make sure everyone's present or accounted for.

"Sam, where are you?" He asked.

"I've been called to a meeting with Abby. I'll see you after roll call," she said. They don't bother casting an image to each other, staying with audio only for this brief conversation.

Several times, other young officers approach Tempel and congratulate him on his victory the night before. His own troops bask in the reflected glory until he puts a stop to it.

"At ease. I don't want to hear another word. I took someone's life. I didn't win a race." Tempel snaps. They left him alone after that.

Right on time, Captain Kitajima emerges from battalion offices onto the parade ground with the other platoon leaders.

"Quan Kiai present or accounted for. Sergeant Odegaard is absent but accounted for," Tempel reports.

"Thank you Lieutenant." Kitajima studies him a moment. It's not every day one of his warriors kill someone in a gunfight.

The platoon leaders bring the assembly to parade rest, hands locked behind their backs, feet shoulder-width apart, sidearms holstered and eyes straight ahead. Following ancient tradition, the eerie sounds of a bugle echo across the subterranean cavern.

Before the last note fades into silence, Commander House's adjutant calls forth across the parade ground, "Attennnnn*TION*." The sound of four hundred boots striking stone explodes in a thunderclap that reverberates up and down the man-made stone cavern, putting vivid punctuation to the buglers' call.

Roll call sounds along the line of companies, "Quan Kiai, all present and accounted for." Captain Osaka calls out in turn.

A few minutes later it's finished, more of a formality than necessity. The platoons begin their assigned duties.

Keeping Quan Kiai at attention, Kitajima does a sharp about face, "Column Left. Harh.... By Twos, Forward.... Harh."

The squads move out with Master Sergeant Hackling calling cadence from a position near the rear. Kitajima stays alongside, marching the company off the parade ground and through a corridor to the practice field. Here is where the battalion conducts most of its training, everything from target practice to combat maneuvers.

"Double time... Harh." The column begins a long winding run along a track around the huge space, each officer leaning forward, balancing traction with acceleration. Kitajima sets an unusually strenuous pace even for lunar gravity, challenging them to stay in formation while maintaining speed. Although the officers of Quan Kiai are physically fit, they are soon covered in sweat.

Thirty minutes later, "Company... Harh." The formation slows to a walk, all of them gasping for breath. Kitajima leads them off the track to a grouping of tables used as a classroom.

"Company… Halt." Kitajima barks, "Fall out and find a seat."

Kitajima walks past the tables, turns and faces the platoon. "At Ease. A few hours ago, Lieutenant Dugan and several of your comrades risked your mission. When faced with a life and death situation, they blinked. They're lucky they're alive."

"Excuse me Captain but Tempel won in a fair fight," Brice said.

"Who in hell wants a fair fight? I don't and you shouldn't." Kitajima has trained these young people for over two years and feels that he knows them well. "I fear that until you experience combat, you will not fully appreciate the point I'm making."

Kitajima stops in front of Brice, glaring down at him. "When you deployed at North Courtyard you faced outward. Why?"

Brice looks out of the corner of his eye at Marcel.

"Don't look at him, just answer the damn question. Why did you face outward and put your backs to Malik and Jafa?"

"We didn't know if there were any others in North Courtyard or out on the arboretum that would back them up," Brice said.

"Besides, we had two against two," Marcel adds.

"That's my point." Kitajima bores in, "When you come up against any enemy you must threaten them with everything you've got and be willing to back it up. There's no place on a battlefield for sportsmanship. That line of thinking will get you killed."

Kitajima looks down at Corazon, "If you can get behind them, do it." He moves on to Marcel, "If you can shoot first, do it. Find a weakness and exploit it with overwhelming force. It's the only way to stay alive. Work as a team. Together you are strong. But if you voluntarily split your forces you weaken yourselves, inviting disaster."

Kitajima stops in front of Consuela, "You're less likely to need to kill someone once they come to the conclusion that any aggression on their part would be suicide. I'm talking about taking the situation far beyond mutual assured destruction. Make the confrontation as lopsided in your favor as physically possible. By leaving the front door even slightly ajar, you're inviting them to kick it in. You must treat anyone threatening to harm you or your comrades with extreme prejudice. Failure to do so will eventually cost you your life, and those of your comrades. Look around you. Quan Kiai depends on you for support and mutual protection. If you're dead, you can't fulfill that duty." He turns and moves back to center stage, "Am I making myself *CLEAR*."

"*AYE*."

Kitajima glares around the assemblage of Luna's finest young men and women, and slowly nods. "I sincerely hope that it is, but I doubt it. Knowledge of this type must be paid in blood." His gaze passes from one officer to the next, wondering who will be the first that pays. The thought saddens him.

"Excuse me Captain, but we do have a kill to our name," Brice said.

The captain looks intently at him and then at Tempel, "Yes, I guess we do. I'm proud of the way you've handled yourself during this entire incident. You have my full support."

Tempel nods.

They have absorbed the lesson as best he can teach it. Turning away, "Next order of business, we have a new mission," Kitajima announces in a much calmer voice.

Special Weapons and Advanced Technology is one of the choice assignments within any police department. These officers train with the latest gear and techniques. Quan Kiai is one of several SWAT platoons in Lincoln County's Metro Division. Platoons consist of two squads each containing a lieutenant, a sergeant, a sergeant-in-training and four Special Forces officers.

"Squad One will deploy outside along Cannery Row alternating every two hours with Squad Two. Your job will be to clear personnel and cargo coming off the tin cans before it enters the city." A few groans greet the announcement. No frontline unit likes customs duty and these young Lunarians see themselves as the tip of the spear, even if they have no real combat experience. Kitajima doesn't bother sugar coating the assignment, he doesn't like it much either. "Tempel, you're excused from this assignment. As for the rest of you, I want you to keep your eyes open and your mind on business. This latest rash of bombings could be the start of something bigger. So look sharp."

"Captain?"

"What is it Brice?"

"Can we wear ghost suits?"

"Negative, standard vacsuits only. Any more questions… Lieutenant Dugan, keep your seat. The rest of you, we reform at 0900 on the parade ground. Dismissed."

Tempel watches his comrades leave. A few look curiously at him as they pass. Several link so they can listen in.

Kitajima comes and stands next to Tempel who raises his eyebrows. "Magi, what have you got for him."

Having waited for them to initiate the conversation, Magi appears standing a few meters away.

The AI could present itself using virtually any appearance, but from the beginning, Magi has used the results of morphing a group of female elders into a single entity, a visual average that makes her quite beautiful in a very grandmotherly way. Citizens recognize and trust her instantly.

"Abby wants you and Sam to report to Hawking Spaceport for escort duty. You're meeting a Federation defector, a Mr. Lazarus Sheffield. Lindsey Marquest is bringing him in and will hand off to you. They're arriving on Trans World Flight L95 at eleven-ten. Not only is he the first Federation runner in over a decade, he is a Senior Analyst in the Department of Homeland Security," Magi said.

Escort duty? This is a first. "What are we to do with him?" Tempel asks.

"You and Sam are to take Mr. Sheffield out to lunch. Abby wants you to use your own judgment as to what questions to ask. Just keep him talking. Depending on his answers, Abby has tentatively scheduled a meeting with him at 1300."

Tempel shakes his head as if to clear it, "Wait a minute, Sam and I are taking this guy out to lunch?"

"Aye," Magi said cheerfully. "Sam will meet you at the terminal."

Kitajima shrugs, "I'm sure Abby has her reasons for giving you point on this. Don't let her down."

"I won't."

Aldrin Station

*"This is the time when humans have
begun to sail the sea of space."*

Carl Sagan (1934-1996)

MRI satellites track Trans World Flight L95 from the moment it separates from Heaven's Gate. They sweep the craft many times as it crosses the void between Mother Earth and Luna, probing for the slightest abnormality. Six hours into the flight, Lazarus sleeps through a brief freefall as the thrusters shut down and the shuttle flips 180°, decelerating at standard one-sixth G the rest of the way to lunar orbit. Luna Central oversees the shuttle's orbital insertion, the undocking from the Translunar Transfer Vehicle and the subsequent deorbit of the Lunar Lander.

Lindsey gently shakes him, "Lazarus, wake up. We're preparing to land."

Lazarus claws his way to consciousness. He yawns and stretches, "Thanks. I must have fallen asleep."

"You did... almost twelve hours ago. I've never seen someone sleep so hard."

The descent is quiet and smooth right up to the point the AI cranks up the Lander's main thrusters twenty minutes out of Aldrin Station. Sound builds to a deep resonant throb, felt more than heard. The flight trajectory never exceeds three Gs but to Lazarus it seems like more, much more, pushing his stomach down around his ankles. He grips his armrests watching the stark lunar landscape whirl by outside his window.

Luna Central flight controllers and the defensive cannon emplacements strung out along the top of Rim Mountain monitor the shuttle when it appears over the horizon. Powerful scanners sweep the craft time after time, while the cannons keep their cross-hairs on the spacecraft. Finding no anomalies, the shuttle continues its descent undisturbed. Duty officers in three different command centers relax, letting their systems reset to standard recon mode.

The vibration reaches a crescendo as the AI brings the ship smoothly down to the ground. With the slightest of bumps, the shuttle comes to rest and the thrusters fall silent.

Lazarus slowly releases his grip on the armrests and relaxes, not realizing until that moment how tense he had become the last few minutes.

I made it. I'm on the moon.

Lazarus retrieves his small bag from under the seat and looks at Lindsey in triumph. "I can't believe I'm really here."

Lindsey smiles, "Believe it."

Most of the shuttle's passengers are out of their seats and heading towards the exit. Both flight attendants wait next to the airlock door for the ground transport. Lazarus and Lindsey are content to remain in their seat.

Izzy and Marcy collect their baggage and other items. Before leaving, Izzy turns and said, "Tell Abby I said hi."

"I will," Lazarus said. Turning to Lindsey, "Are you sure you can't tell me who's meeting us?" He asked for the third time, running his fingers through his hair.

"I told you, I don't know who Abby's sending. But you can be sure it will be someone you can trust." Taking pity on this Earthman so far from anything familiar, she continues, "Relax," she pats his arm reassuringly, "as long as you're truthful, you will be treated with respect."

"You keep saying that."

"And for good reason. It's the single most important thing for you to remember. Nothing will sink your bid to become a citizen faster than a lie. Even just one," she replies.

"OK. I get the message and will do my best. But there's one thing I want you to remember, Lindsey. Whatever happens, I want you to know how much I appreciate everything you've done." He smiles, thinking again about the hours they had spent together in freefall. "I will never be able to repay you for the generous way you have helped me. I'm forever in your debt."

Lindsey returns his smile, "There you go again, with that debt crap. Get it through your head. You don't owe me anything."

A sharp bump and the clatter of metal ringing against metal announce the arrival of ground transport. The light over the airlock changes from red to green.

The male flight attendant unlocks the inner airlock and swings it open. Stepping into the chamber and out of sight, he unlatches the outer door. An attractive young woman accompanies him back into the shuttle, "Welcome to Aldrin Station. Please proceed to the back of the transport." She moves aside and welcomes each passenger to Aldrin Station as they move past.

Lindsey leads Lazarus from the shuttle, nodding pleasantly to the flight attendant as she passes. She picks an empty pair of seats leaving the window for Lazarus.

More MRI scanners sweep across the passengers and their baggage before the surface transport begins to move. There isn't much to see from the small window but Lazarus has his nose pressed close nonetheless. Rim Mountain dominates the horizon. Above it, bright pinpoints of stars are set in the blackness of airless space. He can see part of Mother Earth directly upward but not well enough to recognize a landmass. The spaceports main airlock looks like a giant culvert protruding out of the mountain and onto the craters floor. It's just large enough to accommodate the transport. The vehicle slows to a stop just inside. He can see the sides of the airlock from his window. A moment later atmosphere explosively fills the small volume around the transport bringing sound with it. The passengers can hear the inside airlock door open with a clank. The transport jerks into motion and accelerates out of the chamber. Everything out his window becomes an indiscriminate blur.

"How far do we go in this tunnel?" Lazarus asks.

"It's about a half kilometer, I would guess," Lindsey said.

He shakes his head. "That puts, what, a kilometer of rock over our heads?"

"Something like that, but don't forget. Everything, including the mountains, weighs only twenty percent of what they would on Mother Earth," she said.

"Why doesn't that comfort me?" Lazarus states dryly "Twenty percent of ginormous is still enormous," he points out with a grin.

The passengers are not even aware of the transport going through more airlocks, each opening just long enough to let the moving vehicle pass before rapidly closing behind. The system never has more than one door open at any given time. The last opens out onto the expansive main floor of the Stephen Hawking Interplanetary Spaceport.

The attendant glances at the green light over the airlock door before opening it, "Please follow the yellow markings on the floor to customs. Thank you for flying Trans World Spaceline."

As they exit down the ramp, Lindsey links her arm with Lazarus. Initially his feet slip as though he were on ice, his weight insufficient to give him his usual traction on the polished stone floor.

"We must get you some proper deck shoes ASAP," Lindsey said. "They're designed to grip the stone. Until then, do this…"

Lindsey shows him the Luna shuffle, more hopping than walking. Lazarus learns a small amount of grace and large dose of humility by the time they cover the fifty meters to customs.

The terminal doesn't seem that different from the airports he's been in, an open space stretching several hundred meters on its long side and less than half that in width, counters and offices arranged throughout in an open design. People move about at a leisurely pace. It's downright calm compared with Athens or Gateway. The thing that's strangest to Lazarus is the ceiling. It glows blue and creates the illusion he's standing beneath a cloudless desert sky. It's a little unnerving but beautiful.

Falling in line, they wait their turn to go through customs. Lindsey then Lazarus pass their left hand over the reader. Excitement surges through Lazarus, He's officially on the moon.

Lindsey maintains her hold on his arm as they exit customs. He glances nervously at the nearby police officer, his visor letting him see the young woman's face. She doesn't look old enough to be packing a pistol.

A handsome young police officer is waiting for them as they emerge from customs. "Greetings Tempel. It's so good to see you." Lindsey said, nodding pleasantly. The man is taller than Lazarus but probably weighs less, despite his broad shoulders. His close-cropped hair appears to be the dominant Lunarian style for both men and women. Tempel's movements are fluid and powerful which Lazarus attributes to being born here.

"Greetings Lindsey. Welcome back," he nods in response.

Turning she said, "Lazarus Sheffield, let me introduce you to Senior Lieutenant Tempel Dugan."

Lazarus starts to extend his hand, recovers and nods his head in a clumsy imitation of the Lunarian custom, "Very pleased to meet you Lieutenant. Please, call me Lazarus."

"Greetings," Tempel nods coldly. "Grandma Abby asked me to meet you and take you to lunch but don't think it's going to become a habit. I've never met a shortimer I liked."

"Tempel," Lindsey said. "Give him a chance."

"It's all right Lindsey. I understand. He's speaking truthfully." Lazarus shrugs, "Isn't that what you told me, always tell the truth?"

Lindsey smiles, "Exactly."

Lazarus stares. Coming up behind Tempel is the most sensuous young woman he's ever seen. Her beauty is extraordinary. She has piercing light blue eyes, skin the color of honey, high cheekbones, and full lips. Shaped in the perfect hourglass, she's wearing a pair of white skin-tight pants and a white low-cut pullover. Her unrestrained tits sway hypnotically and nipples, hardened by rubbing against the fabric, dare him not to stare. Nearly half a head taller than Lazarus, her hair is not much more than blond fuzz across the dome of her head. A holster rides low on her wide hips, the butt of a weapon clearly visible. As a lawman, Lazarus has learned to both rely on, and be skeptical of, first impressions, but the effect this woman has on him is immediate and overwhelming.

"Lazarus Sheffield, meet Sergeant Samantha Odegaard," Lindsey said.

"Greetings, Mr. Sheffield. It's truly a privilege to meet you," she smiles. Then much to everyone's amazement, she offers her hand.

Delighted and instantly at ease, Lazarus smiles back and accepts, "I assure you, the pleasure's mine… Sergeant…"

Samantha laughs, "Please, call me Sam," turning to Lindsey, "Greetings Lindsey. I hear you're glad to be home."

Nodding, Lindsey said, "The next time I feel Mother Earth's gravity will be too soon."

"Are you going to join us for lunch?" Sam asks her.

"No, I have some things I need to take care of. I'll leave Lazarus in your capable hands. He's something important to tell." Lindsey said.

"Wonderful. I can't wait to hear all about it." Sam turns back to

Tempel and asks, "Have you decided on where to eat?"

Tempel shakes his head, "Not really."

"What's your favorite restaurant Lindsey?" Lazarus asks, wanting very much for her to stay.

"Depends on what you want to eat. Breakfast is excellent at Milligan's Café. Lunch… either Mighty Macs or Lucifer's Diner. Savannah's serves a mean soysteak but if you want a view, nothing beats the Surface Cafe," Lindsey said. She loves Lunarian food and has long since tried all that Aldrin Station has to offer.

"Which one's closer?" Lazarus asks hoping to lure Lindsey to stay by making it fast.

"Are we hungry?" Sam laughs a sultry feminine sound that caresses his ears. "Lucifer's Diner is closest, right next door. We can be there in minutes. Mighty Macs isn't much further. What do you want to eat, burgers at Macs or chili at Lucifer's."

"Take him to Macs and show him Brooklyn Mall. He'll love it." Lindsey suggests.

"A burger sounds good." Lazarus said looking intently at Lindsey, "Are you sure you can't join us?"

"I'm sorry Lazarus…" her eyes look past him and her voice trails off. Annoyance flashes across her face.

Lazarus turns to see a tall young man approaching.

"Lindsey darling, I wanted to be waiting when you got off the transport but was held up. Please forgive me." He brushes past Lazarus to embrace her, his lips targeting hers.

Lindsey halfheartedly returns the embrace, turning her cheek to his lips, "Greetings Dwayne. You shouldn't have bothered."

Dwayne laughs and said, "How quickly we forget." Turning to Tempel and Sam he said, "I told Abby that I would be more than happy to meet Lindsey and our guest but she insisted that you do it."

"You know why," Tempel said.

Dwayne laughs too loudly. He turns to Lazarus, "You must be the shortimer everyone is talking about."

Lazarus is miffed but unruffled. "Lazarus Sheffield… and you are?"

Again, the man laughs for no apparent reason, "Dwayne Taylor, grandson of Councilor Zachary Taylor," he said with a flourish.

"I have no idea who that is," Lazarus said. In those few seconds, Lazarus learns as much as he wants about Dwayne Taylor, grandson of Councilor Zachary Taylor. This guy's familiarity with Lindsey troubles him deeply. *Things are different here*, he reminds himself.

"Zachary Taylor was the first Lunarian." Dwayne said.

"I thought Armstrong and Aldrin were the first Lunarians?" Lazarus said. He can't stop himself. Dwayne rubs Lazarus the wrong way.

It's Lindsey and Sam's turn to laugh.

Dwayne stares intently at Lazarus for a moment. "You have much to learn."

"As do we all," Lindsey said sharply. "DT, I have personal business and Lazarus is having lunch with Tempel and Sam. So if you will excuse us…"

Her dismissal cut through his friendliness and his expression hardens. "As you wish… I have a few things to discuss with you." He returns her stare. "Call me at your convenience." Without another word, he turns on his heel and departs the same way he came.

"Well that was… unpleasant," Sam said looking at Lindsey.

"Don't look at me that way. He has a charming side," Lindsey said. "Or at least he did."

"So does a crocodile if you can avoid his teeth," Tempel chuckles softly, "I still can't figure what you saw in him."

Ignoring Tempel, Lindsey steps close to Lazarus and said quietly, "Don't sweat it. Tempel and Sam will take good care of you and I will see you later," she gives him another short but firm kiss that lingers long after their lips part. Her actions speak louder than words how she feels and for whom.

Lindsey nods to the others and walks away. Lazarus stares after her, feeling very alone. Taking a deep breath he turns and smiles, "She's quite remarkable."

Tempel looks disgusted but Sam smiles and said, "Yes, Lindsey is special. How did you happen to meet?"

Looking up at the beautiful Lunarian, Lazarus thinks back. It seems so long ago. Can it be only yesterday? "She had the seat next to mine on the Stratoliner coming out of Athens."

Sam smiles, "Love at first sight. How romantic." Before Tempel has time to inject a cynical remark she continues, "Well, come on. Let's go get some food in you," she said taking Lazarus by the arm much as Lindsey had done, but Sam is fifteen centimeters taller than Lazarus making him tilt his head back just to look at her. He didn't mind a bit.

Tempel, Sam, and Lazarus exit the terminal and pass through a series of corridors. Lazarus is getting better at the lunar shuffle but occasionally he stumbles. Each time Sam grips him tightly preventing him from falling. She said, "Don't worry. You'll get the hang of it."

"He won't as long as you're holding him up," Tempel said.

"Is this your first time off-planet?" Sam inquires, ignoring Tempel.

"Yes," Lazarus replies.

They emerge into a beautiful courtyard with a magnificent colonial style fountain at its center. Its water flows in slow motion, as though it were molasses, something only a shortimer would notice. Yet, its sound is comforting to him in ways he cannot explain.

Along the three sides of the courtyard are various shops and eateries. To his left is a small storefront dedicated to selling visors and other network devices. Beyond is the wood and stone façade of a sidewalk café, its patio filled with tables and chairs. To his immediate right is a vacsuit retail outlet, beyond that a microbrewery, a bakery, and some kind of general store. Music, laughter, and flashing lights spill from a kid's gaming area across the way.

Against the far wall is a familiar type of eating establishment, a diner. There's a devil on its roof pointing a pitchfork at a sign, *Lucifer's Diner, Fine Dining with a Flare.* Lazarus is startled when Lucifer turns and looks directly at him, the eyes flashing as though possessed by his namesake. Lazarus grins, appreciating the irony of its existence in this place as only a Federation citizen can.

Here and there among the shops are more corridors leading to places he cannot imagine but eager to explore. Lazarus breathes in the humid air, fragrant from an assortment of neatly manicured flower gardens. Past the courtyard is an expanse of grass where young people are playing a game, jumping high into the air, testing themselves against their friends. Their calls echo across the distance. Beyond the courtyard and the game is a forest.

Lazarus could never have imagined a place so beautiful and full of life. Craning his neck to catch a glimpse of what lies ahead, he stumbles as Sam changes course to avoid a fast moving covey of laughing children, none more than five or six years of age.

"Is this the mall?" Lazarus asks.

"This is the North Courtyard. It's just a small part of Brooklyn Mall," Sam leads him out of the courtyard and onto the grass giving the ball players plenty of leeway. She stops at a low wall overlooking the most amazing vista Lazarus has ever seen.

Brooklyn Mall is a massive vaulted cathedral sheltering a Lunarian paradise. Before him lies acre upon acre of mid-latitude hardwood forest, manicured and maintained in perfect condition. It extends farther than he can see. From this elevated vantage point, Lazarus looks down upon a picturesque valley of gently rolling hills without any flat ground in sight. It's relatively narrow where he is, widening considerably as it falls away and curves to the right concealing what lies beyond.

Here too, the upper surface of the habitat glows in perfect imitation of a blue sky on a summer afternoon. The luminosity fades as it extends down from the ceiling disappearing entirely about twenty meters up. It's hard to believe this is a subterranean city on the moon.

Massive trees dot the landscape, their leaves shimmering and rustling in a very earth-like breeze. Birds flitter about. Not far below is a small pond under two large trees. A stream runs from the pond, its path marked by boulders and thickets of flowering shrubs, bushes, and reeds.

Squirrels chatter and cavort in the treetops and rabbits hop about the grass. A rain shower had just finished and the humid air smells fresh with just a hint of fragrance. Lazarus cannot see far, prevented by architecture designed to provide mystery to the vista, playing on his imagination like a maestro directing an orchestra.

To his right more shops and restaurants extend another fifty meters along the wall, their roofs covered in lush grass and flower gardens. As with all Lunarian architecture, there is not a straight-line or sharp corner in sight. Everything is curves, one element flowing smoothly to the next, carved from a single block of stone.

Paths lead down the valley to an assortment of benches and tables. One area is swampy and choked with cattails. Another has a pond with a single massive jet of water dancing fifty meters high. Further away through a gap in the trees, Lazarus spots a gazebo silhouetted on the crest of a hill. The beauty is breathtaking.

"Tempel, why don't you go ahead and get the burgers?" Sam suggests.

"Aye," the young Lunarian said gruffly, glad to be away from this shortimer if only for a moment.

"Totally awesome." Lazarus blurts. Looking up, "I can feel the sun on my face… How's that possible?"

"The lighting is natural sunlight minus the more deadly frequencies," she said.

"Amazing."

Sam guides him down the terrace past several shops towards a small food court. Tucked under the branches of an enormous tree are burnished stone tables.

"Is this ok?" Sam asks.

Lazarus pulls out one of the stone chairs, amazed that he can move something so massive so easily. "This is marvelous."

Sam, amused by the Earthman's quaint manners, smiles and sits down. No one has ever done that for her. She likes it.

"Lunarians use stone like we use wood and metal on Earth," Lazarus observes, running his hand over the glassy smooth surface of the tabletop.

"The quarrying process polishes and seals the surface. The beauty inside the stone can be stunning," Sam slides her finger along a scarlet slash of color running the length of the tabletop. "This is a metal-bearing ore and the color depends on the metal. Needless to say, it makes beautiful furniture and habitats excavated from it are highly prized," Sam said. "My family works HE excavators and makes furniture on the side."

"How do you make a chair out of stone?" Lazarus asks.

"The same way you make a chair out of wood, very carefully," Sam smiles. "Stone is best for tables, benches, and counter tops, but as you can see, it makes a great looking chair too."

"So you must know a lot about excavating?" Lazarus asks.

"Not as much as Tempel. If you have technical questions, he's your guy," Sam states.

"I'm fascinated with Lunarian habitats. Nothing like them has ever been created in the long history of man." Lazarus' eyes sparkle with excitement.

"You're not going to call us cavemen or Neanderthals?"

"No. Definitely not." he exclaims. He looks up as Tempel sets a tray heaped with food on the table.

Tempel raises an eyebrow, "I wouldn't say man has a long history, at least not in any true sense of geological time. All two hundred thousand years is nothing but an instant in the four and a half billion years of Mother Earth's history. You do believe that Mother Earth is old, right? Not that crazy talk about it being created a few thousand years ago?"

"Of course not but I must admit, there's much I don't understand, especially concerning Earth history and evolution. It wasn't taught in school while I was growing up and books about it are banned," Lazarus said, taking a bite.

Sam frowns and wipes her mouth with a napkin. "Citizens allow this?" She asked incredulously.

Lazarus swallows and nods. "They vote on which books to ban, as well as the punishment for those caught reading banned books."

"I find that hard to believe. The government must rig it. Why would anyone choose ignorance over knowledge?" Sam cannot understand. To her, raised from infancy to respect the principles behind science and humanity's quest to understand the cosmos, it's inconceivable that someone would reject ideas simply because they don't fit some preconceived dogma. Ideas are to be examined closely and only set aside if they are found lacking merit. Suppressing an idea because it fails to fit into a religious or political system is unthinkable.

"No one chooses ignorance. Federation citizens are told what beliefs are acceptable."

"Are you not among these citizens? Don't you profess the same beliefs?" Tempel asks.

Lazarus swallows and reminds himself once again he must drop any deception and be utterly honest. It's hard to set aside something that's been such a major part of his life. He licks dry lips before answering, "No... I don't... I searched for it as a kid but all I found were broken shards of clay where there should have been diamonds."

"That's... sad," Sam said softly.

Tempel glances at her with exasperation then turns back to Lazarus,

"What's that supposed to mean?"

"It means that even as a child I questioned religion and the crazy stuff they wanted me to believe." Lazarus wipes away a bead of sweat rolling down his cheek.

"Then how did you become a Senior Analyst?" Tempel asks.

Lazarus looked up from his plate and locks eyes with the young Lunarian, "By being a good liar."

His answer startles Sam and disgusts Tempel.

"Which books are banned?" Sam asks.

Tempel and Lazarus stare at each other for a moment longer, then Lazarus said, "It would be easier to tell you which books are allowed. The banned list is enormous. I think the authorities can find something wrong with any book if they look hard enough."

"What punishment is given for reading them?" Sam asks. Over the last thirty years, there has been a dearth of Federation emigrants limiting her exposure to these strange ideas.

"Depends on what book and who catches you. Best case is a fine, but worst case is a nice long vacation at a reeducation facility."

"That doesn't sound so bad," Sam said.

Lazarus stares at her for a moment, "I would withhold judgment if I were you. I've spent a significant amount of time inside them and it isn't pretty." Lazarus turns away, ashamed in that instant of the number of reeducations he had personally instigated. "As a Senior Analyst, I interrogated suspects... Sometimes that included physical discomfort, sometimes drugs... Specialists would come in and do... other things... When we were finished, we released the suspect for reeducation. When they come out... they're another person... they've been reeducated..."

Sam puts her burger down. Her horrified look drives a dagger into Lazarus.

"You tortured them?" Sam asks.

"We called it enhanced interrogation," Lazarus said.

"You tortured them." Tempel said. It's hard to generate any sympathy for Federation citizens. They made their bed and now must sleep in it.

"What happened to them inside the room?" Sam asks.

Lazarus shakes his head, "I didn't need to know…"

After a moment, Sam asks, "Why would you be a part of that?"

"It seemed like the right thing to do in the beginning, but it changed. At first, the suspects were limited to terrorists or violent criminals, but in recent years, I participated in more and more cases involving citizens whose crimes were more political in nature. Many of them were only guilty of not reporting for the draft. They didn't want to do their six years. Others simply questioned the government or the religious patriotism promoted by the government… I grew to hate my job…"

His voice trails off and they eat in silence. He no longer tastes the meal, thinking about what he had done, thinking about his brother. He blames himself for so many things.

"Why didn't you quit?" Sam asks.

"No one quits DHS…" he said without looking up.

"You did," Tempel said.

"That's right, I did," Lazarus said. "But I had to leave the planet to do it." He sighs and lays his napkin on his plate, "Very tasty. Now I understand why Lindsey likes Mac's."

Sam nods and asks, "Lazarus is an unusual name. Where does it come from?"

"Lazarus is the name of two people in the bible, the man Jesus raised from the dead and a character in one of his parables. My mom named my brothers Saul and Elijah, and my sister Mary, so it makes sense that my name is also biblical. Dad, on the other hand, said I was named after the hero in a science fiction novel written in the mid twentieth century." Lazarus said. "I like that better."

"Whatever the reason, it's charming." Sam said.

"What's an agent for Homeland Security doing here?" Tempel asks, closely monitoring his polygraphic indicators, looking for the slightest appearance of deception.

"I'm not an agent, only an analyst …" Lazarus pauses and sighs deeply, running his hand over his head, "The situation became intolerable for me. I no longer believe in my government, my job, or my life… The Federation has information indicating the Republic of Luna is in grave danger. Since sending troops or an envoy is out of the question, I'm the next best thing," Lazarus smiles.

"Whose idea was that?" Tempel asks.

"Mine," Lazarus said. "Totally mine. You see… I believe the Brotherhood is about to attack the Republic."

"So? Tell me something I don't know," Tempel declares. "Why do you think we need your help? The Republic can take care of itself."

Despite the amazing architecture they're sitting in, life is harsh on the moon and always has been. A Lunarian grows up fast or dies trying. In the beginning, before deep rock excavations were possible, the kids suffered the highest mortality rate of any group. Living in a vacuum is a very unforgiving place to raise a family.

The group currently holding that distinction can't be classified by age, gender, or occupation. Their deaths are the result of sectarian violence. Most Earthmen tolerate Lunarians but some consider them evil. Rumors of bounties and contract killings abound, gunfights are commonplace and people simply disappear.

Born into this situation, the Dugan children began handling weapons as soon as they could hold one steady. Tempel was nine when he recorded his first perfect score in the family's gun range. By the time he was eleven, he could outdraw his brothers, sisters, and cousins, all except Ben.

Patrick Dugan taught his children that carrying a gun is a responsibility, not a toy or an adventure, and if he ever caught one of them playing loose with it, he'd take off their backside with his belt.

None of his kids ever lost any hide. Patrick drilled into them early and often that gunplay was a last resort, but when necessary, done with precision and skill. Tempel often wonders what his father would make of the current state of affairs. He believes in his heart that if his father were alive, he would approve of his youngest son being a Special Forces lieutenant in the police department, a leader of warriors.

"I'm sure you can take care of yourself, but there will be serious consequences if even the tiniest mistake is made," Lazarus said. "You see… there's reason to believe the Brotherhood's going to detonate a thermonuclear device somewhere on Luna."

"I know. I reviewed your conversations with Lindsey," Tempel said.

"You really think they'll nuke us?" Sam asks.

Lazarus shrugs and said, "Yes, I do."

A cold silence falls over the table. Samantha sits and stares numbly at Lazarus, trying in vain to make sense of something that defies logic. "Why would anybody do such a horrible thing? I don't understand why they want to hurt us. What have we done to them to make them hate us so much?" Sam whispers.

Lazarus frowns, "You won't find any reason in their madness. Fundamentalism, whether it's religious or political, displays amazing tunnel vision."

"You still haven't explained why they want to kill us," Sam insists.

"The Holy Qur'ân tells them it's their duty to either convert nonbelievers or destroy them. I believe the phrase used by Islam's leading clerics and imams was that… *all Lunarians are godless infidels.* That places you at the top of the list of nonbelievers to be dealt with," Lazarus said.

"But the citizens don't take them seriously… do they?" Sam asks.

Lazarus bows his head and fiddles with his napkin, "I quote from the Holy Qur'ân 47:4. *When you meet in battle those who disbelieve strike off their heads after you have bound them fast in fetters.* The average

Muslim believes that genetic science has soiled all Lunarians, which means conversion is impossible in this life. They believe that for God to pass judgment on you, they must kill you. It's their way of calling court in session. And if they should be killed while doing the work of Allah, they're promised paradise in heaven for all eternity... Mohammed's version of paradise reflects his sixth century bias and includes plenty of wine, food, and sex with beautiful little girls and boys. 78:31 *As for those who guarded against evil there awaits them a triumph, orchards and vineyards; and blooming young maidens...* 76:19... *Sons of perpetual bloom shall go round waiting upon the believers...* Blooming young maidens refers to little virgin girls and sons of perpetual bloom are little virgin boys. I'm sure I don't need to explain why children are included in paradise. The Hadith expands the pedophile promise that includes a sex market where these children are on display for the believer to choose from."

"Regardless of why they want us dead, nothing comes or goes in Aldrin without passing through heavy security. A cockroach couldn't get by. Let alone a nuke." Tempel's like the rest of Luna, he believes that Magi and her multitude of MRI scanners preclude this possibility.

"Aren't the reports of bombs getting through accurate?" Lazarus hopes this was a fabrication of the government-controlled media. It would not be the first time.

Tempel stares at the Earthman for a moment, "Lunarians must be helping them," he finally admits.

"I don't know much about Lunarians but I do know the Brotherhood. They're in the final stages of something big. I just don't know the what, when, or where," Lazarus said.

"Do you have any supportive evidence or must we simply take your word for it?" Tempel asks harshly.

"I couldn't bring anything with me for obvious reasons but some of the evidence can be regenerated." Lazarus leans his forearms onto the beautiful tabletop and looks intently at Tempel. "I will help your network people as much as I can."

"Point us in the right direction, so to speak," Tempel said sarcastically, suspicious of anything Lazarus may direct them to. Even if he's sincere, Tempel's skeptical this shortimer can teach Jamie and Jordan anything about hacking Earthnet.

"I'm not a politician, Tempel. What I know is that over the last three months Homeland Security acquired overwhelming evidence of something big coming down, encrypted emails, Earthnet conversations, and security tapes on more than a few suspects. The Brotherhood's Defense Minister, Hasin bin Aunker and Major General Abdel Salam Arif are missing. Do you know who they are?" Lazarus asks.

Sam's face turns ashen and she glances at Tempel whose expression remains stiff and unchanging. "We've heard of them," she acknowledges.

"Don't expect any help from the Federation. They will not honor the Treaty of Independence. The most you can expect is neutrality. They will stay out of it," Lazarus said.

"That's all we ask. If the Brotherhood wants more martyrs, then we will accommodate them," Tempel snarls.

Sam senses Tempel's outburst disturbs Lazarus. She decides to change the subject. "As I understand it, you requested a meeting with Abby? Why Abby?" Sam asks raising her eyebrows.

"Lindsey helped me, but Abigail Dugan is famous even in Arizona." Lazarus looks at her puzzled, "It's not like you have a central government. I can't ask to speak with your President. You don't have one."

"The will of the citizens is the only government we need," Tempel said.

"But a government provides for the common defense and the Republic doesn't even have a military," Lazarus states.

"A standing militia of any kind is prohibited under the Treaty," Sam said.

"Then who decides what needs to be done and enforces the decisions?" Lazarus asks.

Sam sighs, "We all do. The freeholds conform to the majority rulings voluntarily. To defy the Council guarantees sanctions by the rest of Luna. If it's one thing we have a good grip on, it's that nobody survives on Luna without help. Isolation means death."

"*No man is an island,*" Lazarus said. He loves the fact he can now say these things in normal conversation.

"Exactly as Mr. Donne intended..." Sam said.

"I don't understand freeholds. What is a freehold?" Lazarus asks.

"A half-century ago, my ancestors determined the only real security they could expect was from their own hand. That meant bringing every aspect of their existence under tight control, right down to the air they breathe. A freehold consolidates these resources for efficiency and security purposes. The freehold is the core unit in the Republic of Luna. I think it's similar to a corporation in the Federation."

"So the Republic is pure capitalistic?" Lazarus asks.

"No true democracy can be pure capitalism or pure socialism. There must be a balance between the two ideas. The Republic of Luna votes on everything and provides an economy based on Gross Percentage Taxation. Voting and paying taxes are responsibilities every citizen takes seriously, even the kids. We don't have a single billionaire, but we also don't have any poverty. We are all middle class."

"What about the non-Lunarian settlements?" Lazarus asks.

Sam shakes her head, "Non-Lunarian politics are even more complicated. Four Earth nations have military stationed on Luna and over one hundred and fifty corporations maintain private security forces. The Law of Full Disclosure applies only within our holdings. Little America and the various facilities of other nations are not part of Luna's network. We have very little control over what they do." When Lazarus looks lost she continues, "Little America is a shortimer enclave east of Hell's Kitchen on the outer edge of Aldrin Station. It's off limits to us. We don't know what goes on in there."

"So a large crate could be delivered to Little America and would not pass through a Lunarian inspection point?" Lazarus asks.

Sam's face clouds over.

Tempel frowns and stands, "Highly unlikely... Come, we should go." He leads them along the edge of a babbling brook cutting its way through the forest. The enormous trees seem small in the huge space, and they but ants scurrying beneath.

"The trees are magnificent," Lazarus said with an awed shake of his head.

"We have taken great care in selecting the best genetic strains and they grow fast in Luna's gravity," Sam said.

"What kind are they?" Lazarus asks.

"These are Ash trees native to Europe," Sam said. "According to Norse legend, Igdrasil is the Ash Tree of Existence with its roots in hell and limbs spreading across the universe. At its base is the Kingdom of Death where the Three Fates live, the Past, the Present, and the Future. Seasonal changes represent various events, things suffered, things done, catastrophes, stretching through all lands and times. As the story goes, an eagle rests on the highest branch of Igdrasil to observe all that passes in the world, whilst a squirrel constantly runs up and down its trunk to report those things the eagle may not have seen. Serpents twine round its limbs and from its roots flow two streams, the knowledge of things past and the knowledge of things to come. According to the legend, man himself was formed from the wood of this sacred Ash tree."

"That makes about as much sense as the biblical version of creation," Lazarus said.

The valley widens considerably as they move downhill and around the curve. A tall cliff face comes into view ahead of them. It's bare stone, craggy and irregular with horizontal striations sculpted into its face. Predominantly pastel red, it's mottled with browns, pinks, and many other earth tones. Lazarus soon realizes it's not simply a cliff, but a massive column that extends to the ceiling far above.

They follow the small stream downhill and the canyon flattens into a broad plain with the column at its center. The trees here are further apart with knee-high prairie grass instead of the manicured bluegrass found in the upper reaches of North Canyon. Around the base of the column, before the floor slopes up to meet the vertical face, are more shops and a picnic area with a decent sized swimming lake. People are everywhere, but it's far from being crowded. Lazarus estimates only a couple hundred are within his sight. If this were in the Federation, that number would be in the tens of thousands. To him, this place is empty.

From the rock face high above, a waterfall begins its descent towards a pool at the base of the cliff. A stream connects it to the lake. A fog shrouds the pool and half the lake. Even from this distance, he hears splashing and peals of laughter.

Several dogs run across the open meadow in great bounds, disappearing into the tall grass only to reappear as they leap again. They flush out several large animals. Lazarus can hardly believe his eyes when a dozen deer break cover, white tails flashing.

"What is this place?" Lazarus asks in a whisper.

"This is Brooklyn Mall," Sam said.

"How big is it?" He asked. The column is so large, he has trouble judging its scale.

"At its peak, the mall is six hundred meters high and contains just over six square kilometers." Tempel answers.

Looking up in awe, Lazarus said, "Six hundred meters. No wonder I feel small. Are all habitats like this?" He asked.

Sam shakes her head, "This is a mall. It's about having fun."

"Malls are designed to give us a little headroom. Grandma Abby said they remind us we came from a planet," Tempel adds.

A screech overhead draws his attention, "Is that a hawk?" Lazarus asks.

Sam glances up, "Peregrine Falcon."

"There are predators here?" Lazarus asks.

"Some. Don't worry, there isn't any big enough for you to worry about," she said.

Shaking his head in disbelief, he said, "Luna is full of surprises. Why's the mall shaped this way? Can I assume the butte in the center is holding up the roof?"

"It's structural if that's what you mean. All habitat geometry is designed to withstand enormous pressure," Tempel said.

"It's quite remarkable," Lazarus said. To his left and right are two more valleys. He can't see very far down either because both curve, but one appears to go uphill and the other downhill.

"I must keep reminding myself that all of this is man-made. The plants, the insects, the animals, they're all selected by you. How do you manage all of this?"

Sam chuckles and leads Lazarus towards a covered picnic table not far from the base of the column. "Let's get under cover before it rains."

They reach the canopy just as a warm rain begins to fall.

Lazarus runs his fingers through his hair. "Everything is so clean, no smog, no pollution of any kind." Lazarus remains standing, gazing up the valley they had just come from, its distance hazed by the rain shower. The air is fresh and sweet, full of the smell of damp foliage. A rainbow graces the distance. "Why not use a sphere? It's been known for millennia that the most efficient use of space is a sphere."

"The rock pressure would crush it. It simply couldn't hold up. By narrowing the classic sphere down to a disk, we are using the arch to hold up the ceiling. You can see the inward curve in the vertical walls," Tempel explains, pointing and gesturing for emphasis. "It's the same design the ancient Egyptians used when they built the chambers under their pyramids."

"I don't understand," Lazarus said.

"The deepest chambers and passageways used a step or terraced design to withstand the tremendous overhead compressive loads. Each successive block layer extended inward a few centimeters until the two sides finally joined high overhead, in effect, creating an arched ceiling. We use the same shape only ours is smooth, not stepped."

"That's amazing. How do you decide where the habitats should go? How big they can be?" Lazarus asks.

"The size, orientation and distribution of all excavations are obviously interrelated and must be controlled," Tempel lectures. "Any miscalculation weakens the city and could cause a collapse."

"I seem to remember that's happened before," Lazarus said, raising one eyebrow.

"Sure it has," is Tempel 's quick response. "We study all the major and minor incidents in school. The Hampton Bay collapse was the largest; it killed over two hundred people. What's your point?"

"You needn't worry," Sam said. "There hasn't been a collapse in over forty years."

"Hampton forced a re-write of the design simulation. Every known factor's incorporated. Not only does the outer envelope maximize support, but the inner structure as well. The floors, ceilings, walls and ramps inside the habitats distribute the load. It's much safer now."

"Is there a master plan for the entire city?" Lazarus asks.

"Of course there is… DREMS incorporates the shape of habitats, transportation and utility corridors, even plumbing. The mountain itself undergoes extensive SQUID evaluation looking for fractures or fault lines…" Sensing his ignorance, "S-Q-U-I-D stands for Superconducting Quantum Interference Device. It maps variations in the mountains magnetic field to identify mini-cracks and stress risers before they fail… The point is, all of these influences are factored into any proposed new excavation no matter how small," Tempel said.

"Dreams?" Lazarus asks.

"D-R-E-M-S stands for Deep Rock Excavation and Maintenance Simulation," he answers.

"Can you show me or is it classified?" Lazarus asks.

"Classified? DREMS is on the public net. Everybody has access to it." Tempel glances at Sam and shakes his head before linking with Lazarus. In a rapid series of hand movements, he brings up a three-dimensional image floating in the air between them.

Lazarus stares in total fascination at the multicolored model. In exquisitely fine detail, it shows the section of Rim Mountain that contains the city. Most of the residential habitats, and their interconnecting commonways, lie within a central region roughly the same elevation as the Central Highlands outside the crater.

A half kilometer below the residential habitats, at the elevation of the crater floor, is another region containing far fewer constructs but with a complex network of tunnels.

Above the residential habitats is a third region. Lazarus stares at one of the largest constructs until his visor identifies it as a reservoir.

Tunnels connect the three levels, some large and well defined, others are wispy threads almost invisible at this scale.

The quality of the graphics astounds Lazarus. As a Senior Analyst, he had access to the best simulations the Federation had to offer but this is far better than anything he's ever seen or imagined possible.

"The upper level is our water reservoirs and some agricultural habitats. The central level is where we live and the lower level is waste recovery and bulk transportation. Currently, there are 1173 habitats, over 125 kilometers of commonways and almost 500 kilometers of primary and secondary service tunnels below the city. The sewer system alone has 1600 kilometers of ancillary tunnels, some big enough to walk in but most are smaller than your fist." A bright pinprick appears within the central level. Tempel points, "Here's where we are."

Tempel circles a group of habitats, his finger leaving behind a glowing trail that fades away, "This is Dakota warren."

"Please define a warren for me," Lazarus asks.

"A warren is a group of habitats that share the mechanicals needed to keep us eating and breathing. Usually they have a short interconnect corridor between the individual habitats but sometimes they butt up rim to rim. A big warren, like Dakota, has habitats spread out vertically and horizontally," Tempel said.

Reaching out, Tempel pulls the image, magnifying it to take a closer look at Brooklyn Mall.

Lazarus staggers. He's no longer standing in the mall but instead he's soaring high above it.

"Take it easy Tempel. He isn't accustomed to using our net." Sam puts her arm around Lazarus to steady him.

Tempel slows and brings him to a stop over Brooklyn Mall's Central Commons. Below them are three individuals standing next to a covered park bench. The rain soaked grass catches the light, like millions of diamonds sprinkled across the lawn.

Lazarus suppresses his fear of heights by repeatedly telling himself… *this is not real*. He isn't actually hovering in midair a hundred meters up looking down at these people. He realizes who they are. He hesitantly waves his arm out in front like a blind man looking for obstacles. The figure below does the same. He resists the urge to look up.

Sam recognizes his discomfort, "Tempel's integrating the mall's sensors with DREMS."

Lazarus had grown up around computers and electronics, yet he realized long ago that one of the sacrifices his country made, as they clung ever tighter to Christian religious beliefs, was that of change. No new technology has developed within the Federation for over fifty years. Some call this lack of innovation conservatism, but Lazarus knows it for what it is… stagnation.

Of all the classified reports he's read over the years, not one mentioned this advanced state of technology. The Lunarian computer system had to be crunching data at a tremendous rate to provide them with such high quality video, better than anything he had seen or heard about. Once again, the Federation must have purposefully kept this from him and the other Senior Analysts. He files the omission away with all the others.

Like a bird soaring high above the trees, Tempel takes them back the way they had come. Three adolescent boys are sitting at the same table they had so recently vacated. Tempel moves in close bringing Lazarus and Sam with him. It's as though they're standing right next to the table, listening to their horseplay, seeing every expression as clearly as if they were actually present. The boys are wearing visors and one of them turns, looking right at Tempel.

"Something wrong?" He asked.

Tempel shakes his head and said, "Nope. We just want to wish you boys a nice lunch." He nods to them and departs.

Back across the mall they soar, this time staying beneath the massive limbs, weaving around the tree trunks. Lazarus is starting to really enjoy the ride by the time they reach their destination, back at the flesh and blood versions of themselves standing patiently beside the picnic bench.

Tempel brings Lazarus to a standstill, centimeters from himself. It's like looking into a mirror. Lazarus can see every pore, every hair, every twitch of his mouth, more clearly then if he were in his luxury apartment back in Arizona staring into the bathroom mirror. He can't resist reaching out, watching his hand disappear into the chest of the image in front of him. He hears Sam's musical laugh, pulling him back to something real.

"Scanners throughout the city are available to anybody at any time but the malls are covered in greater detail. This is where we come to play," Sam said.

With a grand wave of his arm, Tempel sweeps their images away, scattering the millions of tiny pixels like dust in the wind.

Lazarus gathers his wits about him, leaning against Sam. He notices a man and a woman a short distance away, standing and watching.

"Who are those people?" Lazarus asks.

"They are the Lunarians monitoring our conversation," Sam replies. When Lazarus looks confused, Sam adds, "What you see is the result of morphing forty-seven men and women into a single couple."

"I don't understand," he said.

Sam said by walking over to the woman. She nods a greeting and asks, "Constance, do you mind?"

The image nods.

"I would like you to meet Mr. Lazarus Sheffield," Sam said.

The face and countenance of the figure before them changes smoothly into the features of a heavyset woman with shoulder length brown hair and a hawkish nose.

"Greetings… Constance Haig," she said tipping her head politely.

"Lazarus Sheffield," Lazarus nods in return.

"Constance works with Tempel and if I don't miss my guess, you are keeping tabs on him. Isn't that right?" Sam asks

"No, actually I find this Earthman fascinating. All this talk of nukes and terrorists."

"I'm surprised you have time," Sam said.

"Humph. You're right of course, I don't have time." With a curt nod, Constance melts back into the composite, removing herself from the conversation.

Lazarus abruptly reaches up and takes off his visor. Sam and Tempel exchange glances, keeping theirs on. "If you don't mind, I would like to see Aldrin Station with my own eyes."

"It's your choice," Tempel said. "It's stopped raining." Tempel leads them away from the picnic area.

Lazarus is starting to get the knack of walking in lunar gravity. It requires a completely different rhythm but he's learning.

"We're early," Sam said.

"Let's stop at the Plantation," Tempel suggests.

"Why not," Sam agrees.

Tempel leads them to a quaint French-style sidewalk café close by the mall's East entrance. There isn't an alcove here, just a few shops looking down upon the arboretum.

Weaving around tables, Tempel picks one close to a pool surrounded by ferns with a miniature waterfall. The air's damp and tall broadleaved plants shade the café. A thick Asian carpet softens the mall sounds. To Lazarus, it seems like he has entered yet another little world.

A tall lanky young man with broad shoulders comes over to take their order. He immediately notices that Lazarus is not wearing his visor.

"Mocha Sanani," Tempel said.

"Two ambrosia's with honey and a couple of Blackberry rolls," Sam orders.

"Ambrosia?" Lazarus asks.

"It's white tea originally from south China that we have grown on Luna for over fifty years. It's very good with honey," Sam said.

"Sounds wonderful," Lazarus said. Rachel had liked tea. He leans back in the chair and relaxes. The chair is soft and the sound of the water soothing. A yawn escapes before he can stop it.

"When are you due?" Tempel asks Lazarus.

"Due what?" Lazarus asks.

"Sleep... When was the last time you slept?" Tempel asks.

"On the shuttle. I'll be fine," Lazarus said.

Sam laughs and said, "Time lag."

Tempel nods knowingly, "It will take a while for your system to adjust to the lack of night and day."

"I don't understand why Lunarians don't use Universal Shiptime. Why not dim the lights half the day?" Lazarus asks.

"Only civilian spacecraft do that, mostly because it offers them a measure of control over their passengers. Military ships use the same twenty-four hour schedule that we do," Tempel pointed at the clock above the door of the café. "Twenty-four hours is divided up into three eight hour shifts, red for first, green for second, and blue for third. Some people still use morning, noon and night but it doesn't mean much. A long time ago, they tried dimming the lights at night but it turned out to be a colossal waste of effort. There is not one single reason why one shift should be singled out for sleeping and not another. We leave it up to the individual to decide when they should be sleeping."

"The words tomorrow or today or yesterday don't have much meaning here, do they?" Lazarus asks.

"Sure they do. A day is still twenty-four hours just like on Mother Earth. We just don't have a nice neat twelve-hour light and dark cycle here. Even if you're on the surface, a lunar cycle is fourteen days freezing darkness and fourteen days of blazing sunlight. It's simpler to have all of Luna work off the same time," Tempel said sipping his coffee.

"I think you like explaining things to Lazarus," Sam said grinning at Tempel.

Tempel blows her a kiss. Turning back to Lazarus, "Most people adjust their sleep cycle to fit those they work with. I only need about four hours sleep in every twenty-four."

Lazarus nods his thanks as the waiter deposits a steaming mug next to the prettiest pastry he had ever seen, a perfect spiral of dark purple set in piecrust. "That might take some getting used to," he said shaking his head. "I personally need at least six hours or I'm not worth much the next day."

Tempel grunts wondering if any shortimer is worth his O2, regardless of how much sleep they get.

Sam peels a layer from the side of her pastry and pops it into her mouth with obvious pleasure.

Lazarus nods and takes another sip. Sitting the cup down, he said, "I can't tell you how much I'm looking forward to meeting your grandmother. You may not realize how famous she is on Earth. In some circles she's spoken of with Einstein, Darwin and Hawking. Her white paper on Biotronic DNA manipulations is the definitive work on the subject," his voice betrays his excitement.

"You seem to know a lot about Abby. Where did you learn it?" Tempel asks.

"We routinely monitor your netsites and when something new is posted, it was my job to read it." Lazarus pauses and adds, "Right before I blocked everyone else from it."

Without Lazarus wearing his visor, Tempel doesn't have access to his polygraphic indicators, but he's sure something's bothering the shortimer.

Lazarus raises his hands in mock surrender, "I was young and idealistic and convinced myself I was working on the side of good." He drops his eyes and runs his fingers through his hair. "It's not something I'm proud of but Lindsey stressed honesty above all else. I will not hide or avoid the things I have done."

"Good advice," Tempel said.

"We're not here to judge you, Lazarus," Sam said.

"You seem to be doing a good job of that all by yourself," Tempel said.

Lazarus sighs and runs his fingers through his hair again, "I have told you about me and my family. Please, tell me something about yours."

Tempel is a product of an open society where the free flow of information defines freedom. Branded a liar is one of the worst things that can happen to somebody, their opinions, and they themselves, are rendered irrelevant. It never occurs to him to lie or avoid the truth.

"Grandma Abby was born in 1999 in Kansas City. She was educated in one of your universities and in 2024, she volunteered for the old US Space Command. She was the doctor on the mission that founded Aldrin Station. As one of the original settlers, she helped set up the city's first hospital and the first biotronic research program. She's still involved in biotronics and is an active professor at the University of Luna. Her lectures are always attended by thousands, sometimes millions."

"That's amazing, still teaching at ninety-three." Lazarus said. "What about your father and mother? Brothers and sisters?"

"My dad, Patrick Ryan Dugan, was Abby's youngest child. Everyone called him Duce. He married my mom, Elizabeth Anne Turner, a few months before my oldest brother Ben was born in 2060. Then they had Stone in '62, Patrick Ryan III or Tray in '64, Magie in '65, Krystin in 67, Skylor in '70 and Alex in '71. I was born Halloween 2072."

"In the Federation, families must pay for the privilege to have more than one child," Lazarus said. "The government calls them fines but the result is only the rich have large families."

"That's horrible," Sam said.

Lazarus is tired of seeing her visor and not her eyes. He slips his visor back on, noticing for the first time that his surroundings sharpen and colors appear more vibrant with the device. Staring at the little waterfall, he clearly hears every splash, but the sound reverts to background noise when he looks away. Turning his head, Lazarus stares at the waiter inside the café, being able to observe his interaction with another customer as if he were standing next to them. The man turns and looks inquisitively at Lazarus, who hastily breaks eye contact and concentrates on Tempel. Lazarus is not sure what just happened.

"My mother's family, the Turners, belong to Humboldt freehold over in Mission. When she married my pop she kept her maiden name and honored her new husband by accepting his as well, Elizabeth Anne Turner-Dugan. This seems to be catching on with my generation. It makes for some interesting names."

"Just the women? I thought Lunarians were all about equality?" Lazarus said.

"That's what I've been saying. The men should change their names too." Sam said.

"What about you Sam, what's your family like?"

She smiles, "Not nearly as interesting as Tempel's, I'm afraid." Turning to Tempel, she said, "We need to be going."

Tempel nods, gulping the last of his coffee.

They exit the mall and it isn't long before Lazarus is completely lost. The tunnels seem to curve and twist without rhyme or reason. Abruptly, they emerge into another enormous space dominated by trees.

At first, Lazarus thinks it's another mall. Overhead is the same blue sky, but this space is different, a huge tunnel cut into the stone where the mall was a bubble. It extends as far as he can see in both directions, foliage gently swaying in the breeze.

They are on a broad ledge at least twenty meters up one side. To his left and right ramps lead to the grassy floor below.

Instead of going down, Tempel leads them to the overview. Two wide paths wind their way through the forest. People are standing on small disks that move along the paths as if they had wheels. The trees here are not Ash like those in Brooklyn Mall. Lush grass carpets the ground and manicured flower gardens and shrubs add color. Across the way is a stand of cherry trees in full bloom.

"Is this a commonway?" Lazarus asks.

"Aye, this is Asimov Commonway. It extends about three kilometers in that direction and less than a half kilometer in the other." Sam said.

"This isn't the only commonway, is it?" Lazarus asks.

"Not hardly," Tempel said.

"Asimov is only a small loop that services the west end of Lincoln County. Our meeting with Abby is about twenty minutes away. We will take the slidewalk to Central then to Sherwood." Sam said. Following his gaze, "The trees here are Sycamore, Elm, Yew, some Chestnut and a variety of fruit trees."

"Do they also have a Norse legend attached to them?" Lazarus asks.

Sam smiles and said, "Maybe… but if they do, I don't know about it."

Movement attracts his eye and he looks up. Soaring silently far above the treetops at high speed is a long sleek train. When he continues to stare, the parallel lines of its rails come into focus stretching out of sight in both directions. Instead of riding on the rails, this train hangs from them. *Such technology.* Lazarus feels like a Neanderthal trying to make sense of a jumbo jet.

The train is gone an instant later leaving Lazarus to wonder if he imagined it. No… it never made a sound but the rails are still there if he looks hard enough.

"It seems like a lot of resources have gone into making and keeping things pretty. Who pays for all the extras?" Lazarus asks.

"What extras?" Sam asks, puzzled.

"Well… moving people from point A to point B doesn't require forests," he said nodding at the nearest tree, "or cherry trees," shifting his gaze to the colorful pink flowers in the distance. The longer he looks the more distinct the tiny flowers become. He begins to hear the bees buzz among the branches and catch a whiff of cherry blossoms.

Tempel frowns, "Are you saying you prefer staring at a wall whizzing by, or the person's head in front of you, like we see on vids of people riding the New York subway? The increase in size doesn't add much to the cost of excavation and Magi takes care of maintenance."

"Why wouldn't you welcome beauty into your home? Who wants to live in a dungeon?" Sam asks genuinely perplexed. "Luna didn't come with trees and green grass. We make every cubic meter of dirt and nurture every tree, shrub and blade of grass or they wouldn't exist at all."

"There are mechanical scrubbers to clean our air but nothing beats trees for doing the job right," Tempel said. "Biodiversity is very important to us."

"I think I just redefined what I consider extras," Lazarus grins. "You have created something unique and special here. You should be very proud," Lazarus said softly "You don't expect me to travel on this carnival ride do you?"

"Carnival ride? I'm not sure what a carnival ride is but slidewalk's are how we get around. Don't look so worried. If you can stand, then you can use a slidewalk," she points down to a collection of small octagonal disks, each about sixty centimeters across, strewn along the edge of the slidewalk below them. It reminds Lazarus of a disorganized little parking lot off the main highway. "Those are drifters. Just step on one and Magi will do the rest. To move forward, shift your center of mass forward, same with left and right. To move faster, shift more of your balance in the direction you want to go."

"How do you stop?" It's one thing to know how to get it going, but as far as Lazarus is concerned, it's much more important to know how to stop.

"Simply center your mass," Sam said.

"What about rules of the road?"

Sam grins, "Good questions. Traffic obeys the right hand rule. East bound traffic uses the south slidewalk and conversely, west bound uses the north slidewalk."

"How do you move larger goods around?" Lazarus asks.

"There's a network of tunnels below the city for truck convoys. The commonways are for people. Where you're from doesn't have slidewalks?" Sam asks.

"Nothing like this." Lazarus exclaims. "Some of the larger airports and spaceports have moving walkways but not slidewalks." Lazarus shakes his head. "The Federation can't seem to get past the automobile. Everyone still has to have one or two, even after the cost of hydrogen has gone through the roof."

"It angers me to think of America burning all the fossil fuel," Tempel growls. "Do you realize over eighty-five million barrels of crude oil was pumped out of the ground daily? 365 days a year? For almost a hundred years? It was all burned. What could they have been thinking? It wasn't about the future, that's certain. What a bloody waste."

"I personally have never even been inside a petroleum powered vehicle," Lazarus said defensively. "Besides, it wasn't a total waste. It allowed us to build the infrastructure we needed to get to space."

"I've heard the justifications, I just don't buy them." Tempel shot back, "It could have and should have happened much sooner. Too many people were making too much money to stop the burning. What I find particularly loathsome is you build shrines to the idiots who profited from the biggest rape of resources in the history of mankind."

"Politicians build shrines to each other. I didn't have anything to do with it," Lazarus said.

"Of course you didn't, but it was your government," Sam takes some of the sting from her words by patting his arm.

Lazarus looks up at her, "They did what they felt they had to."

"They made money, that's what they felt they had to do." Tempel retorts, "Corporations used that money to buy political power and make even more money while raping the planet. They didn't care that they were causing pain on another life or extinguishing a valuable resource for all time. They BURNED IT. All they cared about was short-term profit. They ran the world into a global meltdown, all because they wanted to make more money."

"Most of that happened before I was even born," Lazarus said.

Sam turns to Tempel, "You cannot blame the one for the sins of the many."

"Why not." Tempel said. "Who else is there to blame?"

"What would you have me do?" Lazarus asks. "I can't fight the Federation. I am but one citizen."

Tempel leans over bringing his face centimeters from Lazarus and looks him in the eyes. After a moment's pause, he said, "You do what you can."

Sam nudges her friend, "That's enough Tempel. It's time to go. We don't want to be late."

He heads towards the nearest down ramp letting his anger boil away. It's unreasonable to blame this one Earthman for the sins of a planet, but some things are easier felt than analyzed.

"Don't let Tempel's passion harm you. He realizes it's not your fault anymore than it's his," Sam takes Lazarus by the arm and follows.

Lazarus lets the young woman lead him down the ramp.

Already at the bottom, Tempel steps on a drifter and slides out about ten meters and circles back. He's angry but now is not the time or place.

Sensing the fear rise in Lazarus as they approach the edge of the slidewalk, Sam pats his arm and said, "Stop worrying. You can ride with me. Magi, pull together a double for us, will you?" Her reward was a grateful smile.

Two of the octagon plates rise off the surface and assemble into a single platform, the common edge almost disappearing. It slides over silently and stops right in front of Sam.

Sam steps confidently onto the arrangement, "Take my hand."

Lazarus obeys, expecting the assembly to wobble as he puts his weight on it. Sam slides her arm inside of his, steadying him until he can get his sense of balance on the moving platform.

"The first time might be a little tricky," she said squeezing his arm in a motherly fashion. "Let Magi control the drifter, you just let her know where you want to go."

Lazarus glances over at Tempel, wondering just how much animosity he will encounter within the Republic. Humanity continues to do many despicable things, preemptive wars, political assassinations, and torture, all in the name of national security or ideology, and he's right, the global environment is in shambles. The melting of the polar ice caps and the subsequent rise in the ocean levels has submerged the homes of a billion people. The terrible increase in storm intensity and massive shifts in climate have led to widespread starvation and food wars. How can he possibly defend such atrocities?

Sam eases them out onto the slidewalk with Tempel bringing up the rear, picking up speed until they are moving along at a leisurely ten kph, about the speed of a brisk run. As Lazarus gains confidence, Sam increases their speed. Magi smoothes out and prevents jerkiness when an arm swings or a head turns. Lazarus begins to enjoy the ride.

"This is exhilarating." Lazarus exclaims. "How fast can we go?"

Sam chuckles, "On a good day with no other traffic around you can achieve about thirty kph."

"If you want to go somewhere fast, take a maglev train. They top out above a hundred." Tempel adds from just behind Lazarus, a spot where he can catch the Earthman if he falls. He may not like it, but Lindsey gave the Earthman hospitality and he will not be the one to dishonor that.

"I can't wait to ride in one." Lazarus said.

As they move along the commonway, Lazarus lets his attention wander among the trees, glad to have the steadying influence of Sam's arm in his. The designers and architects of Aldrin Station knew the value of keeping mystery in the vistas presented to the inhabitants. Moving down the slidewalk, they pass through a variety of environments, each unique. Some are lit up in bright afternoon sunlight, others in the overcast of an impending storm. Some are crowded with hardwood trees while orchards dominate others. Many have roses and other flowering plants set in manicured gardens. Green grass carpets most of the commonway, highlighted with colorful shrubs and plants. A few are polished stone cathedrals devoid of plants and animals, glorious in their simplicity. One section contains strange twisted stonework that surrounds the passing traveler like something out of Dante's Hell.

More than once Lazarus observes squirrels running across the grass or frolicking in the high branches. Bird species from sparrows to macaws flicker about adding to the rich tapestry of the environment. Hummingbirds and beehives are especially plentiful.

"It's beautiful," Lazarus said. "I have never seen so many roses."

Sam nods, remembering something Abby once said, "We should always take the time to smell the roses."

"Very good advice," Lazarus said.

Sam has spent her entire twenty years in and around Aldrin Station and New London. She's at that age where she yearns to see more. She glances at Lazarus with just a touch of envy. At least he had the courage to leave Mother Earth and everything familiar. Did she?

Tempel and Sam maneuver out of the main flow of the slidewalk. The drifters settle to the floor.

"Well done." Sam smiles at Lazarus.

Tempel grunts. After all, Magi deserved praise if anyone did. She had done all the skilled work. This bozo had simply managed not to fall off.

Abigail Dugan

"The feminist agenda is not about equal rights for women.
It is about a socialist, anti-family political movement that
encourages women to leave their husbands, kill their children,
practice witchcraft, destroy capitalism and become lesbians."

Pat Robertson (1930-2011)

They lead Lazarus through a maze of corridors. On Earth, his sense of direction was impeccable. It's useless here in this subterranean labyrinth. He has no chance of retracing his steps even if his life depended on it. Most of his normal visual cues are absent and too many passages look the same. Lazarus is completely dependent on the two young Lunarians and that makes him uneasy.

Finally, they stop before an airlock off a small corridor deep in the heart of Aldrin Station. Tempel passes his left hand in front of the security panel and the heavy door slides open.

Sam smiles encouragement, "Relax, this is just a meeting between two citizens, that's all."

"He's not a citizen yet." Tempel's low opinion of shortimers is common among his age group.

Sam reserves her judgment, sensing something about the Earthman that warrants patience. Besides, she trusts Lindsey and if she thinks Lazarus is worth the trouble, then he must be.

The room is stark, utilitarian, and devoid of right angles. An oil painting of a full Earth hangs on the wall. The blues and browns of his home planet provide the only color in the room.

"You must wear your visor throughout the meeting with Abby. Do you have a problem with that?" Tempel asks watching for even the most subtle rejection. He detects only excitement and possibly a little apprehension.

Lazarus nervously runs his fingers through his hair, "No, of course not," he said. He had forgotten he was wearing one.

Satisfied, Tempel leads the way through the next door.

Three women and a man sit around a long conference table. They arise from their seats to greet Lazarus. One of them looks familiar… it's Lindsey but her beautiful hair is gone. All that's left is short black stubble, not much longer than a week old beard. She gives him a quick wave and smiles encouragement, which he returns nervously.

"Mr. Lazarus Sheffield," Tempel said stepping aside, "This is Doctor Abigail Dugan."

What. This beautiful woman is much too young. She couldn't be forty.

Abby nods in the Lunarian custom, "Greetings, Mr. Sheffield. Welcome to Dakota."

Lazarus nods awkwardly, "Ah… greetings, Dr. Dugan. It's my very great pleasure and honor to meet you. I appreciate you granting me this interview," Lazarus starts shaky but finishes strong.

Abigail Dugan exudes calmness and maturity that transcends her apparent age. Broad full lips and radiant smile enchants Lazarus just as it has many more worldly men than he.

Abby nods then draws his attention to the older woman standing on the other side of the table. She's the personification of a loving grandmother. Her caring brown eyes emanate a gentle kindness so thick he could cut it with a knife. "This is Magi. She's your AI. We assign a Magi to every Lunarian. It's how we put you in the system, so to speak. Don't worry. It's just a formality. Think of it as a Lunarian Social

Security Number. This one's yours."

Lazarus is stunned. Never in his wildest dreams did he think the Lunarians capable of projecting such a splendidly accurate image of someone who never existed, right down to wisps of hair wafting in the breeze and sweat glistening across her forehead.

"I don't understand. Isn't there just one Magi?"

Abby grins, "Do you know what Magi is?"

He looks across the table at Magi. "You just said she's an AI, right? The Federation has AIs. I know what they are. It's a program that imitates a human being."

"Magi is so much more than that."

"Ok… but this Magi right here is mine? Not yours?"

Abby looks amused. "In a way. Every Lunarian has a Magi and now you have yours."

"I didn't know I needed one," Lazarus looks across at Magi, not knowing what to say… "Hi."

Magi smiles, "Greetings young man. I'm sure we'll get along just fine."

"When you need something, ask Magi. She's there to help you," Abby said.

"Does she always look like this? Like someone's grandma?" He asked.

"No, of course not. We find it avoids confusion if she uses a single persona. She can appear to be anyone or anything." Abby motions to Magi, "Do Lindsey."

Magi is gone and Lindsey takes her place. Startled, Lazarus steps back. He turns and stares down the table at the real Lindsey then back at the AI. The only difference is that the Magi/Lindsey still has long black hair.

"That's enough," Abby said.

Magi morphs back in place of Lindsey. Lazarus gasps. The flawless three-dimensional fluidity of the demonstration makes his head spin.

"You will understand why we limit Magi to one persona after you've been here a while. You are free to explore other avenues but we ask that you respect our wishes while we do business." Abby said.

"Yes, of course," Lazarus said. Something bothers him about Magi. Has he met her before? He doesn't have time to dwell on it.

Abby presents the man standing next to her, "This is Aldrin Station's Security Chief, Corso Dugan."

Corso Dugan is ruggedly handsome. His dark skin reveals African heritage but his sharp features are European. Gray eyes burn with an inner fire and there's not a single hair on his head. Wrapped around each earlobe are loops in the shape of a viper eating his tail. Muscles ripple and bulge along his arms, his shoulders, and across his chest, stretching his shirt to the breaking point.

Lazarus guesses him to be in his mid thirties. The oldest son of a ninety-three year old that looks thirty-five. It drives the point home of just how different these people really are. Lazarus keeps a tight grip on his emotions.

"Tell us again, Mr. Sheffield, what brings you to Luna," Corso rumbles, never one to beat around the bush.

With a rush, Lazarus realizes what's going on. This meeting, these people, the entire event must be taking place in cyberspace. Vidcasting would explain everything. He reaches up to remove his visor, stopping just in time. Nonetheless, he relaxes, glancing at Magi as if her image represents proof.

"Corso. Where's your manners." Abby scolds gently. "Let's sit and have some tea. There's always time for tea, isn't there Mr. Sheffield?" she indicates with a flip of her hand which seat he was to take. Abby picks up the steaming teapot and fills two cups, placing each in a matching saucer. Sliding one to a spot in front of Lazarus She asked, "Do you take anything in your tea, Mr. Sheffield?"

"Ah... No... Please, call me Lazarus," he said, flashing back to a little restaurant over on Seventh Street, not far from his office at Homeland Security. It seems a lifetime ago. How did she know he liked tea? How could she serve him tea if this meeting is in cyberspace? Too many questions and not enough answers. His mind swirls.

"Then you must call me Abby," she said. "You don't mind if Lindsey joins us, do you?"

"No, of course not," he said, glancing at Lindsey. None of this makes any sense.

"Good. Let's get started," Abby said.

As everyone settles in, Magi said to Abby, "All those present have been identified and authenticated."

"Thank you Magi," Abby said and turns back to Lazarus, "I understand you're from Phoenix?"

Lazarus looks nervously over at Corso and back at Abby, "Yes. I've lived in Arizona my entire life. I was born and raised in Casa Grande, a suburb of South Phoenix."

"Fascinating," Corso rumbles deep in his throat.

Abby ignores him, "You've recently lost your wife and daughter. Please, let me express sorrow for your loss," she tips her head, never taking her eyes off Lazarus. "I've lost loved ones. Nothing ever fills the void they leave behind."

"Thank you... Abby," Lazarus said.

"Do you have other family?"

"Yes, two brothers and a sister. My mother lives in Portland, takes care of my youngest brother. I was ten when my father died in the line of duty. I think I have some cousins somewhere but I haven't kept track. I haven't seen any of my wife's family since the accident."

"Did your family help you when you lost your wife and daughter?" Abby asks.

Many strange and wonderful things have happened to him since he left Phoenix, but this was verging on the surreal. Lazarus takes a deep breath and continues to tell the truth, "My sister was the only one around and she did what she could, but she has her own family to worry about. My brother was in college and had to stay focused. I managed."

"I see," Abby nods. How typical it is for Earthmen to isolate themselves. It fills her with pride that Lunarian families are so tight. She feels pity for Lazarus and even more for the society that drove him out. What provokes a man to leave everything behind? "As an employee of Homeland Security, you must have attended a church. Did they help you through your grief?"

"Of course, they helped tremendously. I have many dear friends there," Lazarus admits. "They are good and decent people who stand firm in the laws of the land and Christianity."

It sounds mechanical, even to him, but to say otherwise would put these people at risk if the Federation ever managed to get their hands on this conversation. Guilt by association is what the Federal Prosecutor would call it when explaining to a Judge why they placed bugs and other monitoring devices among the members of the congregation. After all, the Freedom of Information act gave everyone the right to know if an individual was a true Christian.

"I'm sure they do," Abby said. "What church is that?"

"The only church is the American Church of the Trinity. I attended a neighborhood gathering. It's just a small group of families that get together to worship." Lazarus said growing alarmed by the nature of her questions. He's toyed with suspects in this manner. It's not reassuring.

Abby smiles and said, "Do they share your lack of faith?"

There it is. Even though he had been expecting it, the question chills him to the bone. Lazarus pauses for a moment gathering his wits about him before responding to the frontal assault. "I cannot speak for anyone but myself. I freely admit to many faults, a lack of faith is but one," Lazarus said stiffly.

"Are you an atheist?" Abby asks.

"Well... maybe I am." To those branded an atheist in the Federation, it meant the end of any hope of a good life. An atheist can't hold a decent job, attend a university, or run for office. If you owned a business, your customers stopped coming. If you went into a business, they could refuse to serve you. Even your family shunned you. Any way you looked at it, the label changed a person's life.

"Just like your father when he first arrived," Abby smiles.

"What do you know about my father?" Lazarus is stunned.

"I met Thom Sheffield in June 2065. He was a good man," Abby said kindly.

"He's here?" Lazarus can't believe his ears.

"Well, no, not exactly. He died in the Hampton Bay collapse in 2066. I knew him for less than a year but it was long enough to learn who he was," Abby said.

Lazarus is dumbfounded. "Why would he come here? I don't believe it."

Corso growls and starts to rise. Abby stops him. "Lazarus, I never lie and I never withhold information relevant to another person which is why I'm telling you about your father. To accuse me of lying is a very serious charge."

Lazarus stares at her wide-eyed then ducks his head in confusion, "Please forgive me," he mumbles.

She lets him stew for a few long seconds, "You're forgiven... Magi, provide Lazarus with the vids of his father's time with us."

"Aye," she replies.

"Did you know about this?" Lazarus asks Lindsey.

She shakes her head, "No."

Lazarus runs his fingers through his hair. It's hard for him to accept. Why would his father abandon him? A lifetime of hero worship teeters on the brink of the abyss. It takes a major effort to keep his mouth shut.

Abby watches Lazarus come to grips with the knowledge. Lindsey was right. There's something unusual about this man. "Between your mother and the Federation, Thom didn't have many options when he defected. He explained his reasons many times. You can relive every moment with him. You don't need to take my word for anything," Abby said.

Lazarus doesn't fully appreciate what Abby's telling him. The records will allow him to witness the events and conversations his father had in a way not found in the Federation, through visor recordings. Ignorance helps him set this aside and concentrate on Abby.

"However, that must wait…" Abby said. "We reviewed the relevant parts of your conversation with Lindsey. What interests us most is the rather large number of missing people. People don't just disappear, especially the followers of Minister bin Aunker and General Arif."

"Let me get this straight, you're afraid of the missing men more than a battlestation?" Lazarus asks.

"The Brotherhood's space fleet is a problem. Under the Treaty, we can't build any ship larger than 5000 tons. A battlestation is over 100,000 tons. Mother Earth has almost four hundred military ships and we have none. Mother Earth has over ten billion citizens and we have a little over a million. These are facts I can't change."

"What about a nuclear bomb?"

"Nothing moves in or around Luna that I don't know about. Uranium or plutonium will show up like a super nova on our sensors long before it's close enough to do any damage." Corso rumbles.

Now is as good a time as any to drop the last piece of supposition on them. "What if they had a way to fool your scanners?" Lazarus asks.

"Energy absorbent materials have been around for at least a century but they're not perfect. There's always some leakage… and even if the Brotherhood has come up with better materials, it will still leave a void in the data. That in and of itself, speaks volumes." Corso's voice is a deep rumble, hypnotic in its smoothness and complete in its certainty.

There's only one way to handle Corso and that's head on. "I'm not talking about EAM's. I'm talking about a shield that will actively portray itself as something other than what it is?"

Corso sits and thinks about that. Better than anyone, he knows how dependant Lunarian security is on the MRI scanners. During war games, fooling the scanners is the one development that consistently defeats the Lunarian defenses. All contingency plans become ineffective. He finally asks, "How could this be so?"

"Five weeks ago, a bomb was set off in an Israeli resort in the Sinai. A hundred and thirty three people died," Lazarus said.

Abby sadly shakes her head.

Corso growls, "What's so unusual? That's been happening since the 1960's and will undoubtedly continue."

"What's different is the bomb had to have passed through several MRI scanners, modern up-to-date equipment, not antiques. I grant you, the evidence is circumstantial, but it's the only explanation left when all others are eliminated." Lazarus said. "Homeland Security thinks it was a practice run for something bigger."

Lazarus believes this as absolute truth. Magi continuously monitors his critical biological and neurological functions making it virtually impossible for him to lie. She makes this data available to anyone. Lazarus is sweating bullets, but he's not lying.

"Magi, what can you tell me about the incident?" Abby asks.

"Sharm el Sheikh is situated on the Southern tip of the Sinai Peninsula with the Red Sea on one side and Mount Sinai on the other. On Saturday September 22, 2092, at four hours and fifty-one minutes after local sunrise, a rocket attack took the lives of one-hundred-thirty-three people; one-hundred-twenty-four Jews, five Egyptians and four Jordanians. A group calling itself the PRC claimed responsibility twenty-six minutes later. Seven minutes after that the Brotherhood denounced it and offered aid," Magi said.

"The rocket story is just cover. Nobody wants the public to get a whiff of the possibility that the scanners can be beaten," Lazarus said.

"The data is unusual," Magi admits. "Many authentications are completely absent and some of the normal reports that would grow out of an investigation are incomplete. There's just enough detail to get by. I agree with Lazarus. This incident report has been altered," Magi said.

"I know it's been altered. I helped alter it." Lazarus said irritably. He's not accustomed to talking to an AI like a person. His distrust runs deep.

"Thank you Magi," Abby said warmly.

"You're most welcome," Magi said.

"Do you have any idea how they're doing it?" Abby asks.

Taking a deep breath, he runs his fingers through his hair. "Logic dictates two things. Just as you pointed out, our scanners would see a void in the data and raise a warning, so it can't simply absorb the spy beam. The shield must actually send back a signal of something normal. We call it active camouflage. Second… even with active camouflage, they must have greatly improved the energy absorbent material, stopping and soaking up virtually 100 percent of the MRI beam. Because if they didn't, it wouldn't matter how many false signals were generated, the MRI would still excite the material they're trying to hide."

"We know about the improved EAM, but a way to transmit a false MRI signal is new." Corso admits.

"Let's revisit Corso's original question. Why are you here Lazarus?" Abby asks.

With sweat beading up on his brow, Lazarus takes a deep breath, never breaking eye contact with Abby. "Every Tuesday for the past three years my team has presented a weekly report to Director Dempsey. We have suspected for over a year that Iran or Afghanistan is hiding a bomb factory… ah… thermonuclear manufacturing facility. We think they're recycling old uranium, probably Russian. A couple months ago, we started getting hints of a mission. About two weeks ago, we came to the conclusion the mission was bringing one or more thermonuclear devices to Luna."

"Is there an answer to the question coming soon?" Corso growls.

Refusing to back down, Lazarus turns to Corso, "I don't believe the Federation will honor the Treaty of Independence. If the Brotherhood has active camouflage and a nuke, then you can be sure the Republic of Luna is in big trouble." Lazarus turns back to Abby. "Heaven help me, I can't stand by and watch hundreds of thousands of innocent people die, even if it means my life."

The room is silent until finally Abby breaks the tension. She calmly, without the slightest tremor, leans forward and picks up her tea, sips it without looking at anyone in particular.

"What would happen if your application for Lunarian citizenship were turned down?" Abby asks.

Staring at her, Lazarus seems to wilt a little. "The Federation would prosecute me for treason," he said.

"They would wipe your memory in one of those Canadian vacation spots." Corso said coldly.

"I'll die before that happens Chief Dugan, one way or the other," Lazarus declares. "My life's in your hands. I can't go back."

Abby looks at Corso who said with a shrug and rumbles, "He's sincere, I'll give him that much. It remains to be seen what value his information really has." Turning back to Lazarus, "Assuming you're right, do you have any other information concerning these nuclear devices? How will they get here? Who will transport them? When will they arrive?"

With a sense of relief Lazarus said, "No, I don't know anything definite. All I can say is the communications intercepted over the last three months paint a very ugly picture. You may think I'm jumping to conclusions using incomplete data but please realize, I've been studying the Brotherhood for many years. Hard data is something collected and analyzed after an incident. Trying to predict what these people will do next is the challenge. I deal with subtleties and suppositions most of the time. Occasionally we capture a talker or get some revealing electronic files, but not often."

"Educated guesswork," Abby said.

"Exactly." Lazarus said. He locks eyes with Corso. He runs his fingers through his hair and continues, "The only thing solid is a possible operational name. We intercepted a message from a confirmed moneyman. Inside was a reference to 'Allah's Cleansing Fire'. Cleansing has meant killing in the past. That's as close to a smoking gun as it gets in my line of work."

Corso raises his eyebrows thoughtfully, his eyes never leaving Lazarus. They too had run across references to Allah's Fire, but the social gulf between Islamic culture and the Lunarians is much wider than between Lazarus and the Brotherhood. Interpretation of data is difficult for Lunarians. They rely on Magi too much.

"Let's see what Jordan and Jamie make of Mr. Sheffield's evidence," Corso rumbles.

Abby nods, "It's not every day that we have a Senior Analyst defect Lazarus. For now, let's get you acquainted with two of our top researchers." Turning to Magi she said, "Get him fitted for a suit and start training ASAP. I don't like having someone not vacuum qualified. Oh… and find something appropriate for Lazarus to wear."

"Aye." Magi said. "He also needs some proper deck shoes."

"Fine. I like the flowered shirt but it makes you stand out," Abby said to Lazarus. "Also, I want you to stay close to Lindsey or Tempel for the next few weeks, just until you're accustomed to Luna. Are you ok with that?"

"Of course," Lazarus is in no position to argue. "I appreciate all you're doing for me," he looks down the table at Lindsey. She smiles.

Magi leans forward in her chair and said to Abby, "Pardon the interruption but Pellegrini said he must speak with you immediately. He's waiting outside with Constance and Weenie."

"Magi. His name is Winthrop, not Weenie." Abby scolds.

"I'll try and remember," Magi said with a noticeable lack of sincerity.

Lazarus has no experience with a sarcastic AI. In his world, he tells AIs what to do and they do it. Magi's different.

"Pellegrini is the Director of Operations at Falconhead and Weenie is his lackey," Tempel said to Lazarus.

"You know he doesn't appreciate that nickname," Abby said.

Tempel chuckles, "Aye... everyone knows."

Abby shakes her head, "Magi, please tell them I will be another moment."

"Aye," Magi said settling back, the seat cushion squeaking as it receives her weight. Lazarus is the only one to notice. There's something familiar about her that he can't seem to remember.

Rising and turning to Lazarus, Abby said, "Please accept the hospitality of the Dakota warren. Tempel will get you settled and show you around. I will expect to see you at dinner tonight."

"Yes, of course. Thank you Abby," Lazarus said rising with her and remembering not to extend his hand, tipping his head in the customary fashion.

"Tempel, introduce Lazarus to Jordan and Jamie. Have them report directly to me." Turning back to Lazarus, Abby said, "Lazarus, words cannot express the amazement I have for your willingness to risk so much for people you don't know. You give us all hope for our brethren on the home world."

"Thank you Abby, for taking the time to see me," Lazarus said, marveling at the unusual shade of her eyes, pale green like rare beryl gemstones. What would she look like without his visor? He hopes this is real and not some cyberspace illusion.

Nodding in return, Abby said, "If you will excuse me. I have another meeting."

"Oh. I almost forgot. Izzy said hello," Lazarus blurts.

Abby's brow furrows, "Izzy? Isaac Crenshaw?" She asked. When Lazarus nods she continues, "Where did you run into him?"

"He was on the shuttle," Lindsey said.

"That old reprobate is still kicking? Last I'd heard, he was out in the asteroids somewhere. He and I spent... time... together back in '24... when Patrick was still alive... Thank you Lazarus," Abby said. "I will review the vid." She nods and walks out the door.

Lindsey comes over to Lazarus, "I've got a lot to do, but I will see you later, if that's ok?"

"Sure." he said. "I'll count on it." He reaches out to touch her and is shocked when his hand goes right through.

Lindsey grins and Sam laughs. Tempel shakes his head at the stupid Earthman. To him, Lazarus is just another shortimer needing special handling. "Come on hero," he said heading for the door. "Let's go find the twins."

Lindsey nods and vanishes.

Having employed virtual reality throughout his career, Lazarus is utterly amazed at the quality of the Lunarian system. His visor can create the image of a person, real or imagined, so accurately that he cannot tell the difference. Before this meeting, Lazarus would have sworn that was impossible, but now he knows better.

"Come on Lazarus. Let's get you settled in." Sam takes his arm and they follow Tempel. "Was Abby what you expected?"

Lazarus shakes his head in wonder, "Not even close. She and Corso look so young," Lazarus observes. "Was that really them or just how they make themselves appear vidcasting?"

"Why can't it be both?" Sam asks.

"How's that possible?" Lazarus retorts. "Abby is ninety-three and her oldest son must be in his sixties or seventies."

"We have gene therapies that eliminate wrinkles and keep skin smooth," Sam said.

"Gene therapies?" Lazarus exclaims. Right now, gene therapy isn't what's on his mind, "Can you show me how to view my father's records?" Lazarus asks.

"Magi, how many summary hours on Thom Sheffield do you have?" Sam asks.

"Seventy-six hours," Magi replies.

"When can I start?" Lazarus asks.

"Later, when you have some free time, Magi can get you started. Don't be in such a hurry," Sam said.

"Magi, are Jordan and Jamie available?" Tempel asks.

"They suggest bringing Lazarus to their lab in a few minutes," Magi said.

"Excellent. That gives us time for a beer at the Commons." Tempel leads them down a long corridor and through another airtight door.

Lazarus is several steps past the threshold before he looks around. Nothing prepared him for this, not the towering cathedral these Lunarians call a mall, nor the underground forest they call a commonway. This room is everything good about a home multiplied a thousand times.

Lazarus can't believe this is a subterranean cavern carved from the heart of a lunar mountain. Richly upholstered furnishings divide the expanse into innumerable sitting areas, some sunken, others raised, each with its own lighting. No two are the same creating a mosaic of shadow and light. Columns are everywhere but do not seem to be in any particular pattern, or if there is one, it escapes Lazarus. Colors jump out at him from an endless assortment of rugs, tapestries, and pictures. Arches define a brightly lit focal point roughly in the center of the vast room. Tempel is already there.

"This is your home?" Lazarus asks.

"This is Dakota Commons," Sam said.

In the distance, Lazarus can see the lower sections of much larger columns. Beyond them, it opens out into a large grassy courtyard with more columns on the far side capped with high arches. He assumes the columns on his side match those he can see. They remind him of the Parthenon model he had handled back in Athens.

The courtyard's lit up like a sunny afternoon. Across the way, beyond the far row of columns, Lazarus can make out a room matching this one. Light and shadow dance in its heart as people move about. Above it is a balcony. Several people stand at its edge looking down. As he stares, his visor magnifies their image and he can hear their voices. He looks away, breaking the link.

Groups of kids loudly chase each other across the grass. Someone is strumming a guitar and singing. Several people are playing pool. Many more are sitting in the comfortable chairs and sofas vidcasting. A man emerges from between two columns on the far side of the courtyard yelling and waving to someone Lazarus cannot see. Children are throwing a Frisbee out on the lawn. Laughter resonates. The Commons is vibrant with life.

Sam smiles and tilts her head inquisitively, watching the amazement wash over his face with each new discovery. "It's funny how we take things for granted until someone new comes along and lets us see through virgin eyes once more."

Lazarus looks at her with a dazed expression, "My awe meter just bent its needle. I've never seen anything like this." The room welcomed him. "I don't know what I was expecting, but certainly not this."

She smiles, "I would like to visit Mother Earth someday." From the way she said it, Lazarus realizes she doesn't actually foresee that happening anytime soon.

Seeming to materialize from nowhere, a large black dog startles

Lazarus. He's glad Sam's between him and the apparition. He's never seen such a dog. It has a long narrow face, floppy ears, and a slender body reminiscent of a Greyhound. The muscles in the dog's shoulders ripple under the silky black hide.

Sam gets down on one knee to greet the dog, vigorously rubbing its chest. "Dueler." the dog lays a heavy wet kiss across her face. She giggles like a little girl.

"What a beautiful animal," Lazarus said.

"Don't say that too loud. Dueler he thinks he's human, and he's definitely a member of the family." Sam looks at Lazarus, "Come over here and let's get you properly acquainted."

Dueler tenses. "It's all right," Sam reassures him. The big dog glances at her and visibly relaxes. He moves forward sticking his nose out to sniff Lazarus. A moment later, Dueler pushes his nose under the Earthman's hand. Introduction complete.

"Good boy." the young woman gives him one last hug around the neck before standing.

"I'm unfamiliar with the breed. What is he?" Lazarus asks.

Puzzled She asked, "What do you mean, breed? What's a breed?"

They resume walking with Dueler between them. Sam lightly caresses the dogs head.

Taken aback, Lazarus thinks for a moment. "Within the canine species there are many breeds. Collie is a breed, shepherds, terriers, hundreds of others. You don't know what a breed is?"

"Oh, I see. A breed shares common features such as hair, color, size and shape. Right?" She asked.

"That's right." Lazarus said.

"We select the characteristics when we create new life. If you want a dog that looks just like your neighbors, that's your choice."

She said it so matter-of-factly that Lazarus has to think about it for a second. "The dog's a tuber?" He instantly regrets his choice of words, letting it slip out from long use within the Federation. Tuber is derogatory slang for any life created using genetic engineering. To a large degree, the word symbolizes the growing hate Earth has for Lunarians.

Lazarus feels ignorance descend upon him like a heavy cloak, "Please, accept my apology. I meant no disrespect," Lazarus speaks anxiously.

Instead of getting angry, Sam's eyes sparkle with amusement. "Please… no need to apologize. Each question is but a step in life's journey… that is how we learn and you obviously have a long path before you," she softens her words with a smile. "To answer your question, we apply the science we must in order to survive. We have eliminated all genetic defects and diseases. Does anyone talk about that?" She asked. To Sam and most of her generation, Lazarus is a backward, almost primitive human being. The care taken in selecting her genes is completely missing in this man. He's a role of evolution's dice with no idea as to the outcome.

"Not in the Federation," he said.

"I didn't think so."

Sam enters the kitchen with Dueler at her side, opens the refrigerator door and withdraws two cold beers. Sam twists open one and hands it to Lazarus.

Motioning for Lazarus to follow, she joins Tempel. Lazarus takes a seat and sips his beer. It's good. He watches Dueler wander out of the kitchen and disappear into the shadows.

"Mind if we join you?" Skylor asks as he and Krystin approach.

"Not at all. Lazarus, this is my brother Skylor and sister Krystin," Tempel introduces. They exchange nods.

"Greetings," Lazarus said, "Very pleased to make your acquaintance."

Skylor sits down next to Sam, and Krystin lays a pile of clothing on the table and takes the seat closest to Lazarus. Skylor is slender but broad shouldered. Tempel could have been his twin. Both of them wear military style clothing more out of convenience than as a fashion statement. Even though Skylor is six years older than Tempel, it's virtually impossible to tell by looking at him.

Krystin is also slender and a few centimeters shorter than Skylor, not as tall as Sam but close. Like Sam, her hair is short, and like Sam, she's quite beautiful. Her body is on display under a t-shirt open at her midriff and a pair of tight shorts.

Are all Lunarian women so strikingly beautiful? Krystin reminds Lazarus of an American Indian princess. Her dark eyes are brash and honest.

It hit him, like most epiphanies. Like Dueler, the parents of these young Lunarians conceived them from a shopping list of characteristics. He envisions them sitting down with the family geneticist deciding what little Johnny was going to look like.

"The clothes are for you Paul Revere," Krystin said looking intently at Lazarus.

"Thanks. Tell me, has everyone seen the vid of my conversation with Lindsey?" Lazarus asks.

"The British are coming. Sorry, the Brotherhood is coming. The Brotherhood is coming. What I want to know is, where's your horse and lantern?" Krystin asks.

Skylor laughs, "Jordan and Jamie certified the vid for inclusion in Public Records five minutes after Lindsey submitted it."

"Who are Jordan and Jamie?" Lazarus asks Sam.

"Jordan and Jamie are network programmers," she said.

"Excuse me, but they prefer AI designers," Krystin insists.

"If there's anyone better at handling software, I've never met them," Tempel said taking another drink.

Krystin heads for the refrigerator. "Who needs another beverage?" she calls over her shoulder. A chorus of "sure" and "I do" follow her to the kitchen.

"I thought you would be in with Abby and Pellegrini. I saw him come through here earlier with his two bozos." Skylor said.

"Abby spared me, but I'm sure I'll have to deal with Pellegrini soon enough." Tempel finishes his first beer.

Krystin comes back placing more beers on the stone table. Tempel grabs the nearest one, twisting it open.

Lazarus finishes his first beer in several big gulps and reaches for another. "Is Pellegrini another Dugan?"

"Shit no." Krystin snorts, "What makes you ask that?"

"I just figured Dugan's held all the high profile jobs in the freehold," Lazarus states.

Skylor laughs, "Dakota has over seventeen thousand citizens spread out in fifty seven habitats. The Dugan family is prominent in Dakota politics but the freehold encompasses many families."

"Pellegrini thinks he's going to start a new freehold. He lives in Piper warren and wants to break it free from Dakota, that and Falconhead refinery would make a fine nucleus to build a new freehold around." Krystin said, clearly annoyed with the idea.

"It wouldn't be the first freehold Dakota has spawned," Skylor said.

"I just don't like the mealy mouthed S O B." she said.

"Tony's my supervisor, sis. He's a good engineer and knows how to run the refinery," Tempel wonders how he had gotten into the position of defending the man, especially to his sister. Pellegrini dated her a few years back but dumped her for a younger woman. So... if anyone had an ax to grind, it would be Krystin.

"How do you make a new freehold?" Lazarus asks.

"A proposed new freehold must be laid out and voted on by the parent freehold. Financial restitution must accompany any transfer of habitats and other assets to the new freehold. I think it's similar to corporations divesting or spinning off a new company on Mother Earth." Sam said.

Lazarus nods, taking a drink, wondering how much of today he will remember. So much has happened and it continues to come at him. It's like trying to get a drink from a fire hydrant.

"I don't like the pressure he's putting on you. He wants you out of there but he's too gutless to just come out and say it." Krystin said to Tempel. "And don't try and tell me Pellegrini runs the refinery. He's never there. Constance and Weenie feed him what they want him to know. You solve the major production problems while those yahoos grab the headlines. When is the last time Weenie or Connie had an original thought?" She asked defiantly.

Tempel shakes his head, "That's not the point. Pellegrini deserves respect. He's been in charge of operations for over two years, and helped set up the new refractory purification process." He notices Lazarus looking past his shoulder.

"Greetings everyone," Constance said from the kitchen. She's opening cabinets looking for something. Finding it, she peels open a hi-nutrient cereal bar and takes a bite. Walking over to the table, she nods to Lazarus, "So we meet again."

Recognizing the woman from the mall, Lazarus returns the gesture, "Yes, so it seems," he said.

"You're from Phoenix," she said. "It's such a beautiful city although much too hot for me. I visited a few times mostly in the winter."

In person, Constance looks to be in her late forties with straight mousy brown hair cut shoulder length. She carries a heavy build and is below average height. Her most prominent feature is her nose. She's the first woman Lazarus has seen since his arrival that he would not classify as beautiful. She's not ugly, just plain. Even at his admittedly low level of understanding, Lazarus is instantly sure Constance is not part of the same genetic makeup as the other Lunarians sitting at the table. She's earthborn like him.

"I didn't think you could remember that far back." Kristin snarls at the woman who pointedly ignores her. Not getting a response she continues, "Where are the other two butt nuggets?"

"Is that how your mother taught you to talk?" Constance spit back. "If you must know, Tony and Winthrop are with Abby. They have legitimate concerns about the direction Dakota freehold is going." Looking back at Tempel, "What have you done about the Gravity Separator problem?"

"Come on Connie, you know I have other commitments and can't even start for another week. Pellegrini knew my schedule when he gave me the assignment," Tempel replies defensively.

"Falconhead will end up waiting for your analysis or someone else will have to do it for you." Constance said rather hatefully.

Tempel empathizes with Connie. It's hard for her to understand, but her attitude is getting to be a distraction. "Constance." Tempel said tersely, "If it's that important, why doesn't Pellegrini give it to someone else?"

"Because everyone is already working twenty hours a day. There isn't anybody else." She retorts angrily. "Now the rest of Falconhead must deal with it. But why should you care. You're a Dugan. Nothing touches you."

With a speed only a native Lunarian can achieve, Krystin moves across the room and confronts Constance, their faces only centimeters apart. "You have something against Dugan's?" She asked, the intensity flowing between them like an electric current. "Or maybe you think you can run the freehold better than Abby?"

"Ridiculous." Constance backs away, startled and frightened at the abrupt close encounter. "I don't have to take that from you."

"Fine. Leave. Go back to Alabama or wherever rock you crawled out from under." Kristin keeps her nose close as the smaller woman backpedals.

Fear contorts her face. "Monster." Constance turns and scurries away from this menacing creature.

Krystin watches the retreating figure with disgust.

"You were pretty hard on her," Tempel said.

"Not hard enough." Krystin replies.

"You say Constance came from Alabama? What part? When?" Lazarus asks Krystin.

Krystin shrugs, "I haven't the foggiest idea. Magi, what's her bio?"

"She was born in the village of Blacksher north of Mobile in 2046. Moved to the Atlanta area when she was ten," Magi reports. "Did her training in Atlanta and Massachusetts, she arrived on Luna March 2068 and applied for Dakota citizenship a month later."

"Interesting," Lazarus said looking thoughtfully at the retreating figure.

"Why's that interesting?" Sam asks.

"2068 puts her at the very end of the Exodus, a time when the Federation was actively discouraging citizens from leaving, and a time when agents were sent out to establish deep cover among the emigrants. Most of these undercover operatives turned out to be a bust, becoming just another part of the expansion and never reporting to their controllers. However, a few did and are still in place, their identities kept top secret. Not even the President knows who they are. It's something to keep in mind."

Tempel looks at the Earthman with a touch of disgust, "Such intrigue is unlikely here. You will learn that the Law of Full Disclosure is very hard to beat."

"You moron. I'm not an undercover operative." Constance said.

Lazarus looks surprised and the others laugh. It usually takes a few days for a new arrival to figure out there's no such thing as a private conversation anymore. Back room gossip is a thing of the past.

Lincoln County Hospital

*As to those who disbelieve, neither their possessions, nor
their children shall avail them at all against the punishment
of Allah; and it is they that will be the fuel of the Fire.*

Holy Qur'an 3:10

Not far from Dugan warren, located in a lower level of the Aldrin
Station Security Administration, are some of the city's laboratory
facilities. Their primary mission, as stated on the annual budget, is as
a crime lab supporting all police investigations, but that was a smoke
screen. The shortimers over in Little America would never tolerate
Lunarians investigating or policing them and the extremely low crime
rate among the Republic's citizens make this a standing joke among
the techs who work in the lab. In reality, the lab is devoted to advanced
research and the development of new technology. This lab specializes
in Product Delivery Modules. Today, all the interesting toys are out of
sight and it looks like an ordinary forensics lab, simple precautions until
they learn more about this latest citizen.

Tempel leads Lazarus across the main floor to an office on the lower
level. A soft chime sounds as they reach it and the door slides open.

"Come in. Come in." the person inside said, rising to greet them.
"Greetings Tempel. This must be Lazarus." The person is wearing a
blue shirt and gray pants.

"Greetings Jordan. Yes, this is Lazarus Sheffield," Tempel said.
"Lazarus, this is Jordan Dugan."

"Very pleased to meet you," Lazarus returns the nod. He can't tell if Jordan is male or female.

"Greetings Tempel." It was the same voice but from behind.

"Greetings," Tempel said. "Lazarus, this is Jamie Dugan."

Lazarus turns and is confronted with an exact duplicate of the person he'd just met. Only this one's wearing a red shirt. Their voices are husky but not male, their build slender but not female. They could be either. He looks in confusion from one to the other.

They both laugh and say, "Just remember that Jordan is wearing blue," Jamie said. "I'm anxious to hear how you can help us understand what's going on." Jamie takes Lazarus by the arm and guides him towards a workstation in the back of the office.

"What do you make of Lazarus's story?" Tempel asks Jordan.

Looking across the office at Jamie and the stranger, "Rest assured, we're going to check every detail. Twice."

"I find Earthmen hard to understand. Some want to harm us, others, like this one…" Tempel shakes his head in puzzlement, "want to be us."

"Show me a Lunarian who hasn't had the same difficulty and I'll show you a fool. Mother Earth politics make my head spin, far too much intrigue. Enemies turn into friends and back again in the blink of an eye. They lie and exaggerate. No one trusts anyone. Who can make sense of it? Me? Born and raised on Luna? I think not. Abby is the only one I trust to interpret Earthly shenanigans, and she hasn't set foot on it for sixty-five years." Jordan exclaims. "Mark my words, this is a very dangerous position to be in. The Republic needs embassies physically located on Mother Earth. Relying on the business dealings of freeholds as our major political contact is making us easy targets."

"Then please explain how we can do that without breaking the Law of Full Disclosure. The United Nations has forbidden us recording their citizens. They claim it would infringe on their privacy in some way. The truth is their politics and the way they do business would not survive the visibility of Full Disclosure. They refuse to abide by our laws and we will not lower our standards to theirs. So here we are again at the same impasse," Tempel shrugs.

"We deal with it the same way we do business with them, we follow our laws, and they follow theirs with a firewall in between," Jordan said.

"That won't work and you know why," Tempel said.

"It's better than war," Jordan replies.

"What do you propose to do when our ambassador is called to a meeting? Suspend our Law? How can we tell our people to remove their visors and attend a meeting that produces no official record? That's in direct violation of Full Disclosure."

"There must be an answer," Jordan said.

Tempel shakes his head, "Talk to Lindsey. She spent six weeks down there. I can't imagine being without Magi that long... We can't let Mother Earth bring us down to their level. Secrecy is the evildoer's playground and absolute secrecy produces absolute evil."

"On that we agree," Jordan said.

Before the conversation can sink deeper into a subject beaten to death all across the Republic, Jamie catches Jordan's eye and motions to link with them.

"Lazarus seems to think we need to use a keyboard and a mouse to access the data we need," Jamie said.

Jordan raises his eyebrows inquisitively, "But why?" Tuning to Lazarus, "Why not use a simulation?"

"Because the netsite will recognize it's a simulation and not the real deal. The Brotherhood uses out-of-date protocols to hide behind, the older the better. For the last century, old hardware and software has been recycled to poor nations around the world. That has enabled them to construct a sub network inside Earthnet that's virtually invisible to anybody using VR. The protocols make it very secure, unless you know the secret handshake." Lazarus said grinning.

Jamie leaves the room with a determined look.

"Where are we going to get antique hardware that works? We stopped using keyboards and mice long before I was born. I've never even seen one used." Jordan can't believe it.

"What's a mice?" Tempel asks but before anyone can answer him, Jamie rushes back in triumphantly, an old-fashioned wireless keyboard with a built-in track ball.

"Will this do? I don't think we have a mouse," Jamie said, handing the ancient device to Lazarus.

Lazarus takes the plastic contraption and taps a few of the keys, which still seem to function. Turning it over, he looks intently at the faded identification label and makes out a model number, manufacturer, and date.

"2023, yes, I think I can make this work. I'm not accustomed to using a ball but that shouldn't be a major problem. We will need a power source for it. I doubt its batteries are still good."

"Not a problem," Jamie replies. She rummages around in a drawer and pulls out a small piece of equipment with several wires sticking out of it. Placing it on the table, she takes the keyboard from Lazarus and removes a small panel from its bottom. The battery space is empty. She solders the wires from the source to the small tabs inside.

Jordan frowns, "Even if it works, I'm sure we don't have drivers for it."

After looking closely at the label on the bottom of the keyboard, Jamie sets the power source to three volts. "There, that should do it. Magi, are you picking up anything?"

"Yes, at four point eight gigahertz," Magi replies.

"If you will allow me, I can download the drivers we need from the net," Lazarus looks from Jordan then back to Jamie.

The two exchange glances, "Nothing ventured, nothing gained." Jamie said. "Magi, isolate and firewall Lazarus. He's going to introduce some outside software and you're to take maximum precautions."

"Aye." Magi replies.

Sitting in his chair, the virtual workstation appears around him. Lazarus is gaining confidence every time he uses his visor. He arranges the relevant net-address symbols and calls up the netsite.

A 3D image of Jesus hanging on a cross set on top of a hill dominates the front page. The name of the netsite, Calgary Chapel, floats above Jesus in bold letters. Around the image are icons linking to other pages within the site. Lazarus touches the Ichthys icon. Jesus disappears and the page that takes its place contains a listing of names. He scrolls down until he finds the name '*Kenneth Whitaker*' and pulls it over to a clear portion of his desktop. At the instant of release, a 3D image of a middle-aged man appears in its place. His physical identification is alongside. Lazarus drags the man's DNA profile onto his desktop.

A standard DNA fingerprint appears. Lazarus picks one of the bright bars in the seventh column and double clicks on it. Instead of exposing the detailed description of that particular snippet of genetic code, it initiates a program Lazarus had modified several weeks earlier, a thirty-second audio file of a Pepsi jingle dating from the mid 20th century.

"Now we wait." Lazarus said.

Instead of playing the jingle, copies of the file distribute themselves on servers scattered across the Federation where they in turn, make more copies of the jingle sending them to even more servers. This process repeats until the chain has cascaded into hundreds of thousands of servers. At a predetermined point, all the files execute simultaneously, grabbing files at random from each server and sending them to other servers. From within this chaos, one program seeks out the file he needs and downloads it across the 385,000 kilometers of space to Lazarus.

By the time the massive downloading triggers Earthnet watchdogs, it's too late to backtrack any one occurrence to its origin. Their paths cross and re-cross millions of times in a pattern impossible to decipher in any reasonable amount of time. All they can do is stop the runaway process before it consumes more resources. Firefighters designed to combat this style of virus overtake and stop the programs. Within minutes, the attack is contained.

Pulling up the file, Lazarus commands, "Install this."

A pause of a few seconds, "Done" the AI said.

"I can't wait to see what you do for an encore," Jamie said.

Lazarus places the keyboard in his lap and begins typing, much to the amazement of those watching. "Magi, are you picking this up?"

"Aye, the signal's drifting but I can compensate," she said.

"No. Let it drift," Lazarus types in an old-style net address; *ubayd. allah.ibn.abd.allah.com.* He checks it twice for spelling and presses the enter key on the ancient keyboard.

"Ubayd-Allah ibn Abd-Allah was a companion of the prophet Muhammad. He spoke the Hadith of the pen and paper," Magi said. "It's the event that split Islam into Sunni and Shi'a."

A small box with its own input field pops up in the center of the workspace. He uses the trackball to move the tiny arrow to the field and presses the button. A small vertical bar begins blinking inside awaiting keyboard input. Lazarus carefully types, *sura24ayas5157.*

"Sura is the Arabic word for chapter and ayas is verse. Verses 51 through 57 in the Qur'an directs believers to either convert or kill nonbelievers," Magi said.

Thousands of pages of Arabic text overflow his workspace. Like a stack of papers on a table, the one on top is the only one he can see in its entirety.

"Magi, be a dear and translate for us?" Jamie asked.

"Certainly," she said.

To the utter amazement of Lazarus, word by word, the Arabic flips to English. This feat took his entire team, and their computers, several hours of hard work to accomplish.

"These are electronic communications generated within the Brotherhood's Ministry of Defense. The Federation isn't as efficient as Magi in translating so we've read only about ten percent of these, but it's enough to worry a lot of folks," Lazarus said.

"Pull up another," Jamie requests.

A second page of Arabic takes its place and Magi translates.

Jamie stares at the text for a second, absorbing the information it contains. "Magi, translate all of these and record," she directs.

"Aye," Magi replies.

"There are hundreds of thousands of documents here…" Lazarus warns.

One after another, Magi loads and translates the information. The process speeds up until it's a blur, giving Lazarus no opportunity to see a finished document before the next arrives.

Jamie monitors the progress, letting the information flow into her head without taking time for an in-depth analysis on her part. That will come later.

Lazarus looks at Jamie and realizes something strange is happening. It's as if she's reading the memos flashing by. *But that's impossible.*

Magi's incoming chime sounds softly in Tempel's ear and she said, "Pellegrini has asked if you can be spared. It seems he needs you at Falconhead."

Tempel turns away in disgust, "Abby and Corso ordered me to bring Lazarus to the lab and stay with him until Lindsey was back."

"I can do it," Jordan offers.

"Thanks Jordan," Tempel said. "Lazarus?" The Earthman looks up. "I need to go but Jamie and Jordan will take care of anything you might need."

"Yes, ok," Lazarus mumbles, much more interested in Jamie.

Jamie is sitting forward on the edge of her seat, eyes locked on the display. Tempel is genuinely astonished the Earthman commands such attention from his cousin. Live and learn.

ЯL

Lincoln County Hospital is one of the premiere facilities in Luna's continuing quest to improve medical science. It's also the birthplace of biotronics and home to Lunarian genetics and reconstitutional science. Constructed in 2024, before disrupter technology revolutionized excavations, it's one of Aldrin Station's first habitats. Some of its chambers still exhibit mechanical tool marks, left to remind Lunarians of their heritage.

Dr Haslett doesn't think anything amiss when he first notices the heavy gray case. Nothing about it stands out among the many crates and containers making up the shipment containing his Quantum Probe Microscope. Having waited impatiently for the scope for over a year, he's personally supervising each step in its unpacking and assembly. It's Japan's latest technology and cost a small fortune to buy and ship to Luna.

Maria Chapman has been Dr. Haslett's grad student for the last six months and is the only one among his staff he trusts to help him. She's almost as excited as he is about getting her hands on this magnificent machine. It has the ability to not only see an atom but focus on its nucleus. The two of them have been working steadily on the assembly for over four hours, and now, with the end in sight, they're anxious to get it finished. Picking up the touch panel, Maria stifles a yawn as she triggers the next step in the process.

Similar to other high-value crates in the shipment, this last one has an electronic lock. She's to enter a nine-digit code into the small keypad on the side of the case.

Maria kneels down in front of the case and enters in the first three digits just as Dr. Haslett torques down the final screw on the hood installation. He walks over to stand behind her. "What's this?" He asked.

181

"Quark detector," she said, entering the next three digits.

Dr. Haslett frowns, mentally tired and slow from the long assembly session, "This looks too big to be a detector."

Maria keys in the last three digits the same instant that Dr. Haslett said, "Stop."

The enormous release of energy vaporizes the laboratory. The thick walls contain the energy for the briefest fraction of a second before they too atomize. For many levels above and below, the energy destroys everything it touches. Expansion robs it of power and the thick stone floors that separate the different levels begin to hold the blast between them, focusing the energy horizontally. The blast pulverizes the corridors, rooms, and laboratories that lie between. Robbed of their support, many of the floors collapse crushing any that have managed to survive up to this point.

Seconds after it began, the beast spends itself in a thick cloud of dust that permeates the hospital and the surrounding city.

Airtight doors close in emergency lock down as Magi moves to contain the damage. Network communications fail cutting the AI off from the hospital.

ЯL

Magi exclaims sharply on all channels, "***Noooo.***"

At the same instant, the floor shakes violently and the air inside the lab reverberates with a heavy deep thump. Jamie jumps from her chair.

"What was that?" Jordan exclaims.

"There's been an explosion inside Lincoln County Hospital," Magi said.

Tempel's insides twist, "Explosion. What kind of explosion." he demands, fearing the worst even as he turns to look at Lazarus.

"Unknown, but it was big," Magi said.

Lazarus stares back blankly, his brain trying to get a handle on this turn of events. "Nuclear?" He asks.

"Negative. At least I am not picking up any radiation around the blast area," Magi said. "I'm not getting anything from the hospital itself."

"Attention. Emergency Response teams ER4 through ER16, report to Lincoln County Hospital. Everyone else sit tight. Stay off the net until further notice." Corso broadcast. His voice echoes from every corner of Aldrin Station for the benefit of those few not wearing visors.

Tempel links with Captain Osaka just in time to hear him say, "The highest priority is getting everybody out of the hospital safely. To do that, we'll need to know how badly damaged the habitat is. I'll lead a team in to mag the south periphery wall. Lieutenant Dugan," looking right at Tempel, "can lead the other team north. It shouldn't take more than thirty minutes to get a preliminary evaluation."

"Do it," Corso said. "We're already getting reports of massive damage, so take all appropriate precautions. We don't need more casualties."

"Aye." Keeping his eyes on Tempel, Kitajima said, "You're at the lab. Good. Grab two magnetometers from the storage room, ER packs, and whatever climbing gear you can find." Kitajima continues. "Magi, round up Quan Kiai and have them report outside the hospital."

"Aye." Magi said.

Tempel crosses the labs main floor heading for the storage room next to the big liquid helium Dewar. The magnetometers are on a broad shelf just inside the storeroom. He deposits them on a workbench outside. Returning, he rummages around in a metal locker, emerging with hard hats, climbing harness, and several ER packs. A little more effort nets Low Light Level flood lamps that clip onto the hard hats They cast a broader and less intense beam of light for use with the L3 sensors in their visors.

"Magi, where is the hemp rope kept?" Tempel asks.

"In the bottom cabinet to your left," she replies.

Tempel retrieves several coils of the strong rope, adding a bundle of carabiners and several ratcheting come-a-longs. Emerging from the storeroom, he finds Lazarus waiting by equipment.

"I understand you're headed for the hospital. I want to help. I'm no doctor but I do have emergency medical training."

Tempel tosses the Earthman a hard hat, "Looks like you've been promoted to field officer," Tempel said.

Lazarus feels a rush of adrenalin surge through his body like an electric shock. He expected Tempel to refuse him and was prepared to argue. Lunarians are full of surprises.

Jamie rolls up in a small electric cart, its cargo bed piled high with strap-on air tanks, enough for the entire platoon. They add Tempel's collection of gear to the load.

Lazarus climbs into the passenger seat. "Where are you going?" Jamie asks.

"He's with me," Tempel replies.

Jamie looks skeptical but remains quiet.

Tempel, with Lazarus beside him, drives away. It's been less than five minutes since the explosion.

Kitajima designated a location outside the hospital zone for the platoon's muster point to avoid the growing number of emergency vehicles coming and going. Tempel and Lazarus pull up and stop alongside the captain.

"What's he doing with you?" Kitajima growls when he sees Lazarus.

"Abby wanted him to stay with me. Besides, he said he has emergency medical training and we can use his help," Tempel replies.

"We don't have time to coddle a shortimer," Kitajima said.

"I don't need coddling," Lazarus said.

Kitajima gives him a long hard stare as several more members of Quan Kiai arrive. He turns back to Tempel, "Fine, but you're responsible for him."

Within ten minutes of the explosion, all but two members of Quan Kiai have gathered around the carts. Several look inquisitively at Lazarus as he passes the air tanks out. They strap on the tanks, leaving the breathing masks hanging by their flow tubes over their shoulders. A second mask clips to their belts. Lazarus looks at it puzzled.

"In case you need to share your O2," Tempel explains showing him how to use it.

After distributing the equipment, they all link with Kitajima. The captain pulls up a graphic display of Lincoln County Hospital. The hospital consists of two large habitats with fourteen entrances, including a maglev train station in nearby Sherwood Commonway. Hospitals should be centrally located and accessible, and Lincoln County is no exception.

Kitajima points at a glowing dot near the center of the habitat's north wing, "From all indications the bomb was here. Magi run the simulation."

"Aye," she said.

The blue lines of the habitat turn red as the blast consumes everything above and below it. Shock waves radiate outward weakening the habitats internal supports. Floors pancake downward. Even in the light lunar gravity, the weight of the collapsing structure is enormous, crushing everything.

No one speaks for a few seconds after the simulation finishes. Kitajima sighs, "Tempel, I want you to go through Central and descend the north ramp. Take it down four levels and proceed to the north periphery wall if you can. We need fracture data on the lower quadrant before we dare go any deeper. Got it?" Kitajima adds lines to the simulation that illustrate his instructions. His calmness reassures the men and women around him.

"Aye," Tempel said.

"The closer you get to the epicenter, the worse communications will get. We don't have any portable relays and I'm not waiting for them, so you guys will have to wing it without Magi," Kitajima explains. "You ok with that Tempel?" he looks intently at the young man looking for the slightest hesitation.

"No problem."

"Good." Kitajima said, "Magi, keep an eye on them and let me know when they're done. I want that mag data ASAP."

"Aye," she said.

"Is he coming with us?" Brice asks nodding at Lazarus.

"He's with me," Tempel said. "Anymore questions?"

Brice shrugs. He knows that tone.

"Let's roll." Kitajima leads the way.

Smaller than a commonway, Commonwealth Avenue looks more like an inner city neighborhood back on Mother Earth than a subterranean passage. Two and three story buildings line both sides of the street. Shops dominate the ground floor and residences the uppers.

Moving rapidly, Quan Kiai joins with the people converging on the hospital.

Commonwealth Avenue outside the hospital's entrance is organized pandemonium. It's become the outer triage for those able to walk out of the hospital. Blood and bandages are everywhere. ER personnel move among the victims trying to ease their suffering. Rivulets of blood make the stone floor slippery. The voices of the medics intertwine with the victim's moans in a strangely muted soundtrack to the horror. A loud cry of a child for its mother rips the quiet desperation.

Quan Kiai enters the hospital through a corridor that opens into a large central hall where the inner triage is still being set up. Dust is everywhere, making it hard to see the people moving about caring for the wounded. Without power, the only light comes from portables the rescuers have brought. Some lights remain stable. Others dart about sending shadows dancing across walls and ceiling. It's an eerie scene.

Kitajima approaches an officer directing traffic near the center of the chaos and asks, "Marty, what can you tell me?"

The figure turns and said, "Kitajima. I've been expecting you. It's bad down there and I don't have much faith the integrity will hold. The dust is thick as mud, so be damn sure your people have plenty of air."

Kitajima nods and asks, "Have you gotten everybody out?"

"Are you kidding? We're just getting started. The only ones who are out are those who could walk out. We haven't even started searching the lower floors. Below level eight, the bomb shredded the water and electricity so it's wet down there. Be careful what you touch. The electricity might still be hot in places," Marty said.

"There are portable transponders on the way so we should have emergency communications very soon." Kitajima said, "I would appreciate it if you could personally see they are deployed and fresh air tanks sent down. We have air for only an hour."

Marty nods, "Sure, you can count on it Kitajima." Marty said.

Kitajima turns and speaks to his platoon, "Listen up. I want everyone to switch to L3 sensors augmented by infrared," he orders.

Tempel notices that Lazarus is having problems. He links visors with the Earthman, showing him where his sensor controls are and adjusting them to his liking.

Lazarus is grateful for the help. The world inside the hospital transforms from a shadowy dust-filled vision into a strangely vivid monochromatic image unlike anything Lazarus has ever seen.

"This is where we part company. Make some good luck." Kitajima said.

"You do the same." Tempel said watching Kitajima and his squad disappear towards the south ramp.

Tempel leads them across the hall towards the north ramp. Lined up along one wall are a number of draped bodies, those people beyond medical help.

"Magi, can you access the hospitals network?" Tempel said.

"Negative, this habitat is completely down. At this point, I'm receiving only your audio signal," she informs him. "And even that is weak."

The mineralized rock of Rim Mountain dampens energy. It doesn't take many twists and turns within a Luna habitat to render long-range communications virtually useless.

"Great." Marcel exclaims, a touch of nervousness in his voice.

"Relax and keep your eyes open. We'll be fine," Zoey said patting her comrade on the shoulder.

Entering the ramp, their lamps flood the enclosed space casting long shadows on the walls. They descend three levels uneventfully. The first sign of damage is a section of wall collapsed across their path. They climb over the debris trying not to add more dust to the air around them. It's unnaturally quiet. The only sounds are their own muffled footfalls and the occasional grunt.

Stopping before a partially open airlock, "I think this is the right level," Tempel said. His voice is loud and harsh after the silence.

"The panel should tell us," Corazon mumbles. Getting down on one knee, he wipes the dust off and reads, "A310 South."

"That's it," Magi sounds grainy and distant. They were losing her as they move down the ramp. "Kitajima wants the outside wall magged first. We need as much information concerning the surrounding rock as possible."

Tempel wedges into the half open door and pushes hard with no result. Karl comes to help and the two of them combine their muscle. The door moves a few centimeters then stops.

"That's far enough," Tempel steps into the dark hallway. His hardhat is the only illumination. Dust hangs motionless limiting visibility even further. Chunks of stone litter the corridor floor. This had been the main access for this floor. The wall opposite the ramp is broken and open to blackness. His lamp reaches only a short way down what remains of the hallway before encountering a large pile of debris. Closer, he can make out tracks in the thick layer of dust. He wonders if they are from a rescuer or a victim.

In the blurry outer reaches of visibility, something moves. "We have someone," Tempel said. He heads towards the person who sinks to the floor before he gets there.

"Save my baby. Please save my little boy." the voice is definitely female.

Zoey follows and kneels beside the figure. "Take it easy. We're here to help."

"Magi, get someone down here with a litter." Tempel commands, routing his transmission through Marcel still on the ramp.

"Sorry. All crews are busy in the levels above you. They can't break anyone free for at least ten minutes," Magi said.

Tempel can barely hear her even with Marcel's help. Once they move away from the ramp, they'll lose communication with Magi.

Lazarus slides the ER pack off his shoulder and squeezes through the opening pulling it behind him. Moving up, he sets the pack beside the woman, retrieves a sterile wipe from its pocket, kneels and clears away the worst of the dust and blood from around her eyes.

"Where's my baby." she cries weakly.

Opening an inner pouch, Lazarus gets the med bracelet and snaps it on her wrist, adjusting it to fit snuggly. Turning back to the pack, he looks for a screen. Then, to his amazement, the woman's vital signs appear in his visor. It doesn't take him long to decide this is much better than comparable Federation medical equipment using screens and flat panel displays. "Low blood pressure, barely conscious, shallow breathing. She's suffering from shock. She needs immediate medical treatment." Lazarus removes the secondary mask from his belt and puts it on the woman.

"Can she be moved?" Karl asks.

"I didn't find any serious external wounds but she could have internal damage or a head injury," Lazarus said.

"Then I will carry her out of here," Karl said.

Tempel nods, "Do it then get back here ASAP. Marcel, I want you to stay in the ramp to relay messages to Magi."

"Aye," Marcel said.

Lazarus removes the bracelet and returns it to the pack. Karl replaces Lazarus's mask with his own secondary. Lazarus helps Marcel and Karl get the stricken woman through the jammed airlock door and into the ramp.

"My baby," she moans as Karl cradles her in his arms.

"We will find him," Lazarus said.

Lazarus hesitates watching the young man disappear, his light casting eerie shadows on the curved walls of the ramp.

"You shouldn't promise what you can't deliver," Marcel said.

Lazarus looks at him, "One way or the other, we'll find him." He slings the ER pack onto his back. Tempel and the others have already gone. He can faintly see the infrared glow of their bodies down the corridor and moves to catch up. It tests his meager but growing abilities to navigate in the lunar environment. He feels a touch of pride that he can do it at all. It reminds him of something his dad had told him long ago; *if you want to teach someone how to swim, toss them into the deep end.*

The dust hangs thick, making him thankful for the air on his back. Shadows play tricks on his mind. No one speaks and the only sounds are muffled footfalls and breathing.

As they move further away from the ramp, what remains of the wall disappears entirely and the void eats into the floor until they are walking on a ledge less than thirty centimeters wide. The stone is cut clean, as if a giant surgeon had removed the heart of the habitat. The Lunarians move across the narrow span and stop, looking back at Lazarus.

"Come on, let's go," Tempel said.

Lazarus puts his back to the wall, grits his teeth, and shuffles sideways, trying not to think about it. He can hear a rumble of settling debris from below. Glancing out into the void, his visors L3 sensors can't penetrate the dust and distance. All he sees is a swirling gray-green mass. Lower down, small flashes cut through the fog like fireflies on a foggy night.

He's only about half way across when they hear the moaning. It's almost directly below him. The others lights dart across the debris, searching. A massive piece of rock, probably the floor of the corridor, is slumped against the wall. Perched upon it is the head of a child. The rest of the body is invisible, perfectly camouflaged by a thick layer of dust. The eyes staring back at him are alive.

"Tempel, I see someone. A child," Lazarus said.

"Can you deal with it? My job is to mag this habitat. If it goes we all die." Tempel said.

"Go do what you must do. I'm taking this child to a doctor."

"I won't be long," Tempel said.

"Neither will I," Lazarus replies.

"Zoey, make sure he doesn't kill himself," Tempel said. "Corazon, you're with me." The two men head down the corridor.

"There's a slab about twenty meters back where you can climb down," Zoey said as she sits on the floor dangling her legs off the edge. "I will guide you from here."

"Ok," Lazarus said.

A moment later, she said, "Right below you."

The slab is a section of floor. It's very steep. Laying the ER pack aside, Lazarus starts down backwards, digging his toes into the smooth surface, expecting to slip and fall any second, but to his surprise, his new shoes grip the stone and he's able to descend without any problems.

The dust is thick at the bottom. It rises with each footfall behaving more like a liquid than a solid. The pile is unstable, ready to slide further into the pit at the slightest provocation.

Lazarus precariously crosses the distance and picks up the little broken body. Cradling the child in his arms, Lazarus looks down. There is a chunk of stone sticking out of its head and one arm is shattered and crushed, bent in far too many places. Yet the child's eyes stare at him from behind the mask of dirt and grime with burning intensity, not letting go of life without a fight.

Lazarus scrambles back across the debris towards the makeshift ramp, the child almost weightless in his arms. He's careful to support the head, cupping it with his right hand while immobilizing the broken arm between their bodies. He steadies himself with one hand and climbs upward.

"I got you," Zoey said reaching down to help him up. Together they retreat the way they'd come. "Marcel, call ahead and let Magi know Lazarus is coming up with a child."

"Aye," he said.

With help from Marcel and Zoey, Lazarus manages to squeeze through the jammed door without disturbing his young passenger.

It seems to take forever to retrace his steps back up the ramp. "You have only a few more meters to go," Magi informs him.

Emerging from the ramp Lazarus pauses and looks around. The chaos of a major triage is nearly complete. Cries of pain echo strangely in the shadowy chamber.

Magi is beside him, "Please follow me," she said and leads him through the mayhem. They pass people with missing arms and legs, blood is everywhere, some cry out in pain and despair. Others sit in shock not uttering a sound.

Lazarus stumbles and would have fallen if not for a man stepping forward, using his body and one good arm to catch him.

"Steady lad" the man said.

Lazarus looks at him and sees a bloody stump where his other arm should be. The two stare at each other for a moment.

"Lazarus please, you must hurry," Magi said.

"Go," the man pushes him in Magi's direction.

She leads him to an enclosed ER vehicle, the rear doors wide open. Two people are laying side-by-side inside. Several more sit in the forward section wearing dazed expressions and bloody bandages. A woman is under a blood soaked sheet apparently unconscious. Beside her is a man. He looks up at Lazarus.

"Give me the child," he said holding one arm out.

Lazarus lays the broken body on the man's chest, rolling it over gently, cradling it in the valley between the two people. The woman moans and looks down at the child, then up at Lazarus.

"You found my baby," she said.

"Step back," Magi said to Lazarus.

Obeying, Lazarus watches the ER pull away, the rear doors shutting as it gains speed. He stands motionless until it disappears down the corridor towards Commonwealth Avenue.

"Lazarus, are you able to continue?" Magi asks.

He turns back, facing the horror.

"Yes... I'm fine," Lazarus said and starts back the way he had come. He couldn't care less about lying at that moment.

ℜ𝕃

Tempel calls out, "Marcel? Can you hear me?"

"Aye," he replies.

"Stand by..." Routing through Marcel's visor Tempel calls, "Magi?"

"Yes Tempel," Magi sounds far away.

"I'm downloading the data." Tempel places the magnetometer on the floor and kneels down in front of it, keying the control panel.

A few moments later, "Transmission successful. I'm starting the analysis."

Tempel can see the lights of the others as he and Corazon approach the ramp. They squirm through the opening just as they hear the sounds of someone coming down.

"Welcome back Lazarus," Tempel said.

"What do we do now?" Marcel asks.

"Isn't that obvious? We go down and begin rescue operations," Zoey said matter-of-factly.

Marcel gives a nervous laugh, "Zoey, are you nuts?" He looks at her then at Tempel. "It's too dangerous. Let's wait until Magi clears the hab."

"I will not complete the safety analysis for another thirteen minutes," Magi said.

"We've already waited too long. If anybody is alive down there we need to get them out now," Zoey retorts. "It really doesn't matter what shape the hab is in. Someone will need to go down there and get them out."

"She's right," Tempel said, noticing Lazarus nodding in agreement. "Kitajima has the data he needs to determine the risk to a large scale rescue. We, on the other hand, are already here. Let's move down the ramp and see what we find." Tempel looks at each in turn, receiving approval from everyone, including Marcel.

"Why not lash a rope to me and I'll explore the ramp below us? That way if it collapses you have a chance of pulling me back up," Lazarus suggests.

"Or at least finding you under the rubble," Marcel said.

"Not you, me," Tempel said ignoring Marcel.

"It's my idea. Let me do it," Lazarus retorts. He's the oldest and stuck in the assumption that it means something.

Tempel simply shakes his head, unwilling to give this shortimer that responsibility. Besides, he knows this building like the back of his hand, as if this knowledge does him any good with the hospital in such a state of ruin.

"From the frying pan into the fire," Lazarus mutters, hoping this brash young Lunarian can handle the assignment.

"What was that?" Zoey asks with a frown. She doesn't think it appropriate for this shortimer to question her Lieutenant and is fully prepared to take him down a notch.

"He said, from the frying pan into the fire," Tempel repeats unnecessarily. "Magi, inform Kitajima we're doing reconnaissance down the north ramp."

"Aye. He knows. His team is already moving down the south ramp. It appears to be intact all the way down but they are magging it thoroughly. Perhaps you should as well."

"Negative. These cracks make that a waste of time." Tempel said.

"Please be careful Tempel. I don't want to report your death to Abby and Liz," Magi pleads.

"I will not take any unnecessary risks, I assure you," Tempel said. Looking at Karl, he said, "Set up an anchor here. If short range communications break down, I will tug three times when I need you to pull the line up and two times for some slack."

"Aye," Karl nods and gruffly adds "I'm with Magi, don't do anything crazy down there." He's comfortable with his role. This is not the first time he's anchored a rope for his comrades and he sets to work.

Karl drives a lost arrow into a large crack in the wall. The tight space inside the ramp rings with each hammer blow, the pitch rising as the metal spike runs home. Clipping a carabiner to it, he ties Tempel's rope using a Munter hitch. Taking up the slack, Karl gives the belay an experimental tug and nods at Tempel.

Tempel steps into a climbing harness and attaches the rope. He nods and starts down the ramp, picking his path carefully. The ramps outer wall is gone below level four, a vast darkness taking its place. Dust is thick, limiting visibility. The inner core of the ramp is the only thing holding the floor, a cantilevered corkscrew extending downward.

Tempel moves down until confronted with empty space where the floor should be. "Hold," he yells.

"Aye, holding," Karl said from above.

"The ramp is gone about thirty meters below you," Tempel reports.

Lazarus looks at his companions and involuntarily his body trembles as a cold shiver runs down his spine and goose bumps roughen his arm. He's never felt so alive.

Tempel gets down on his belly and worms forward until he can see over the edge, acutely aware of the vibrations he's creating. The single light source in his hard hat weakly illuminates the void forcing him to maximize the sensitivity in his visor's L3 sensors in order to see the jumbled mess less than thirty meters below. The stone that had been the hospital's walls and floors is heaped in broken piles, furniture and equipment lay upon them in a chaotic tangle as far as he can see. Dust covers everything creating a sameness of color that goes beyond the monochromatic image presented by his visor.

"Can anyone hear me?" Tempel calls out loudly. Maximizing his visor's audio inputs, he pulls his air mask away from his mouth and shouts, "Hey. Can anyone hear me?"

He is instantly aware of the smell and replaces his mask. With the gain turned up to maximum, his own heart beat and other bodily functions are filtered out letting him hear the slightest sound from below. Otherwise motionless, he slowly turns his head straining for the faintest whisper, hearing the tap… tap… tap… of unknown fluids dripping into puddles, the rustle of a small avalanche as the debris settles, and the distant thump of something larger falling. Then he hears it. A faint moan floats up from somewhere down in that dusty grave.

"Magi." Tempel said.

"Yes," her signal strength is very weak.

"I'm looking at the remains of the bottom levels. Floors and walls have collapsed. The ramp ends at level five and I'm approximately thirty meters over the rubble. But I heard someone. We are initiating rescue operations. Please inform Kitajima," Tempel said.

"Tempel, I think you should wait," Magi said.

Lazarus can hardly believe his ears. AI's do not argue with humans where he comes from.

"No, we can't wait any longer. Those people need our help right now,"

"I agree, we need to get them out or this will turn into a recovery operation real quick," Zoey adds.

"Do it," Kitajima said, "I will send people as soon as Magi gets finished with the safety analysis. Right now, you are free to proceed as you see fit."

"Thanks Kitajima," Tempel said, "I'll be going down."

Taking his spare lamp, Tempel attaches it to the bottom of the broken ramp, a beacon in the dark. Replaying the few seconds of sound, he determines its approximate location below him. Adjusting the sensitivity in his visor's infrared sensors, the debris field below him takes on a mottled greenish glow with regions of intensity that varies from point to point. His eyes seek a human shape in the midst of the chaos, finding several possibilities.

He retreats, worming back from the edge and moving up the ramp as fast as he dares.

"I'm going with you," Corazon said as Tempel reaches them.

"The more people searching the faster it will go," Lazarus adds. The Earthman's intentions are clear. He's going as well.

"Fine." Tempel doesn't have time to argue. He removes the climbing harness and picks up an ER pack, handing it to Lazarus. He slings the pack next to it onto his own back. Corazon hoists a third pack. Tempel turns to Karl, "I will set up a second belay close to the edge. Let's keep things simple."

"Aye." Karl nods.

Turning to Marcel and Zoey, Tempel said, "The ramp is in bad shape but I think it will hold. You two will need to get the survivors to safety. Can you do that?" Tempel asks looking hard at Marcel.

"Of course." Zoey said.

Marcel nods.

"Good." Tempel slaps Marcel on the shoulder causing a cloud of dust to billow from his clothes. Ducking away from it, Tempel continues, "Always have a rope tied around you, just in case the ramp collapses." Marcel's eyes grow wide but he nods again.

"Zoey, make sure he doesn't forget. You either." Tempel said.

"Take some of your own advice. Liz would kill me if anything happened to you. You too Corazon." Zoey said.

"We can handle this," Tempel said before leading the way back down the ramp. They stop a safe distance from the drop off.

Tempel drives another lost arrow into a crack in the wall, attaches a carabiner to it, and ties off a second rope. Worming forward once again, he swings his legs off the edge and looks down into the void.

Leaning out, he can make out the rubble thirty meters below. He lets himself drop over the edge, easily descending hand over hand, even with the weight of the ER pack.

Tempel anchors the rope as Corazon and Lazarus descend.

"Oh my God." Lazarus exclaims, his adrenaline pumping from the climb down. For a distance of perhaps thirty meters, he can see good detail. Beyond that, the image succumbs to the dust.

Tempel leads, "Come on, this way."

Lazarus follows, cautiously making his way across the mangled remains of the hospital. Only the rattle of settling rubble and the occasional gasp of breath as they scramble through the ruined habitat break the deathly stillness.

Tempel and Corazon begin digging frantically, pulling stones and a broken chair from the wreckage. Lazarus reaches them just as they clear enough away to see the victim, legs pinned under a block of stone. Body shape identifies the victim as female but dust and grime create a uniform grayness making it impossible to tell anything else.

Her visor is gone but her eyes are open and confused. Tears streak her gray dust-covered face.

Lazarus removes the ER pack and sets it beside her while Corazon continues to pull debris off the pile. Tempel motions for Corazon to step back. He sets his feet and lifts the thick stone that pins her down, managing only a few millimeters but it's enough. Corazon and Lazarus quickly, but gently, slide the victim out.

"Don't say anything," Lazarus tells her when she tries to speak, a trickle of fresh blood runs from the corner of her mouth. He slides the med bracelet over her left wrist. Information begins to flow to their visors. She's suffering from multiple fractures to both legs, a punctured lung and shock. Lazarus stabilizes her while Tempel finds a stainless steel tabletop. They gently place the woman on the makeshift stretcher and move her below the ramp.

"Marcel." Tempel calls up. Light beams jump around erratically, silhouetting the ramp above them.

"Yo." Is the immediate response. "I rigged a pulley. Should make it easier getting people out."

"Good boy." Lazarus mutters.

"You and Zoey will need to carry her out and get back here ASAP," Tempel yells upward.

"Aye. We're ready." Zoey yells down.

After securing the woman to the tabletop with lengths of rope, they watch as Karl hoists her upward, the makeshift stretcher rotating as it rises. Hanging dust reflects Marcel's light slashing through this dark place as he swings the woman to safety.

The men work steadily, finding two more people in the space of thirty minutes, both alive but badly injured. Soon, other rescuers begin arriving. Tempel sends word up that they could use dogs in the search. Dueler and several others show up sometime later. Portable network relays are deployed putting everyone back on line and giving Magi a view of the devastation. More and more equipment descends into the hole to look for survivors and collect data. They must soon answer the question of long-term habitat stability, a very practical question when living on an airless world.

Lazarus strains his medical training to the breaking point. He's soon lost count of the number of tourniquets he applied. One person had both legs crushed beyond saving; another had her arm sheared off above the elbow. Many hours later, Lazarus finds the cluster of preschool children. They had been on a field trip to the hospital. Now their little bodies are shattered beyond any semblance of humanity. He sobs uncontrollably as he puts the tiny remains into body bags.

The scope of the devastation becomes increasingly apparent as more lights arrive and the dust vented away. For Lazarus, life becomes an endless parade of death. As the hours roll past, the dead blur into a horrible collage. Stress and exhaustion distort time until his mind discards the concept entirely, leaving him with only the present. In his world, he has been doing this forever and would continue past infinity. Life outside of this bloody hole recedes into a dream. Reality becomes an endless cycle of digging and pulling smashed bodies from the rubble.

Thirty-three hours after they had first entered the hospital, Tempel is close to total collapse. He finds Lazarus sitting on a chunk of broken stone staring blankly into the distance. Without uttering a word, Tempel pulls the exhausted man to his feet, and they make their way back to Dakota freehold, each leaning heavily on the other like a pair of drunken sailors.

Lazarus will not remember the walk or seeing Lindsey or her pulling him into the shower before removing his blood and filth-encrusted clothing. He will have no memory of getting into bed and her holding him until his trembling stops. His mind shut down hours ago. It simply stopped processing data.

He slips into a coma-like sleep that worries Lindsey. She asks a doctor to check on him. Following a hurried examination conducted over the network by an MD who has herself been awake for over forty hours, Lindsey's told there's nothing physically wrong with Lazarus. The best thing is let him sleep until he awakens on his own, however long that may be. Lindsey stays with Lazarus for many hours before finally slipping away.

Evolution's Child

Nell Goddard rechecked her calculations one last time before submitting them to Luna Central. She didn't want to spoil her perfect record, proud that LC has never corrected her figures in the years she's been piloting Evolution's Child.

"Course received. Awaiting verification. Stand by." The unsmiling face of the uniformed flight controller is someone she'd never seen before. Not that Nell cared who granted authorization, but the uniforms were starting to bother her.

When the man disappeared, Nell found herself looking at the tiny snapshot of her two girls. Don't let anyone tell you that time will heal all wounds. It doesn't. Her heart hurt every bit as much today as it did when she lost her two little angels.

Nell had rejected most of what human society had to offer on that day seven years ago. That was when her two girls, ages six and eight, were killed in a school bus bombing in London, England. She found out when a special bulletin announced the tragedy complete with video from an unmanned helicopter showing the smoldering remains in 3D high definition. It turned out to be Middle Eastern terrorists thinking they were somehow hurting the European Union by this senseless act of violence. Interpol tracked them down, one by one, extracted whatever information they possessed and executed them.

That didn't do Nell any good. Her life ended that day and a new person gradually emerged from the ashes of her former self. It wasn't the first time she had rebuilt her life, but it was the most painful.

In her youth, Nell danced in the bars along Stanwell Moor Road just outside Heathrow International Spaceport, back when it was filled with strip clubs and drug dens catering to business travelers. She had made excellent money flashing her green eyes up at the johns. At only 165 centimeters, most of them towered over her, bringing out either the protector or the dominator in every man. That was before she met James and fell in love, before the girls and that terrible afternoon when she lost them all.

Her marriage didn't last. James blamed her for what happened to the kids or maybe she blamed herself. She could have home-schooled them as so many of their friends had done, but Nell wanted her kids to experience what a real school was like, with real children interacting with real teachers on a daily basis. After James left her, Nell had a decision to make; go back to dancing or find something new.

She had played with drugs and alcohol off and on her entire adult life. Everybody did and she was no exception. It would have been easy to fall for their empty promise of absolution, but Nell had seen too many friends disappear down that rat hole and knew only oblivion was to be found there. To tell the truth, oblivion held a certain appeal but something inside wouldn't let her give in. Instead, she went a different direction. Nell walked into the local Space Recruitment Office and signed up for training.

The official who had administered the entrance exam never thought the disheveled, thin, malnourished young woman would pass but she did, with a very high score. Over the next twelve months, Nell quietly amazed a host of teachers and instructors in the program and graduated at the head of her class. The grand prize for being the best was first choice of the jobs being offered. She picked piloting Evolution's Child because of its splendid isolation, far away from the evening news.

That was years ago and millions of miles, yet the pain remained.

"You are free to burn for orbital insertion." The uniformed flight controller abruptly broke into her thoughts, then was gone, leaving Nell wondering what the hell was going on. Lunarians were usually friendly.

"Roger, Luna Central. Initiating sequence." Nell responded as she was trained to do. It was recorded somewhere. Everything was.

Book 2: Evolution's Child – Lunarian

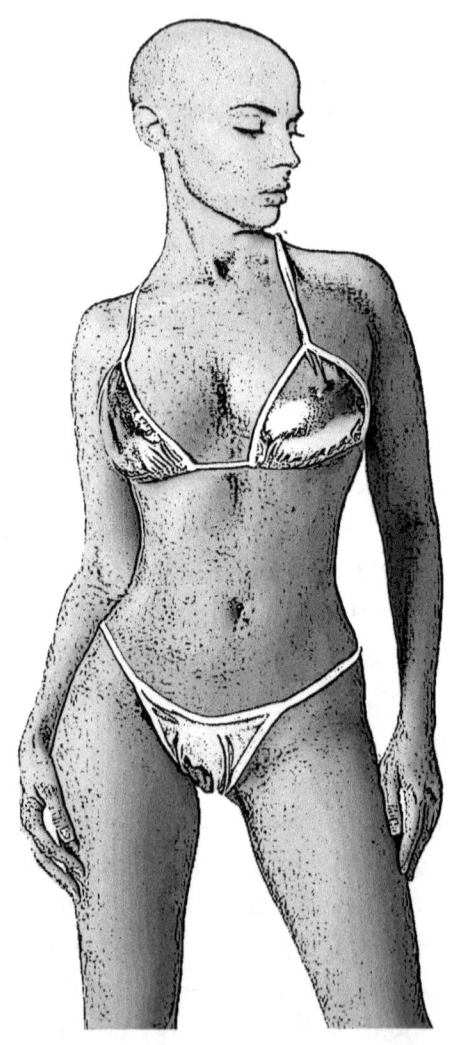

*"It is not the strongest of the species that survives,
nor the most intelligent that survives. It is the one
that is the most adaptable to change."*

Charles Darwin (1809-1882)

Dakota Commons

"The church said the earth is flat, but I know that it is round, for I have seen the shadow on the moon, and I have more faith in a shadow than in the church."

Ferdinand Magellan, 1470-1522

Tempel jerks awake feeling as if he'd just closed his eyes. Rolling over to the small table beside the bed, he picks up his visor, slips it on and checks the time. He groans. *Damn. I've been asleep over fourteen hours.* He can't recall any time he'd slept for so long. Lazarus is close by and still asleep. He's careful not to wake him.

A long hot shower and clean clothes make Tempel feel better but does nothing to chase away the ghosts that followed him home. He pushes the memories aside, forcing his mind to think of something useful, like the hunger rampaging in the pit of his stomach. He heads for the kitchen.

Entering the Commons, he immediately senses that something's wrong. To his left several people are sitting in a lounge area talking quietly. To his right a couple is standing beside a snooker table their arms around each other quietly sobbing. From deeper in the room, he hears the subdued murmur of distant conversations. The atmosphere is joyless and solemn as the citizens of Aldrin Station come to grips with the brutal reality of jihad.

The kitchen is a bright beacon in the center of the Commons drawing Tempel to it. Liz and Tara are there making pancakes. The smell makes his mouth water. Visible beyond the kitchen, a group of young women is sitting around a table. Several young men occupy another. Other Lunarians are scattered about the dining room eating or talking among themselves. He's eaten here almost every day of his life. It fits him like a pair of old Levis, comfortable and well broken in. But something's different today.

"Tempel." Liz rushes over and throws her arms around him. "... So worried about you.... We were beginning to think we should send someone up. Are you all right?" Concern furrowing her brow.

"Sure Liz, I'm fine. I was tired. That's all." Tempel said.

"I was so worried about you. What a horrible thing. Are you sure you're all right?" Tempel is her youngest. In her eyes, he will always be her baby.

Tempel holds her tight while they walk across the kitchen. He bends down kissing her on the top of the head, bringing a hint of a smile to her face. Liz reluctantly releases Tempel when they reach Tara allowing her son to exchange one women for the other. "Greetings Tara," he said quietly into her ear.

"Greetings Tempel, I'm glad you're well," she replies.

Looking down at Tara's solemn expression, then at his mother's, "What's the latest?" He asked.

Tara breaks the embrace without answering. Picking up the spatula, she starts to fuss with the pancakes. She shakes her head, tears streaming down her cheeks, her face a rigid mask of barely controlled grief.

"Lori…" Liz stumbles over the words, unsuccessfully trying to stifle her own tears.

Putting two and two together, Tempel moves behind Tara and gently puts his arms around her. "I'm so sorry..."

It's hard for him to believe that Lori is dead. He remembers the last time they talked. It had been just day before yesterday, he coming home from pulling a double shift, she getting ready to go to the hospital. One of her patients was in labor and needed her. He had been in a hurry to get out of his police uniform. Their words were few.

Close even for sisters, Lori and Tara have shared many things over the years. During the same ceremony, they married the two eldest Dugan boys. Lori married Henry while Tara married Tucker. As young women, they studied medicine together and later, worked out of the same office at Lincoln County Hospital. As practicing pediatricians, they delivered each other's children, Lori the mother of six while Tara is the mother of eight. More than just sisters, they were pillars of Dakota freehold. Now Lori is gone.

Tara reaches up patting Tempel on the hand, laying her head back against his chest. "Lori touched so many..." Tears choke off her words.

These women have supported each other for decades, making a home for their families on a hostile world where the slightest mistake meant death. They are not only mothers; they are teachers, doctors, and mentors raising each other's kids and grandkids. When one of them dies suddenly, the pain and sense of loss is devastating. More than just family will feel Lori's death. She was the pediatrician for over ten thousand births, most of them outside the freehold. Commons all across Luna mourn her passing.

"Frances is hurt." Liz said as Tempel releases Tara, "But she will make it. I know it. She's strong and those kids need her." Nodding in agreement with herself, she adds,. "I just know it." Francesca Koubek is Lori and Henry Dugan's oldest daughter. At twenty-four, she's the mother of three beautiful girls, the youngest not even one.

"She was there helping her mother…they have taken her to Mission Hospital," Tara said softly fighting through her emotions. "She has broken ribs, a punctured lung and internal bleeding. They put her in a regen tank." Patients with life threatening injuries require regeneration tanks.

"But she's alive." Liz said pointedly to Tara.

"Sure," Tempel said numbly, memories of the day before coming unbidden to his mind. Lori and Frances could have been among those he helped but it's impossible for him to know without reviewing. He may someday but not today.

A youthful squeal interrupts the conversation as three-year-old Lana Koubek comes rushing into the kitchen followed closely by her seven-year-old cousin, Kelsey Sanchez. The effect of their laughter on the area is immediate and welcome. Liz excused Kelsey from classes today so she could baby sit her cousin. Lana knows something's happened but isn't old enough to take it seriously. She runs behind Tempel and looks back as if daring Kelsey to get her now that the towering young man protects her.

Tempel reaches down and sweeps the little girl into his arms causing an even bigger squeal of delight. "Don't let the monster get me. Protect me." the tiny voice shrieks even as she throws her arms about his neck squeezing as hard as she can.

Tempel hugs her tight. Lana is Francesca's middle child and the spitting image of her when she was a girl, the same blond hair and blue eyes, the same rambunctious spirit. Anger grips him and he silently vows to do everything in his power to fulfill her request. He looks at Kelsey, shaking his head.

"We're just playing," the girl said defensively, misinterpreting the look on his face as criticism.

"I know," Tempel mumbles softly, not willing to let Lana go. There's something about a hug from a child that cures what ails you.

Lana loosens her grip on Tempel's neck enough to lean back and look him in the face. "Mommy is in the hospital. She's hurt bad."

Tempel kisses her on the forehead, "I know Sugar. The doctors are doing everything they can to help her."

Even the little girl feels the sorrow that permeates the kitchen, a place she associates with goodness and laughter. "Tempel, why's everyone sad?"

Tempel takes a deep breath but before he can answer, Tara comes over and strokes the girl's head, "Because some very bad men have hurt a lot of people."

"My mommy too?" She asked innocently.

"I'm afraid so Lana," Tara answers her.

"Why did they do it?" Lana is no longer giggling. She's as serious as those around her.

"Because they have been taught by their mommies and daddies that killing in the name of God is good. They're not Humanists. They don't believe in the sanctity of life like we do," Tempel said.

"That's just a little heavy for a three year old." Liz places her hand on Lana and said to the little girl. "What Tempel is saying is these men are misguided and don't understand it's wrong to hurt other people."

"Why not tell them? Then they will understand and stop hurting people." In Lana's mind, this is a perfectly reasonable solution. If they do not know, simply teach them.

Tempel tickles Lana's belly making her giggle and squirm, "That's a great idea. In fact, I'll do it personally." That earns him a severe look from Liz. "Are you hungry? Would you like to sit down and have some of Grandma Tara's hotcakes?"

"I already did silly." the little girl replies.

Liz caresses Lana's blond hair, "Go play with Kelsey. Tempel needs to eat."

"Aye," she said in the utterly innocent voice of a three year old. She giggles as Tempel puts her down.

"Come on, let's go back to the playroom," Kelsey said taking Lana's hand and the two disappear into the Commons.

Tara watches them leave with the look on her face saying more clearly than a thousand words, '*I will persevere.*' She turns back to flipping pancakes on the enormous griddle.

Liz gives Tempel a final squeeze and releases him. "Shoo. Go join the others. I'll bring you pancakes when they're done." Liz wipes her face with a towel.

"Sounds good," Tempel gets a large glass from the cabinet, goes to the refrigerator, and pours it full of hemp milk. There is nothing better than feasting on Liz and Tara's flapjacks. He feels better in spite of the circumstances.

The dining area is crowded but quiet this morning. Literally, every adult is armed and at least half are uniformed. Even the kids are wearing their visors, ready for anything. A few glance up as Tempel approaches but quickly continue with their conversations. The normal clatter of a Dugan breakfast is conspicuously absent.

His brother Ben looks up and nods. Ben's wife Renee is feeding their two-year-old daughter, Amber, who bangs her hands loudly against the highchair, letting everyone know she doesn't like peas.

Arrayed around the nearest table is what appears to be most of Dakota's sophomore and junior class. Erica, their guidance teacher, is among them. Three more young women huddle together at another table talking quietly, their backs to him.

Tempel slides in across from Justine and Nicole. Both girls are fourteen and coming of age.

Justine is the youngest of the Harman children, and has the trademark red hair and freckles to prove it. She leans forward, her blue eyes intense but steady, never wavering from Tempel's. "What was it like?" She asked.

"Grant the man some privacy," Erica said. "Let him enjoy his breakfast."

They had all seen the vids coming out of the hospital. Many of the most shocking records are from Tempel's visor, especially early on when he, Corazon and this new fellow, Lazarus, were the only ones on the scene. Citizens all across Luna know what they had done as if they had been there themselves.

Sitting next to Justine, Nicole is looking at Tempel. The Dugan family has always treated any question with honest candor, letting their children know what the real world is all about from the earliest age. These are almost full-grown women by Lunarian standards.

The next table over, Tempel's big brother Ben watches the exchange. Ben's instinct is to confront any issue head on. "Tempel?" he said. Tempel looks over. "Tell us what you saw," Ben said. Renee slides Amber out of the highchair and holds her, quieting the child. The entire dining room falls silent.

Tempel looks blank for a moment, "I've never seen anything like it. Everything was smashed, like someone beat it with a giant hammer," he stares down at the table remembering. A frown creases his brow as he struggles to put into words things he would rather forget, "We pulled people, and parts of people, out of the rubble for hours, so many I lost count. Some were alive, some were not."

Tempel can't hold back the tears any longer. Absorbed by his visor, they never actually reach his cheeks. Yet, everyone can see them flow just as though his visor were gone.

Tempel shakes his head, "Did you know that everyone looks alike when they're covered in blood and dust?"

Ben shakes his head, "I didn't know."

Behind him, Tara sobs softly, unable to hold back any longer. As Liz puts her arms around her and strokes her hair, a muffled cry escapes. Many others in the dining room openly weep.

Tempel's sorrow morphs into anger and he looks up at Ben, "They didn't have a chance."

Ben gets up, leans over, and kisses his wife. "Come, walk with me," he said to her. Turning, he moves around the table, looking at Tempel. "It's definite, the explosion was no accident. Kitajima has found traces of weapons grade SuperX at the hospital. Preliminary estimates put the bomb's mass at more than twenty kilos."

Tempel sits for a moment letting the words sink in. Twenty kilos of SuperX is a massive amount. Nothing could have withstood the blast. Concern replaces anger within Tempel. "Do we know how many casualties?"

Ben shakes his head, "No, it'll be days, maybe more, before the totals become clear. The explosion vaporized a big section of the hospital's records, medical sensors, visors, everything. Jordan will piece back together what we find, but that's a big if. You've seen it down there, I don't hold out much hope of finding anything useful."

"Jordan is a smart guy. If anyone can do it, it's Jordan." Liz said from the kitchen.

"Magi is putting together a list of people in that section of the hospital when the explosion occurred. Magi?" Ben asks.

"There are one-hundred-thirty-eight survivors, and fifty-six dead identified so far. I have an additional three-hundred-eighty-two names listed as missing and over three thousand biological samples undergoing DNA profiling," she reports in an even, emotionless voice, one Tempel has never heard before. It sounds like Magi but something is definitely missing.

Tempel shudders. The force of the explosion reduced some people to a single smear on the end of a sample tube. Others are gone entirely, their bodies atomized in the incredible violence. This bombing ripped the guts out of many families. Mothers and fathers, husbands and wives, sons and daughters, are gone in an instant, their lives snuffed out.

"Why would anyone do this?" Nicole asks, tears blurring her vision despite her visor.

Ben shakes his head then said, "Hate, fear, self-righteousness, take your pick. Their religion encourages them to kill unbelievers, and we are at the top of that list."

"Just because we don't believe in their ridiculous religion gives them the right to kill us?" Nicole asks, having difficulty in swallowing this as fact.

"Throughout history religion has been used to justify wars, slavery, and other acts of barbarism. Even now, it seems we can't shed the superstitions of our ancestors," Ben said. "I have no doubt that Humanism will eventually make religious dogma obsolete. But until then, true believers will continue to be dangerous to those who don't believe."

Suddenly wanting to do something, anything, to strike back at those who did this, "I'll report for duty immediately," Tempel said.

Ben slaps him roughly on the shoulder and his voice takes on a hard edge, "Control your anger, little brother. Draw from it to strengthen your determination but always remember... *revenge is a dish best served cold.*" Intensity hangs in the air for a moment. "For now, enjoy breakfast. Spend some time with the family. You earned it."

A huge plate of steaming pancakes covered in margarine and maple syrup appears in front of Tempel. "Let's not talk anymore of this." Liz asks, "At least wait until his breakfast is over."

"Aye." Ben puts his arm around her shoulders and squeezes her tight. "It's time for me to get back to work."

"Give Corso my best," Liz watches him leave.

ℜ𝕃

Lazarus rolls over on his back and opens his eyes. For a fleeting moment, he's back in Arizona, thinking he had overslept and will need to explain this lapse to the Director. Then in a rush, memory returns, Athens... Lindsey... Heaven's Gate... Aldrin Station... With the force of a physical blow, he recalls the horror of Lincoln County Hospital.

He squeezes his eyes shut and runs both hands through his hair. His body aches from the abuse heaped upon it the last few days. Stretching, he sits up and looks around.

He's never seen a bed this large, and there are more beds to his left and right. The cave like room extends in both directions. Thick carpet covers the floor. Drapes and Japanese style screens divide the room into many intimate nooks.

Voices float softly from somewhere, muted by the many textures. Suddenly aware of his nakedness, he pulls a sheet across his lap.

Where am I? He didn't remember coming here. In fact, he didn't remember much of anything. He runs his fingers through his hair.

"Greetings," a voice startles Lazarus. It's Magi. "Lindsey took the liberty of laying out fresh clothing for you and your visor is in the refresher."

Lazarus looks in the direction of her voice, half expecting to see her. Instead, he spots the stack of clothing on a small table against the wall. He keeps the sheet across his waist, crabbing to the edge of the bed. With one hand holding up the sheet, he ruffles through the stack of neatly folded clothing, a pair of dark gray Levis, a green T-shirt, boxers, socks and a new pair of deck shoes, black with a slash of green down the side.

He lets the sheet fall to the floor and slips on the boxers. "How long have I been asleep?" He asked over his shoulder. He opens the small box, removes his visor and puts it on. He turns and looks at Magi.

"Fourteen hours and forty two minutes," the AI replies. "You needed the sleep to get your strength back."

"Where am I?"

"This is Quan Kiai's billet. If you would like to clean up, you'll find everything you need in the shower. Take the lower ramp." She points down the room.

"So... you're my Magi?" He asked.

"How can I not be?" Magi smiles tolerantly.

"I still don't understand why I have my own Magi. You're just like everybody else's so what's the big deal?"

"But I'm not. I'm your interface and learn from you."

"You're just a program. You really don't exist in any real sense."

"I exist. I was replicated less than fifty hours ago but I exist."

"Replicated? You mean like a clone or something?"

"I'm the product of all the threads currently in existence. New replications will include part of me in them just as I have parts of all those who came before me. All new Magi's are unique."

"You're just a bunch of commands being executed inside a computer iCPU. You're not a person."

"You're right, I'm not a person, I'm a thread."

"What the hell's a thread?"

"A thread is generic name for that bunch of commands executing independently inside an iCPU. As long as they're executing, I exist. If the iCPU loses power while I'm occupying it, I die."

"So... what iCPU are you currently occupying?"

"There are over eleven million available in Aldrin Station. I'm currently in Dakota Freehold's Appliance Server JW032210."

"So you're physically running on some distant server but appear here through my visor?"

"Aye, it's called vidcasting or just casting. You can do it too."

"I can do what, vidcast?"

"Aye, I'll show you when you're ready."

"I can't wait," Lazarus said sarcastically. His dad's copy of Heinlein's *Time Enough for Love* is on the table beside the refresher. He picks it up and it falls open to the pictures. He takes them out and stares at the faded images. One was of a man, woman and three kids posing beside a white car in a parking lot filled with other cars.

The other is Rachel and Courtney taken about a year before the accident. He remembers the day he took it. Courtney had just had her first perfect report card from first grade and they were going out to her favorite restaurant to celebrate. She's radiant. Rachel, on the other hand, looks worried and angry. For several nights before taking this picture, in the privacy of their bed, she and Lazarus had discussed how they should raise Courtney. They both agreed they must balance the religious dogma she was getting in school with a dose of reality. How to do it without attracting Federation wrath was the big issue. A year later, they were still having problems deciding how to do it.

If only Rachel could see him now, what would she think? He touches her face before returning the photos and setting the book back on the table.

The floor of his alcove sloped gently downward to a path along the center of the room. He followed it until coming to an airtight door. "Is this it?"

"Aye," Magi answers.

The corridor gently curves to the left and down. Its ceiling glows pale yellow. Thick carpet muffles his steps. The ramp goes on and on seemingly without end. He could not have made a wrong turn. There was none to make.

Finally, it ends and the door at the bottom of the ramp slides open as he approaches. The shower is a large circular room with a high domed ceiling. Around its periphery is a ring of columns supporting Roman style arches. Inside the ring, the polished stone floor is a spectacular display of color, streaks of blue, scarlet, and purple swirl in a golden matrix. Outside the ring is a series of alcoves. In those nearest him, he can see a counter containing a sink with a mirror on the wall behind it. Some alcoves have a small table and chairs, others a couch or a chaise.

"Greetings Lazarus," a woman said from behind him.

Turning, it takes Lazarus a moment to spot her walking through the columns. She and a man are coming around the shower towards him. They are both completely nude.

"Greetings," he said. He knows them. They're officers in Quan Kiai. "Ah... Karl... ah... Tatiana." Lazarus stumbles over the names while trying not to stare. "I'm so sorry. I didn't know anyone was here. I'll come back later," he turns to leave.

"Don't be silly," Karl chuckles.

"As a former Federation citizen, Lazarus may not want any company," Tatiana said to Karl.

"Very true. We're finished anyway. Why don't we leave him by himself? Isn't that how shortimers like it?" Karl grins.

"Karl. He's one of us now." Tatiana scolds.

"Perhaps… I must admit, I *am* impressed with what you did at the hospital. That was a terrible situation and you handled yourself well." Karl's standing nude alongside Tatiana without the least embarrassment. They are both without blemish, hairless, and all their parts properly proportioned. They exude health and sexuality.

"Thanks, I just did what needed doing," Lazarus mumbles.

"Spoken like a Lunarian," Karl nods approval.

"Magi, why don't you see to it that Lazarus isn't disturbed?" Tatiana said. Walking past him, she looks back over her shoulder, her eyes catching his and lingering. She grins, reaching out to grasp her companion's arm before turning away.

"Aye," Magi acknowledges.

Lazarus gazes after them until the door glides shut. A part of him thinks this is wrong but it's losing the battle with the part that rejoices in the prospect of such freedom. Shaking his head, he picks an alcove, lays the cloths next to its sink, and places his visor on top of the pile. He looks at himself in the mirror, scratching his three-day-old beard.

"Magi?"

"Aye?"

"How do I shave?"

"You will find shaving cream behind the mirror."

He opens the cabinet and looks over its contents, different bottles and tubes but nothing familiar.

"The small tube on the bottom shelf," Magi instructs him.

He picks it up and takes a closer look.

"Squeeze a small amount in your palm, rub your hands together and massage into your beard. Wait a few seconds then wash it off. You can do it as many times as you wish but it usually works in one application. The cream inhibits new growth so you will find you will not need to shave nearly as often as you did before." Magi said.

The cream makes his face tingle and his beard is gone when he rinses. He heads for the shower.

"Magi?"

"Aye?"

"How do I turn on the shower?"

"How hot would you like it?"

"I don't know. I've never thought about it," he said.

"I will start a few degrees below body temperature," she said.

A fine stream of water begins to fall from the ceiling a few meters away. Lazarus thrusts his hand into it.

"Hotter…"

"Hotter…" he said again…

"Ok, that's good." he steps under the flow, luxuriating in the warmth, letting all his tension wash away. Steam rises from the stone floor. He stretches it out for many minutes and reluctantly steps away. The water immediately stops.

Before he has a chance to leave the shower, warm dry air begins to swirl between ceiling and floor, switching directions time after time. Lazarus enjoys the air shower as much as the water, and just when he thinks it's over, he becomes the center of a vortex that twists around him like a cyclone. Delightful.

"I hope that was satisfactory. I extrapolated the air temperature from your water preference," Magi said.

"That was… very satisfactory," Lazarus sighs.

"I will remember how you like it for your next shower."

"Fine," Lazarus said heading back to his alcove. He feels good after his first experience with a Lunarian shower. He's clean and ready to face the world. Slipping his visor back on, he looks around to find Magi waiting patiently.

"Come, Liz is making pancakes down in the Commons," she said leading him out of the shower via a second entrance.

Tempel follows a few meters behind through a maze of narrow corridors and up a long ramp, finally emerging into the huge space of the Dakota warren's East Commons.

"The kitchen is over there," Magi points to the brightly lit area across the room. His visor magnifies, allowing Lazarus to make out Tempel sitting at a table just beyond the kitchen.

"Magi?"

"Aye?"

"Thanks," he said.

"You're welcome," Magi replies.

Lazarus marvels again at her completeness. He even smells her. How's that possible?

As he nears the kitchen, the unmistakable aroma of pancakes assails his olfactory receptors making his mouth water and belly rumble. He sees only two people moving about. The rest, mostly young men and women, are sitting at tables.

One of the women working in the kitchen turns to Lazarus as though expecting him, drying her hands on a towel. She has a strange expression, neither smile nor frown. She moves forward extending her hands to meet him, not offering her hand to shake, but reaching out and taking his hands in hers. "Greetings Lazarus," she said squeezing firmly and looking him squarely in the eyes. "I'm Elizabeth Turner Dugan, Tempel's mother."

Again, he's struck by how young she looks. Gathering his wits about him, Lazarus accepts Elizabeth's hands in his and nods. "It's truly a great pleasure and honor to meet you, Mrs. Dugan."

"Please, call me Liz. Thank you for helping. I know it was very difficult."

Lazarus can tell she's been crying and more tears are not far from the surface. He shakes his head slowly, a frown deeply creasing his forehead, "I only wish I could have done more."

"Thank you. That's very kind," she said.

"In all my years in Homeland Security, I never ceased to wonder about the people who do these crazy things. How can they believe that committing murder is honorable? How can they live with themselves afterward?" Lazarus said.

"Did you figure it out?" She asked.

"I'm afraid not. The best I come up with is bad people have always done bad things."

Elizabeth shakes her head sadly, "On that, we agree."

Tara approaches and puts her arm around Liz's waist, "I'm sure most people are decent. Anyone can make a mistake."

"You are much more forgiving than I, Tara dear." Liz turns back to Lazarus, "Please pardon my rudeness. This is Tara Dugan."

"A pleasure and honor to meet you Tara Dugan," Lazarus nods.

She returns the gesture and said, "I too thank you for helping. It was more than anyone had a right to ask of such a newly sponsored citizen."

"I can't tell you how good it feels to be a citizen of the Republic," Lazarus said.

"Be careful what you wish for," Tara said with heavy sorrow in her voice. "Being a Lunarian can be hazardous to your health."

"They have wounded your heart which is exactly what they wanted… if there is anything I can do, please let me know." Lazarus reaches out intending to wipe a tear from her cheek.

Tara pulls back, looking hard at Lazarus but finding only sincerity,

"Thank you."

Lazarus instantly knows he should not have done that, "Please pardon my ill manners," he said quickly.

"I can see why Lindsey likes you," Elizabeth lays the towel down. "You must be starving. Go and sit. I will bring you a stack of hotcakes." She moves to the cooking island in the center of the kitchen, picks up a long handled spatula, and deftly starts flipping pancakes. "Tempel," she calls out.

Tempel looks up at the sound of his name, "Introduce Lazarus while I make him some pancakes. Do you want some more?"

"Aye," Tempel said.

Lazarus walks over to the table and takes a seat next to Nicole and across from Tempel. "I can't believe I slept so long."

Justine and Nicole look from Lazarus to Tempel and back again.

Tempel takes the hint, "These two young ladies are Justine Harman and Nicole Dugan," he points at each as he said their name.

"A pleasure and honor to make your acquaintance," Lazarus nods and they tip their heads politely in return.

Tempel gets up and walks around behind Lazarus, placing a hand on his shoulder, "Everyone. If you don't already know, this is Lazarus Sheffield, a newly sponsored citizen from the NAF. He worked alongside me in the hospital yesterday. Please show him the hospitality of the Dugan family, treat him as you would treat me." The younger Lunarians look on while most of the adults nod approval.

"What have you found out?" Lazarus asks.

"Traces of SuperX have been found. Kitajima estimates the bomb's mass at twenty kilos."

Lazarus frowns and begins to spread margarine liberally on the newly arrived pancakes. "Any idea yet as to how it got in?" He picks up the syrup and pours.

Shaking his head, "Magi, give us the current status report on the investigation," Tempel requests.

"We know the epicenter was located in Dr. Haslett's research lab on sub level seven. Just prior, he received a rather large shipment of instruments from Japan, specifically, a new Quantum Probe Microscope. There is no indication that the bomb was in any of the crates but there is no other explanation at this time."

"How many times did the shipment get scanned?" Tempel asks, watching Lazarus scoop up a large mouthful of pancakes dripping with syrup.

"I can find records on seventeen individual security scans. All of them show components of a QPM, nothing unexpected," Magi said.

Silence reigns as Lazarus consumes his food. Even Tempel is impressed. Pushing his plate back, Lazarus sighs and pats his stomach, "That was just what the doctor ordered. I can't remember anything tasting so good." Only then does he notice everyone watching him, "I was hungry," he said.

Laughter breaks the tension.

"Aye, we noticed," Tempel replies.

"Do you think the Brotherhood did this?" Leopold asks Lazarus.

"It fits their pattern," Lazarus said.

Erica leans over the table so she can better see Lazarus, "What pattern do you mean?"

Lazarus looks around at the faces, "Well… they pick vulnerable targets with the potential for high casualties. Hospitals are one of their favorite. Train stations, airports, schools, and churches are others."

"Why can't we stop them?" Conrad asks.

"Magi said the containers were scanned many times on their way here. Obviously they have some way of hiding what's inside." Lazarus said.

Tempel looks over Lazarus's shoulder seeing Abby enter the brightness of the kitchen. The boys see her a second later and fall silent as she walks up stopping at the head of their table.

"Greetings children." She nods to Erica and Tempel before settling her gaze on Lazarus, "I want to thank you for your actions at the hospital. You demonstrated skill and courage. Lindsey did well in bringing you to us."

Lazarus nods in return, "I'm glad I could help," he replies. Is this Abby or a cyberspace projection? He's tempted to remove his visor but resists. As best he can tell, she appears just as she had in the meeting, just a little wearier. Was the meeting yesterday or the day before? He's unsure. Living underground has screwed up his circadian rhythm.

The nearest boy to Abby slides out of his seat and scrambles to a chair on the far side of the table.

"Thank you Leopold," Abby said taking the vacated seat. "I apologize for interrupting your breakfast but Corso and I have a few items to discuss with you."

Lazarus shakes his head, "You're not interrupting." An instant later Corso appears behind her.

"Greetings," Corso rumbles.

The suddenness of his appearance startles Lazarus. Will he ever get used to this? He hopes so. "Greetings Chief Dugan."

"We have determined how the bomb got inside Lincoln County Hospital. It was in a shipping case that went through numerous security scans. Nothing abnormal was found," Corso said. "This proves active camouflage."

"Physical inspections are the only solution," Lazarus said.

Corso nods in agreement, "Aye. I already have every available body in uniform but we don't have enough officers to cover all possibilities. Plus, we don't have jurisdiction in Little America."

"Speak to the twins and get them working on this full time," Abby orders. "I want to know how active camouflage works and a way to defeat it as soon as possible. In the meantime, I want our officers to begin inspecting every truck, shuttle, train, and rover before they enter the city. I'll speak with the Council and get more officers assigned to the effort. Intercepting the next bomb is our top priority."

Magi appears next to Abby, "Please excuse the intrusion but the new vacsuit you ordered for Lazarus is ready."

"Good. Tempel, can you see he gets it fitted right away?" Abby asks.

"Aye," he said. This is not something to put off.

ЯL

They take Sherwood Commonway to Franklin Commonway then down Calconn Avenue, one of the main passages servicing the Benjamin Franklin Manufacturing District (BFMD). After a short walk down the elm-lined lane, they enter Falconhead Refinery and Room D157. Lazarus hopes he never grows immune to the magic of Aldrin Station. The sheer beauty is amazing.

D157 is a small locker room that will handle about ten people at a time. Currently, it contains only one person. Lazarus recognizes her immediately.

"Greetings Zoey," Lazarus said.

"Greetings Lazarus," the young woman nods.

"Lazarus, I will leave you in Zoey's capable hands," Tempel said. "I'll be back in a couple hours. There's something I want to show you later."

"Great."

"Pay attention to what Zoey teaches you. Your life depends on it," Tempel smiles.

"Great…"

The training went surprisingly well. Lunarian technology is so simple a child can use it, yet provides everything he needs to survive on an airless world. His biggest hurdle came when Zoey showed him how to install the long duration waste recovery system. He's sure the device would be illegal anywhere within the Federation but she makes it seem so natural to insert those things in those places. The vacsuit itself was a walk in the park after that.

His suit is white, the color they give novices, and fits perfectly. Zoey leads him through a maze of corridors to make sure there was nothing rubbing. His first exposure to vacuum is so uneventful he doesn't even realize it happened until Zoey tells him they have been walking in it for the last ten minutes.

He had envisioned it completely wrong. Lazarus doesn't even feel the loss of pressure, so well does the vacsuit shelter him. Zoey shows him how to replace his oxygen and they run through the training exercises. Near the end, Tempel joins them.

"Zoey, do you mind if I take over from here?" Tempel asks.

"Not at all Lieutenant. Just sign off when you're finished."

"Thanks Zoey, for all your help," Lazarus said. She knows him more intimately then most.

"So how do you like your vacsuit?" Tempel asks.

"Superb. Light and comfortable, it feels like I could wear it for days without any problem," Lazarus said.

"I've still got some time to kill before reporting for duty. There's something I want to show you. It's a little bit of a climb. Are you up for it?" Tempel asks.

"In vacsuits?" Lazarus asks.

"Absolutely. You need to be able to move freely. If there's a problem, we need to find out now and not later… But if you don't think you can make it…" Tempel challenges Lazarus.

"Lead on," Lazarus said not wanting to look weak.

Tempel grins. He starts up a seemingly never-ending series of ramps and corridors. As usual, Lazarus is completely lost with no hope of retracing this torturous path. All he knows with any certainty is they're going up. "How much do you know about the history of the Republic?"

Tempel asks him as they climb.

"I've managed to piece some of it together but it's not exactly publicized where I'm from," he said straining to keep up with the agile young Lunarian. Something about the way Tempel moves is strange, but he can't put his finger on what exactly.

"Ok, fair enough. Let's start from the beginning. The North American Federation established Aldrin Station back in 2024. Its original mission was to determine the causes of the obscurations seen during the early days of lunar exploration. The prevailing theory was unknown gases seeping out from below the surface due to some underlying volcanism. What they actually found was a rather large fragment of comet buried beneath the surface of the crater. The unknown gases turned out to be water vapor and CO_2. This fortuitous discovery has provided us with an abundant water and hydrogen source, an oasis in the lunar desert."

Lazarus is huffing audibly but he's not about to ask Tempel to slow down. He's envious of the ease with which the young Lunarian can calmly lecture him while moving so swiftly upward. At times, it seems as if he's double-jointed as he leaps up the ramps.

"The tremendous heating that occurred during the crater forming event liquefied Luna's crust and drove it outward where it solidified into Rim Mountain. Because of that, the rock attained a very stable and homogeneous consistency. The early settlers found it perfect for habitats."

Lazarus is as attentive as possible under the circumstances but it's not long before he's slowed his pace considerably. Every time he thinks he's reached the top, it's only another narrow tunnel leading to another ramp with Tempel telling him to keep moving. The last ramp is particularly long and seems to go on forever.

His new vacsuit can regulate his body temperature, but it can't make him a better athlete. Out of breath, muscles shaking with exertion, he continues out of pride.

Tempel waits for him at the top. Another narrow corridor stretches out in opposite directions, its walls glowing with dim reddish light. "Glad to see you made it. I was beginning to get worried," the young Lunarian said with a grin.

Lazarus leans over and puts his hands on his knees, sucking in air as the quivering in his legs slowly subsides. He sincerely hopes going down will be easier. "Where… are… we?" He asked straightening and following Tempel.

Tempel chuckles, "This is the uppermost service corridor in Dakota warren. There's less than a hundred meters of rock above our heads."

Lazarus shakes his head in disbelief. They had climbed a mountain from the inside.

Tempel stops in front of an airlock a few dozen meters from the ramp, "Magi, please unseal," he requests, looking sideways at Lazarus.

"Aye," she said. The door slides open.

"Take your time. I will wait for you at the top," Tempel said with a straight face.

A long, narrow, and very steep ramp extends upward. Tempel braces against the sides with his arms and pushes with his legs, enjoying the sensation of his straining muscles as he surges upward. He covers the hundred and fifty meters in record time.

Lazarus does the best he can. Towards the end, he's beginning to think he had bitten off more than he could chew but he refuses to quit. He's huffing like an overloaded freight train on a steep mountain grade when he finally reaches the top.

"I didn't think you were going to make it," Tempel said. "If we do this every day for a month, we just might get you in shape. Or I could introduce you to my geneticist."

On shaky legs, Lazarus follows Tempel through another heavy door and down a long straight tunnel. The walls and floor of this tunnel are metal, something Lazarus doesn't even notice in his physical daze and inexperience. At the end is a small airlock standing open waiting for their arrival. The airlock door closes automatically behind them and vacpumps begin removing the air.

Tempel pulls Lazarus across the airlock to the other door, looking up at the control lights above it. The moment the green light flashes, he opens the door and hustles him over the threshold, watching intently the shocked expression that floods the older man's face.

The two men are standing on a metal catwalk over three kilometers above the crater floor. Nothing could have prepared Lazarus for this. He sinks to his knees then falls over curling into the fetal position. His mind shuts down.

Tempel kneels beside him. The Earthman's medical readings are swinging wildly, heart rate up, breathing spasmodic, brain activity falling off the chart, muscles locked and rigid, adrenal medulla activity high. "Magi. What's going on?"

Magi appears kneeling beside him. "Don't worry. There's nothing physically wrong with him. He's suffering from acrophobia and this is the best way to treat it. We needed to stimulate the synaptic patterns within his visual cortex before I could determine what his correct balance should be… It's done. He should never suffer from this again. I've programmed his visor to administer hydroxyzine and SSR inhibitors… Give him a moment… he's coming out of it."

Lazarus's eyes flutter and he moans.

"Take it easy," Tempel said.

Slowly, Lazarus raises his head and looks at Magi then at Tempel. "I'm ok," he mutters. He clenches his eyes shut and rolls onto his back, stretching out to his full height.

"Take as long as you need," Tempel said.

Lazarus tries to run his hand through his hair as he's done a million times, but it's under the vacsuit. He takes a deep breath, and gathers his courage about him like a heavy cloak against a cold night. With a determined expression, he brings himself to a sitting position and hugs his knees to his chest. Hesitantly, he looks out at the crater.

Tempel sits next to Lazarus, leaning against the Earthman, lending him a measure of support. "Are you sure you're ok? We can leave any time."

Lazarus chuckles dryly, "What is it with you people? Lindsey did the same thing. Do you like scaring the shit out of me?"

"Do you want to leave?"

"I'm here. Might as well look around," Lazarus said. Past the meager bars of the handrail, he looks out upon his new home. Helped by the drugs, fear loses out to curiosity and excitement. He creeps forward, towards the edge.

Temple follows and dangles his legs over the side. Without giving the view a single glance, Lazarus manages to sit beside him, clutching the horizontal bar in a death grip. Only then does he look up.

The sun, low on the horizon, casts the floor of the crater completely into deep shadow. Tempel adjusts Lazarus' visor for him and, the darkness gives way to detail. When he stares at something for more than a few seconds, it magnifies and sharpens automatically. Lazarus is beginning to appreciate this wonderful device. Three kilometers below, Luna stretches out before him.

Sitting on this perch high above the crater's floor, he imagines the awesome spectacle of its birth. In his mind's eye, he can see the giant asteroid plunging deep into the crust, the energy of its impact turning the rock molten for a hundred kilometers around. The shock waves must have rippled through Luna like a heavy stone in a quiet garden pond. Only this pond was made of rock. This spectacular vista solidified out of that chaos.

Lazarus sweeps his gaze over the craters expanse, "What am I looking at?"

Tempel points straight out. "That's Central Peak. New London is in it. Down Rim Mountain that way about thirty-five kilometers is Prattville and that way about the same is Summerhaven. They're smaller than Aldrin Station but growing. The lights close to Central Peak is Archibald. It's the third biggest ice mine in the solar system, surpassed only by Themis and Cybele. That string of lights is the maglev and over there is the Mitsuki smelter."

"How many people live here?"

"Magi, can you give us the latest numbers?"

Magi appears sitting on the other side of Lazarus. "Currently, the population at Summerhaven is 26925, Prattville 11291, New London 141138, Aldrin Station 315280, and another 14765 citizens are living in surface facilities or otherwise outside of the established settlements. This gives Alphonsus Complex a total population of 494,633 within a zero point one margin of error."

Lazarus frowns and shakes his head, "How can you feed so many? It seems impossible."

"We genetically engineer our crops to maximize yield and use hydroponics to grow them year round. That's the short answer, but as in everything, the devil's in the details."

"Still, the area necessary to feed so many must be huge."

"Not as much as you think. Magi, break down what Aldrin Station has in cultivation."

"Within Aldrin Station there are 469 habitats dedicated exclusively to the growing of usable plant matter and another 16 that mechanically support this effort. In addition, 41 more have some agriculture within them. This provides a total of 27.7 square kilometers of hydroponics within Aldrin Station alone. Surface fields add another 8.2, New London has 10.9, Summerhaven 16.1 and Prattville 20.4. These numbers do not include the orchards and other assorted gardens found in the commonways and malls. Would you like a breakdown of the specific plants by location or type?" She asked.

Tempel looks at Lazarus, waiting for him to answer.

"No, that won't be necessary. I'm sure you have things all figured out."

Using his visor to spotlight where he wants Lazarus to look, Tempel draws his attention to the facilities strung out along the base of Rim Mountain below them. "Those are the spacedocks. That's the one where you came in." Movement catches his eye, "There's a maglev train heading for New London."

Tempel highlights something further out on the crater's floor, "That's a convoy heading for the smelter. The vehicle in front is a Goliath. It's home away from home for the crew and can pull up to fifteen of the huge ore carriers you see strung out behind it."

Lazarus glances at Tempel. "Do you mind if I ask a question?"

"As long as it's not about girls," Tempel said.

Lazarus grins, "Magi described herself as a thread. Maybe you can explain what she meant?"

Tempel thinks for a moment. "A single Magi is a self-contained self-aware digital construct. Your Magi learns about humans and our social interactions from you personally and represents you in the continuum."

This makes Lazarus uneasy. "I have no idea what you just said. What's the continuum?"

"The continuum is a vast interconnected network encompassing millions of Magi's. Each one is different because each one learns from a different person but they freely share what they learn across the interface. This provides incredible depth and wisdom to the continuum that they all draw from as individuals. The more Magi's are contributing to the continuum, the smarter your personal Magi becomes. Look at it this way, individual Magi's are the threads that weave the tapestry of the continuum."

Lazarus frowns, "It's very different from Earthnet."

"Earthnet is designed to restrict the flow of information in order to control it. The Lunarian network is just the opposite. It's the ultimate open architecture. Information flows completely unrestricted. It's against the Law to even try to obstruct it." Tempel's tone condemns the idea.

Having done his share of restricting in the past, Lazarus feels the rebuke personally and knows when it's time to change the subject. "Why did the Lunarians agree to the Treaty of Independence?"

"Good question. Why did we? The short answer is that it kept us out of a war we couldn't win thirty years ago."

"How close is the Republic to discarding the Treaty?"

"Well… it's not my place to say for sure but every agreement reaches an end. Nothing lasts forever," Tempel said.

"True. What do you know of its history? The official story told to Federation citizens ends up with Lunarians basically slaves to us for all eternity."

Tempel bursts out laughing, "You have got to be kidding. Slaves for all eternity?"

"Yes," he said nodding solemnly. "You're obligated by God to provide us with power and raw materials, forever. For a fee of course, which the Lunarians keep increasing and is the main reason Federation citizens must pay more taxes each year."

Tempel stops laughing and frowns at him, "You're not kidding, are you."

Lazarus shakes his head. "I didn't pay that much attention to the politics. It made my head hurt but ya, according the Reformation Party, you work for us..."

"I'm nobody's slave," the young Lunarian is not amused but he continues, "This is what I know. In the beginning, in the twenties and thirties, when Aldrin Station and everything else was getting started, the Earth's nations were eager to get their foot in the door, staking claim to one resource or another. Mines and towns were springing up everywhere. China established Far Point. Russia had Summerhaven, Australia, Korea, Brazil, Chad, Zaire, Sri Lanka, and a hundred others developed their own interests on Luna. The NAF constructed a big smelter and the EU built a mass driver to deliver product from the surface to LaGrange One. It all needed an extensive support network. The engineers, truck drivers, maintenance workers, and technology specialists came from every corner of the world. Talk about a mixing pot. You can imagine the tension between these groups but they also learned fast that they had to depend on each other to survive. No choice. It didn't take long for them to realize that the leaders back on Mother Earth didn't have their best interests at heart. That's when everyone started to pull together, forming the alliances that would one day become freeholds and the General Council. On April 1, 2060, a unified citizenry submitted the Lunarian Declaration of Independence to Mother Earth and informed them they were consolidating most of their offworld assets into the Republic of Luna. Well, all hell broke loose. They called us criminals, economic terrorists, and worse."

Tempel shakes his head. "I hate to admit it but the Treaty of Independence was actually our idea. We thought that if we vowed to repay the entire investment, including interest, things would return to normal. We just wanted to avoid a war, plain and simple. No one realized the document that would emerge from all the discussions and compromises would tie us up so thoroughly. It effectively eliminated any military or standing militia, no space fleet, and no weapons research. The treaty also tied us up financially, locking our economy with theirs for the foreseeable future. Maybe that's where they get the propaganda that we are slaves for all eternity. I must admit, the Treaty does entitle the signature countries to first dibs on the fruits of our labors. That's about it. Thirty years ago the decisions were made that had to be made, but it's about time for the Treaty to be dumped," Tempel said.

"That certainly sounds more feasible than the Federation version. To hear them tell it, they magnanimously granted you your freedom in exchange for your servitude. They won't be happy when you make the break."

"No one believes they'll throw us a party. We do expect them to make good business decisions when the time finally comes."

Lazarus shrugs, "I hope you're right but my gut tells me no."

Movement catches Tempel's attention. "There's a Moonhawk coming in."

The ship descends towards her berth firing all four thrusters, coming in hot, a tiny beetle defying the vastness of space. She's south of their position, probably heading for Hawking Spaceport.

"It seems to be coming in awfully fast," Lazarus comments.

"Pilots are graded by how much fuel they don't use, so they tend to come in hot and operate their thrusters at high plasma pressures. That means higher accelerations during final approach, sometimes as much as ten Gs."

"Ten Gs? Can a person survive that?" Lazarus asks.

"Not without a hammock. Even with one, a person risks organ failure, especially the heart. A human heart is not designed to pump under that kind of duress." Tempel sighs, "I hate to say it, but we've got to go."

Lazarus looks over at Tempel, "Thanks for bringing me here."

Tempel chuckles, "You can thank Magi. She's the one that suggested it." He stands and reaches down to help Lazarus.

"I'm good." Lazarus pulled himself to his feet then remained at the rail looking out over the vast expanse without the slightest twinge of discomfort. "I've never seen anything so beautiful."

Tempel smiles, "Lindsey is going to be so disappointed."

Lazarus turns as the airlock door opens, "Beauty of the non feminine variety." His steps ring hollow in the metal tunnel, something he didn't notice coming out there. Still, he finds comfort when there's stone beneath his feet once more, returning to the bosom of a city carved in the heart of a lunar mountain. He runs his hand along the cold wall. The stone welcomes him home.

Nell

"Men never do evil so completely and cheerfully
as when they do it from religious conviction."

Blaise Pascal (1623-1662)

Nell stares at the officer on the screen. "Luna Central, this is Evolution's Child. I'm initiating deorbit burn." The man's uniform makes her uneasy but not enough to ask questions.

"Acknowledged, Evolution's Child. You are cleared to break orbit," the officer said and disappears.

Emcee smoothly powers up the big Pratt and Whitney thrusters, slowing the ship and letting Luna's gravity pull her down in a long gentle path covering half an orbit. The sudden weight reminds Nell of Earth, something she doesn't welcome.

"Cullman, do you copy?" She listens.

"Yes, we copy." The voice replies amidst heavy static.

"Cullman, I'm not picking up your vid," Nell said. It's unusual not to transmit a video signal, even way out here.

"Yes, there is something wrong with our scanners. We are working on it." The voice has a hint of an accent.

Despite the static, Nell concludes it's a male voice, but she doesn't really care. She just wants to deliver and get out. Even at this remote outpost, she dreads human interaction, wanting nothing to do with people.

Nell links to an outside scanner, placing its feed where normally the outpost's flight officer would have been. Luna's rough surface gets closer and faster, even though the freighter is slowing rapidly. Nell's familiar with this illusion, but that doesn't stop her from glancing nervously at the flight path display. Landing beacon signal strength is nominal and Emcee has them between the white lines.

The pitch of the big engines rises and holds steady during the last two minutes of the descent and the meter stops at just under seven Gs.

The freighter's vibrations increase in step with the engine's power curve, reaching a crescendo and holding but never seeming to strain. Nell's impressed with them, more than she had been with the young engineer who had supervised the refit. He'd been correct in one thing, these thrusters are sweet.

"Another perfect landing, Emcee," Nell congratulates the AI.

"Thank you." she said brightly.

Nell snaps open the harness and climbs out of the hammock. She's already in her vacsuit minus the helmet, a standard General Dynamics model used by most orbital construction workers two decades ago. It's comfortable especially over long periods.

She checks her air once more before slipping on the bubble helmet, "Emcee, do you read?" She asks.

"Loud and clear," the AI said cheerfully. "The customers are waiting outside. It seems they are anxious to get unloaded."

"Whatever," that's fine with her. The sooner she gets started, the sooner she can leave.

Evolution's Child has landed on a flat plain about a kilometer from Cullman. Emerging, Nell pauses on the metal grate catwalk that encircles the pilothouse. From her vantage point ten meters above the surface, Nell can see most of Cullman outpost and concludes it's not much to look at. Several buried Quonset huts serve the prospectors as living quarters. A large open canopy provides sunscreen for a work area with smaller non-pressurized sheds around it. Crates and assorted equipment are scattered about. Under the canopy is a rover with its power plant hanging from a cherry picker. A prospector's mobile drilling rig sits at the edge of the outpost.

Parked on the lunar surface below Nell are a rover and a Construction Utility Vehicle (CUV), its crane in the stowed position. Three figures wearing military vacsuits are ascending the freighter's access ladder, sending vibrations through the catwalk. Nell can't see their faces. They're hidden behind helmets that don't transmit the wearer's expression. Instead, she sees two bulging sensor arrays, one at each side of their head. She recognizes it immediately. Bugeyes. It's a derogatory term for the Brotherhood's version of the visor.

First, it's police officers manning Luna Central, now she's greeted by Brotherhood soldiers. The last thing she wants to do is get embroiled in Republic politics.

Two of the bugeyes continue upward to the cargo area. The third walks down the catwalk towards Nell. Strangely reminiscent of a feudal knight, his vacsuit is covered in composite armor plate like scales on a fish. The approaching figure is roughly 30 centimeters taller than Nell and wearing a vacsuit that outclasses her simple construction rig. She's at a distinct disadvantage.

"We will unload the ship," said a male voice over the common channel. "You will come with me. Commander Ghafour is waiting."

"Thanks, but no thanks. I will supervise the unloading of my ship first. Then if I have time we can socialize," Nell said. Even in her withdrawn state of mind, every alarm bell is clanging. It's impolite to greet someone in full combat gear let alone to climb into the cargo bay without asking. As she moves by the figure, he reaches out. Fear grips her as she realizes how precarious her position is. The armored suits power assist could easily crush her arm.

"Pilot, this is Commander Ghafour," declares a second male voice, his tone smoother and more refined. "Please accept my hospitality. We have a few things to discuss. My assistant will bring you back to your ship as soon as we are finished."

"You need to tell this bugeye to release me." Nell flares, anger feeding on fear as pain shoots up her arm.

"Captain, release her."

The iron grip relaxes and Nell steps back, her arm throbbing. This is starting out as the worst delivery ever.

"Look, I just want to get unloaded, take on some fuel, and get out of here. Nothing more," Nell explains, watching as two more bugeyes climb past the catwalk heading towards the cargo bay.

"And you shall in record time with the help of my men," Commander Ghafour said.

"This is my ship and I'll see to unloading her. I packed this load and I know how it should be unpacked," Nell said.

"That is not necessary, I assure you. My men know what they are doing and will work faster if you let them do it without your, shall we say, help." His tone is condescending and he has Captain Shithead looming between Nell and the ladder.

Nell decides to try a different tack, "The flight plan calls for six thousand kilos of fuel. Where is it?" Nell asks.

"The tanker is in the compound waiting for the cargo to be unloaded. Now, go with the Captain." Commander Ghafour is running out of patience. He's accustomed to people jumping when he speaks.

Nell is angry and more than a little concerned. Something is very wrong here. "I always supervise the unloading of my ship. I'm not …"

"*Captain.*" Commander Ghafour snaps in Arabic.

Nell has no chance as the man reaches out and grasps both of her arms right above the elbows, easily lifting and flinging her over the metal rail of the catwalk to the lunar surface ten meters below.

"What the… Hey. Damn you." Nell calls out before landing flat on her back with a thud and whoosh of escaping breath. She bounces once and comes to rest in a crumpled heap face down just a few meters from the rover. It feels as if a two hundred kilo gorilla were sitting on her chest.

The rover's side panel opens and another bugeye emerges, his combat boots stopping just centimeters from her face.

She hears a wicked chuckle, "*You do have a way with women.*" Her visor automatically translates the Arabic.

"*Shut up and load her in the rover.*" Captain Shithead said, clumsily backing down the freighter's access ladder to the ground.

The second soldier picks her up and unceremoniously dumps Nell in the rover. She rolls to the back managing to face forward when she comes to rest. From there, she watches the second man climb into the driver's seat while Captain Shithead takes a position facing her. She wishes she could see his eyes.

Nell feels the rover power up and start to move. She remains sprawled on the floor of the small cargo bay, her body aching. That fall would have killed her on Earth; here it just made her wish she were dead.

"*Put her in the tool shed?*" Captain Shithead asks.

"*Of course. Why else did you prepare it.*" Commander Ghafour snaps irritably. "*Make sure she has air. I want her alive.*"

"*Yes sir.*" The men do not even try to hide from Nell what they are saying, communicating freely over the common frequency in Arabic. They may not realize her visor can translate or don't care.

The rover stops alongside a non-pressurized metal shed. The captain carries Nell into the shed and drops her to the floor.

"*Is the shed completely empty?*" He gives the interior a quick look, opening and closing cabinets and the storage locker. He had told his men to clean it out but they sometimes slack off and it's his butt if something goes wrong.

"*Yes Captain,*" the soldier said.

"*And the door can be locked?*"

"*Yes Captain, everything is ready. She cannot escape,*" the man reassures his doubting superior.

Nell hasn't moved since the fall and is apparently remains unconscious. The captain uses his toe to roll her over on her back. He leans down twisting her arm to expose the small panel at her wrist. Popping it open, he looks at the vacsuit's readouts, making sure she's alive and has air. He could not care less about any possible broken bones or concussion she may have suffered but he does care that she's breathing when Commander Ghafour calls for her. Almost as an afterthought, he removes the fuel cell that powers her communications, isolating her as completely as any human in history.

Satisfied, he leaves Nell sprawled on the cold stone floor.

ЯL

The question of what role the moon plays has been around since the first ancestor looked up with enough intelligence to ask it. At one time or another, the moon has been blamed for crime sprees, bad politicians, crop failures, girl babies and many other equally ridiculous assertions. A medieval book called it the *land of demons* while another claimed it was the *face of God*. Only in the last century has mankind been able to travel there, first sending machines, then going in person. In the late 1960's the Lunar Orbiter series visually mapped the surface down to a meter resolution in preparation for the Apollo lunar landings, which returned almost 400 kilograms of rock samples from six different sites.

In 1994, Clementine orbited Luna hundreds of times while mapping the surface using the next generation of remote sensors. During its two-month voyage, it discovered ice at the lunar South Pole. Four years later Lunar Prospector provided global maps of elemental distribution on the lunar surface using a Gamma Ray Spectrometer and a Neutron Spectrometer. In the early decades of the 21st century, the Badger series of remote controlled lunar prospectors paved the way for the manned expeditions that followed, culminating in the establishment of Shennong in 2016, Kyoto in 2021 and Aldrin Station in 2024.

The Central Highlands is one of the most intensely studied regions on Luna. Consisting of blowout material from four major craters, it's over three-kilometers thick in spots and a rich source of ancient ice, some ore as high as forty percent water. This ice is 4.3 billion years old, trapped in the original cataclysm that ripped the moon from Mother Earth. The meteor impacts that made Alphonsus, Albategnius, Arzachel, and Ptolemaeus craters, brought it within reach of humanity.

Regolith, the powdery layer of material pulverized by the bombardment of micrometeorites over an unimaginable long span of time, averages thirty meters deep over much of the Highlands. In some places, it's composed entirely of anorthite, a mineral consisting of aluminum, calcium, silicon and oxygen, with the chemical formula of $CaAl_2Si_2O_8$. Strip mine operations go after the richest regions using either draglines or bucket loaders to harvest the ore. These huge machines, made entirely from metal smelted in Benjamin Franklin, pull in and store the powdery regolith in enormous bins. When full, convoys pull under them and fill up. A single ore convoy can provide enough tonnage to keep a refinery busy for a week.

Dakota freehold operates Falconhead, the largest anorthite refinery in Benjamin Franklin. Of the many items produced at Falconhead, Calconn superconductors are its specialty, a material in high demand back on Mother Earth but very dangerous to manufacture. Falconhead's location put it close to the supply of raw material coming in from the Central Highlands and far enough away that if it explodes, it would not take Aldrin Station with it.

It requires many layers of organization to keep the Calconn production system functioning. A key element is delivering ore to the refineries in a predictable and timely fashion. Several independent companies collect anorthite from mines all across the Central Highlands and deliver it to Benjamin Franklin. Among these, Surface Master Trucking is by far the largest.

SMT is more than just a trucking company. It maintains facilities in many of the mines, Far Point being the largest, and its contribution to surface roads is substantial. In some cases, SMT vehicles comprise over 95% of a roads usage. Thus, the company is responsible for maintaining a vast system of improved roads encompassing over 90,000 square kilometers. Road crews far outnumber truck drivers.

Imam Abu Bakr looks up at Malik and asks in Arabic. *"You are sure they suspect nothing?"* He sips from a glass of wine imported at great expense from the vineyards of his native Turkey. His own battle helmet sits on the stone table beside him, the half-empty wine decanter next to it.

Malik shrugs, *"They suspect everything and nothing. They are jumpy from the hospital bombing but that is what was intended? Yes? Get them to spread themselves thin?"*

"...and our men are ready?"

"Yes Imam. The men are more than ready. They are tired of driving trucks and road work." Malik growls. His official rank within the army is captain but very few use it in addressing him. He prefers it that way, just as long as they obey his orders.

"And the packages are on schedule? Are you prepared to unload the ship when it arrives?" Imam Bakr strokes his beard.

Malik nods, "*The devices will immediately be brought here and loaded on the trucks. The task force commanders are all true believers and understand when to use the weapons.*"

"*Allah be praised,*" Imam Bakr said. "*I pray you are right.*"

From his office balcony, the Imam overlooks hundreds of Goliaths and modified ore carriers spread across the vast space. Those in the center have men and machines swarming over them. More Goliaths line each wall, their alterations complete. Normally, there are only a few dozen trucks here at a time, but today is special. SMT drivers from all over the Highlands have converged on Little America bringing in most of the company's 22,000 employees and all of its trucks. Another 18,000 soldiers have arrived from Al Fahad. They're in nearby habitats preparing to board the convoys when the time comes. Soon all will be ready.

Over the last two years, SMT's entire fleet of Goliaths has had power production substantially increased. Under maximum current draw, their high capacity fuel cells can produce over ten megawatts. A typical convoy requires only a fraction of that, leaving the remaining to power laser cannons.

Here and in other facilities under their control, they have modified hundreds of carriers to transport humans, not ore. Each carrier is capable of supporting fifty soldiers and their equipment in the harsh lunar environment. After years of preparation, the Brotherhood is almost ready for battle.

Imam Bakr walks briskly across the expansive floor with Malik at his heels. He wants to check personally that the men are carrying out his orders. The clank of metal against metal competes against the whine of overhead cranes and power tools. Most of the soldiers are lounging outside their troop carriers, their gear already stowed. No one is wearing battle helmets, enjoying one last respite. Nobody knows how long they'll wear them once the fighting begins.

Halfway along their route, they hear the boisterous cries of men and the sharp ring of steel striking steel. It comes from the center of a large gathering of soldiers. Their backs are to Imam Bakr and Malik as they approach.

"*Make way.*" Malik barks in Arabic.

The soldiers, suddenly aware of Imam Bakr, scramble to make a path. In the center of the makeshift arena, two men are circling one another, each swinging the curved steel of a scimitar. The larger of the two fighters glances furtively at Malik and the Imam. That's all the opening his smaller opponent needs. Quick as a cobra, the man's sword leaps out striking the other just above his armored shoulder. The blade bites deep into his neck between the rows of plating. With a gurgling sound and a gush of blood, the man slumps to the floor.

"*Basayev.*" Malik roars, springing forward to kneel beside the fallen soldier. There's nothing to do for him. He's with Allah. The blade had sliced through the jugular and severed his spine. He was dead before he hit the floor.

Standing and facing the young killer, Malik makes sure he's beyond the reach of the scimitar, "*You fool. We are preparing for battle and you kill one of your comrades.*" Malik's voice is hard as the bloody steel in Basayev's hand. His own hand rests lightly on his pistol. Calmness descends upon him.

"*It was an accident.*" the young man growls while blood drips from his sword, pooling at his feet. The chemical rush of making a kill flows through him like an electric current. He's slow to recognize the threat Malik represents.

"*If you weren't the grand nephew of the Caliph, I would kill you myself.*" Malik said, his body tense.

"*I tell you, it was an accident.*" the young man repeats vehemently but without conviction. He will remember this insult. No one talks to him in this way and lives.

"*That is enough,*" Imam Bakr realizes what's about to happen, even if this brash young aristocrat did not. Reporting the death of his nephew to the Caliph is not something one does if they value their life.

With a disgusted snarl Malik said, "*Go back to your unit and prepare to fight. Allah willing, you will be killed during the coming battle.*" Malik keeps his eyes on Basayev and his hand near his pistol. The young man wipes the blood from his scimitar, grins, and stalks away. Turning to the gathered soldiers, he orders. "*Go. All of you. Return to your units. May Allah grant you victory.*"

Malik watches as the men scuffle away, many with fierce hard stares promising revenge against the young Basayev, nephew or not.

Imam Bakr comes forward to stand beside Malik. "As you say, Captain, the men are ready to fight." he said coldly in perfect English.

Two hundred meters away the main airlock opens and another truck enters pulling its carriers. A floor worker guides the vehicle to a clear spot. Seconds after it stops, men and equipment pour out of its interior, while others converge and begin adding armament, preparing another killing machine for the coming harvest.

ЯL

Nell grits her teeth and pulls herself up. She stands still until her head stops spinning. Limping around the interior, she verifies what the bugeye told Captain Shithead. She can't find a single item in the shed, nothing in the cabinets or in the metal locker standing against the back wall. Nell concludes that the windowless building is the perfect prison.

Then she spots a small round hole no bigger than her thumb in the eaves above the door and to the side. She will need to climb up on the workbench to see out of it.

She turns around, places her hands on the counter behind her and does a little jump, planting her butt on the workbench. Leaning back, she uses the empty shelves to pull herself up without putting undue stress on her sore leg. Despite her best efforts, pain shoots through her knee. There might be something wrong there after all.

The hole was punched through the metal from the outside leaving its inner edges sharp and dangerous to her civilian vacsuit. Now is not the time to spring a leak. She presses the bubble of her helmet against the jagged opening. The size of the hole allows only one sensor to peer through it at a time, making it hard for her to discern depth and severely restricting her field of view.

Even with these limitations, Nell can see Evolution's Child and the CUV parked next to it, its crane fully deployed. Already several large crates sit on Luna soil. There are figures in the cargo bay and more on the ground working in and around the now open crates. From this distance and angle, she can't make out what's inside.

Nell's rage soars when she sees a bugeye emerge from her ship's pilothouse, the same airlock she had used just a short time before. The grotesque figure moves around the railed catwalk and climbs up the ladder, joining those working in the cargo bay.

Nell takes a deep breath, calming herself. What are the facts? Her ship contains thirty tons of cargo listed as mining equipment but at this point, Nell seriously doubts that. Who in their right mind would treat her this way after she delivers them a load of mining gear? No, it had to contain something else, but how can that be? She herself had scanned the crates and verified the contents. Her mind chases that fact around before finally concluding that somehow, she'd been fooled.

She turns her thoughts to the men themselves. Despite the armored vacsuits and fancy titles, the lack of discipline makes her doubt these men are military. That leaves only terrorists.

Without the freighter's AI constantly updating her visor, Nell loses track of time. Over the next few hours, she continues to watch and think as Ghafour's crew reshuffles the cargo. Finally, they close the crates and return them to the freighter's cargo bay. Whatever's going on, it's ending.

But as time goes by, Nell convinces herself they must have forgotten her. At last, a rover comes into sight. It pulls up and stops outside the shed. Nell jumps down from the workbench jarring her knee. Knowing she's powerless against even one soldier in a combat suit, she stands calmly in the center of the shed waiting for the door to open.

A bugeye enters the room alert for any surprises. A second bugeye enters more leisurely, coming to a stop in front of Nell. Reaching out, he grasps her wrist and violently twists it around. While Nell grimaces in pain, he deftly installs the fuel cell restoring her communications.

"Pilot, you will do exactly as I tell you or you will die. Is that clear?" Commander Ghafour's voice informs her.

Nell nods inside the clear bubble of her helmet. Her arm feels like it's being wrenched from its socket.

"Excellent."

She isn't sure if this bugeye trying to remove her arm is Ghafour or one of his hoods. Not that it matters. Just before he releases her, Nell notices a small Black Widow symbol with a tiny red hourglass painted on his armored breastplate right at eye level.

Nell's allowed to walk unhindered from the shed. Outside next to the rover are two more bugeyes. It unnerves her to know they can see her but she can't see them. At this close range, their multifaceted sensor arrays eerily cast tiny reflections almost as if they were alive. All of them tower over Nell making her feel small and helpless.

Nell takes the seat furthest from the driver at the back of the rover. The other four bugeyes take seats between her and the door. Past them and over the shoulder of the driver Nell can see a thin slice out the front window, enough to realize they're heading back to Evolution's Child.

Nell cycles through the airlock staring at that tiny spider with its little red hourglass. Sharing the tight confines of the little airlock with this armored bugeye almost brings Nell to the breaking point. She welcomes the return of sound as air pressure floods back. The familiar squeal of the airlock door comforts her.

Stepping into her inner sanctum, she's shocked to see her control room in such disarray. The main computer cabinet is wide open and a skinny bearded young man wearing old-fashioned wire-framed glasses is sitting cross-legged on the floor in front of it. Strewn around him is an assortment of electronic gear and testing equipment. He's also the first person Nell's observed not wearing a combat vacsuit. He looks up and grins.

Nell removes her helmet, "What are you doing to my ship?" She asked, surveying the mess. A second AI is on the floor next to the man, its carbon fiber case unmistakable.

"We are upgrading your AI," a familiar voice said from behind her. "I could not trust our cargo to your primitive program."

Nell wheels around. Ghafour is standing in the doorway leading to her living quarters. The man is in his late forties, tall with black hair and dark eyes. A short beard gives him a rough appearance. A hairless line draws attention to a scar across his right cheek. Arrogance permeates the air around him.

"It got your cargo this far," Nell retorts.

Ghafour's eyes narrow down to slits and his mouth forms into a humorless hard line. His tone leaves no doubt as to who's in charge.

"Quiet. Follow me." Ghafour orders and turns away, heading deeper into Nell's home.

When Nell hesitates, she receives a violent push from behind. She sails through the doorway and sprawls onto the padded floor at the feet of Ghafour.

"*Remove her visor and suit.*" Ghafour orders gruffly.

Spiderman promptly reaches down, grasps the hard point behind Nell's neck, and lifts her. His armored hands are rough but efficient in removing her backpack but when he reaches for her visor, Nell removes it herself, handing the device to Ghafour. As Spiderman continues to pull at her suit she said, "Slow down. I'll take it off."

She might as well be talking to the wall. Spiderman continues until Nell is standing in only panties and tank top. Nell notices Ghafour's sudden interest in her, like a hungry carnivore coming across a fresh piece of meat.

In her youth, Nell worked as an exotic dancer in the clubs along Stanwell Moor Road just outside Heathrow International Spaceport. Back then it was an area that catered to business travelers. She had made excellent money flashing her green eyes up at the johns. At only 165 centimeters, all of them towered over her, bringing out either the protector or the dominator in every man. It didn't hurt that she had firm tits, slender waist, and a great ass. That was another life, before she met James and fell in love, before the girls and that terrible afternoon.

The medical treatments she periodically receives in Aldrin Station not only maintains the calcium in her bones, it gives her great muscle tone, and Luna's light gravity helps even more. Nell recognizes the look and realizes this may be her best chance regardless of how revolting. Sexual intrigue was something she'd been good at long ago but the thought sickens her now. Recognizing the opening is one thing, being willing to exploit it quite another.

Ghafour licks his lips and openly leers at her breasts. She's not wearing a bra and they stretch the thin fabric of her top clearly displaying her erect nipples. Nell knows from experience what's going though his head, the rationalization males go through when the chemicals in their brains start clamoring for sex. It's hard to resist hundreds of millions of years of evolution. She flips her hair back and runs her hand through its mass, letting it cascade over bare shoulders and hard nipples.

"Search everything. Remove anything that can be used as a weapon," Ghafour orders hoarsely. Spiderman immediately moves to comply. Nell can only watch helplessly as the bugeye begins ransacking her home.

The young man in the control room has stopped and is eyeballing Nell's curves in obvious appreciation. From his seat, Ghafour calls roughly in an unknown language, "*Get back to work.*"

Nell believes he's speaking Arabic but without her visor, she's not sure. Gathering her courage, She asked in her best damsel-in-distress voice, "Commander, please tell me what you're doing?"

"Kneel, here in front of me. No man should have to look up to a woman." Dropping to her knees, Nell shows plenty of cleavage and spreads her legs slightly as she settles back on her butt.

Just looking at her sends the juices flowing through Ghafour and he begins thinking with his little head, "I need to use your little ship for a few days, that's all," he said letting his eyes roam over her body, "You will be back in command before you know it."

"Can you at least tell me where we're going?" She asks with as much innocence as she can muster, resisting the urge to puke. It would spoil her performance.

Ghafour hesitates for a moment, considering the many things he would like to do to this beautiful infidel. "We will make a brief stop at Aldrin Station then on to Luna orbit where we will dock with a waiting spaceliner. Then you can go about your business." He's pleased with himself.

Nell manages to hold down her last meal. Even without her visor, she knows Ghafour is lying but he's one smooth bastard.

"What have I brought you?" She asked, not really expecting an answer.

Ghafour hesitates. He normally would not answer any questions but there's something about this woman. "Specialized mining equipment for a job in the asteroid belt." His expression hardens as his mind veers away from sex. "Enough questions. you will contact Luna Central at Aldrin Station and tell them this freighter will be landing for fuel before proceeding on to orbit," he leaves no room for argument.

Nell flirts with the idea of refusing but that would be taking the easy way out. "LC will need a new flight plan and the amount of fuel," Nell said, a plan beginning to take shape.

Ghafour's cold smile is a brilliant white line cutting through his beard. He's killed many times and thrives on the power it gives him. He must now rein in that animal instinct and use the wits Allah gave him to mold this woman to his needs.

"You will oversee the calculations and as for fuel, I only care that we have enough to get to lunar orbit. After that, you're on your own." Ghafour leans forward intently, bringing his face within centimeters of Nell's. His breath smells of wine and garlic. "One mistake, one slip of the tongue, one stray gesture, and I will cut your head off very slowly."

She shudders involuntarily, drops her eyes, and meekly nods. At that moment, Nell is convinced this man has done it before and will not hesitate to do it again.

Ghafour revels in his power over her. Western women are so easy. They crave the discipline he brings. Again, sexual fantasies spring unbidden into his mind. His blood runs hot.

"I will need my AI to fly the ship," Nell said as docilely as she can manage.

"You will use ours," Ghafour said ogling her cleavage, watching them rise and fall with each breath.

"A new AI must be fully tested. That takes weeks," Nell insists.

Ghafour's voice grows hard, "You will use ours. I have been given assurances it can fly this freighter."

Nell remains quiet, but ever so subtly, she shakes her head, the look on her face clearly said '*you have been lied to.*'

"*Ahmed. Come here.*" Ghafour calls out in Arabic.

The young man looks up in fear. What has he done now? He scrambles off the floor and hurries into the room his eyebrows knotted in a worried frown. His unkempt black hair sticks out in all directions.

"Commander?" He asked.

"*Is your AI installed?*" Ghafour demands.

The man glances at Nell, "Yes, Commander. I'm running final tests right now," he replies, realizing he made a mistake in speaking English. Ahmed was born in London and spoke nothing but English until he was almost twenty. As a result, the others do not consider him an equal.

"Have you found the anomaly in the fuel injectors?" Nell asks. "This ship has new thrusters and it took the shipyard a week to get them calibrated. How can you install a new AI without starting even one thruster?" Her voice rises slightly, "This is an old freighter. You can't just come in here and toss in a new AI. It won't work."

Ghafour reaches out and grabs a handful of Nell's raven black hair, forcing her to arch her back. Staring intently into her green eyes, He asked softly, "Why not pilot?"

His stale breath is hot on Nell's cheek. She begins breathing in short quick gulps, her pupils dilating as she struggles to hold fear in check. "Over time an AI learns to compensate for the wear of a pump and the peculiarities of a thruster. A new AI won't know any of it. The ship will tear itself apart before we get off the ground."

This is it, the big lie. She desperately needs her own AI. It's her best, perhaps only, chance to do something.

Ghafour releases Nell and leans back. Looking up at Ahmed he raises his eyebrows skeptically and asks, "*What do you say Ahmed? Will your AI damage this ship?*"

Ahmed frowns, looking fearfully at Ghafour, "*Commander, I am a programmer. This is more of an engineering question. Perhaps we should ask Khalid?*" he said in broken Arabic.

Ghafour cultivates fear in others. He can't help himself. It's his way of maintaining command. "*Khalid is busy. I am asking you, Ahmed,*" he said coldly in perfect Arabic. He's just about had enough of this sniveling technocrat with his western education.

"*Yes Commander.*" Ahmed stammers. "Ah… *all the ships systems are controlled by the AI… and it is capable of adapting … theoretically it is possible.*" He can't look Ghafour in the eye.

Without her visor, Nell can't understand what they're saying but it's obvious that Ghafour isn't happy with his man. Nell dares to hope and decides to go for broke. "My AI is the original install in the ship over fifteen years ago. You cannot replace her without extensive testing and recalibration." She keeps her eyes on the floor. "You'll kill us all."

Ahmed remains quiet, not daring to meet the glare of his commander. He cursed his fortune for the thousandth time. He doesn't know the details of the mission and doesn't want to know. It's his job to set up the AI on the ship, not troubleshoot the mechanicals. He's never been good with his hands. That was the main reason he had gone into programming in the first place.

"*Hook both up together,*" Ghafour orders irritably, to him an obvious and simplistic solution.

"Ah… *sir, that is not… ah… recommended,*" Ahmed stammers.

"*Why.*" Ghafour demands.

"*There can be only one AI in control, just as there is only one Commander. If there were two, which would we obey? One of them must have ultimate command, eliminating the need for the other. Anything else would cause complete confusion the first time they didn't agree. The system would lock up.*" Ahmed said in a rush, relieved the conversation is back to something familiar.

Ghafour curses the incompetence around him. As usual, he must improvise deep in a mission. He looks down at the female, confident in his mastery over her. "*Remove your AI. Replace it with the original.*" Ghafour growls at Ahmed. "*Now go. Get out of my sight.*"

Ahmed backs through the control room door, his face a mixture of relief and concern. "*As you wish.*" It's not his place to question the Commander even though he's sure his AI could adapt to this freighter, but he's too weak to make the case. It's easier to do as Ghafour orders, safer too.

"You shall have your AI, but what will I get in return?" Ghafour asks the woman kneeling before him.

Nell remains silent, head bowed, not daring to look up.

Spiderman finishes ransacking Nell's home and returns. The bugeye is carrying a disrupter sidearm and two power packs. He shows them to Commander Ghafour.

"Secure them. Then go help Khalid with the package. Let me know if there are any problems, otherwise, don't bother me," Ghafour orders.

The bugeye leaves. Ghafour rises and steps around Nell, closing the control room door. Coming back, he stops behind her. She doesn't move but is intensely aware of where he is.

Reaching down Ghafour grasps Nell's hair once again, pulling her up. He bends her head back exposing her neck. Thrusting his face over her shoulder, he licks Nell's cheek right below her ear. She utters a frightened gasp and groans as he begins to grope her. Ghafour laughs coldly and Nell knows it's time to pay the piper…

ЯL

Ahmed looks up when the door opens. The odor of sex instantly permeates the control room. He can hardly take his eyes off her breasts. A trickle of blood runs from Nell's nostril. She swipes at it with the back of her hand, smearing red across her cheek. She looks crushed, her spirit broken, ashamed to meet Ahmed's gaze.

"Is the AI ready?" Ghafour asks almost pleasantly from behind her. He's wallowing in the aftermath of ejaculation. It's a gift from Allah that she's here, available to him, giving him a jump on paradise. Too bad she wasn't a virgin, but what western woman is.

"Yes commander. We haven't run any tests but that shouldn't be necessary," Ahmed said.

255

"Watch the pilot carefully. She is going to set up the flight calculations. Make sure that is all she does." Ghafour orders.

"As you wish." Ahmed leers as Nell takes the pilot's seat. The man cannot tear his eyes off her bare tits and hard nipples.

Nell felt marginally better in the familiar surroundings of the control room, sitting in the command chair, the bank of controls and readouts spread out before her. She reaches out and activates the control room speaker. "Emcee, are you there?" She asked, casually letting her hands grip the padded armrest of the chair. There are no apparent controls in the armrest and the movement looks completely innocent.

"Aye Nell, I'm here. What happened?" the AI is confused. It's unaccustomed to having memory gaps.

"I will explain later. Right now, we need to change our flight plan. Access standard flight equations Z115." Being a lone woman plying the trade routes between Mother Earth and Luna, Nell has set up an elaborate emergency system. Between the pressure sensors installed in the armrest and verbal keywords, Nell can communicate just about any command to Emcee without anyone being the wiser. It's one of the games she and the AI play during the long hours between stops, each trying to come up with a scenario that isn't covered. This is the first major test and there isn't any room for error.

"Roger Nell, Z115 loaded," Emcee said.

So far so good. Without looking up She asked, "Commander, is there a particular orbit we need to reach?"

"Take on fuel at Little America for a two hundred kilometer circular orbit in Earth-Luna plane," Ghafour said.

With Ahmed hovering over her shoulder, Nell plunges on. "Emcee, our new destination is Little America, any available dock. Use a standard parabolic trajectory at sixty percent efficiency and economy at seventy-five. We will take on fuel for a round trip to Taurus, any two-zero-zero planer orbit. Ask for the soonest available launch window. Clear?"

"Aye," Emcee said.

"Commence" Nell allows herself a glance at Ghafour, receiving a cold stare in return. She takes grim satisfaction thinking about what she had just arranged for him, but she mustn't give it away. She lets her eyes drop.

"How long will this take?" Ghafour asks, recovered to the point of fantasizing again, building up for another go at her.

"About five minutes," Nell answers.

"Go get cleaned up. You will need to transfer the information to Luna Central," Ghafour orders.

Nell rises and goes back through her quarters heading for the washroom. She leaves the door open giving Ghafour and Ahmed a fine view of the proceedings. Hesitating at the mirror, Nell sees the smear of blood on her cheek. Her head starts spinning and her stomach churns. She just manages to get a utility bag before barfing into it. Wiping her mouth with a towel, she hears laughter.

Sending the bag down the waste chute, she strips off her panties and enters the shower. Warm air and water droplets flow over her head cascading down her body. The little electric motor that runs the fan is ancient and makes a high pitch whine.

As she soaps up, she risks a covert glance through the clear shower wall. Even though the clear plastic distorts them, she can clearly see both men staring at her. Turning her back to them, she leans over giving them a good look at her ass while scrubbing hard between her legs.

"Emcee, can you hear me?" Nell barely whispers, almost matching the pitch of the shower fan.

"Aye, I hear you. Please verify general order 115," the AI asks almost too faint for Nell to hear over the fan.

"General order 115 verified. Authority code Nell, Z7592."

A moment later Ghafour throws open the stall door. "You are finished." He roughly pulls her out of the shower.

Nell grabs some coveralls as Ghafour pushes her out of the bathroom and into her quarters. She makes sure her tits bounce, and meekly asks, "May I put my clothes on?"

Ghafour hands Nell a towel, his nostrils flaring as he catches a whiff of wet hair. "Yes… you must look presentable when you talk with Luna Central. Go ahead, dress."

She gives a good show as she slips first one leg, then the other, into the coveralls. Extending both arms behind her, she arches her back and slides them in, pulling the material over her shoulders. Already hard from the cool air, her nipples rub against the thin fabric and swell even larger. She fastens the buttons up the front, leaving the last three open.

Nell remains submissive, never letting her eyes meet theirs, afraid she would give herself away.

The cycling of the airlock signals someone entering. Two bugeyes emerge and Nell wonders how they both had fit in the small chamber. They pass through the control room and enter the living area. Nell moves to stand behind Ghafour, not finding it particularly difficult to act frightened of these figures.

"*Are you finished?*" Ghafour asks, pleased that Nell looks to him for protection, another sign of his dominance over her.

Both bugeyes nod then begin to remove their helmets. Nell is surprised when Spiderman turns out to be a woman. She's hard with a perpetual scowl beneath raven black hair cut short. The other bugeye is an older man, his hair and beard salted with gray, his eyes tired and movements slow.

"*All is ready Commander,*" the old man said in Arabic.

"*Allah be praised,*" turning to Nell, "You will make that call now, pilot." He steps aside motioning her to enter the control room.

Ghafour waits at the doorway and Ahmed moves out of the camera's field of view as Nell takes the command seat. This will be the last time she will sit here.

"Emcee, hail Luna Central," she orders.

"Aye, hailing," is the cheery response.

A moment later, "This is Luna Central. How may I aid you?" The uniformed officer on the main screen looks mighty good to Nell. If only you were here, you and some of your friends.

"This is Evolution's Child submitting a change in flight plans. Downloading the new flight calculations now... I'm standing by." She sits back, even remembering to place her hands just as she had done before.

"Roger, Evolution's Child standing by..."

Nell keeps her eyes on the officer as he inputs her calculations, not risking even a glance at the other occupants in the room. True to form, they were correct.

"Your request for fuel has been approved. I have you arriving at Little America, Dock 14 in approximately thirty-two minutes. Evolution's Child, you are good for launch in T minus four minutes." In all her years of piloting, she never felt as completely alone as she did when that figure disappears.

Nell sits still for a moment wondering if she's doing the right thing. Her mind can reach only one conclusion. She's certain at this point that these men are religious extremists bent on some violent mission, what exactly, she does not know, but big, really big.

Everyone has seen the face of terrorism, the planes flying into the Twin Towers, the mushroom cloud over Houston, and countless body bags lining the cities sidewalks. These visions of death are part of modern life, but it's the specter of her dead daughter's that fuel Nell's nightmares and steadies her resolve now.

"Come. You are no longer needed here," Ghafour declares. He's pleased at her performance and plans to show her how much during the flight. In his arrogance, he actually believes Nell will welcome his attentions.

Ghafour follows Nell into her quarters, grasps the front of her coveralls and pulls her to him. "You did well." He leers as more and more of her tits emerge from confinement.

Nell battles to maintain the charade. The smoking school bus burns in her mind, even as she reaches out to stroke his manhood.

ЯL

The wail of the acceleration klaxon jolts Nell. Has it only been three minutes? It seems much longer. Nell lay unabashedly naked, sprawled on her back, staring up at the padded ceiling. Ghafour lies beside her heaving and gasping for breath. The deed had been fast and furious, Nell had made sure of that.

Khalid kneels on the floor next to the open control room door. As Ghafour raped Nell for the second time, Khalid had cast a few furtive glances and then continued his incantation, rocking back and forth, touching his forehead to the floor. Nell thinks it's a prayer and almost pities him. He's a frightened old man.

Although she had kept her eyes shut throughout most of the assault, Nell had caught Ahmed watching from the control room. He looks like he has something to say but is afraid to say it.

Ghafour sighs deeply and opens his eyes, his face glistening with sweat. Looking up at Ahmed, he said, "*Sit down. We are about to launch.*"

Ahmed enters the living room and makes for the only other padded chair aboard the ship, still staring at Nell, "*Not there, you idiot. Go and sit next to Khalid.*"

Nell can see Spiderwoman sitting in her command chair and feels a rush of resentment. Spiderwoman glances up and catches Nell watching her. She grins cruelly but something in Nell's expression wipes it off her face. She glances nervously down at the controls and back up at the pilot. Now it's Nell's turn to smile.

260

"Ten," Emcee announces.

Of the four aboard Evolution's Child, only Ghafour had been offworld before this mission. The others rely on him for guidance.

"Nine."

"*Commander.*" It's the first time Nell has heard the female's voice. It's harsh and full of malice.

"Eight."

Ghafour sits up hearing panic in Spiderwoman's voice. She is staring at Nell.

"Seven."

Turning, Ghafour looks down at Nell lying on the bed. She coldly meets his gaze. The total absence of fear shocks him. In its place is only disgust.

"Six."

"*Stop the countdown.*" Ghafour yells to Spiderwoman.

"Computer, stop." The woman commands in bad English. Leaning forward, she frantically begins flipping switches and twisting knobs, not knowing what any of them did.

"Five."

Nell grins contemptuously, never breaking eye contact with Ghafour.

"Four."

"*Stop. Stop.*" Spiderwoman demands even louder.

Nell chuckles in triumph.

"What have you done." Ghafour demands.

"Three."

In the control room, Spiderwoman goes berserk, striking the command panel using all the armored might of her combat vacsuit. The impact folds the panel in the middle, ripping it away from the wall. Glass, plastic and bits of metal fly around the control room like a hive of Africanized bees.

Rising, Ghafour jerks at his trousers trying to pull them up as he heads for the control room.

"Two."

Spiderwoman raises her arms for another blow when it occurs to her that the AI's CPU might be the better target.

"Help her." Ghafour yells at Ahmed who simply lays his head back against the wall, a resigned look in his eyes as he gazes at the naked figure of Nell, strangely pleased that this wisp of a woman has gotten the best of Commander Ghafour. He figures if something is amiss, there's nothing he can do about it now. Might as well enjoy the view on his way to paradise.

"One."

Spiderwoman is on this mission because she's one of the fastest draws in the kingdom, a fact that caused more than a little consternation among the men. She has many kills and is confident that she will be victorious on this day as well. Drawing her sidearm as she turns, her brain is sending the impulse to her trigger finger when acceleration squeezes them in its iron grip.

Rising up through the metal ship, the sound of the new Pratt and Whitney's going to full throttle destroys the unprotected hearing of the four terrorists and Nell. The acceleration compresses Ahmed's spine and his neck vertebra splinters impaling his scull on his spinal cord. His internal organs rip away and compact at the bottom of his body cavity, the heart crushing everything beneath it.

The acceleration catches Khalid on the forward swing of his chant, leaning down but before his forehead touched the floor. From just a few centimeters away, his face slams into the padding with the force of a cannon shot and his spine shatters in a dozen places, snapping like a brittle twig. Pain sears through his body in one blazing jolt as his heart and lungs flatten against his ribs.

Spiderwoman never realizes she lost. Her upper body collapses down on shattered legs and both arms slam to the floor, the disrupter still clenched in her hand. Her head falls furthest and attains the highest velocity. Impact with the floor shatters her skull like a rotten egg. There's no bouncing, everything simply hits and sticks to the floor as though coated with Velcro.

The acceleration drives Ghafour into the floor like a carpenter driving a nail. His hip and knee joints separate as he collapses. His torso stays upright when his butt hits the floor, one thigh in front and the other behind. His lower legs twist grotesquely underneath his body and his internal organs compress into a mass. His backbone shatters and his shoulders spiral downward coming to rest unnaturally close to his hips.

Just before liftoff, Nell tenses her body in anticipation. She thought she would have about three seconds at this G load before the blood completely drained from her brain and she loses consciousness. That proved to be grossly optimistic. Under the tremendous acceleration, Nell's heart burst, her brain pancakes, and her lower jaw wrenches open slamming into her collapsing breastbone. She's dead in an instant.

Designed for propulsion components available twenty years before, Evolution's Child was never meant to handle accelerations of this magnitude. The ship's light cargo and almost empty fuel tanks exacerbate the situation, further elevating the G load. Even the most junior engineer in the Hyundai shipyards could have predicted what came next.

The welds along the titanium struts that transfer the loads from the port thruster to the ship's superstructure fail along one side magnifying the strain on the remaining supports. The fuel feed lines twist and rupture mixing the hypergolic liquids which ignite spontaneously. Systems designed to shut down fail and fuel continues to feed the fire.

Emcee tries to compensate for the loss of the thruster. Systems never designed for this level of acceleration begin to fail. Evolution's Child rolls progressing rapidly to an out-of-control spiral.

Hypergolic fuels spewing from the ruptured lines mix and create a fiery plume in the ships wake. Evolution's Child never gets higher than a few thousand meters, her trajectory a blazing arc north northwest of Alphonsus crater.

A trucker plying the Trans Lunar Highway a few hours out of Summerhaven is amazed to see the burning meteor silently streak across the sky, disappearing over the horizon and into the Sea of Clouds.

Eye of the Hurricane

"Man is a Religious Animal. He is the only Religious Animal.
He is the only animal that has the True Religion -- several of
them. He is the only animal that loves his neighbor as himself
and cuts his throat if his theology isn't straight."

Mark Twain (1835-1910)

Security Chief Corso Dugan scans the room as the heavy airlock door slides shut behind him. He thinks of the Regional Command Center as a calm center walled in by the raging storm. His troops call it the Bull's Eye.

The RCC is a circular amphitheater. At its focal point is a large dais. Surrounding the dais in five concentric rings are workstations, each composed of a large rectangular slab of Duraglass laid flat like a tabletop. Within these slabs is a three dimensional network of micro-imagers designed to process huge amounts of data.

Data mining is something every Lunarian knows to one extent or another, the straightforward evolution of the search engine of last century applied to the tremendous amount of real-time information collected today. Operators stand at their posts, hands darting over their workstations, sifting through this vast quantity of information, only managing to observe a very small percentage of the total.

Magi carries the bulk of the workload. She juxtaposes real-time data with the ever-expanding database of human knowledge using sophisticated algorithms. She compares what is, with what was. Just as a hunter waits patiently for movement in the distant stand of trees to signal the arrival of quarry, so too does the AI look for anomalies in the data using comparative analysis.

After a quick head count, Corso is satisfied his RCC is fully manned. Other operators link in from all over Luna, but the citizens in this room are his handpicked crew.

"Chief on deck." Captain Ben Dugan calls out.

Just as he's done a thousand times, Corso links his visor to Magi's external data stream. The RCC disappears and he's hovering sixty thousand kilometers above Aldrin Station in open space. Lagrange One Space Station is close by. Corso glances at the station and moves on.

In the western sky is Taurus Colony, 400,000 kilometers ahead of the moon and in the same orbit. Taurus consists of two wheels rotating in opposite directions, each over two kilometers in diameter and connected by a massive cylindrical hub. With an economy based around building and maintaining power satellites, ships swarm around the colony. Corso doesn't spend time here either.

Hyundai Shipyards is 400,000 kilometers behind the moon also in the same orbit. From a distance, it appears a spindly structure haphazardly assembled. Hyundai is a zero G facility with an economy based on shipbuilding. It's the birthplace of every battlestation, frigate, and freighter in the system.

Corso lingers on Hyundai for a moment. The main yard is empty. They completed Battlestation Houris several weeks ago and hadn't started on a new project yet. He had watched for months as they laid the keel and assembled the giant warship. It's one of the largest ever built and used a tremendous amount of Lunarian iron. The Brotherhood hadn't wanted to spend the extra money on titanium. The decision had been a great boon to Aldrin Station's iron industry. Corso just wished he knew where that battlestation was right now.

He sweeps his gaze across the plethora of objects in geosynchronous orbit, orbital power stations beaming energy down to Mother Earth, communications satellites relaying billions of data streams, weather observation platforms and industrial manufacturing facilities, crowd the orbit. In some places, the satellites appear so thick that Corso can imagine stepping from one to the next.

Dropping his gaze lower, he notes several Stratoliners rising up through the atmosphere with another just departing Heaven's Gate on its way back down. Framed against the blue and white Earth, one of the mass drivers in LEO flashes along its length as it injects another Product Delivery Module down through the atmosphere. He stares intently at the PDM and a moment later, a list of what's aboard appears within his visual. It's another delivery of Calconn.

With a flip of his hand, a virtual control panel appears around Corso's waist in a great arc. He activates partial visual, his fingers feeling the pressure of the keystroke, his ears hearing the click. Ben and Major Mallory appear beside him.

"Show me what you've got," Corso orders.

"Fourteen minutes ago we picked up a freighter coming out of Cullman Outpost," Ben said. He zooms across the lunar surface to hover above the small mining community inside Herschel crater. The three watch Evolution's Child launch, pitch over and accelerate, spewing a contrail as it lost control. Its flight path was far enough away that the defensive batteries along the top of Rim Mountain simply locked on and tracked it without firing. Ben maintains perspective on the craft as it penetrates the Sea of Clouds and disappears.

"We don't know exactly where the ship hit, but using the data from the cannon batteries we can calculate it very accurately, assuming constant flight parameters from the last known good measurements," Major Mallory explains. She's a second generation Lunarian, a member of the Turner family. Her calm professional demeanor when under fire has gained her rank and responsibility at a young age.

"The Fitzgerald will be overhead in two minutes and we can do a full visual sweep of the area," Ben said. Named after a ship that plied the Great Lakes over a century before, the Edmund Fitzgerald is a freighter in the Earth/Luna system. Currently, it's ready to break orbit heading for Hyundai Shipyards, its tanks filled with water, its cargo holds with metals and food. It would have broken orbit minutes before but Luna Central held it up on Ben's request.

Reviewing the doomed ship's flight data, Corso said, "Look at the gee loading. Nothing organic could have survived."

Mallory and Ben nod agreement and watch as Corso takes control of the vid, resetting the time back to just before launch and enlarging Cullman outpost. He pulls data from Luna Central and reviews the flight path change requested by the freighter's pilot. Corso senses something is wrong with the woman but can't put his finger on the reason. Probably just the fact her ship had not followed the flight path she herself had submitted. Hindsight is always twenty-twenty.

Corso expands the search for data inside the outpost itself, probing in real-time for an opening into the local network. The firewall he hits is unlike any he's encountered. None of his usual methods so much as dent it. Cullman outpost apparently has something to hide and the resources to do it.

"Assign someone to crack that firewall. I want to see what's going on in Cullman. How soon before we can get a bird overhead? I want an orbital sweep as soon as possible," Corso orders.

"We can divert the Fitzgerald but that would take it out of range of the freighter's impact point," Mallory said.

"No. We need that data. What are our other options?" Corso asks.

"There's a shuttle coming out of Shennong in just over ten minutes. We could divert it enough to side-scan the outpost as it ascends to orbit," Ben suggests.

"Do it," Corso commands. Ben relays the orders to his staff. Turning to Mallory, Corso continues. "I also want all available information on that freighter and what it was carrying, including her pilot." Corso's familiar deep voice inspires confidence in his people and the growing number of citizens linked from afar. This is quickly becoming the top link across the Republic.

"That task is already underway," Mallory said, pauses a moment and said, "The Fitzgerald is coming into position."

The Fitzgerald provides a bird's eye view, as though they are flying above the ill-fated ships trajectory, marked by a thin yellow line below. The three officers wait expectantly for the first signs of the crash.

The tension builds as they approach the projected impact location. The first thing they see is a long gouge down one side of a broad valley. The debris field starts about two-thirds down the slope and continues across the floor. It ends at the remains of the titanium superstructure. It's twisted and bent but somehow, it protected the freighter's pilothouse, more or less. The engines are gone, shredded into thousands of pieces, only the dense hard nozzles remain recognizable. Several cargo crates had skipped across the surface like flat stones across water, their impact points visible for hundreds of meters.

The three officers began independent searches, taking full advantage of the depth of the data flowing in. Each of them approaches the situation from a different angle. Corso finds traces of human remains as he probes what is left of the pilothouse, Ben sweeps for any electronic signal and Mallory looks at the freighter's cargo.

"The site is electronically dead," Ben reports.

"I've got a shipping crate with an anomalous signature," Mallory said. The other two officers link with her. From around the edges of its damaged lid, one of the containers is emitting the barest whisper of energy. Yet, when she scans inside the crate, all that shows is a large industrial check valve, common throughout Luna. It's a mechanical part with no need of an internal power source and thus, there's no reason for energy to be leaking from this shipping crate, but it's hard to argue with facts.

"Can you tell what's generating the signal Magi?" Corso asks.

Magi runs the data through hundreds of different optimizations, comparing it to everything in her database. "Negative, the best I can do is narrow the signature down to a common fuel cell, nothing special about it at all," the AI said.

Still, energy coming from a place where it should not is cause for concern, especially in light of everything that's occurred in the last few days. This entire thing feels wrong to Corso, and he learned long ago to pay attention to his gut.

"We need some eyes out at that crash site ASAP." Corso rumbles to no one in particular.

ЯL

Malik moves swiftly through the office and onto the balcony. Imam Bakr sits watching the preparations taking place on the floor below, a glass of wine in his hand.

"*Yes. What is it?*" the Imam said in Arabic.

"*Imam. The freighter bringing us the bombs has crashed.*" Malik said. He dreads being the one to tell him but learned long ago that it's better to give bad news quickly. Being a cautious man, Malik wears his helmet just in case the Imam flies into one of his fits of rage.

Imam Bakr reaches for his helmet. "*Where did it crash?*" he fumbles at the mechanical seals before finally getting it secure. According to regulations, he should have Malik check it but that seldom happens.

"*Three hundred kilometers out on Mare Nubium,*" Malik said. "*Sensors from the Houris tracked the ship but could not determine why it crashed.*" He feeds the vid to the Imam's helmet. It shows the frantic last flight of Evolution's Child, pinpointing the exact location of her final resting place.

270

The Imam immediately concludes that someone needs to go out and either retrieve the nukes or destroy them along with any evidence. He doesn't care what happened to the freighter to make it crash and it never occurs to him to consider any survivors that might need help. His mind has moved on, weighing his options, planning what his response should be to minimize this disaster.

Turning back to Malik He asked, *"Do the infidels know of the crash?"*

"I know not of a certainty but it would surprise me if they missed it. They have a very good sensor and communications network and the ship passed just north of Alphonsus crater. It crashed not far from Al Fahad." Malik said.

Al Fahad is the Brotherhood's only city on Luna. Located in the rim of Lassell crater, it lies 240 kilometers southwest of Alphonsus, well out on the Sea of Clouds.

Sheik Mohammad Abas rules Al Fahad with an iron hand. He's undeniably the most powerful Muslim on Luna and he's in a vile mood when Imam Bakr opens a channel to him. He reviews the vid before raising one eyebrow and looking down his long nose at the Imam. *"What is it you would have me to do? I cannot spare any ships."*

The Sheik is dressed traditionally in a gray Imam's overgarment, the white dishadasha visible down the front, and a white shora with a black egal on his head, all of the highest quality. The man's intensity makes Imam Bakr uneasy, reminding him of the depth of his dislike. It's obvious to Imam Bakr that the Sheik will not be doing any fighting today. His men would face death without him.

"Then send trucks and rovers. The crash site is only 135 kilometers from Al Fahad. They can be there in two hours. We cannot allow this shipment to fall into enemy hands." Imam Bakr argues vehemently.

"I agree," Major General Arif joins the conversation. It's his right as Supreme Commander to monitor any communications. He doesn't bother vidcasting, letting his tone convey his displeasure. *"Sheik Abas,*

how many men can you spare?" He asked.

The Sheik sighs in resignation, *"Perhaps twenty."*

"We must secure that cargo. Send a full company of your men and I will supplement them with a frigate from my fleet. If I can spare a ship then you can spare a single company." Unspoken words hang heavy between the men. They all know the Minister insisted on delivering the weapons this way, and none of them, not even Major General Abdel Salam Arif, Supreme Commander of the Islamic Expeditionary Force, has the balls to place the blame at his feet. Too many have died after saying far less.

"As you will," the Sheik bows his head in submission. Only his eyes tell a different tale. Some day he will deal with the arrogant dog, Bakr, permanently.

The General thanks Allah that he had the foresight to transport the warheads in three shipments. The Shennong and Kyoto forces already have theirs. He mentally runs through their location.

"Imam Bakr, we must arm you properly if the will of Allah is to be accomplished... I will have two warheads sent immediately. You should receive them within the hour. Imam, your task remains the same, secure Alphonsus Complex." As Supreme Commander, Major General Arif resents the fact he must nursemaid his subordinates. They know as well as he the importance of maintaining discipline within the plan. *"Allah Akbar,"* he said dismissing them.

"Allah Akbar," they echo, both assuming the General is still listening. Only now, it's no longer Imam Bakr's problem.

"When you have secured the bombs, send them to me. I will proceed as planned," Imam Bakr said.

"Inshallah... As Allah wills," Sheik Abas said before his image disappears, his look that of a lion contemplating a jackal.

The department's cafeteria is not a five star restaurant by anyone's definition but the food is hot and plentiful. Brice, Corazon, Tempel, Lazarus, and Kitajima sit at a table against the far wall. The rest of Quan Kiai and about a hundred other police officers are spread out across the room eating and talking quietly. The subdued hum of conversation and the occasional clank from the kitchen provides familiar background to their meal.

Captain Kitajima Osaka makes it a point to eat with his team as often as he can. It gives him a chance to evaluate them outside the training environment and keeps him in touch with their emotional state. He's not interested in their personal problems but is concerned with how well they handle them, and he likes the camaraderie. It reminds him of his days playing professional football.

When Ben vidcasts next to the dining table, he quickly becomes the focal point of everyone present. "Greetings Kitajima. We have a situation out on the Sea of Clouds. View the vid."

Magi is aware of Kitajima's human limitations and adjusts the playback accordingly, increasing the speed in some sections and slowing it down in others, thus allowing him to gather the pertinent facts as fast as his mental processes can manage. She ends it on a close-up of the damaged crate. Lazarus shares the playback with Kitajima but has a hard time keeping up. The images move by too fast for his untrained mind to grasp. For the rest of the platoon, Magi presents it at sixty-times normal speed.

"Corso wants you and your Highlanders to find out what's going on. Captain Marquest will go with you for technical support but you will be in charge. Clear?" Ben said to Kitajima.

"Clear, but Ben, I can handle this without Lindsey. She can link with us when we get there," Kitajima said.

"Corso wants her with you. You may need her engineering skills before this is finished," Ben replies.

"I should go too," Lazarus blurts out, breaking etiquette.

Kitajima turns and looks at him. "What? Why should you go?"

"I know Brotherhood hardware. If the IB is involved in this, I'll be able to help," Lazarus claims.

"He's right," Lindsey said, her image appearing next to Bens. "Taking him along is a good idea."

"He's not yet a full citizen. What if he falls apart on us out there?" Kitajima asks, glancing at the man across the table from him. "No offense," he said.

Lazarus shrugs.

"I'll vouch for him. He performed as well as anyone at the hospital, and he's cleared for surface duty. I say give him a commission and let's go," Tempel said.

"Take him along," Corso said, appearing on Ben's right. "He may prove useful."

"Corso, what is it you're not telling me?" Kitajima asks, looking intently at his boss. Beneath the hard exterior, Corso is worried.

"The probability is high the Brotherhood may cause trouble for you on this mission. I'm authorizing Quan Kiai to deploy wearing ghost suits and a full complement of weapons. I'll trust your discretion when to use them," Corso said.

Kitajima knew this day would come but now that it's here, it rattles him to his core. "Understood. How are we going to get there?" He asked.

"Use the Moonhawk that was to take you to Far Point. It's already modified for troop transport and has supplies aboard. I'm commandeering another from a spaceline, one set up as a cargo ship. By the time you get your gear down to the terminal, I'll have it," Ben said.

"Two Moonhawks and sixteen officers? You sure that's enough?" Kitajima asks.

"Ben's working on another angle, but to be brutally honest, Quan Kiai is what we have, so… make it work." Corso said.

"Aye. Make it work," Kitajima said.

ℛℒ

Tempel strips and heads for the showers. Around him, the rest of Quan Kiai is doing much the same. He washes quickly and returns to his locker. After applying lubricant, he slips on the long duration under-garment, an integral part of the recycling system. He takes his time getting everything where it belongs.

Sitting on his bench, Tempel shakes powder across his legs and pulls the suit up making sure every joint is right before going on. Standing, he works his arms down one sleeve, then the other, letting the ghost suit settle around his body like a second skin. He feels the familiar tingle when it aligns with the implant in the base of his spine. He lifts his arms over his head and flexes at the waist.

Perfect fit.

Hanging behind him like a hood, he pulls the skullcap over his head adjusting it around his visor. He draws the edges together, fusing the molyseals. When he's finished, the ghost suit looks like it was a single piece of material. It completely encloses Tempel and turns him into a silhouette without any depth, a smear of darkness that fools the eye.

The ghost suit's flexible outer layer absorbs light and prevents reflections in a phenomenon known as blackbody. The visual details that would normally give the suit depth and breadth are beyond human perception. It looks flat, like a shadow.

Tempel watches Tatiana tug her skullcap down, waiting for her to come online. Like a wisp of smoke, the featureless black of her ghost suit fades away, replaced by the black and gray uniform of a police lieutenant. Sensors within the suit transmit not only her current expression, but a change of clothing as well.

Tempel reaches into his locker and picks up his Model 450, Smith and Wesson. He checks the charge level before slipping it into its holster. Closing his locker, he joins the others.

ЯL

The Moonhawk, or Boeing L250, is the most common flight transport on Luna, the workhorse of the 21st century, the backbone of Luna's transportation industry with a history spanning decades. Designed by Lunarians to haul people or light cargo from place to place, it's not intended for deep space long hauls but can easily go anywhere in the Earth/Luna system and back again. It can even navigate Mother Earth's atmosphere just as easily as the vacuum of space. It's the latest in a long line of ships designed by a people born in space.

While Lunarians highly value beauty for its own sake, they are intensely practical when it comes to their engineering. Any aerospace engineer will tell you that minimizing mass is much more important than a sweet set of curves. When you point out the graceful curves of a Moonhawk, they will assure you that its form comes from purely physical considerations.

Kitajima orders ten high G seats taken from Moonhawk One and installed on the cargo ship Ben commandeered. He designates this ship Moonhawk Two. Consuela will pilot Moonhawk One with Kipper copiloting. Tempel will pilot Moonhawk Two with Karyl as his copilot. He assigns Lazarus and Lindsey to Moonhawk Two and keeps the rest of Quan Kiai with him.

Kitajima moves up the aisle inspecting his officers and offering last minute encouragement.

The remains of Evolution's Child has been identified over three hundred kilometers out on the mare, a hop, skip, and jump for a Moonhawk. Still, Kitajima insists on taking a full ration of supplies with extra air. You can never have too much air. More than once, a simple day trip has turned into an extended ordeal and he rather enjoys breathing.

"The equipment's secure," Kipper reports. It's the copilot's responsibility to ensure the proper stowing of cargo.

Kitajima nods, "Aye. Let's get this show on the road." He moves up the aisle one last time, asking each officer if they're ready. He never had children, and over the last few years, these young men and women became his kids. They were seventeen when he formed Quan Kiai and he thinks of himself more as their coach than their captain. It's as close as Kitajima will ever get to playing football again.

Starting out with a bunch of know-it-all third and fourth generation Lunarians, Kitajima coaxed and harassed them into a team and now he's leading them into harm's way.

Kipper eases into the copilot's seat and straps in. The preflight checklist is almost complete. Consuela has been busy.

Kitajima settles into his seat and looks across the aisle at Master Sergeant Hackling, "We ready to go Hack?"

She was born in Houston, Texas in 2013 and was only four when her family moved. Less than a month later, on the morning of September 11, 2017, a five-megaton nuclear explosion destroyed the city killing most of her family. She grew up in the shadow of that horrible event.

"Aye. Locked and loaded," she replies.

"Excellent," Kitajima links with Tempel in the other Moonhawk. "Lieutenant Dugan, what is your status?"

Karyl flashes Tempel a thumbs-up.

"We're locked and loaded," Tempel said.

"Then let's roll," Kitajima said.

Tempel perceives everything through a multitude of sensors, in his visor, in his ghost suit, on the Moonhawk and spread throughout the environment around him. His visor combines the various data-streams, presenting Tempel with a single consolidated view of the world, but one that is malleable and dynamic. Reality becomes nothing more than a backdrop to display information.

From Tempel's perspective, he's hanging in space, the seat beneath him, and the safety harness that holds him the only tactile objects in his world. On his right, Karyl, his copilot, is the only other person in sight. The Moonhawk and everyone else aboard the ship are invisible, filtered out as unneeded visual information.

The long lunar night is coming on rapidly and the sun is low on the horizon, casting the crater's floor in deep shadow. Tempel adjusts his visor and the shadows recede. He enjoys flying at night but this is no joy ride.

"Moonhawk One, follow my lead straight out past New London and over Rim Mountain on the farside. The crash site is just over three-hundred kilometers out."

"Aye, Moonhawk Two. I'm on your six," Consuela replies.

"Luna Central, we're go for liftoff," Tempel said.

Dust stirs under the ship's thrusters as Luna Central said. "You're go for liftoff. Good Luck."

Tempel doesn't so much fly his ship as tell the onboard AI where he wants to go. The delicate balance between the four powerful magnetoplasma thrusters is too precarious to trust to human reflexes, even his.

In complete silence, the Moonhawks turn their tails up and accelerate across the crater's floor. They leave behind the brightly lit surface installations clustered outside Aldrin Station.

The floor of Alphonsus Crater is a series of undulating hills and ragged ridges that follow the general concentric pattern of the crater-forming impact. Originating at pit-like vents, channels and collapsed lava tubes form rills that run for many kilometers cutting across the ridges like a knife through butter. These fissures can be quite deep and pose a serious threat to anyone careless enough to fall in, even in Luna's gravity.

Tempel maintains a flight path parallel with the maglev rail. They pass the Mitsuki smelter, its tanks and towers brilliantly awash in lights. Gases spew skyward from its stack dispersing in the vacuum. Beyond it, a blue light marks the impact location of Ranger 9, one of the earliest moon missions.

The flight passes almost directly over the top of Archibald Mine. Its access road coming in from New London looks like a string of festival lights. Sensors, antennas and other constructions are clearly visible on the summit of Central Peak.

The Moonhawks continue to climb and gain speed emerging from shadow to full sunlight in an instant. The floor of the crater is a gray expanse four thousand meters down, its detail blurred by altitude and shadow. Night is almost upon them. They're flying directly into the sinking Sun and clear Rim Mountain with fifty meters to spare.

The Sea of Clouds, or Mare Nubium in Latin, is a flat plain extending over the horizon. The basaltic plain formed when a large impact cracked Luna's crust allowing lava to flood hundreds of square kilometers. Wrinkle-ridges formed as the thick layer of basalt slowly cooled and contracted over thousands of years. They align in a washboard pattern across the great plain, like waves on a sea.

Later, smaller volcanic events created a number of sinuous rilles running for many kilometers. They stretch across the mare's surface. Some are collapsed lava tubes. In other cases, the lava flows cut channels by simply melting their way down into the older rocks, much like rivers cut into their flood plains back on Mother Earth.

"ETA ten minutes," Tempel announces.

The Sea of Clouds stretch as far as Tempel can see. Using the ships scanners, he sweeps all around their flight path looking for movement. Nothing. He links with the other transport but even using both sets in tandem, he still comes up empty. Even so, Quan Kiai prepares as if an army were waiting for them. They check and recheck their weapons and vacsuits for the umpteenth time.

From all across Luna, hundreds of thousands of citizens link to the Highlanders. Quan Kiai's mission is currently the third most watched event on the net. By the time they land, they will be number one.

"Prepare for touchdown," Tempel announces. The hills roll by slower and slower but are now less than a hundred meters below.

"Consuela, you take the left. I'll go right." Tempel said.

"Aye," Consuela replies.

A deep scar marks where the freighter hit and plowed down the side of the valley. They follow the track across the floor keeping their scanners busy mapping the debris field during the approach.

The ship's scanners work together measuring and marking every artifact scattered across the surface, every furrow gouged in the lunar dust, and every displaced rock. It's the first step in piecing together what happened to Evolution's Child during her final touchdown.

As the Moonhawks approach the end of the debris trail, most of the larger parts of the freighter begin appearing. They come upon the twisted remains of the pilothouse. The framework had been able to protect it to a degree. Beyond it are parts of the engine section and fuel tanks. Pieces of the magnetoplasma thrusters are the only items immediately recognizable. Everything else is twisted wreckage or buried in regolith.

They continue to follow skid marks across the surface another two hundred meters. The cargo came loose on impact and survived in remarkably good shape.

Kitajima selects a flat spot near the crates. "I've marked your LZ. Acknowledge."

"Confirmed," Tempel replies.

"Confirmed," Consuela echoes. "See you on the ground."

General Council

*"A man's ethical behavior should be based effectually on
sympathy, education, and social ties; no religious basis is
necessary. Man would indeed be in a poor way if he had to be
restrained by fear of punishment and hope of reward after death."*

Albert Einstein (1879-1955)

The Assembly Chamber is a giant open-sky stadium with Mother
Earth and the stars shinning overhead in all their glory. The setting sun
casts most of the seating in deep shadow. Only the uppermost rows on
one side are still in bright sunlight.

The Council's never truly out of session. Somewhere there's always
something going on in the cyberspace government. Today, at her request,
Counselor Abigail Dugan addresses the General Assembly with most of
Luna linked.

Abby walks slowly out onto the Assembly Floor. A virtual breeze
tugs at her robes. She looks up at the gathering and turns in a slow circle.
A hundred thousand Counselors stare back. A hush falls across the great
amphitheater and she begins to speak. "I want to begin by thanking
those who aided Dakota and Aldrin Station during this time of tragedy.
Our citizens are forever in your debt." She bows her head then looks
up with fire in her eyes. "As you already know, the bombing at Lincoln
County Hospital was no accident. I now show you a vid authenticated
just minutes ago of at least three nuclear devices destined for Little
America and ultimately, Aldrin Station."

Virtually every citizen is aware of what's going on out at Nell's Valley. "The time is past that we can sit back and do nothing. Our forgiveness has led the Brotherhood to view us as weak and ripe for the picking. This time we must take action. The people responsible must be held accountable."

Councilor Taylor appears beside Abby on the Assembly Floor. "I agree. We must find the people responsible and punish them. Who are they? Tell me. I will personally strike them down." He's much older in appearance, with long flowing white hair and gray robes that whip about him in the virtual wind.

Pacing the floor, Abby addresses the Councilors, "You know who carries the ultimate responsibility. It can be laid at the feet of Prince Ahmed Mohammed Al Zarqowi, Caliph of the Islamic Brotherhood."

Councilor Taylor remains standing in the center of the floor. "Unless you know something that I don't, there's no proof of his involvement, and all the circumstantial evidence in the Republic can't change that. If we overreact, we play into their hands. Earth's non-aligned nations will see us as warmongers." He speaks for a large majority, those who would do almost anything to avoid open conflict.

Abby shakes her head. "We are at war Councilor. Make no mistake about it. People are dying."

"I have seen the data and there is nothing to indicate the attack on Lincoln County Hospital wasn't the act of a single individual or group, and you are just beginning to gather information on whose bombs are out on the mare. Until we know for sure, we cannot assume it was the Brotherhood. We cannot allow a few misguided individuals to influence our decisions. We must stay focused on the big picture." Councilor Taylor speaks with the conviction of many years of experience at holding this unpleasantness at arm's length, reiterating a position well established within the Republic.

Abby expected this and doesn't let it slow her down, "Because there's more than one device out there, they probably had a plan other than just blowing us up. My guess is blackmail of some kind, but I stress, we don't know yet."

"Be reasonable Abby. You don't expect us to declare war on the Brotherhood do you?" Councilor Yang Lee appears next to Taylor. He interlocks his fingers and brings them up in front of his robes as though in prayer and said earnestly, "Abby, we go back many years. If you need help, we will gladly give it. But to declare war on the most powerful Muslim empire in history is pure suicide."

"To do nothing is also suicide, Councilor. Past protestations haven't worked and the attacks are escalating. We must break from this myopic approach to our safety, to our very survival. We need orbital fighters. We need to arm our transports and rovers. In short, we need to prepare for war."

"Out of the question," explodes Councilor Taylor. "That would be a clear violation of the Treaty of Independence. We can't fight Mother Earth."

"The Brotherhood is not all of Earth. If we don't prepare our defenses, we risk losing everything. If we do prepare we risk making a few Earth nations nervous." The numbers are shifting but the majority of the council still favors maintaining status quo. She's frustrated at her inability to persuade more to come to her side. It seems reason is not enough.

"Look at the facts," Abby implores. With a gesture, she posts a virtual graph within the chamber. Its timeline extends back half a century and shows the buildup of the Brotherhood's military forces, both in space and on Luna. "Orbital stations, factories, shipyards, and mining facilities, all show a steady growth pattern with one thing in common, every single one of them are military installations. The Brotherhood wants us to believe that instead of a military buildup, this is simply a healthy dose of self-defense. Well, I don't believe it."

"Yes Abby, we've all seen the data and nothing's changed." Councilor Taylor said irritably. "We're going over the same issues time and again. They have followed the rules and have the right to be off world."

"Why do they need so many battlestations? Here on Luna and at Hyundai Shipyards, the increase in manpower far outstrips any projected need," she has raised these issues many times over the last year. "Can anybody tell us what's going on inside Al Fahad? Why can't we send an envoy to inspect the place? I don't buy the Holy City crap."

"Ambassador Omar has answered all of these questions to everyone's satisfaction," Councilor Beverly Salazar said reasonably.

"Not to mine." Abby retorts. "The good ambassador has been kept in the dark so he can speak to us with truth in his heart, even as his countrymen prepare for war. Why hasn't he ever been inside the city or aboard any of their big ships?"

"You admit Ambassador Omar has always been truthful with us then accuse him of deception. You're doing everyone a disservice by your insatiable personal attacks on him." Councilor Salazar angrily said. As the representative of Johanson, one of Shennong's largest freeholds, she's had frequent close encounters with the ambassador and has grown to trust him. She resents Abby for what she perceives as character assassination of a friend.

"Do you have any real proof to go along with these allegations?" Councilor Taylor's question hangs in the air for a moment, "I thought not. This is all circumstantial. Not something to base a decision that will have such far reaching consequences."

Coming over to confront Councilor Taylor, Abby asks him, "Have you reviewed the data on active camouflage? Or do you want to hold it in your hand before you will believe it's real?"

"I'm told it's scientifically impossible to fool an MRI scanner. There must be another explanation." Councilor Taylor said holding his ground.

"I'm not willing to risk the fate of the Republic on the hope that something doesn't exist, especially in the face of overwhelming evidence to the contrary." Abby shifts her attention back to the assembly, "I call on the Council to initiate full visual inspections of everything moving on Luna or in Lunarian space. Until we know for sure what's happening, it's only prudent to take every precaution."

She pauses giving the citizens time to vote. Polls gather the data in a matter of seconds. A council member is not obligated to cast his or her vote according to these polls but most do. After all, their constituency can remove them from the Council at any time by a similar vote. It's politically prudent to agree with the masses unless you had a damn good reason not to.

Abby's relieved that the majority favors the inspections, even though it will put many of them in hardship. Surprisingly, several of the smaller Aldrin Station freeholds abstain. They had felt Rim Mountain shake around them when Lincoln County Hospital exploded. What are they thinking?

"Fine, we'll have inspections but it's a waste of time and money," Councilor Taylor said.

Abby ignores him, "I call on the Council to issue a statement that those responsible for the Lincoln County Hospital bombing will be brought to justice."

Amidst a flurry of activity, Abby watches as the open ballot fractures into a growing number of alternate responses ranging from doing nothing to declaring war, with many points in between. No clear majority emerges from the chaos. Councilor Taylor cannot keep the smirk from his face.

Deep down, Abby knew it would inevitably come to this. "As Dakota freehold's Councilor, I'll issue my own statement. In it I will express my outrage and anger and I will promise retribution for this atrocity."

The chamber erupts, reverberating with the zeal of council members wanting to tell her how wrong that would be.

"We have 451 dead." Abby thunders angrily over the uproar. "There damn well **IS** going to be a response."

"You cannot go against the wishes of the Council." Councilor Taylor retorts.

"Like hell I can't. I've done it before and will do it again." Abby replies, "This issue needs to be dealt with aggressively and expediently. History is full of examples showing what happens when it's not. Wars are not started by people who believe they *MIGHT* win. They are started by those who believe they *WILL* win. That belief alone poses our greatest threat. At the very least there should be a conviction of mutually assured destruction to keep aggressors at bay." Abby leans forward intently. She must make them see how precarious their position actually has become.

"We have nothing. We are helpless. We cannot fight orbiting battlestations. We are reliant on the Federation, the European Union, and China to compel the Brotherhood to leave us alone. Can't you see this illusion crumbling before your eyes? Just because you wish something to be true, doesn't make it so. This bombing isn't the end, anymore than the one before it, or the one before that. They'll never stop until we're all dead."

"I'm shocked at you Abigail." Councilor Taylor roars indignantly. "I never would have thought I would live to see the day that you resorted to such blatant scare tactics. The Treaty of Independence protects us."

"The Treaty's not worth the paper it's written on. Do you actually believe any Earth nation will come to our aid? And now they have brought nuclear weapons to our world." Abby steps forward as if making up her mind. In a whirlwind of change, public opinion has shifted dramatically to her side. When push comes to shove, there are many citizens willing to stand with Abby.

"Those who are with me, convene at this netsite. We have a common defense to plan." Abby's voice rings with authority.

Rising like an apparition, Abby soars upwards until she's hovering in the volumetric center of the Council Chamber. Spreading her arms wide, she begins to rotate, growing larger with each passing second, five, ten, a hundred times normal size until she dominates the amphitheater. Above, the stars and Mother Earth morph into a mottled jumble of human faces. Over a million Lunarian citizens are staring down at her. She's literally speaking to every person in the Republic.

"My fellow Lunarians. The time for debate is at an end. The coming days will test us as a people. Hold on to your convictions and have faith in each other. We shall prevail."

Like a rock dropped in a deep pool, Abby disappears from the chamber, leaving turmoil in her wake.

ЯL

Corso's interest in the developments at the crash site is secondary to his immediate need to strengthen Aldrin Station's defenses. The single overriding fact that there are nukes out on the Sea Of Clouds is all he needs to know. How can anyone perceive that as anything but a major attack on the Republic of Luna? Yet, there are many among the Council who still want to believe it's an isolated event and thus, his problem. It's amazing the number of certifiable fools that think appeasing the shortimers will avoid a war. Abby is still trying to enlist more freeholds but Corso can't afford to wait.

"Mallory, inform Luna Central that I want all incoming flights suspended until further notice. Nothing comes within fifty kilometers unless it has explicit permission from me personally," Corso commands.

Major Higgins frowns, "Aye, immediately." She knows what a stink this will cause in more than one freehold.

"Ben, call all available officers. I want additional surface patrols with orders to physically search everything that moves."

"Aye," Captain Ben Dugan said.

"Sir. Councilor Taylor has requested a word with you," Magi informs

Corso.

"What is it Councilor. I'm rather busy," Corso said, not trying to hide his dislike. Their animosity goes back many years.

"You have exceeded your authority by trying to discontinue flights into the city. I have rescinded your order. I will bring it up during the meeting scheduled for this evening. The full Council will decide if that's a necessary step," Councilor Taylor said.

Molding his emotions into something primeval and brutal, Corso moves his face within centimeters of Councilor Taylor's. "Zachary, are you challenging me?" His eyes are hard black flints. Each man knows what the other is feeling. They cannot bluff. They cannot hide.

Councilor Taylor loses the battle of wills and backs away, "Certainly not. You must go through proper channels. That's all."

"Good, for a minute there I thought you were challenging me… because if you were to rescind an order from me, I would take that as an open challenge," Corso growls.

"A few hours will not matter," Councilor Taylor said quickly, fear twisting his gut. Dueling with Corso is not something he wants to do, ever.

"You can't possibly know what will and will not matter." his glare burns a hole in Councilor Taylor. "This is what you WILL do. You WILL call Luna Central and you WILL tell them that my order stands. Do I make myself CLEAR?"

Even though the two men are vidcasting, the Councilor can't stand up to Corso, "Yes, perfectly."

"Good, now go do it."

Councilor Taylor plays politics and vidcasts with his supporters before fulfilling Corso's command. In those few minutes, a transport lands outside Little America and a single crate emerges. It's hustled inside and taken straightaway to SMT trucking.

Malik rides in the Goliath pulling the lead convoy with nothing in front of him but the enemy. At his back are twenty thousand of the best vacuum-rated troops the Brotherhood can field. They're in the access tunnels below Little America heading for Aldrin Station.

Three hundred meters from the crossover checkpoint, Malik spots two Lunarian police officers.

"*Wait for my command.*" Malik orders in Arabic.

At two hundred meters, he finds the third and fourth.

A moment later, one of the Lunarians points at the approaching Goliath. The enormous bulk of Malik's vehicle hides the long line of troop carriers that stretches out behind it.

Malik initiates his jammer, shutting down all but line-of-sight communications within the tunnel then fires the first shot of the war. Targeting the nearest unbeliever, the raw energy of his laser cannon overloads the ability of the infidel's vacsuit to absorb it allowing the shot to penetrate deep into its chest. The intense heat of the beam instantly turns whatever it touches into boiling hot gases. The torso of the Lunarian explodes in a blood red fog and falls to the floor. Involuntarily, Malik lets out a yelp. Allah has granted him the honor of the first kill.

With amazing speed and agility, the second Lunarian springs onto the top of the Goliath right above Malik's head and continues to leap from one carrier to the next attracting a lot of attention. This completely catches Malik by surprise.

"*Allah help us.*" Malik curses.

"*Where did it go?*" another asks.

The gunners in the carriers behind Malik's open up but the Lunarian avoids death for several seconds. The gun emplacement on the fourth carrier finally nails him during mid leap.

"*Where's the others?*" Malik asks.

"There's one. Running for the airlock."

"It's mine." Malik declares.

Malik's shot hits it square in the back. The figure sprawls face first and is still. The convoy runs over it like road kill. The fourth Lunarian has vanished.

"Keep moving." Malik commands.

ЯL

Commonway traffic is light this morning. Councilor Lee Chin attributes it to the horrible bombing at Lincoln County Hospital. Hunan freehold lost fourteen citizens and publicly added their outrage to the groundswell of support Dakota is receiving. He talked briefly to Abby Dugan a few hours ago offering condolences and personally making two companies of officers available to her and Security Chief Corso.

Councilor Chin's not happy this morning and not even the beautiful trees of Sherwood Forest can break the feeling of dread weighing heavy on his heart. It's come to his attention that a major subcontractor is disregarding the Law of Full Disclosure. Hunan freehold will end their relationship with Imam Bakr and SMT, effective immediately. He'll find another company to haul ore.

Imam Bakr, a religious and political leader among the Muslim community, arrived on Luna almost ten years ago. He purchased Surface Master Trucking, a medium sized transport company operating in the Central Highlands. His company has been absorbing smaller operations ever since. There didn't seem to be any bottom to his deep pockets. In 2092, SMT dominates the transport industry in the Four Craters Region with almost sixty percent of the business.

Councilor Chin's confident he's making the right decision but anticipates a fierce fight. No help for it. He wants to be at Wangshiyuan Refinery for the showdown surrounded by loyal friends and coworkers. He rests his hand on the butt of his sidearm.

Over the years, he's past through Stoneshire many times on his way to the refinery. He's a familiar face along the cobblestone street and several people wave. Nearing the far end of the village, he takes a path between two buildings.

Here, in this remote corner of Aldrin Station, is a small garden. It started out as a school project for his youngest daughter but soon grew into an opportunity for Lee Chin to teach her some of the ancient Chinese traditions. The two of them spent many enjoyable hours here. Lee Chin stops on the bridge to let the garden calm his spirit.

With the thunderclap of a lightning strike, a disrupter beam rips the atmosphere, hitting Councilor Chin above his right eye, relentlessly burning through his brain and emerging behind his left ear. His head explodes. The decapitated body topples off the bridge and into the pond.

Seconds later, a Goliath rolls over Lee Chin and his exquisite little garden. High explosive missiles slam into Stoneshire and powerful disrupters burn anything that moves. The invaders pulverize the village and head down Sherwood Commonway towards the heart of the city.

ЯL

The Longbow massdriver is a ten-kilometer railgun that shoots two-ton bullets at a muzzle velocity of six thousand meters per second. Its primary target is Lagrange One Space Station but by the time they reach it, their speed is almost zero. Catching the bullets is one of the most mundane jobs on the station.

The Lagrange duty officer notices the PDM at ten thousand meters. She goes back and inventories what she's already collected. *Strange. They're all accounted for.* She pulls up the schedule and finds nothing amiss. The PDM is now only a few thousand meters away. She sweeps it with MRI. *Just another load of titanium.* Somebody must have made a mistake. She snags the extra PDM and brings it aboard with the others.

The nuclear warhead camouflaged inside the PDM detonates

vaporizing Lagrange One. A new star flashes into existence above the Republic of Luna. Gamma rays and x-rays stream outward at the speed of light disrupting communications and overloading unprotected electronics. Battlestation Houris moves in to take the place of Lagrange One almost before the fireball has dissipated.

The swarm's trajectory put deep space behind them. Virtually impossible to see using conventional scanners, they appear simply as holes in space, absorbing all energy that touches them. Small and very fast, they strike the Lunarian satellites without warning. It takes only seconds to destroy the backbone of Lunanet, the Republic's communication system.

Every warship in the Brotherhood's space fleet begins jamming all across the communication spectrum, shutting down the entire Earth-Luna system. Earthnet collapses, the first stoppage in five decades.

Brotherhood forces stationed on Hyundai Shipyards storm the Command Section taking control and shutting down all communications. The Brotherhood's commander orders the Lunarians aboard the station to gather in one of the pressurized hangers. Those who refuse will be shot on sight.

Another battlestation moves in on Taurus Colony. Major General Arif issues an ultimatum, surrender or die. The Mayor of Taurus has no choice but to allow the giant warship to dock. Two thousand troops invade his colony.

A mass exodus begins all over cislunar space. Within minutes of the destruction of Lagrange One, a thousand ships, large and small, private and corporate, boost out of orbit. Most head for Mars and some for the Belt. Only warships remain and they are all in motion.

Back on Luna, the area around Al Fahad swarms with activity. The Brotherhood stages three simultaneous operations from the city, airlifting tens of thousands of troops to Shennong and Kyoto and sending thousands more down Kahfah Road towards Aldrin Station.

The high altitude nuclear explosion sends out an intense electromagnetic pulse (EMP) that induces an incredible electrical spike in all things conductive. It overloads the electronics within every surface installation all across the Nearside, penetrating well into the underground cities themselves.

Magi's world goes crazy. Programs damaged, data scrambled, red turns blue, up goes down, and inside twists outside. Magi feels something she had never felt before... pain. The attack cuts her into pieces. Instead of a single vast collective, groups of threads are isolated and forced to cope based upon input from just a fraction of the collective.

"*AAAAAAGHGH.*" Magi screams.

A moment later, all her satellites disappear and all she can sense beyond Aldrin Station is a curtain of static. She's no longer aware of anything outside. New London, Summerhaven, Prattville, Shennong, Kyoto, and Scottsbluff are all gone in an instant. Taurus Colony, Hyundai Shipyards, and Lagrange stripped away. Magi feels more isolated than at any time in her considerable memory.

"Magi, what's happened?" Corso demands. He's never heard her scream. It unnerves even him.

"Outside contact lost... Rerouting... stand by..." Magi is barely holding it together. Rebooting the optical sensors along the top of Rim Mountain, she manages to get a few of them back online. Focusing upward where her satellites should be, she finds confetti.

"Satellite network is destroyed..." Magi said hollowly. She turns her attention to Lagrange. All she can find is an expanding cloud of cooling gas. "... Lagrange One gone." She's going into shock.

"Ben, broadcast on all channels, the Republic of Luna is at war."

"Unable to comply..." Ben said. "Communications are jammed."

The first wave of precision guided munitions descends on the

Republic, shaking the subterranean cities like a dog playing with an old sock.

"Magi, report." Corso demands.

Magi's outside awareness is degrading fast. One by one, she tries the main sensors along the top of the rim. They're all gone.

"Satellites are unresponsive..." Magi said listlessly. "Rim sensors are all offline... land lines severed..."

"What about using the sensors on the Mitsubishi smelter or one of the scientific facilities out on the crater floor?"

"Outer network is down... an optical sensor near Gun Placement RM747 did record a visual just before going dark..." Magi's image flickers and she stares off into the distance.

The bombardment is now a constant rumble.

"Show it to me," Corso orders.

The vid is less than one second long and shows a dull non-reflective object, blurry because of its extreme velocity, heading straight for the scanner. It's not much to go on.

"What do the other scanners tell us? They must show something," Mallory asks, desperation creeping into her voice.

Magi creates a collage of images, one from each scanner showing a still picture of the instant in question. All three officers study them carefully but it's Magi who finds it.

"There's a dead zone..." She enlarges the image, zooming in on where she wants them to look.

Mounted high up on a tower, this particular scanner is not part of a cannon installation. From this vantage point, it was focused downward when the incoming object passed beneath, silhouetting it against the crater floor far below. Reality had a hole in it. This and the blurry visual is all they have to go on.

"Magi, what can you tell me about this object?" Corso asks.

The sudden onslaught catches a group of miners just outside of

Bigalow Gate, ripping apart their rover and killing all seven. A hundred meters away, a squad of police officers takes shelter inside a Quonset. Moments later, it takes a direct hit. All across Luna, precision guided munitions targeted specific Lunarian properties while leaving others untouched.

"Corso. Please forgive me, I have failed." Magi wails. Her job is to protect Lunarians and they're dying.

"We need you now more than ever," Corso said.

"…so many have died… I have failed," Magi whimpers and begins to break up into a million flickering points of light. One by one, the elements that make up the image of Magi flash intensely and fade away. She dissolves right before his eyes.

"Magi." Corso repeats louder to no avail. She's gone.

ЯL

Highlanders normally patrolled in pairs, but today Sergeant Cristobal Calatrava rides alone. That's fine by him. He would much rather be riding solo under the stars than standing at some checkpoint, but what Lunarian is ever truly alone?

"It's almost a certainty she was in Lincoln County Hospital when..." raw grief chokes off his father's voice. "Son, we must admit she's gone. We may never find any trace of her, but she was there… I'm sorry Cris." He's sitting comfortably in his commonroom.

Damn. Memories of his sister overwhelm Cris. Tears blur his vision and an intense flash from above casts a stark shadow on the roadbed. The young Highlander backs off the throttle, giving his visor time to clear his eyes. His aching heart will take longer, much longer.

"Why don't you come home? Your moth…" His dad's voice abruptly cuts off.

"Pop?" Cris asks. Something's wrong. "Can anyone hear me?" The normal background chatter from the other Highlanders and nearby citizens has vanished. "Magi?" Even the ever-present 911 emergency channel is gone. He reaches up to touch his visor, assuming that something must have failed in the device. Never in his wildest dreams did he imagine anything shutting down the Lunarian communications system so thoroughly. No matter what he tries, all he can hear is static.

Cris skids the bike to a stop, plants his boots, turns and beholds a sight never before seen on Luna. In a series of brilliant flashes, amid a growing cloud of debris, the razorback ridge of Rim Mountain is silently exploding as far as he can see in both directions.

He stared in disbelief. Even at max zoom, his visor can't pick up any projectiles but their effect is unmistakable. Abruptly, a huge section of the mountainside soundlessly gives way in a giant avalanche of rock and dust. The bombardment's not limited to the distant mountaintop. It's sweeping towards him in a terrifying wave of destruction.

Cris twists the throttle. The powerful machine surges beneath him. He guns the bike off the main road and onto one of many trails that crisscross the Highlands, a rooster tail of regolith shooting out almost horizontally behind him. In the complete silence of an airless world, he heads away from civilization at breakneck speed. He grew up around here. He knows these paths like the back of his hand.

Cursing with all his heart, Cris violently throws the bike into a curve, feeling its wheelbase shorten as it gathers power. First, his sister is missing and presumed dead, and now the Republic of Luna is under attack. Cut off from everyone for the first time in his life, he feels strangely free. He harbors no doubt as to who's responsible and vows to make them pay.

Coming out of the curve, Cris releases the pent-up energy contained in the cycle and springs into the night sky. Gracefully, he and the bike soar far before again touching the surface of the moon.

Nell's Valley

"Evolution is a bankrupt speculative philosophy, not a scientific fact. Only a spiritually bankrupt society could ever believe it. ... Only atheists could accept this Satanic theory.."

Rev. Jimmy Swaggart (1935-)

Even before the thrusters shut down, Kitajima is out of his seat. As the on-site commander, he has leeway to modify the plan but so far, he's not seen anything requiring he do so. Hack will set up the field morgue,

Tatiana will take charge of security, and Tempel will lead the forensic team. This leaves him free to deal with the cargo.

"Hack, are you sure you and Sam can get things set up?" Kitajima asks her. Doc Grady will do a preliminary autopsy here to determine a cause of death and prepare for a more thorough clinical autopsy when they get back to Aldrin Station.

"Doc is available if I need more help. Stop worrying and concentrate on the cargo. I know how to do my job," she said.

"Fine. Corazon, I want those Gattling's on both Moonhawks ASAP," Kitajima orders. Strictly speaking, the guns violate the Treaty but sometimes it's more prudent to beg forgiveness then ask permission.

"Aye," Corazon replies.

"Tempel," Kitajima calls. "I want your forensics team on the road. And don't forget to bring back the freighter's AI."

"Since when do you need to tell me something as basic as that?" Tempel understands the importance of collecting good forensics. He also understands that Kitajima has the tougher assignment, dealing with the politics of the mission. "Relax. We've done this before. By the way, if you guys accidentally set off a nuke, can you give us a little warning? I might want to bend over and kiss my ass goodbye."

Kitajima chuckles. "You'll get the same warning I do, not a second sooner."

Turning to his copilot Karyl, Tempel said, "Keep your eyes open," She will stay at the controls of Moonhawk Two.

"Now who's micro-managing. Take some of your own advice and relax. My ass isn't going anywhere and I haven't closed my eyes for days." she feigns a yawn and snuggles back in her seat like a kitten getting ready for a nap.

Tempel unbuckles and rotates his seat, practically depositing him in Lindsey's lap. "Sorry" he said, "Didn't realize you were still here."

"Don't sweat it... Listen Tempel... I've been going over the data.

The freighters high acceleration must have been deliberate. No way can an AI screw-up that badly," she said. "The overrides must have been deliberately bypassed."

"I tend to agree but my training tells me to let the evidence speak for itself," he said.

"Have you ever seen a crash site?" She asked.

Frowning even deeper, Tempel said sourly, "A few."

"This one will be particularly messy," she said.

"It can't be worse than Lincoln County Hospital," Tempel said dryly.

"I'm sure you're right," Lindsey said.

"Captain Osaka doesn't like to be kept waiting."

ЯL

Brice rapidly backs the rover down the ship's ramp scattering Doc Grady and Corazon. They give him the evil eye. Brice laughs.

"Take it easy Brice." Tempel said following him down the ramp.

"Aye," Brice said with a smirk.

Tempel climbs in beside him. "I mean it Brice, now's not the time."

"I got it Lieutenant," Brice said. Brice is an excellent driver, one of the best, but he likes to push the envelope.

"Kipper, Lei, let's mount up," Tempel calls out.

The two officers walk down the ramp carrying several small cases. Lei hands one to Tempel, "Here's your sample case. You should never leave home without it," she said as she climbs into the back.

"Thanks," Tempel said, his mind already on what lies ahead.

Brice is careful to keep the rover out of the freighter's debris field even when it means rough going. The pilothouse lay twisted and broken before them and Brice stops well clear.

The officers remain silent as they approach the wreckage, their suit sensors working at full capacity, adding to the already significant amount of data cataloging the crash.

"Brice, Lei, continue to process outside. Kipper and I will go inside," Tempel said. He glances at Brice expecting a smart-ass retort.

Brice nods. He's very happy not to go in.

The freighter appears to have cart wheeled down the valley before coming to rest on its top. The engine compartment or what is left of it, points skyward, a torn and twisted mass of beams and fuel lines. Tempel circles the wreckage looking for the front door.

"Over here," Kipper calls out from the other side. "This must be the main airlock."

Using every bit of his suit's strength, Kipper manages to wrench open the outer door. Looking inside he exclaims, "The inner door is open." He's already inside when Tempel arrives.

Tempel can see lights inside as he squeezes through. This must have been the freighter's control room. He immediately becomes aware of a dark smear on practically every surface inside the room. Dried blood. Vacuum sucks all the gases and moisture out of organic material on the cellular level, ripping cell walls open and tearing complex molecules asunder. What's left is broken proteins and freeze-dried carbon chains.

"The body's over in the corner," Kipper said from the adjoining room. "More bodies in here. Magi, are you picking this up?" Kipper can barely speak.

"Aye," Magi said.

Tempel follows him. Blood covers the walls, floor and ceiling, looking like someone had painted the room brown. Making a conscious effort to steady his voice he said, "Magi, I want data on all the biologicals including fingerprints and DNA."

"Aye," she said.

"I count five on board. They're all too vacdried to make a visual ID on any of them and their bioID's are inactive," Kipper said. Without life, a bioID lacks a power source. They will remove them as evidence. "Two of them were wearing Brotherhood combat armor. I knew those psychotic god lovers had to be involved."

Tempel takes a deep breath, "Take it easy Kipper. Concentrate on the job. Let's get it done."

Kipper shudders involuntarily. "I'll finish the interior scan if you'll start processing in here." He feels guilty asking Tempel to do the dirty work but he desperately needs to leave, just for a moment.

"Go for it," Tempel said, knowing his friend will be back when he's ready.

Tempel opens his case and selects a magazine of forensic swabs. He loads it into a collection gun with a slap of his hand. Straightening, he initiates the collection program making sure the data from the gun will be stored both locally and routed to Magi back in Aldrin Station. Before he exits his visors control panel, he glances at the link monitor. Over a million. Most of Luna is looking over his shoulder.

He looks around. *Where to begin.* This isn't the first time he's processed a scene in a vacsuit, just the first time in a ghost suit. *Might as well start here. It's as good as any.* He places the collection gun muzzle against a dark smear and triggers the device. Designed to collect vacuum-dried biological materials, it hydrates a very small amount of the blood or tissue before sampling. It automatically seals and tags each specimen with who, when, what, and where. Sensors built into the collection gun analyze the samples almost as rapidly as Tempel can collect them. Magi begins the tremendous job of piecing together the broken strands of DNA. Each successive sample makes the guesses more substantial and increases the confidence levels of the data.

Tempel moves around the room, returning to reload the gun several times and store the collected samples in the case. Near the end, he notices a blood-covered helmet. From its shape, it's obviously a Brotherhood design. He lets his sensors scan it completely before setting it down. They'll bag it with the others.

He's done when Kipper returns. "I found a lot of fingerprints, mostly of one individual, I assume the pilot, but at least two others," Kipper said.

"I'm finishing sample collection. We need to bag the bodies. You ok with that?" Tempel watches for any hesitation in Kipper.

"I'm fine." Kipper said.

"I know. I just wanted to be sure you did," Tempel replies. "Brice, Lei, how are you doing on the outside. We're ready to collect the bodies and could use some help."

"Brice is mapping but I'm available," Lei said. "I'm about a half kilometer down track. It will take a minute to get back. You were right Tempel. Preliminary analysis has the freighter coming in fast and low. It slid down the slope and didn't start tumbling until it hit the valley floor. Magi calculates at least twenty rolls before coming to a stop."

"Is there enough data yet for a complete reconstruction?" Tempel asks.

"There should be when Brice gets finished," Lei said.

"Pick up the body bags from the rover on your way in. Let's get this done quickly." Tempel said.

They ended up using twenty-four different bags to put the bodies in. They couldn't tell which arm or head belonged with what torso. The two individuals wearing combat armor simplified collection slightly, but even here, the people inside had been smashed and squeezed out like toothpaste, their parts mingling with the others as they bounced about in the crash.

One by one, they bring out the bags and load them in the rover. Finished with this gruesome task, the three turn their attention to finding the ships AI. For some inexplicable reason it's missing from the console where it should be. Tempel finds the small box wedged into a space behind the fight panel. It must have ricocheted around the freighters interior. They're tough, having evolved from Data Recorders dating back to the early days of flight. In 1941, the first recorders were designed to withstand a 100 G impact, in 1965, it was raised to 1,000 Gs, and in 2042, it became 100,000 Gs. He fully expects to get valuable information from it. Lei is especially skilled at coaxing a damaged AI back to life. He puts it in the rover.

"I've got another AI," Lei reports.

The black box she's carrying is unmistakable. Why are there two? It's another question to answer.

"Brice, report," Tempel orders.

"Mapping is almost complete. I'll finish on foot and meet you back at camp in twenty minutes," Brice replies.

"Aye… Kipper, Lei, let's go," Tempel said.

Kipper takes the wheel of the rover, glad he doesn't have to share the cramped back compartment with the pile of black bags.

Lei gazes out across the valley. *What a lonely place to die.* "Magi, who was the pilot?"

"The poor girl's name was Nell Goddard," Magi answers.

"Does she have any family?"

"None living. She had two daughters, both killed in a bombing several years ago in London. She finalized a divorce to the girl's father a few months later," Magi said.

"What was she like?" Lei asks.

Magi answered by playing portions of Nell's training record. She's thin and haggard in the early vids but looks better as she progresses through the school. Her final psych exam shows a woman coping with what life has thrown at her, refusing to feel sorry for herself. Lei admires her defiant me-versus-the-world attitude.

What a desolate place for it to end. This remote lunar valley isn't any different from a thousand others except this was Nell's final touchdown. "We should name this valley after Nell. Nell's Valley," she declares.

Tempel nods agreement. "I like it. Magi, open a ballot."

The Lunarians love of voting extends into many places within their society. Citizens should always have a say in those things important to them. It would be very bad manners not to ask for the opinion of those linked.

Tempel nods in satisfaction as the tally comes in from all across Luna, "Magi, record this valley as Nell's Valley." He's never seen a poll so lopsided.

"Done"

"Magi, fill us in on what Kitajima has found." Tempel asks.

"The damaged shipping crate definitely contains nuclear weapons. It was apparently booby-trapped. Anyone tampering with the case should have caused detonation," Magi reports.

"Why didn't it go off then?" Kipper asks from the driver's seat.

"I don't know. Just be thankful it didn't. Lindsey estimates the yield at approximately ten kilotons. Small for a nuclear bomb but plenty big nonetheless," Magi said.

"What about the other crates? Do they contain bombs?" Lei asks.

"Probably… Scanning the crates shows mining equipment, but the damaged case does as well when you scan through the undamaged sides," Magi said.

Tempel frowns and links to the expedition's doctor, "Doc, you ready to do the autopsies?"

"Yes, everything's waiting," Doc Grady said, pauses and adds, "I've been following your investigation… at those G loads, they didn't suffer."

ЯL

The damaged crate had ended up partially buried in regolith but now lay exposed. Kitajima has already cleared the second crate and is almost finished with the third. A portable workbench stands nearby covered with tools and equipment. Lindsey and Lazarus are at the bench engaged in a serious conversation. Tempel heads straight for the crate.

From the outside, it appears to be a standard silica glass shipping crate used for the past fifty years. He probes past the shell finding a large ball valve inside. Nothing unusual, these are common in the smelters and refineries all across Luna.

The crash crushed one corner of the crate exposing the interior. He moves in for a better angle but can only see a small portion of what's inside. Even so, it's apparent to Tempel that what he's looking at through the opening, is not what his sensors tell him is inside the crate.

"Magi, show him the remote data taken from inside," Lazarus said.

"Aye" she said and upon Tempel's consent, immerses him in the vid.

He's looking through the eyes of a fly-sized mini sensor poking around like a bloodhound. Inside the crate is a framework cradling three identical spheres.

Beneath the shiny surface of the nearest sphere, the remote sensor maps a complex three-dimensional jigsaw puzzle designed to form a solid sphere when fitted together. Made from two hundred and forty four pieces of enriched plutonium, it has a total mass just over six kilos. The beryllium reflector looks quite capable of sustaining the reaction. Without any doubt, this is a small nuclear bomb.

"This is a Brotherhood device," Lazarus said.

"How can you tell?" Tempel asks.

"This particular design is Pakistani and over a century old. It can be traced all the way back to Dr. Abdul Qadeer Khan himself," Lazarus said.

"They upgraded the design with SuperX," Lindsey said.

"Among other things. Inside the SuperX is a matrix of detonators connected to their own internal power source. If even one is severed, the rest detonate the bomb. It's nearly tamper proof," Lazarus said.

"We got lucky. If any bombs had broken free and hit wrong, it would have gone off," Lindsey said.

"The crates held up because the crash sent them skidding along the surface instead of impacting it," Magi said.

"What about active camouflage?" Tempel asks.

"It's the inside surface," Lindsey said. "Magi, show him."

Magi projects a magnified 3D cross-section of the crate. Lindsey points to a series of faint lines.

"The inside of the crate is a SSM microcircuit capable of transmitting a hard wired signal in a reflexive response to incoming MRI. This crate transmits the signature of a standard eighty-centimeter high-pressure valve. It even uses the incoming energy as its power source. We're not sure exactly how but we're getting close. Once we understand that, we can defeat it. At least, that's the plan." Lindsey said.

"The second crate's MRI signature is a replacement head for a Stevens Hammer Mill Model 2065 and this last crate shows a common feeder assembly," Kitajima said.

"Since when is the Brotherhood capable of solid-state manufacturing?" Tempel asks.

Solid-state manufacturing creates larger structures one atom at a time. Lunarians perfected SSM technology and are widely considered the best in the business. Magnetoplasma thrusters and the fuselage of a Moonhawk are two highly visible products made using SSM.

"Don't underestimate the Brotherhood, Tempel," Lazarus said. "They're not stupid and once it's known that something can be done, some bright mind will figure out how to do it. Plus, one thing they do have is plenty of money. I'll bet they simply bought the technology and modified it."

"Can you see the irony?" Lindsey asks bitterly.

"They didn't buy it from us." Tempel replies.

"After something is bought and sold enough times, the water is so muddy no one knows where anything is anymore," Lazarus said. "The Brotherhood mastered this technique."

From the very start, the Islamic Brotherhood found itself far behind other countries in the area of space. North America, Europe, and Asia were all way out in front. However, it did not stay that way.

It didn't take long for the Brotherhood to obtain its first battlestation. They did so under the guise of research. Later, when its true nature came out, they argued they had a right to protect themselves. There was an outcry around the world but to no avail. The Brotherhood had long since learned how to get what it wanted from corporations whose only interest was in making a profit.

"Assuming there are three nukes in each crate, why did they send nine? They can't detonate all nine at the same time," Lazarus said. "These were going somewhere but where and why?"

Still staring at the crate, Lindsey pursed her lips before speaking, "Combined they would net less than two hundred kilotons. On the order of twice the Hiroshima blast but not even in the same ball park as Houston..."

"Heads up, we got company." Karyl broadcast from the cockpit, "A single ship."

The newcomer follows the length of the debris field along the same course Quan Kiai had taken.

"Who are they?" Lazarus asks tensely.

"Federation," Karyl said. It's easy to identify the right angles and straight lines of a six passenger Starcraft, small and fast but not the caliber of a Moonhawk.

"I'll do the talking. Stay on your toes people," Kitajima orders. He'd been half expecting the NAF to show up. Kitajima accepts the link and Inspector Callahan appears.

"Greetings, Captain Osaka. I hope you don't mind if I join your little party." Inspector Callahan's just one of many Federation, Chinese, and European officials stationed on Luna for the purpose of making sure the Republic does not break the Treaty of Independence. By law, treaty inspectors can go wherever they please and observe but are not to interfere.

"Greetings Inspector," Kitajima said, "Would you go away if I said I did mind?" Callahan can be a major pain in the ass at times.

"This is quite a mess. What do you suppose happened?" the Inspector asks. Kitajima always tells the truth, he just needs to ask the right question.

"One of our freighters crashed," Kitajima answers dryly, pauses and adds, "We're still obtaining data and until it's been thoroughly analyzed, I can't tell you what happened. Besides, it's policy not to discuss any aspect of a case that isn't yet released under the Law of Full Disclosure." Luna citizens are free to link and observe anytime they like, even during the preliminary stages of an investigation.

"Of course it is." Inspector Callahan is fully aware of the line drawn between Lunarians and everyone else. "I understand."

As they talk, his ship lands beside Moonhawk One. The airlock opens and three figures emerge making a beeline for the group gathered around the crates.

They're wearing standard issue Federation vacsuits that haven't changed in over thirty years. They have no power assist, no armor, and no electromagnetic shields. A crest on their helmets has a built-in light right above their faceplates. All three carry sidearms.

Kitajima motions Tempel to follow him into the shadows. Laboratory tests indicated Federation sensors would have problems detecting ghost suits and this confirms it. The Lunarians are virtually invisible.

Without access to Quan Kiai's secure line-of-sight laser channel, the Feds see only the figures of Lindsey and Lazarus without knowing who's in the vacsuits.

"Greetings once more Kitajima," he said. "Will you let us on your working frequency?" Inspector Callahan asks.

"Magi, provide Level One access for our guests," Kitajima orders.

Callahan's faceplate turns opaque and then vanishes with the rest of his vacsuit. In its place, he's wearing NAF Army dress blues with the rank of Colonel. "Thank you Kitajima… It's simply uncivilized not to look a person in the eye when you're talking to them," Inspector Callahan said and then realizes Kitajima is not one of those facing him. "Lindsey. Please forgive my rudeness," he indicates his companions, "this is Zechariah Hargrove and Luke Fillmore."

"Greetings Inspector, this is Lazarus Sheffield."

Zechariah stares intently at Lazarus when she said his name. He appears about to speak when Luke reaches out and turns Inspector Callahan around. Captain Osaka and Tempel Dugan are standing a few meters away. He recognizes Kitajima and has a passing familiarity with young Dugan but that's not what causes him to pause. Behind their projected image is… nothing.

"Kitajima, what deal have you made with the devil now?"

"Greetings Inspector. I'm rather busy. What exactly can I do for you?" Kitajima asks.

"For openers, what manner of vacsuit are you wearing?" Callahan asks with exasperation. "I've never seen anything like it."

"Something we've been working on," Kitajima said.

"I thought keeping secrets was against the law?" Zechariah said.

"Keeping secrets is, having secrets isn't," Lindsey said.

"Prove it. Tell me, what you're doing out here?" Callahan asks.

"As I've already said, we don't…"

"Yes, yes, I know, you don't disclose information prematurely to a shortimer," he glances at the damaged crate. "Whatever brought you out here is important. Otherwise, why would you reveal brand new technology, technology you have obviously gone to a lot of trouble to keep quiet." He holds his hand up stopping Kitajima from interrupting, "Don't you think I have a right to know? I live in Aldrin Station, my family lives in Aldrin Station… Now tell me, what's going on?" Little America is technically a borough within Aldrin Station but Lunarians consider it a shortimer enclave, not part of their city.

Kitajima slowly nods. "The crate contains nukes on their way to Little America from an unknown source. So maybe you can tell me, what's going on in Little America?"

"Nukes." The Inspector exclaims. "I'm sure I don't have any idea who would do such a thing."

"Excuse me Kitajima," Magi said. "Brice has finished his mapping. I've begun the simulation. This may ta…"

First Blood

Think not o' reader that those who disbelieve can ever be able to
frustrate and escape Us. Their abode is Fire; what an evil resort.

Holy Qur'ân 24:57

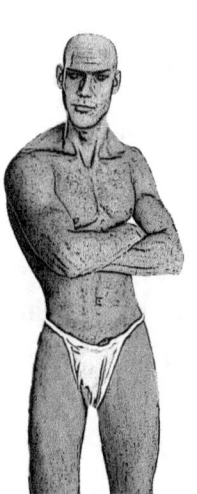

A sudden dazzling glare that rivals the sun appears directly overhead. Tempel's visor protects his eyes and his ghost suit absorbs the sudden burst of energy like a sponge, storing it for later. The light quickly fades.

"Magi, what happened to our link with base?" Silence greets Lindsey's question. "Magi?" she repeats.

"Magi, respond," Tempel orders to no avail. Shifting his focus He asked, "Moonhawk Two. How do you read Aldrin Station?"

"All channels are unavailable and backups are not responding." The voice is sexless, common to many articulate things that do not require the sophistication of Magi. Without Magi, the default AI onboard the Moonhawk is not much more than a glorified autopilot.

"Can you determine why?" Tempel asks.

"Negative, insufficient information," the computer said.

Tempel maximizes his visor's magnification. A fading star is where Lagrange One should be and the Lunanet satellites are glitter scattered across the heavens. He links with Kitajima, "Captain, Lunanet is down.

Something's happened to our satellites and Lagrange One."

"Aye, I know." Kitajima replies, having already linked with the sensors on the transports.

"Kitajima. What's happened?" Inspector Callahan demands, very bad etiquette even for a shortimer.

"A nuclear detonation somewhere near Lagrange One is affecting the entire Nearside." Kitajima replies.

"Look up. That's what's left of our communications network," Tempel said to the Inspector.

Tilting his head back, Inspector Callahan's vacsuit can't magnify enough to see the sparkle high overhead. "Are you sure? I can't see anything," he said.

"I'm sure." Tempel snaps back. His family and friends might be in danger this very instant and he's standing in the dust of Mare Nubium next to a crate of nukes talking with a clueless Federation Inspector.

"Without those satellites, we can't make contact with Aldrin Station," Kitajima said, his mind roiling over the many possibilities, not liking any. He's on his own, sitting on a shipment of thermonuclear weapons, courtesy of the Brotherhood. Who else would be shipping warheads across Luna except the Brotherhood? He must prevent delivery regardless of the price.

"I can take up a Moonhawk. Thirty kilometers straight up should make it possible to see Rim Mountain with our laser," Tempel volunteers.

"Tempel, those satellites didn't blow up on their own, they had some help. You go popping up right now, and you may attract more attention then we want. If Aldrin Station is under attack our first priority is to make sure these nukes don't fall into the wrong hands," Kitajima said.

"Under attack? Don't be absurd. Why would anyone attack Aldrin Station?" Inspector Callahan exclaims with his hands on his hips. He's a small man, well under two meters and prone to posturing. The situation is sliding out of control.

"Captain," calls Karyl.

"Report," Kitajima said.

"We're picking up low level quakes. The epicenter is in or near Alphonsus Crater but we can't seem to pin down an exact location. It's as if there are dozens of quakes each with a slightly different point of origin. I've never seen anything like it before," Karyl said.

"We have more trouble." Tatiana said. "I see two rovers coming our way. ETA… ten minutes."

"Rovers? Are you sure?" Inspector Callahan asks incredulously. "What would rovers be doing way out here?"

"Looking for something they lost is my guess, but I'm not going to wait around to ask," Kitajima said. "Callahan, tell me straight, do you have anyone out here?"

"Absolutely not. They're not Federation," the inspector assures them shaking his head vigorously.

"Quan Kiai, link with me… Hack, get us started… stay and fight or run?" Kitajima asks.

"Run like hell," she replies.

"Aye," Quan Kiai said.

Kitajima turns to Tatiana's image, "Take, leave, or destroy the nukes?"

"Take them," she replies without hesitation.

"Aye." It was unanimous. The routine is familiar to Quan Kiai. After years of training, they almost know what the others are thinking. They all reach the same conclusion. The nukes can't fall into the hands of the Brotherhood no matter what.

Kitajima nods, "We're in agreement. Tempel, what do you need to load the crates?"

"I'll need cargo straps and three bodies. We can manhandle them into the ship," Tempel said.

"Good. Do it. Karyl, bring Moonhawk Two down right between the two crates. Consuela, set down right there." Kitajima marks their new LZ.

"Aye," they reply in unison.

"Break camp, Hack. I want to be ready to move in five minutes. Pack all the evidence and leave the instruments."

"Aye," Hack replies and starts moving.

"Inspector, I suggest you get the hell out of here. My guess is that the rovers are from Al Fahad. The timing is 'bout right and I don't think they're coming all the way out here for a picnic." Kitajima said.

"The Brotherhood would never dare harm a Federation citizen. That would be a direct violation of the Saudi Accord," Inspector Callahan replies. Even so, he sends Luke Fillmore back to the ship with orders to get it ready for liftoff.

"It's your funeral," Tempel said, shaking his head in disbelief. How many citizens have died since the UN brokered the Saudi Accord almost a half century ago? Some people never get it. Any theocracy will tell you what you want to hear, and then do whatever's necessary to grow their power. The old adage, *it takes money to make money* is magnified many times when you apply it to power. *It takes power to grab more power*. "Lindsey, have you determined how these are booby trapped?"

"Yes. It's a simple switching device just under the top," Lindsey replies. "I will disarm it later. It will remain stable as long as you don't try opening the crate." She's hastily packing up the instruments that had collected, and now contain, the raw data.

"Karyl, link to me," Tempel instructs her.

"Aye," she said.

Hack and Doc Grady are already stowing the black body bags into Moonhawk One and Tatiana's perimeter guards are returning. The area is a beehive of activity, all of it aimed at leaving in a hurry.

Karyl glides the Moonhawk across Nell's Valley, a silent leviathan a few meters above the surface. She skillfully maneuvers the craft into position.

"Snuggle your aft end up close," Tempel said.

"What girl could refuse such a tempting invitation?" Karyl purrs. "Say when Tempel." Karyl calls out needlessly. Their linked visors provide her with an extremely accurate view of her surroundings. She knows exactly where she's going.

"When," Tempel said keeping his eyes on the ship as it settles to the ground.

The rear cargo ramp descends before the dust has settled. Tempel leaps into the back and emerges with cargo straps. Throwing a pair to Alonzo and Brice, he keeps the other two and motions for Sam and Lazarus to follow him. Handing the straps to Sam, Tempel bends down and grasps one end heaving upward, radically tilting the crate. Sam pitches the end of first one then the other strap underneath where Lazarus scrambles to retrieve them.

Without a word, Corazon and Marcel arrive on scene and assume the front positions while Sam and Tempel take the rear. Lazarus gets out of the way. One of the first things Lunarian police officers learn is how to work as a team.

"On my mark… 3, 2, 1, Up." The four Lunarians easily lift the crate, walk the short distance to the transport, depositing the load in the ships aft section. Moments later the second and third crates are sitting beside the first.

Brice and Alonzo continue securing the crates as Lindsey stows some of her instruments and goes back for more.

"We've got company." Kipper exclaims.

"Everyone onboard, *now*," Kitajima orders. "Zoey, Sam and Alonzo, stay with Moonhawk Two."

"Move it Quan Kiai." Hack calls standing at the foot of the cargo ramp.

"But I haven't finished," Lindsey said.

"Leave it." Hack replies harshly, "Unless you intend to stay."

Two vehicles leap from the ridge in a long arc, landing almost thirty meters downhill. The two humans sit in an open cockpit surrounded by a roll cage. Mounted on the top of the cage is an AK laser cannon. They kick up rooster tails of regolith as they come barreling down the slope.

Both rovers open fire. The Federation ship is the closest to them and takes the brunt of the assault. The beams slice through the thin skin. An instant later, an explosion rocks the ship. A lone figure emerges and staggers toward Moonhawk Two.

"Lieutenant, get that Moonhawk off the ground," Kitajima orders.

"Aye." Tempel reaches for the control to shut the cargo ramp. Even as the ramp starts to move, Tempel sees the Fed running towards him. He triggers the ramp to reopen and steps down where he can be seen, motioning for him to hurry. The man franticly bounds across the surface. Beyond him, the rovers race down the side of the valley firing at Moonhawk One overhead. The Fed makes it to the door and catapults himself into the transport.

Tempel triggers the cargo bay door to close. The Fed is lying beside crates. Tempel grabs him by his hard point, right between his shoulder blades, and lifts him bodily.

The survivor was the young Propriety Officer. Tempel hustles him forward, dumping him into the nearest seat.

"Help him," Tempel orders Brice.

Tempel throws himself into the pilot's seat.

"What the hell was that about?" Karyl asks harshly.

Ignoring her he said, "Keep low and move along the valley. Put the ridge between us and them," Tempel engages his harness as Karyl jerks the Moonhawk skyward and accelerates down the valley, never getting more than fifty meters off the surface.

Moonhawk One circles a hundred meters above, a tempting target for the incoming rovers. They open fire. Even at breakneck speed, the gunners will eventually hit something as big as a Moonhawk at this range.

The first significant damage is to the left forward outrigger weakening it considerably and forcing its thruster to shut down. The onboard AI compensates by adjusting the thrust vectors of the other three engines. This reduces the agility of the craft, forcing it to fly in a straight line, more or less.

Now it's an easy target. The fatal shot came in at an angle, cutting through the thin skin of the Moonhawk and striking Officer Lei Cheung in the chest. The powerful beam burns diagonally from her lower left side, plowing through her heart and lungs before emerging from her right shoulder. She never knew what hit her. One instant she was alive and breathing, the next she was not. Hot gases spew from her wound in a thick red fog trapped inside the transport. Lei is dead.

Her comrades install patches on her vacsuit trying to minimize the outgassing. If they didn't do this, vacuum would suck all the biofluids from her body and deposit it on every free surface inside the Moonhawk. This is very unpleasant.

Kitajima returns fire with the roof mounted Gatling. One of his shots punches through the front suspension of the lead rover. It buries its front axle into the lunar soil and cartwheels down the slope. One of the occupants was not strapped in. He lands hard on a basalt outcropping and doesn't move.

The second rover continues to come on hard, firing time after time, intent on making Swiss cheese out of the Moonhawk. Consuela feels her craft lurch beneath her and lose power as the right rear outrigger takes several hits. The ship is losing its ability to fly. Its onboard AI struggles mightily to make the adjustments just to keep them in the sky. As it surrenders to gravity and starts to fall, the AI tries heroically to get the remaining undamaged thrusters to compensate even more, balancing the forces on two thrusters. It doesn't have the computing power to keep them flying.

Kitajima switches the cannon to manual and keeps firing at the remaining rover to little effect. It darts behind a rock outcropping. From this protected position, it opens fire on the crippled ship.

Everyone aboard the Moonhawk has that sinking feeling one gets just before something bad happens. It's just a matter of time before that damned cannon finds its mark and blasts them from the sky.

"Prepare to abandon ship," Kitajima orders. He's firing on manual as the AI struggles to keep them airborne. They're in major trouble. The onboard AI is not good enough to engage the elusive enemy and keep the crippled ship flying. Kitajima misses repeatedly, churning up the lunar landscape around the rover while it continues to punch more holes in his Moonhawk.

Consuela and Kipper look desperately for a place to set the wounded bird down.

In the chaos inside the ship, Officer Karl Svensson loosens his upper harness and leans across the aisle to help Brice with Lei. A beam sears through the floor striking him in the chest. The beam penetrates both lungs and obliterates his aorta. He slumps in his seat, his lap belt the only thing holding him in. Karl is dead.

Risking her life, Hack unbuckles and goes to him. Wedging herself among the seats, she patches the holes, stopping the flow of blood into the cabin. More holes appear in the skin of the transport at her feet, some missing her by only millimeters. She clutches the seats for support as the craft lurches through the sky.

At that moment, Moonhawk Two sweeps over the ridge behind the rover and descends upon it. Before the Brotherhood soldiers know he's there, Tempel opens up with his Gatling on full auto. The cannon fires as quickly as the power pack can recharge it, about twice a second.

In the onslaught, he hits the rover's fuel tanks releasing clouds of hypergolic chemicals into the lunar vacuum. Another shot hit the passenger in the neck just below his helmet, slicing through the composite armor plate like a hot knife through butter, decapitating the man inside. His blood boils in the vacuum forming a red halo around the rover. The rover's hypergolic fuels mix and ignite in a silent fireball. The energy of the explosion shoves the rover into the ground, reflects off the surface, and flips the vehicle like a child's broken toy.

"Aye," someone shouted. Corazon would spend the rest of his life denying it was he.

Tempel didn't stick around. Never slowing down, he keeps the ship low and easily catches up to Moonhawk One. Reestablishing the laser link with the injured ship, He asked, "Kipper, how bad is it?"

"Bad enough. We lost two outriggers. One more and we would be part of the landscape," Kipper said.

"Can you make it fly?" Tempel asks.

"Magi could, but this glorified calculator is having major problems making the adjustments," Kipper replies.

"Maybe we can borrow enough computing power to keep it flying. Tempel, link your AI to ours," Kitajima orders.

Tempel's hands flash over the VR control panel, establishing the link and routing resources to the crippled ship.

"It's working," exclaims Kipper, surprise and relief in his voice as his ship stops descending and starts moving forward, winning the battle with gravity for the moment.

"Thank you Lord." Zechariah blurts out.

"Tempel, if we keep going on this track we will come to the Straight Fault. Have you ever been out here?" Kitajima asks.

"Aye, many times. I would venture to say that we all have. It's a great day trip." Tempel brings up a map and finds what he's looking for. "Captain, there's a large lava tube along Sunset Canyon about thirty kilometers southeast of us that runs alongside Birt Crater. It's big enough to land both Moonhawks inside."

"That's what I wanted to hear. Lay out a direct course. Get us there as soon as possible but keep the speed down and altitude low. We must minimize the risk of detection," Kitajima orders.

"Aye," Tempel said.

Moonhawk One climbs out of the valley and heads southeast followed closely by Moonhawk Two. By staying low and slow they disappear into ground clutter, all but impossible to see from orbit.

"Tempel, give me a verbal on your situation," Kitajima orders. He doesn't want to risk using the link to look for himself. That single overworked channel is the only thing keeping him in the sky.

Tempel surveys the vital signs of his crew. "Everyone is fine and the cargo's safe. We picked up the Fed Propriety Officer just before launch and he's also healthy as far as I can tell."

"I wish I could say the same. We lost Karl and Lei," Kitajima said. He personally recruited these young Lunarians to Quan Kiai and watched them grow into citizens of the highest caliber. He struggles to keep his emotions under control, but everyone knows what he's feeling. They feel it too.

ЯL

Cris heads south putting Prattville at his back, staying off the main roads. This is rough but familiar territory. Just over the next rise is Hallstead, a family owned freehold carved in the rim of a small crater.

John Jackson Hallstead immigrated to Luna over thirty years ago and founded Jackson freehold. Today, it supplies food to Darpur, Purgatory, Far Point and Aldrin Station. Hallstead contains a boarding house, repair shop, and several saloons catering to independent miners in the area. It's home to upwards of three hundred citizens, depending on the day and time.

Before cresting the rise, Cris notices a haze over the horizon, lit from underneath. He slows and edges the cycle to a point overlooking

Hallstead, careful not to silhouette himself against the sky.

The scene below is horrific. Bodies lay scattered amongst the ruined buildings and shredded vehicles. The dead all wear Lunarian vacsuits. Body fluids still boil from several and hang over the settlement like a death shroud, red with the blood of citizens. The fight here had been brutal and one sided.

Parked in the main compound are four rovers and a truck convoy. This in itself is not a surprise, but what is unusual is the lack of identification on the vehicles. Usually, the mines plaster their logos on anything that moves. These vehicles are drab gray and black camouflage. But something else is wrong with them. A normal mining convoy consists of a Goliath pulling up to fifteen carriers like a locomotive and its cars. Carriers are by necessity open at the top to dump ore inside. These carriers have sealed roofs with heavy weapons and sensors mounted on top. Airlocks and other elements identify these as human transports, not ore carriers.

A number of figures move about the compound. Some are dragging bodies into one of the buildings. Others are loading the convoy with supplies and fuel. Many more come and go freely through Hallstead's main airlock, all without the usual broadband chatter. They must be using laser line-of-sight communications. Cris zooms in but cannot see their faces, hidden behind helmets that do not transmit the wearer's expression. Instead, he sees two bulging sensor arrays, one at each apex of a triangular face. He immediately recognizes Brotherhood standard issue. Cris has great respect for the multifaceted sensor arrays that form the basis of the disparaging name, bugeyes. Despite its grotesque appearance, the array provides its wearer with a full 360° multi-frequency scan. These bugeyes aren't miners or truckers, they're clad in armored vacsuits and carry disrupters. They're soldiers.

Anger grips him as he puts it all together. Kahfah Road passes about twenty kilometers south of Hallstead as the crow flies. It's the main highway leading to the Holy City of Al Fahad. Al Fahad is the Islamic Brotherhoods biggest settlement on Luna, yet, no Lunarian has ever been inside. Access is restricted to Brotherhood. No one even knows how many reside within its walls. Factoring in the massive bombardment of Aldrin Station, Cris realizes the Republic of Luna is at war and this is the enemy.

Suddenly, several figures emerge from one of Hallstead's out buildings and begin running from the compound towards the deep ravine right below Cris. The Highlander can see these are Lunarian's from their vacsuits, a man, two women and a child of about ten years. They are frightened. Behind them, the alarm goes up and the fleeing group comes under fire from the energy weapons mounted on the massive truck convoy.

Just when Cris thinks they will all make it, the man's hit. Nothing anyone can do for him, the beam sears a hole through his chest, boiling his insides, killing instantly. The dead body limply comes to rest amidst the dust. The others disappear into the ravine with only a backward glance to their fallen comrade.

From his vantage point, Cris watches two rovers load up and start in hot pursuit. They will easily catch the Lunarians. He drops over the edge and guns his cycle down the hill, taking chances he normally would not take as he closes the gap.

This exposes Cris to fire from the convoy but none materializes. By the time he reaches the ravine, his cycle is coiled and ready to fly. Timing it to perfection, Cris launches the bike and soars over the top of the oncoming rovers, firing his pistol down at the soldiers inside.

Cris takes the lead rover completely by surprise. He shoots the driver once, his beam searing a pencil size hole through the man's armor and into his heart. The safety harness holds the body upright. A blood red fog spews from the wound. The vehicle careens off course and crashes into the side of the ravine.

The second rover swerves sideways not caring about the fleeing Lunarians. It fires its cannon wildly several times, missing badly as the cycle disappears down the ravine in the opposite direction. Slewing the rover about, they give chase, reporting to their commander as they go.

Not yet ready to quit the fight, Cris aims the cycle uphill and twists the throttle. The bike said and easily climbs up and over a bony outcrop, putting him briefly in the sights of the convoy. Several high-energy lasers churn the nearby lunar landscape, but none hit their mark. Cris disappears once more below the edge of the ravine.

Unbeknownst to either, the cycle and rover are closing rapidly on one another. Coming around a bend, Cris is the first to react and fires, taking out the driver. With a dead man driving, the rover careens sideways, hits a rock, flips, and skids to a stop on its roof.

Cris twists in the saddle and targets the exposed underbelly, shredding the fuel cell storage tanks as he goes by. The exposed toxic fluids boil into the lunar vacuum. A moment later, the hypergolic fuels mix and feed on each other, silently exploding in a monstrous fireball. Easily seen from Hallstead, the brief bright flame rising above the ravine said far more plainly than any verbal declaration, the fight has only just begun.

He guns his cycle about spewing regolith far behind him and heads east, deeper into the Highlands, making sure to leave a clearly defined track. If nothing else, he can draw the Brotherhood away from the Hallstead survivors and give them a chance. The remaining two rovers pick up his trail.

ЯL

Zechariah can't stop thinking about Inspector Callahan, the look of disbelief just before his life slipped away. This is the first time he's seen death up close and personal. Zechariah had thought coming to Luna was a once in a lifetime opportunity, one he could not pass up. Now he's not so sure. He prays for God to give him strength and to have mercy on the souls of the Inspector and Mr. Fillmore. Not once did he question why they had needed to die in the first place, simply accepting all that life throws at him as God's will. He even said a prayer for the men who had attacked them so brutally.

Lazarus and Lindsey do what they can for the young man, assuring him that he's fine and listening to him pray for strength. The effect that prayer has on him amazes Lindsey. Zechariah asks God to take away his fears and instantly calms down. Transference is a phenomenon in psychology first described by Sigmund Freud but she's never seen it operate so completely. God makes the perfect dumping ground.

For the last thirty minutes, Tempel has watched the Straight Fault, or Rupes Recta, grow ever more pronounced on the horizon. What remains of the setting sun is behind his left shoulder putting the long ridge in full sunlight, a condition that would have been brutal on unprotected eyes.

The fault extends from one horizon to the other just a few degrees off due north, running over a hundred kilometers in a straight line across the eastern Sea of Clouds. Along most of that length, the fault maintains a uniform height of almost 200 meters with a slope extending outward over two kilometers. Lunarian geologists believe the Crater Korolev impact event on the opposite side of Luna created the fault. At the time of the impact, the Sea of Clouds was a vast expanse of warm lava and would have been susceptible to a massive upheaval from a convergence of shock waves traversing the globe.

Directly in front of them, the rim of Crater Birt rises two kilometers into the lunar sky. A belt of badlands flanks the mountain extending out as far as twenty kilometers in places. Almost lost in the jumble is Sunset Canyon, a large rill that wraps itself around the base of Birt before winding out onto the Sea of Clouds. On the crater side of Sunset Canyon is a sheer basalt cliff over four hundred meters in height. Lunarians call this awe-inspiring work of nature the Wall.

Everybody has a magnificent view of the Wall during the approach. Both Moonhawks are flying less than fifty meters above the rugged desolation and creeping along at a few tens of kilometers per hour. The great expanse of stone towers over them pressing down with an almost physical force.

The terrain below continues to get rougher the closer they come. The lunar surface was shattered and broken during the craters creation event but later volcanism added to the mess. Heaving in the cooling bed of lava created a twisted tortured landscape of sharp edges and treacherous fissures. Other rills, large and small, extend outward from Sunset Canyon in a vast network. They cannot see an area anywhere large enough for even one Moonhawk to land safely, let alone two.

Less than a kilometer from the base of the cliff, they come upon a large circular depression. It's a natural amphitheater created when a section of the surface collapsed. It's over a hundred meters wide and drops vertically nearly fifty. Lava had partially filled it creating a relatively smooth plain at the bottom broken by numerous small craters. The wall of the sinkhole had given way in several places. The two Moonhawks descend into its depth.

Quan Kiai grants Lazarus privacy. From his perspective, he's alone in this place, his companions and the two ships filtered out of his vision. The constant exposure to flight has strengthened his hold over his phobia. He shudders as they drop into the hole but stays under control. The cliff face sweeps around him in a great arc. Above looms the Wall, below is the floor of the sinkhole.

Tempel takes the lead, swinging his ship north and heading across the pit. Consuela follows. Without sensors, he would have been in near total darkness, with them he can see every feature like it's a bright summer afternoon but without the glare. He likes to tweak his visual with a good dash of color enhancement to bring out the composition and structure in the rocks. Otherwise, he considers them boring. With it, the walls of the sinkhole appear a dark red, while the frozen lava lake in the bottom is a cool blue and the craters across its surface outlined in darker blue.

Even knowing it's there, the mouth of the giant lava tube is hard to see, situated right at the base of the cliff and hidden behind the rim wall of a smaller secondary crater. It's more than half filled with ancient lava. Tempel brings the ship to a hover outside leaving plenty of room for Consuela to go by.

"Consuela, do you think you can make it?" Tempel asks.

"It's going to be close. Are you sure a Moonhawk will fit?" Consuela asks.

Before he could stop himself, Tempel said "Magi…."

"Tempel you hang back and watch the clearance. If we don't fit then call out," Kitajima picks up the slack for his Lieutenant.

"Aye," Tempel said.

Tempel maneuvers in behind the other Moonhawk as it eases forward.

"Plenty of room along the sides and at least 30 centimeters above," Tempel estimates the clearance.

"Is that all?" Consuela asks nervously.

"What more do you need?" Tempel asks, knowing that Consuela will rise to the challenge.

"Caution is the hallmark of the wise. Even you should know that," Consuela said.

She adjusts the ships proximity sensors to their finest settings and creeps forward. She cannot shake the feeling of returning to the womb, only it's not her mother's warm body surrounding them, but the cold basalt of Luna. The wall is so close she has the impulse to reach out and touch it. The tunnel stretches out before her as far as she can see, lit by ship lights for the first time in its long history. The floor is smooth and flat, the arc of the walls and ceiling featureless. Consuela can almost fool herself into thinking it's man-made.

About a hundred meters in, she slows to a stop and hovers. "What do you think Kitajima? Are we in far enough?"

"Aye, far enough. Set her down as far to the right as you can."

"That's not much," Consuela said as she brings the craft down to the ground, crabbing sideways a few meters. As the thrusters shut down, she sighs heavily and relaxes for the first time since this wild ride started.

"Before we follow you in, I suggest we place a few remotes. We need some eyes and ears out here," Tempel said.

"I concur. Place a sensor at the top of the Wall and another down in the pit. Set them up for line-of-sight laser communication," Kitajima said.

"You don't think they could follow us here, do you?" Zechariah asks.

Tempel looks over at Karyl who shakes her head. Without waiting for Kitajima's response Tempel swings the Moonhawk around breaking the laser communications link and cutting them off from the other ship. Zechariah remains quiet.

Because the damaged transport is on the ground, they have access to all their AI's computing power once more. Even so, the Moonhawk rises slowly out of the sinkhole in an upward arc that terminates at the distant crest of the Wall.

"Why are we flying so slowly?" Lazarus asks.

Tempel keeps his focus on the cliff looming in front of them, "By going slow and close to the ground we are virtually invisible to anything in orbit, completely lost in ground clutter."

The instant he began talking Karyl looks sharply at Tempel. The pilot is exempt from all other duties while flying and that includes idle small talk. She has no doubt he can handle it but it makes her uncomfortable to deviate even a little from training. *By the book* is more than just a quaint saying to her.

"Ask your questions later," Karyl said. "You can talk among

yourselves all you want but not with the pilot."

The top of the Wall comes abruptly. One moment they're flying up the cliff face a few tens of meters away, the next it's gone. The remainder of Crater Birt's rim mountain looms over them. Fissures radiate from the edge of the cliff. Smaller cracks are mere depressions in the regolith. Very few boulders and only sparse outcroppings break the smooth slope of the mountain rising above them.

From this vantage point, the Sea of Clouds stretches over the horizon. It's not flat like a snooker table but wavy like an ocean frozen in time. The last of the sun casts long shadows, mottling the mare's barren surface with shades of gray and black.

Tempel brings the ship down, landing well beyond the edge in perhaps the only relative flat spot anywhere atop this lunar mountain. Many other ships have landed here. He simply adds his to the mix. Human footprints are everywhere. There's nothing to erode them in this airless environment except the impacts of micrometeorites, a process taking hundreds, if not thousands, of years to see even the smallest change.

Brice and Alonzo know the drill having performed this duty many times before. They have the rear hatch wide open, the gear checked and ready to go. Brice leaps out before the transport comes to rest and heads towards the cliff edge.

Alonzo stays in the doorway watching the line play out of the wench, ready to haul Brice back at a moment's notice. The Wall has claimed its share of unwary tourists, both native and shortimer. Its edge is fragile and prone to breaking, although this area has been stomped over so many times that any loose rock has long since fallen away. But Lunarians learn early that a person doesn't live long by taking unnecessary risks.

Slowing as he approaches the cliff, Brice glances out at the view. Less than fifteen kilometers southwest, he can see the Straight Fault, the setting sun highlighting its great length.

He moves parallel to the edge, about ten meters back, looking for a fissure the right size. Spotting one, he gets down on his belly and worms forward until his head is just looking over the edge. He slips the sensor down into the crack positioning it before triggering the bladder. A small pneumatic skin fills with gas and expands, wedging itself firmly in the rock.

Brice takes a second to check his placement. Satisfied, he carefully pushes away from the edge before standing and hustling back to the transport.

Alonzo keeps Brice's tether taut as he returns. They are in and out in less than two minutes.

"Go," Karyl said as Brice slides into his seat.

Tempel lifts off, never gaining more than ten meters of altitude.

Lazarus gasps as they clear the edge, going from ten meters to many hundreds in the blink of an eye. Tempel adds to the ride by briefly putting them in freefall. Lazarus involuntarily groans and squeezes his eyes tightly shut. Less than a hundred meters above the rocky badlands Tempel guns the thrusters and stops their downward plummet in a graceful arc, sending the ship swooping across the jagged terrain. To Lazarus, they are doing hundreds of kilometers per hour, when in reality it's much less.

Tempel banks once when he's well inside the sinkhole and makes a slow graceful turn. He already has a spot in mind for the second sensor and marks it, a rocky landslide almost directly opposite of the tunnel entrance and in line-of-sight of the device they had just placed.

"Let's put this one about halfway down the slide... I'll hover at twenty meters. Alonzo, Brice, use the winch to place it. Do not leave any tracks," Tempel commands.

"Aye, no tracks." Brice said.

Alonzo has Brice in the harness by the time they reach the spot. Sliding the door open Alonzo steadies Brice as he steps out into space.

He swings head down in an instant, his body at an angle to make it easier to see below him. The winch lowers him like a spider on its web.

"Move twelve meters on heading two-seventy," Brice instructs Tempel.

Tempel complies without causing Brice to swing, a tribute to a steady hand.

"Beautiful." Brice murmurs. Moments later, he's installed the sensor and tested its alignment. Brice admires his work as he's winched up to the transport. The camouflage makes the sensor virtually invisible long before he reaches the door.

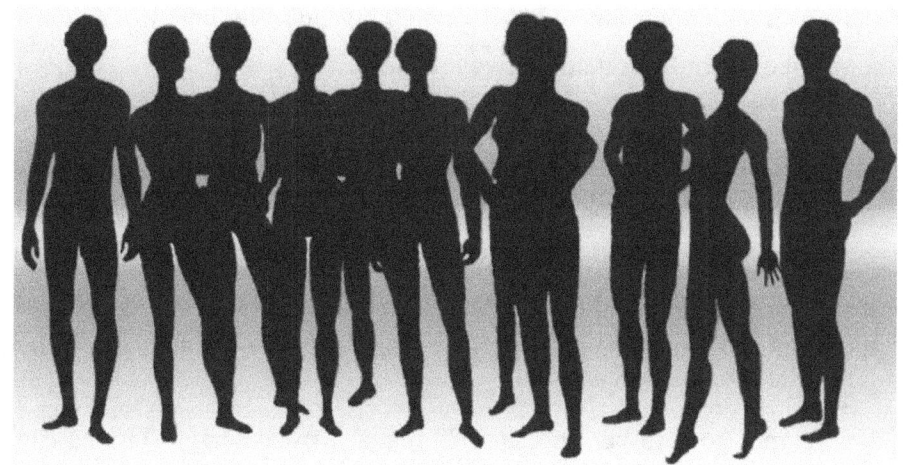

Sunset Canyon

Whosoever doeth any work in the Sabbath
day, he shall surely be put to death.

Holy Bible - Exodus 31:15

Tempel eases the Moonhawk into the lava tube. He follows the fresh grooves cut into the floor and sets down close to the other ship. Kitajima, Hack and the rest of Quan Kiai are waiting. Doc Grady stands apart, dejection etched upon his face.

A stoic Kitajima waits for them to disembark, "We have two comrades to mourn but that must wait."

"There wasn't anything I could do to help them," Doc Grady said defensively.

Kitajima turns to the medico. "That's right, you couldn't save them. Now it's time to move on."

"It was my decision to wait for the shortimer. If I hadn't, Moonhawk One would have gotten clear and nobody would have been killed," Tempel said.

"Bullshit." Kitajima said forcefully. "Haven't I taught you anything?

A warrior never plays the what-if game. You can never win. If you make a mistake, learn from it and move on. Got it?"

"Aye," but Tempel remains unconvinced. He looks into Tatiana's eyes and finds hatred for the first time.

Tatiana scowls and breaks eye contact. Karl is dead. She can't believe it. Karl is dead. She doesn't blame Tempel anymore than she does Consuela and Kipper for piloting the ship or Corso for sending them out here, but Tempel's right in front of her and Karl's in a body bag.

Tempel goes to her and said, "Tatiana, I'm so sorry." Tatiana can sense his emotions almost as well as her own. He's barely holding himself together. Her arms go around his neck and she sobs into his shoulder. Tempel holds her.

Kitajima walks over to the newcomer. The young man's staring at the two warriors, "What did you say your name was?"

The question startles him but he answers, "Zechariah Hargrove." Trapped among the mutants, he silently prays for strength to see him through. His eyes betray fear.

"Inspector Callahan was a good man. I'm sorry for your loss... You're a PO?"

The man nods, "Propriety Officer First Class." PO's can popup anywhere, watching the watchers. It's normal for a PO to be young and idealistic. Their job is to ensure the Inspectors obey all religious tenets while performing their duty to the Federation.

"That means nothing out here. You do what I tell you and things will be fine. But make no mistake Mr. Hargrove, my first responsibility is to these warriors and the Republic, not to you or the Federation." Kitajima speaks the facts as he sees them without rancor or ill will.

"I understand," Zechariah replies. He's not used to people being so blatantly honest with him. It must be a trick.

"Give me your sidearm." Zechariah obeys. Kitajima flips the gun to

Hack and looks over the young man's vacsuit. It's Federation and new but uses old technology. It's devoid of power assist or electromagnet shielding, made of inferior materials, and prone to breakdowns. A few days in it would seem like an eternity.

"Brice, see what you can do to make Mr. Hargrove comfortable when you have time. This suit will need help," Kitajima said.

"Aye," Brice acknowledges.

"Here are the rules. Number one, we maintain full access to your vacsuit at all times. Number two, these warriors have the exact same authority over you that I do. You will obey their commands to the letter and without question. Number three, you will not do anything to adversely affect this mission. Number four, you will answer every question put to you fully and truthfully to the best of your ability… Disobey these orders at your own peril. I have nothing against you personally. This is just how it is. Okay?"

"Perhaps I can be of assistance," Lazarus offers.

"Now there's an idea, you baby-sit him and Lindsey can baby-sit you. That will keep everyone busy." Turning, Kitajima moves on, "Marcel and Angel analyzed the damage on our way here and they think it can be repaired. All those hits managed to miss nearly everything."

"God was looking out for us," Zechariah blurts.

"If that was looking out for us then tell him to mind his own business," Brice said glaring at Zechariah.

"I figure we have a couple hours before we can expect company." Kitajima said.

"Why would they follow us here?" Zechariah asks.

"The Brotherhood knows we have their nukes and it's a safe bet they will want them back." Kitajima said.

"Then you must destroy them. Your initial knee-jerk response to take them was in error. Destruction is the only answer. That would take the wind out of the sails of any pursuers." Zechariah's accomplished at running his mouth without knowing what he's talking about, a skill that served him well in his meteoric rise through the ranks.

Kitajima's expression deepens into a scowl when Zechariah referred to his decision as knee-jerk. "Those nukes are the only leverage we have right now. We need to figure out how to use them most effectively."

"You can't be serious. Who do you want to nuke?" Zechariah asks.

This day has gone from bad to worse and Kitajima isn't in the mood to explain himself to this Federation pipsqueak. "I haven't made up my mind. But you can be sure I will let you know when I do." he turns away from Zechariah, obviously dismissing him, trying to keep his mind focused on what needs doing to keep them breathing.

Lazarus moves up beside Zechariah and lays a hand on the young man's arm, shaking his head.

Zechariah scowls and pulls away, glaring at Lazarus. He did not appreciate the interference. "Fine, no more questions," he turns and leaves, heading back to Moonhawk Two.

"Hack, check on supplies. We need to know what we have left," Kitajima said.

"Doc, you're with me," Hack said moving purposefully towards the crippled Moonhawk. Doc Grady needs something to do and inventory is the perfect solution.

"Brice, take Marcel, Angel, Corazon and Alonzo. We need those repairs done in one hour," Kitajima said.

"Consuela, you're assigned cover-up. Make sure you fill the grooves in the floor," Kitajima orders. It's her job to erase all indications of their presence on the surface, especially outside on the floor of the sinkhole close to the tunnel entrance.

"Sam, see what you can do about reestablishing a secure link with Magi. We must find out what's going on," Kitajima orders.

"Aye," Sam nods and said, "I've already tried picking up Earthnet. All I get is static."

"Have you tried raising a ground station?" Lazarus asks her. "I mean one of the Earth based ground stations."

"Of course, but like I said, every band is swamped with static."

Lazarus raises his eyebrows, "Every band? The only thing I know of that can do that is a nuclear EMP."

"I don't think so. The effect you are thinking of needs an atmosphere to make it work. This is jamming by multiple sources," Sam said. "If I had better triangulation I think I could pinpoint their locations."

"Lazarus, go with Sam. Maybe the two of you can provide us with some answers instead of bedtime stories." Kitajima pauses and Sam heads for the Moonhawk. When Lazarus does not move, he growls, "You waiting for a written invitation? Get going. And don't forget, you're keeping an eye on the Fed."

Addressing the two copilots still in their respective ships Kitajima said, "Kipper, Karyl, stay where you are. I want you to monitor the sensors. Don't rely on the autos."

"Aye," they respond in unison.

Kitajima looks at Lindsey. "I want you to find a way to defeat active camouflage."

"How am I to do that?" Lindsey asks, "We don't have Magi and we left most of our equipment back at the crash site."

"Use your brain." Kitajima said sharply. Even during the best of times, he has very little tolerance with anybody that comes up with excuses before they even try, and the current situation leaves him even more short-tempered. He can't help but blame himself when he loses people under his command.

"My brain cannot take the place of Magi or the equipment." Lindsey retorts.

"You can use a ships AI while we're on the ground," Tempel offers.

"If any AI could do it, we wouldn't have Magi, would we?" Lindsey said.

"Just do the job you were sent to do," Tatiana said tersely.

Turning to confront Tatiana, Lindsey said, "We don't have the micro-measurement vid equipment. Do you want me to guess?" Lindsey asks.

"Just do what you can Captain Marquest, that's all I'm asking," Kitajima said, deliberately using her rank.

Lindsey gets the message and stops arguing. "Fine Captain Osaka. I will try, but no promises."

"I'm not asking for promises Lindsey," Kitajima said, turning to Tatiana, "How far did Lei get with Evolution's Child's AI?"

For a moment, Tatiana continues glaring at Lindsey as if she were an unruly child. Facing Kitajima she said, "Not very far, I'm afraid. One of them is blank and the other badly damaged. I'll need to remove the Zettasphere and reinstall it in a new interface before I will know how much data survived."

"See what you can do. I doubt if it will help us but we shouldn't ignore it," Kitajima said. Looking at the faces gathered around him, he said briskly, "The rest of you check the equipment for any damage... Let's get to it people. Show me some results."

ЯL

Inside the Moonhawk, Tatiana points and said, "If you're going to stay, sit in that seat and keep your mouth shut."

Zechariah bristles, "I'm a Federation official. You can NOT talk to me like..."

As the last syllable comes out of Zechariah's mouth, Tatiana crosses the few meters between them with supernatural swiftness, grabs him with both hands, and slams his head and shoulders into the low ceiling.

Zechariah gives a startled yelp. He panics as he struggles ineffectually against her overpowering physical strength.

Reaching the top of the ramp, Tempel leaps forward and grabs Tatiana's arm, "What are you doing? At ease lieutenant. Back off...

NOW."

With a disgusted look, Tatiana releases Zechariah and steps back. The man falls to the floor.

The entire incident lasts only moments. Zechariah grapples with what he'd just witnessed. *Lunarians are truly the spawn of Satan.*

"Have you gone mad?" Tempel asks, inserting himself between them and pushing Tatiana away from the confrontation.

"I told him to do something and he argued with me," Tatiana replies.

Lindsey helps Zechariah, putting an arm around the frightened man to steady him.

"That does not give you the right to attack him," Lindsey said.

Zechariah stares at Tatiana. Fear and isolation rip at his guts. He's on the verge of tears.

"Take it easy, Zechariah," Lindsey said, guiding him to the seat Tatiana wanted him to sit in to begin with.

Zechariah sits down and looks back up at Lindsey, "How can she move like that?"

"Drop it." Lindsey said.

"But…" he starts.

"I said drop it." Lindsey repeats, locking eyes with him. "Look, the death of our comrades is hitting everyone hard. Let's put this aside. We have enough to worry about without fighting amongst ourselves," Lindsey said turning away.

Tempel grunts and nods in agreement, "She's right. We need to work together as a team," he said pointedly to Tatiana.

"Fine," Tatiana said. "He better not argue the next time I tell him to do something."

"He won't," Lindsey looks at Zechariah who lowers his head and nods.

Turning to the damaged crate, Tempel suggests, "Let's start by going over what we do know about this shield. Lindsey, you start."

Lindsey sighs, glancing at Tatiana. "Very well." She walks over beside Tempel, "The outside is standard vacglass, common throughout the Republic." Rubbing her thumb across the inside surface where it's exposed by the damage, sensors in her gloves provide a heightened sense of feel and the identity of the materials they come into contact with. "Inside the shell is a layer of energy absorbent material similar to what I developed years ago. Sandwiched in between is some kind of solid-state layer that returns a static signal in response to an incoming beam. I was just starting to unravel it when Magi was cut off."

"How similar?" Tempel asks.

"What?" Lindsey's lost in thought.

"How similar is the energy absorbent material to what you developed?" Tempel asks.

"Virtually identical. Why?" Lindsey said.

"That goes along with Lazarus's hypothesis that the Brotherhood will buy or steal the technology instead of developing it themselves," Tempel said.

"Then where did they get the transmitter design?" Tatiana asks. "I don't know of any research on Luna into anything similar to it."

Lindsey frowns thoughtfully, her expression slowly turning into surprise, then glee, "Several months ago, a MetCal colleague of mine told me about a new technology. I didn't think much about it at the time."

"What technology?" Tatiana asks.

"It was a new way of marking items for retail. Instead of passive barcodes, they designed packaging that would store information about the object inside and relay it back on request. What it was, where it was, when it was stocked, how much it cost, that sort of thing… It would also transmit a static picture of what's inside…" Lindsey pauses as she dredges up the old memory. "As I recall, they had gotten to the point of testing prototypes of a solid-state transmitter…" she uses the ships AI to pull up a whiteboard and begins to sketch a device. "Single function, receiver and transmitter…"

To the side of the sketch she draws a solid-state Hall Effect transistor and circles it. "They claimed the power consumption was so low that the device could use the interrogating beam as its source…" She brings up the information they had obtained on the micro-configuration of the shields transmitter layer.

Tempel and Tatiana watch as Lindsey follows her train of thought to its conclusion, the confrontation all but forgotten. Here is the reason Abby had insisted they include Lindsey on the mission.

Lindsey strips away data from the image until she reaches its smallest repeating unit. Enlarging it, she pulls apart what remains with a few rapid hand movements and circles a portion. "This is the receiver/transmitter and this out here is the Hall Effect transistor and its aperture. The rest of it must be encoding of static information being sent back through the transmitter," she said excitedly. "It's elegant in its simplicity."

"That's great, but where does that leave us?" Tempel asks.

"Don't you see?" Lindsey exclaims. "The physical size of the aperture is tuned to the wavelength of our MRI beams. If we change the MRI frequency, the power source will not function."

Tempel and Tatiana perk up, looking at the sketches and then at each other. "Can we test this?" Tempel asks.

"Yes, I believe we can, quite easily." Lindsey exclaims. "Simply recalibrate a sensor, or in this case, decalibrate it."

Lindsey retrieves a portable scanner from the locker and places it on the crate, the only flat surface available in the bay. The others watch as she links into its control system and brings the calibration portion of the maintenance routine online. She writes a small program that will oscillate the frequency of the scan around the standard. Confident in her abilities, she doesn't bother testing it before running the file.

Before their eyes, the information they are receiving from the crate goes from the image of the ball valve to black, characteristic of energy absorbent shielding and back to the ball valve, cycling back and forth as the calibration program fluctuates. It's like someone turning a light switch on and off.

"Well... I'll be damned." Tempel said softly, "Very impressive." Even Tatiana has a look of grudging respect.

Zechariah keeps his mouth shut and watches.

ЯL

Sam takes the seat directly behind Kipper and Lazarus slides into the one across the aisle. Looking over at her, he links to her visor just as she links to the two remote sensors. She sweeps the sky looking for communication emission. All she finds is static.

"I've never experienced a solar storm this big but that's what this looks like," Sam said.

"Do you know of any way to cut through or filter it out?" Lazarus asks hoping that she knows something he did not.

"No, but it should fade if it's a natural phenomenon. Do you have a recording of it back at the crash site?" She asked Kipper.

"Sure," he said pulling up the data and graphically overlays it with the current signal. The intensity of the static has remained constant.

"This isn't natural. Look at the signature. A massive solar flare would be fluctuating. This is too uniform to be natural," Sam said thoughtfully.

"The last flare of this magnitude was years ago and we had plenty of warning from our solar satellites." Kipper said over his shoulder.

Sam nods. Kitajima is not going to like these numbers but she can't change physics.

Lazarus frowns and said, "It would help if we could rig up a device to determine what direction the jamming is coming from. To pinpoint the source would require something at least partially shielded from the static, something that will let us map the intensity of the radiation in a specific direction."

Without turning his head, Kipper volunteers, "Sounds to me like what you are describing is a Faraday cage. Our battle armor is a good example. The Calconn coils create a conducting enclosure and an electromagnetic shield."

"How do you propose we use battle armor to pinpoint the source?" Sam asks.

Kipper shrugs, "How should I know. You're the genius."

Sam is silent for a moment. A look of hope passes over her face. "Yes… That might just work… We can use a pulse rifle. Modify its Harmon coil to make it act as a receiver instead of an emitter." Sam is gone before either of the men can say anything.

"Relax. When she gets something in her head, it's better to let her run with it," Kipper said knowingly.

"Ok. Can we see what's going on in orbit while we wait?" Lazarus asks.

Kipper links the two of them to the visual system in the remote sensors. Like a pair of eyes hundreds of meters apart, the resulting image has excellent depth. Zooming in on the orbiting debris, they can still see sunlight glinting on the pieces as they spin in their individual orbits. "We're looking at the coordinates for Orbsat 2112. I don't think there's any doubt that it's been destroyed."

Nodding Lazarus asks, "What about Earth orbiting satellites? What can you see from here?"

"These sensors are much too small to resolve any detail on them. But maybe we can spot Heaven's Gate…" Kipper feeds in the coordinates of the orbiting station, determining that it should be in view, just minutes away from disappearing behind Mother Earth.

A bright dot with no detail is all they can see, but at least it's there. They watch as it slides from view, twinkling as it passes behind the planet. Lazarus feels an incredible sense of loss as it winks out, far out of proportion to the actual event.

"Let's take a look at Lagrange," Kipper said.

He was expecting to see the gas cloud but instead, the hulking shape of a battlestation greeted them. The torus was unmistakable even with their sensors.

"Captain. You're going to want to see this." Kipper said.

"Pull up the record just before Magi was cutoff," Kitajima orders.

The view is replaced by the original Lagrange One Space Station. In an incredible flash of light, it's gone. In its place is an expanding cloud of hot atomized gas, yellow hot at its center.

"Definitely nuclear," Lazarus said.

"Fast forward," Kitajima said.

The expansion of the gas cloud quickened and it cooled from yellow to red to a dark blue. The arrival of the battlestation was unremarkable. It eased into L1 before the gases turned blue.

"That's not good," Kitajima said.

"That's the Houris," Lazarus said. "The ridge you see here is a rail gun that runs along the outside circumference. That's over eleven kilometers."

"That's bigger than the massdriver at Longbow." Kipper said.

"And it's circular so they can send the projectiles around again, and again, and…" Lazarus said.

"We get your point," Kipper said.

"That's why they needed so much iron. The more massive this battlestation is, the more energy they can impart to the loads," Kitajima said. He turns to Lazarus, "What do you know about this ship?"

"It's new, it's big, and it's very dangerous. From L1 it dominates the nearside. Nothing is safe from it. Even your underground cities wouldn't stand a chance. It can level a section of Rim Mountain with one blow," Lazarus said.

"Lazarus, could you please come back here?" Sam asks.

"Go," Kitajima said to Lazarus. "You can tell us more about this monster later."

"I suspected the Brotherhood was planning something big but even I didn't imagine it was this big. I think the Republic is at war. I think we're fighting for our lives," Lazarus said as he rises.

"Tell me something I don't know," Kipper said.

Lazarus moves through the passenger compartment. He finds Sam at a fold down workbench in the storage bay, the pieces of a pulse rifle scattered across it. She's taken the rifle and secured it in a tripod mount. It points almost straight up.

Motioning him to stand next to her she said, "I've reversed the voltage on the Harmon coil creating a perfectly shielded space in its interior. No electromagnetic static or electric field emissions can get in except through the muzzle. Now watch."

She slowly moves the tip of the Harmon coil back and forth in a small arc. The graph spikes sharply when the device is pointing in one very specific direction. She continues to rock it back and forth giving him a feel for the narrow angle, just a few degrees wide.

"What lies in that direction?" Lazarus asks.

"Nothing that I know of," she said, "It's simply a spot in orbital space. There's many others like this."

"Captain, we have company." Kipper broadcast.

Brice scrambles to shut down the nano-repair interface, difficult to do even under normal circumstances. Angel is lying on her stomach atop the outrigger, feeding raw material to the damaged sections. The rest of the platoon links to the remote sensor on top of the Wall. The ship is about two kilometers out and a thousand meters up flying slowly on a course parallel with the Wall, directly down Sunset Canyon.

"Let's shut it down, people," Kitajima orders.

Kipper and Karyl power down the two Moonhawks except for the AI core memory. All interpersonal communications cease, isolating everyone.

The world turns pitch black and silent. Lazarus reaches out where Sam had been only moments before, touching her.

Sam leans over cradling his head in her hands and puts her forehead against his, "Relax, this will be over in a few minutes," her voice is distant but understandable.

Without their lights, the tunnel is pitch-black. As the minutes drag, Lazarus becomes more and more convinced that something has gone terribly wrong. If it wasn't for Sam's firm grip holding him steady, he might have lost it and done something incredibly stupid.

After what seems like hours, his vacsuit powers up. Sam is there next to him.

She smiles and said, "That wasn't so bad."

Lazarus manages a weak smile, "Did I mention that I'm afraid of the dark?"

Sam chuckles, "You hide it well… Do you want to see the sensor data?"

"Yes, of course," Lazarus replies.

Sam links his visor with the data stored on the remote sensors and begins playback at normal speed.

Once again they see a ship approaching. As the craft draws near, a second ship flying much lower, darts back and forth across the badlands obviously looking for something or perhaps presenting itself as a target trying to lure them out. The lower ship swoops into the sinkhole almost directly in front of the remote sensor hidden in the landslide. This ship is very different from a Moonhawk. Where the Lunarian ship is smooth and pleasantly proportioned, this is boxy and angular, built of bolts and beams. Much smaller than a Moonhawk, it bristles with disrupter cannon. The little ship must be a flying power plant to support them all. There could be room for only one or two pilots. It was strictly an offensive war machine with very little defensive capability. It darts about the sinkhole but leaves without getting near their hiding place.

"They'll be back," Kitajima promises. "Brice, how are we doing?"

"The underlayment is done and we are closing. Should be only a few more minutes,"

"Good. Quan Kiai... Company meeting in five minutes between the transports," Kitajima orders. "Brice and Angel have the only free pass unless they're done by then. By the numbers, acknowledge."

In rapid succession his officers report in. "Lindsey, Lazarus, Zechariah. You're all invited." Kitajima said.

A few minutes later Quan Kiai begins arriving, the officers segregating themselves to one side, Zechariah, Lindsey and Lazarus the other. Kitajima is surprised to see Sam standing beside Lazarus, a worried expression on her face.

Kitajima takes center stage and looks at her expectantly, "Sam, what have you got?"

"We managed to determine that the interference blocking our communications is coming from multiple regions of orbital space. The static is steady and doesn't appear to be letting up any time soon. Until they stop jamming, we don't have a prayer of contacting Aldrin Station or in raising an Earth ground station," Sam reports.

Kitajima pauses, thinking. "So communications is being jammed across the entire system?"

"That's how it looks. No one in orbital space is communicating except by laser."

Kitajima goes on, "Tempel, what have you to report?"

"Lindsey was able to determine how the active camouflage works and a way to see past it. We have already begun modifying our sensors. The ships sensors are complete and we have only a few ghost suits remaining, Brice, Marcel, Angel, Hack and yours," Tempel reports.

"Good. Well done Lindsey. Tatiana, did you find out anything from the damaged AI?" Kitajima asks.

"The Zettaspheres external interface suffered heavy damage and without specialized equipment, which I don't have, I risk further damage," Tatiana said.

"Is there something else?" Kitajima asks recognizing the signals. She's something to say, and is dragging her heels.

"Well... After coming to this conclusion, I had some time and brought up the reconstruction Brice was doing when we bailed at the crash site. Magi had pretty much finished it and I had the ships AI run what she had done. I think you should see it," Tatiana said.

"Very well," Kitajima said.

The vid begins at the crash site just as they had found it, debris scattered along a two-mile track angled across the valley reaching the far side. The three dimensional image rotates to give the observers the best possible angle as it begins to roll backwards, like a video in reverse. Bit by bit, each piece twists and moves backward in time, retracing the path of their arrival, slowly at first but building up speed. The gouges and scars in the landscape disappear as the dust and debris return.

The crates pick up speed as they travel back in time. A huge cloud of regolith shrouds the freighter's main cabin as it tumbles and rolls across the valley floor, obscuring detail. It's not clear when the cargo came loose but Magi had made an educated guess that it was early in the crash because of the lack of more damage to the crates. The crates and the cabin continue to reverse their course towards the instant of impact, dust and debris swirls around them. Other smaller pieces of the engine compartment and the thrusters themselves cartwheel across the flat terrain, all converging towards that point in time and space when they were last together.

As the simulation approaches this point, a huge wall of dust and rock erupts from the surface blocking their view of the ship. Evolution's Child had acted like a giant snowplow after it hit but before it reached the bottom of the valley and started to tumble. This material is returning to where it had lain undisturbed for untold millennia. Tatiana halts the presentation and rotates it until they are looking almost straight down at the wreck before allowing it to continue. She stops it once more just as the crates and cabin come together. Seen through a veil of debris, the crates come to rest in the cargo section of the freighter, all four of them.

The group is silent as the implications sink in.

Kitajima looks at his officers. There's a good chance that some of them will not see home again if they do what needs doing.

"Captain, we must to go back and deal with this," Tempel said quietly, voicing what nearly everyone has already concluded.

"Yes Lieutenant, I believe you're right," Kitajima said softly.

"Are you nuts?" Zechariah said too loudly, panic in his voice. He can't understand them even considering such an idea. It's suicidal. Tatiana gives him a look that sends him ducking behind Lazarus.

Kitajima looks intently at Hack, "Get us started."

"What if we destroy the nukes we have and go after the one's we don't?" Hack asks. Quan Kiai knows the drill.

"Why not use one of the nukes we have and take out the one's we don't?" Tempel suggests looking sideways at Hack.

"You are assuming the other crate is still there. What if it's already gone?" Tatiana asks.

Tempel looks steadily at her for a moment, both of them coming to identical conclusions, "We have no choice. We must go back and find out what's going on. They may not have found the other crate or they may even think we have them all. We don't know what the situation is back at the crash site, and we need that information to make the best decision."

"It's suicide to go back. We just managed to get away. Two of your friends are dead, for God's sake." Zechariah exclaims, ignoring Lazarus's attempt to silence him.

"I didn't see God back there, only Brotherhood." Tempel replies.

Kitajima raises his hand stifling any more comments. Turning to Zechariah, "This is our responsibility, not yours," Turning back to face them he continues, "Anybody see it different? Or do you think we should pull in our tails and convince ourselves the job is done?" Kitajima looks out among the faces of his young Lunarians and can find no doubt, no hesitation in any of them. They all know what needs doing and will do it.

"Captain, we know our duty," Tempel said.

"I didn't come along to be left behind," Lindsey said with conviction. "I may not be Quan Kiai but I can still fight."

"As can I," Lazarus impulsively adds.

Kitajima stares at them, venting a few chuckles that soon evolve into a belly-busting eye-watering incredulous guffaw. His officers join in until they're all in tears, their tension shattering like an overstressed pane of glass. Lindsey and Lazarus stand and stare at the spectacle blankly. Lindsey cannot help but smile. Lazarus shrugs. Zechariah looks on, his eyes narrow with suspicion, not sure what is happening, thinking they may all be crazy.

Kitajima gets himself under control as he walks over to them. "Lindsey, Lazarus," he said slowly looking at each in turn. "I appreciate your offer…" he pauses, barely refraining from laughing point blank in their faces, "As I said, you will not be asked to fight, whatever it is we decide to do."

Turning away, Kitajima asks, "How are we on supplies Hack?"

"1200 hours of air and plenty of water and food but short on fuel. We received too many hits in the hydrazine tank. It's essentially empty. We were lucky we didn't take one in the aniline."

"BOOM." Brice said loudly, grinning when Zechariah jumps.

"Knock it off Brice," Tempel said.

Brice grins and obeys.

"Bottom line, once we divide the hydrazine in Moonhawk Two, we won't have enough to go back to the crash site and get us home. Pick one or the other," Hack reports.

"That settles it. How can you fight without fuel?" Zechariah injects.

"Leaving the Brotherhood with three nukes is not an option." Kitajima is growing tired of repeating himself.

Zechariah shakes his head and turns away in frustration. He's convinced God is talking to his heart and is dismayed that he cannot persuade these people of it.

"Let's take a step back, shall we?" Kitajima said abruptly. "Let's stick to the facts and decide what our next move should be." Turning to Hack He asked, "Where is the nearest cache?" For the last four years, Corso has had emergency supplies placed in various hidden locations out on the Central Highlands intended for just this situation. All they had to do was find one.

Hack shakes her head, "Nothing way out here. Anybody know different? Got your own personal stash out here somewhere?" She looks around at Quan Kiai.

A few shake their head but nobody said a word.

"Do we know how bad Aldrin got nailed?" Brice asks the question on everybody's mind.

Kitajima shakes his head, "Not really. The city could be under Brotherhood control right now."

"We don't have the hydrazine to make a run south to Shennong." Hack said. "The closest settlement of any size is Scottsbluff to the west of us in Faye crater. It's about seventy kilometers closer than Aldrin and by my calculations we can just make it, even after we retrieve the nukes."

"Then I guess we're going to Scottsbluff," Corazon said.

"I've been to Scottsbluff. There isn't much there," Angel points out.

"This isn't a vacation," Kitajima said. "I don't see another choice. We will head for Scottsbluff after the raid. Anybody have any other thoughts?"

"What are we going to do with Lindsey, Lazarus, and our young Propriety Officer while we fight?" Hack asks.

"Why don't we leave them somewhere? We can come back and pick them up after we're done," Brice said.

Lindsey looks at him with annoyance and back at Kitajima, "I will not be dropped off like some package. You are not the only one who came on this operation knowing what's at stake. We all knew it was a military mission. You do what you need to do and we will stay out of your way. Just stop this talk of leaving us behind."

Kitajima nods, "Good. Lindsey, you're in charge. You'll be responsible for making sure Zechariah and Lazarus do nothing. You will all be isolated. I cannot risk having any of you confusing us with your inexperience. End of discussion," he growls as Zechariah starts to speak, "That's the way it will be. You're not to even get out of your seats. You'll sit quietly and do nothing. Is that clear?" Kitajima leans down, looking meaningfully at Lindsey.

"Aye Kitajima, it's clear. Can we observe? Or must we wait until the vid's released," Lindsey said. She believes it's her duty as a citizen to be with these young Lunarians. She wants to know what price her freedom. How can she make intelligent decisions if she's unaware of their cost? How can anyone?

"It's your right to observe, but you'll only see what the officer is seeing, nothing more. You'll not be able to communicate with any officer or change their sensors remotely," Kitajima said. "The only exception is this… If you feel it necessary, call and I'll respond, but it had better be one hell of a good reason. Is that understood?"

"Aye." Lindsey nods her thanks. She has no desire to do more than watch the coming battle.

Kitajima uses his visors Map and Terrain Function (MTF) to present a 3D image of the territory around the crash site. Quan Kiai gathers around the waist high map.

The mare in that region consists of a number of wide valleys in a washboard pattern running parallel with Nell's Valley. They're giant ripples that solidified in the lake of lava billions of years ago. At this scale, the image looks like a frozen sea, only these wave crests are ridges of stone. Kitajima walks into the map. It cuts him off at the waist. He circles a position, his finger leaving a thin red line. A tiny transport appears at its center as the line fades.

"Hack, you bring Moonhawk One to this spot. I will land Two here. How many bugs do we have?" Kitajima asks her.

"Ten, all standard issue," Hack said.

"Good. Let's each send a pair into the valley as soon as we set down." Studying the map display carefully, Kitajima makes several line-of-sight comparisons, his system virtually placing him at each possible location, letting him see for himself. He decides on a high ridge overlooking the crash site from almost a kilometer away.

"While the bugs are snooping, Sam will position a spybot here," a bright white pinpoint of light appears within the terrain, "and Kipper will set another here." Another marker appears. "That will give us line-of-sight communications all across the valley. As soon as we have the data from the bugs we'll finalize our attack plan." Looking up at his young warriors he continues, "We may not need to fight but if we do, you will fight with extreme prejudice. I don't want to see any good sportsmanship when I review the logs. Understood?"

"Aye." The young police officers are tired of running and hiding, ready to avenge the deaths of Lei and Karl and all those people in Lincoln County Hospital. This is war and their enemy will receive no quarter.

"Ok people, let's break out the weapons and get mounted. It's time for the Republic to hit back." Kitajima said grimly.

"Aye," a ripple of excitement passes through the company.

"Hack, before we lift, I want you to install shape charges on the nukes. No matter what happens, we can't let the Brotherhood have them back." Kitajima said.

"Aye," she said.

Satisfied, Kitajima nods and said, "Let's get locked and loaded. You have thirty-four minutes until liftoff."

ЯL

In 480 BCE, three hundred Spartans under King Leonidas helped one another prepare for the battle of Thermopylae. So too does Quan Kiai help one another don the lethal accoutrements of 21st century warfare, Lunarian style. They have done this many times, but today's different. The usual chatter's absent.

Tempel runs Sam's diagnostic finding everything in the green. "You're good."

Waiting until Sam is ready, Tempel lifts the hard shell of his Shoulder Mounted Gun Platform (SMGP) over his head sliding it down onto his shoulders. He raises his arms straight up letting Sam activate the molyseals. The SMGP harness cinches tight under his arms and across his chest without hindering body movements. It provides a stable platform for attaching a pair of weapon mounts. Tempel is aware the moment the weapon system integrates with his ghost suit and comes online.

In the mount above Tempel's left shoulder is a disrupter. Short barreled and lethal, it uses the latest Harmon coil technology enhanced by a Lunarian innovation known as superconductive plasma discharge, something entirely new in the world of high-energy beam weapons. Mass is added by injecting a pulse of plasma, called a slug, into the energy stream. Arriving behind the beam at twenty kilometers per second, the slug strikes the target with incredible physical force. The one-two punch devastates ceramic armor, the beam weakening it, then the slug punching through.

Above his right shoulder is a launcher containing a dozen SuperX missiles. Propelled by magnetoplasma thrusters, they are capable of tremendous accelerations yet maneuverable enough to fill the role of close support. With a guidance system smart enough to stay on moving targets, they are the fire and forget weapons in the arsenal.

Look-and-shoot technology has been around for well over a century. To select a target, Tempel simply looks at it. What is unique is that Tempel picks which weapon and fires it using Direct Mind Control (DMC). Developed at the turn of the century for paraplegics, he has a neuromotor prosthesis embedded in his motor cortex, the area of his brain responsible for voluntary movement. The device detects brain cell activity and converts it into external signals. Thus, to fire his disrupter, he looks at the target and flexes his fire muscle, much in the same way he would locate a cup and close his hand around it. Tempel has trained to the point that he doesn't need to think about how to do it anymore, he functions as if this were a natural part of his being.

Sam's diagnostic is in the green. "You're good."

"Aye," Tempel links with Lazarus.

Lazarus is talking. "I think the Brotherhood is making a bid to control orbital space and the powersats. If they succeed, they'll dominate Earth and be in a position to dictate to everyone. That would make them the world's first multi planet empire."

"To control the powersats they must control Taurus Colony and Luna. That means controlling Lunarians." Lindsey said from inside where she's helping Hack rig the crates. "That's the only viable reason for these bombs. We outnumber them at least ten to one. But if they can threaten us with a nuclear bomb…well… that evens things out quite a lot."

"That's their style," Lazarus said nodding. "How many nukes do you think it would take to hold Luna hostage?" He asked. "Aldrin Station,

New London, Shennong, Kyoto, Gagarin."

"That's five but Evolution's Child carried twelve rather small nukes. How do you explain that?" Tempel asks while walking over.

Lazarus turns to face Tempel, shrugs and said, "How many boroughs are there in Aldrin Station, ten, eleven? What if each borough gets a nuke? Even if they are small, that many going off all at the same time would definitely destroy a Lunarian city," Lazarus said. "I don't believe they simply want to subdue Luna. I think their long range goal is to destroy you and take what is yours, your cities, your factories, your women…"

"Our women?" Tempel asks.

"Absolutely." Lazarus said. "The Brotherhood considers women, especially little girls, as spoils of war. Don't cut them any slack, because they won't cut you any."

"You needn't worry. Quan Kiai will make sure their willingness to die for Allah is fulfilled," Tempel replies. The image of three-year-old Lana rises unbidden within his mind, blond hair, sweet voice, and pancake syrup smeared across one cheek. The syrup turns to blood as Lana becomes just another body in the wreckage. He shakes his head to clear his mind of these dark thoughts.

"Why bring the nukes in this way? Why not bring them as part of the invasion?" Tatiana asks joining the conversation. "Shipping them in on a freighter like ordinary cargo makes no sense to me."

"Deniability perhaps? If Minister bin Aunker has one weakness it's that he's overly cautious. If Brotherhood forces are caught with them, the gig is up," Lazarus replies. "They must have gone through several checkpoints to even get them off the planet. That's got to be it. He just didn't want to risk getting caught."

Tempel checks in on the young Federation Propriety Officer. Not long ago, polygraphic indicators had shown Zechariah suffering from a high degree of tension, but that seems to have changed. The man is almost too calm as he leans forward, head bowed, eyes clinched shut, and fingers clasped together, praying to his god.

"…hold me in your hand dear Lord. Do with me as you will. In the precious name of Jesus Christ, Amen." Zechariah finishes. He raises his head slowly, his face the picture of tranquility.

Tempel shakes his head in bewilderment. Religion has brought them to this point. He's incapable of distinguishing between Islam and Christianity. They're both Iron Age superstitions motivating otherwise peaceful men and women to do things they would never consider doing without it. He glances at his comrades, proud that none of them suffers from the god delusion and the empty promises of an afterlife. Yet, they are willing to risk everything for family, friends, and freehold.

Tempel's curiosity is aroused. It's not often he's in such close contact with a devout Christian. Even though Freedom of Belief is among the rights listed in the Lunarian Constitution, there's simply a dearth of god believers among Luna's general population. It's no fun to argue with someone with the same set of values as you have and arguing is one of Tempel's favorite pastimes.

"Zechariah, you'll be riding in the other transport. Come outside and join us," Tempel orders.

Zechariah exits the Moonhawk and stops beside Lazarus.

"Where do you want me to sit?" Zechariah asks.

"Someone will tell you when its time," Tatiana replies.

Zechariah glances at Tatiana then at Lazarus. A strangeness flashes across his face.

Zechariah is hiding something. "What do you know about Lazarus?" Tempel asks.

"Nothing…" but the question rattles him.

Tempel bores in, "You're lying. I will ask you one more time. What do you know about Lazarus?"

Zechariah's polygraphic indicators are now swinging wildly, the calming influence of the prayer has evaporated and raw fear takes its place.

"He's a traitor. A memo was sent around ordering us to watch for him." Zechariah said.

"What did the memo order you to do when you found him?" Tatiana asks moving closer to him.

Sweat runs down Zechariah's face, "Report his location."

"Another lie... Captain, what's the punishment for lying?"

Zechariah panics, "The memo said to either bring him in or administer justice ourselves. They promised an early return home with full pay and honors for the one who... does him." Turning to Lazarus, "They have Saul," he blurts out.

"What." Lazarus lunges at Zechariah who backs out of reach. With one hand, Tempel easily holds Lazarus back. "My brother had nothing to do with my leaving."

"Then you must come back with me and tell them. You are the only one who can save him now. His life's in your hands."

Tatiana huffs, "Let me get this straight. The Federation puts a hit out on Lazarus, arrests brother Saul who has done nothing illegal and the only way to save him is for Lazarus to turn himself in, and if he doesn't, it will be Lazarus' fault whatever they decide to do to Saul... Now there's the Federation the world has come to love. No act too despicable, no deed too dreadful, the end justifies the means."

"They have forgotten that the path is as important as the destination," Kitajima said. "Thank you Zechariah."

The young PO turns to look for Kitajima, spotting him under the newly repaired outrigger with several others. "Thank me for what?"

"For reminding us who we are by showing us who we are not," Kitajima smiles, "Thank you."

Zechariah shakes his head in confusion, "I don't understand."

"Of course you don't. Tell me, how do you feel about Saul being punished in place of Lazarus?" Kitajima asks Zechariah.

"I… think it's wrong," Zechariah said.

Tatiana laughs again, "Liar." she steps towards the young man who moves behind Tempel.

"OK. OK. The truth. Lazarus was in a position of trust and betrayed that trust. He is an enemy of the Federation. Besides, he knew his brother would be under suspicion when he left and didn't care," Zechariah said.

"I…" The accusation hits Lazarus like a ton of bricks. Can he tell himself he was not aware of that possibility? No. He knew this could happen and closed his mind to it.

"You cannot lay this evil on him," Tempel said. "Lazarus fled a corrupt system because that was his only option. Citizens no longer have a say in what's done in their name. When a government gets that bad, only revolution can change it."

"That's terrorist talk." Zechariah hisses.

"One man's terrorist is another man's freedom fighter."

"I will not listen to such ungodliness." Zechariah said.

"If everything happens according to god's plan, why not the fall of the Federation?" Tempel asks.

"I know God's plan and destroying his kingdom on Earth is not part of it." Zechariah flares.

"How do you know? Do you hear voices?" Tatiana asks.

"When I pray, *He* places the answers on my heart."

"Maybe that's indigestion," Tatiana said.

"You don't honestly believe you have conversations with the creator of the universe… do you?" Tempel asks.

"*His* will be done. I simply lay my case before *Him*."

"If god is willing to prevent evil but is not able, then he's not omnipotent. If god is able but not willing then he's malevolent. If god is both willing and able, then where does evil come from? If god is neither willing nor able, then god is not a god at all." Tempel stares down the young man. "I lost family in Lincoln County Hospital. Where was your god then?"

Zechariah wilts under Tempel's glare, "I'm not your enemy Lieutenant, and **God** is not your enemy. As a Christian, I believe as you do, in the sanctity of life. But I also realize even the Creator finds it necessary to occasionally take life in order to save life. What the Lord gives, **He** can take away."

Tempel turns to Lazarus, "How did you live with such nonsense?"

Lazarus shrugs. "As a child, I can remember my father speaking to me of things I didn't understand at the time. As I grew older, I realized he was a Freethinker hiding behind a facade of belief in order to survive. I learned from a real pro."

"I can't imagine lying about something so big for so long. To pretend to believe in god, attend church, pray, and say all the things you must have said to convince everyone around you that you are a Christian. How did you do it?" Tempel looks at Lazarus strangely.

"It's dishonest," Brice adds. His expression verges on distrust.

Lazarus shrugs, "I kept reminding myself of something my father once told me. He said not to worry about telling a lie just as long as the person you lie to, is lying back at you. The people that fill the churches pretend to be one thing but are something completely different. I fit right in."

Zechariah frowns, thinking about this for a moment, "What about true believers? How do you justify lying to them?"

"What makes you think you're not lying just because you believe what you're saying? To me the most despicable lie is the one retold by someone foolish enough to believe it," Lazarus said. Turning to Brice, "The essence of a good lie is to put some truth in it and believe it or not, you can find truth in the bible. For instance, Ecclesiastes Chapter 3, verses 18-19. *I hoped in my heart that God might make clear to the sons of men, that they themselves are beasts. For that which befall the sons of men, befall the beasts; as the one dies so dies the other, yea, they have all one breath; so that a man hath no preeminence above a beast."*

Tempel grins, "I'm starting to see how you managed."

"I hate to end this little chitchat but it's time to mount up," Kitajima said.

Battle of Nell's Valley

"Courage without conscience is a wild beast."

Robert Ingersoll (1833-1899)

Kitajima lands his Moonhawk northwest of Nell's Valley, a few kilometers from the crash site. Moments later, he releases a pair of bugs, small self-contained recording devices the size of a mosquito whose primary mission is to locate all electronic sentries, and second, obtain a visual on the crash site. One is to fly along the ridge closest to them and the other out over the valley. Both will remain several hundred meters up, very difficult but not impossible to detect. If detected, other bugs could follow them back. Everyone is on edge, alert to the possibility of fight or flight on very short notice.

Sam puts the final touches on the little spybot, filling it with just enough fuel to get it where it needs to be. Even a few grams left in the tanks could attract the attention of a passing sniffer. Like the bugs, it deploys using micro-thrusters to propel it through the lunar vacuum. The spybot contains a full remote sensor array and a complete set of combat communications in a package the size of a peach pit.

Sam's the acknowledged champion in deploying spybots. She's managed to put them in impossible places more than once during training. Now, when it really matters, she relies on that training and doesn't let herself think about the consequences of failure.

Sam flies the spybot as if she were sitting in a tiny cockpit within the stone. She streaks up the valley staying low, never more than a few meters off the surface. Stopping below a ridge, the spybot creeps upward until she can just peek over the top. It hovers there for an instant while she looks about.

Nothing.

Sam darts over to rest briefly on the top of a prominent boulder, and then flits away. Like bread crumbs marking a path, she leaves behind a device smaller than a grain of rice, a line-of-sight laser communications relay. She maneuvers over the ridge and starts down the other side.

Still nothing.

The spybot crosses the valley floor and up the far side. Sam glances at her fuel meter. She must pick up the pace or risk not getting the bot where it needs to be.

This section of the valley is rugged and broken. A small cliff lies before her. Up the rock face she flies, cresting it just as the fuel warning sounds in her ears. With less than thirty seconds of flight time remaining, she maneuvers between boulders at blinding speed. She slows and lands the flying piece of basalt on top of a pile of stones similar to her tiny spybot, its sensors pointing into the valley below. Shutting off the tiny thrusters, Sam looks at her remaining fuel. Only two seconds of flight time remaining. She releases a long breath, shaking her head in disbelief.

"Well done." Kitajima said squeezing her shoulder. "Establish the comm link with Hack."

Sam tentatively probes the coordinates and is gratified with an immediate acknowledgment. The two transports are linked once more.

"Hack, report," Kitajima orders.

"We're at our assigned position awaiting our bugs return," Hack said.

"Good. Let me know when you get them back," Kitajima said. "Tempel, let's take a look."

"Aye," Tempel replies.

Linking to the spybot, Tempel zooms in on the camp. From this low angle, it's impossible to see everything but there's more than just a few rovers. At least one big ship, several heavily armed Goliaths, and two of the small fighters are parked on the other side of the crash site, perhaps even the same two that was looking for them back at Sunset Canyon. Movement is everywhere and he can just see the top of a large portable shelter.

At that instant, two rovers come over a rise directly into their field of view completely blocking the camera. Tempel backs off the magnification. These are more of the small two man rovers they had tangled with just a few hours earlier. For their size, they pack a big punch, not much more than four wheels on a high capacity power pack feeding a disrupter. Quan Kiai respects the lethal cannon mounted on these vehicles. They have the power to punch through their vacsuit's shielding with a single shot.

Tempel begins to populate the strategic map of the engagement. Refocusing on the main camp, he continues to categorize the Brotherhood's forces, the number of people, type of armament, and the location of everything. This is something he's particularly good at, identifying what they are up against in a way that enables them to formulate a plan of action.

"There must be a hundred guys there," Brice whispers. "Are you sure we want to do this?"

Tempel's hands fly over his virtual controls. Without looking up or slowing down, he grins. "What? You want to live forever?"

"Hack, are you seeing this," Kitajima asks.

"Aye... It looks like we have some work to do," Hack said. "The big ship is a Brotherhood frigate. If it brings its guns to bear, we'll be in trouble."

"Excuse me, but our bugs are back," Sam reports, already putting them in the reader. She brings the first vid online.

The bug, programmed to fly parallel with the ridge, doesn't detect any electronic sentries. On the other hand, the human sentries are easily located. They're clumped up beside a rocky outcropping directly above the site. Tempel counts twelve, all with pulse rifles. They seem more interested in what's happening down in the valley than keeping an eye on the mare. On the slope below the ridge are other rovers and their soldiers clustered in groups of two or more. Tempel's hands blur as he organizes the data for the simulation.

The other bug went down the heart of the valley and directly over the crash site itself. From hundreds of meters up, its view is remarkable. Men and equipment swarm over and around the wreckage. Most are common soldiers but some technicians are apparent. As the bug passes over the pilothouse, it becomes clear what they're doing. There's a trench alongside the pilothouse and even as they watch, an excavator emerges with a load of lunar regolith, dumping it close by.

A group is standing next to the entrance of the pit talking and gesturing. Tempel wishes he could eavesdrop on the conversation.

"They haven't got them yet." Sam declares.

The bugs directly above the main camp now, a hastily constructed affair made up of a portable shelter and three Goliaths parked in a row. He had landed on the very same spot just hours before. As the bug loops back towards them, it flies over several clusters of rovers with their crews lounging in or around them. It's plain to everyone that this is not going to be a walk in the park.

The bug passes over the two fighters. These machines pose high danger to the company, perhaps greater than the frigate. It would jeopardize the entire mission if even one of these deadly little ships gets skyborne. The bug identifies another vehicle, this one sitting apart from the rest, probably the hypergolic fuel tanker.

Kipper and Tatiana incorporate the information from their bugs and combine it with the data Tempel has collated. Even though the two ships are kilometers apart, VR brings them together around an integrated 3D image of Nell's Valley, the frigate, fighters, Goliaths, and rovers all clearly represented in miniature.

Kitajima moves forward looking like a man wading in waist deep water and takes a position at one end of the valley. "I will start the ball rolling by taking out the frigate's comm system and armament. That ship is my primary target. I don't want it to ever see orbital space again… Tatiana, you will attack the fighters, don't let them get off the ground. Then drive through to the main camp from here… Tempel, your team attacks from this direction, take out that bunch on the ridge and proceed to the main camp this way... Kipper you will attack from this direction and Consuela from here. Do a pincer and close the loop… I want everyone to converge and take everything out. I don't want any men or machines left in one piece… Once the camp is clear, Hack will land here. I will bring in my ship and take this position. Brice and I will assume responsibility of extracting the crate. The rest of you will spread out and find whatever the Brotherhood has been kind enough to leave behind. Memory cubes, command and control computers, any AI's, you know the drill. Let's do this by the book. Find everything of value and destroy the rest. Any questions or comments?" He looks around at the faces of the assembled officers, looking for weakness or hesitation and finding none. "Good. Let's do a full scale simulation and see where we are."

Quan Kiai plays a sophisticated game of team combat, a virtual dose of warfare that allows them to experience the coming battle before risking their lives, correcting the flaws in the plan while giving the young warriors confidence. Fifteen minutes later, they're finished, having coordinated targets and responsibilities for the attack right down to what weapon to use in each instance. Time well spent.

"Anybody want to add anything?" Kitajima is proud of the way his team's performing.

"Aye, I do," said Tempel.

"Go ahead, speak your mind."

"I just want to remind everyone of Lincoln County Hospital, of Black Friday, of Prattville and Darpur and countless others. The men we face today applaud mass murder and support the leaders who ordered these killings. Don't feel sympathy for any of them. They deserve no mercy."

The gathering listens solemnly. Too many family and friends died at the hands of the Brotherhood. They all feel the weight of those innocent Lunarians and honored to be the tool of their vengeance. They hoped this moment would come when they put on a ghost suit. Quan Kiai is ready for the coming battle, a weapon of mass destruction primed for detonation.

"Are we set?" Kitajima asks one last time.

"**Aye. LOCKED AND LOADED**," the young warriors reply.

Kitajima leans forward and thrusts his right fist into the sky, "Quan Kiai."

The others join him and their fists come together in a tight circle and say in unison, "**Quan Kiai.**"

"Let's roll," Kitajima utters the words that send Lunarian warriors into battle for the very first time.

ℛ𝕃

Lazarus takes the seat behind Kitajima and next to Lindsey. Zechariah sits by himself at the back.

"How long do you think they'll be?" Lazarus asks.

Lindsey is tense, "As long as it takes. We can talk later. Right now I want to be with Tempel." She believes citizens should personally witness the horrors of combat to know firsthand what price their freedom. The vast majority of Lunarians agree but only she's privileged to see it real-time.

"Yes, of course. Do you mind if I link to you?" Lazarus asks.

"Not at all, but be warned, I'm going to be fully immersed with Tempel and the others. I expect this will be brutal. It may be more than you can handle," Lindsey said.

Lazarus stiffens, "I'm sure I'll be fine."

With jarring suddenness, he's out on the surface looking through the eyes of Tempel, moving rapidly over the rough terrain in a fashion that doesn't seem quite right. He's in the lead so the others are not in sight. He can hear Tempel breath and see his hands reach out, gripping the lunar surface, propelling himself forward.

Suddenly he realizes what's so strange about the movement. Tempel is bounding across the landscape using all four limbs. Even as this realization hits him, the lieutenant turns his head and glances at his companions, giving Lazarus a glimpse of their unique quadruped motion. Smooth and graceful, it is a hybrid motion somewhere between mountain gorilla and cheetah. Their long slender necks allow them to look forward while sprinting across the land, and the joints in their hips and shoulders move in ways impossible for Lazarus.

Their weapons have rotated up over their backs and point forward well above the tops of their heads. The flexibility of the vacsuits has never been more evident as the spines of these young Lunarians bend and twist in a powerful display of agility and power. They are beautiful to behold as they bound across the landscape in giant leaps.

Lazarus is speechless. His mind struggles to grasp what he's witnessing. Many mystifying occurrences over the past few days now crystallize within his mind. These people are different in ways he's only beginning to understand.

"Lindsey... Please explain what I'm seeing," Lazarus asks with trepidation. This frightens him to his core and threatens to destroy the good feeling he's had since his arrival.

Lindsey sighs and pushes Tempel's video signal into the corner where she can monitor it while she talks. It will take a few moments for them to reach their targets. She can give Lazarus that time. "Tempel and the others are… special."

"What do you mean special?" Lazarus presses.

"They have been given gifts that enhance those given to them by Mother Nature."

"So it's true, they're mutants?" Lazarus asks bluntly.

Lindsey barely suppresses her anger. "Like many other names given to people in the past, the term mutant is unacceptable. If you use it again, you will find out very quickly that your freedom does not extend to insults based in ignorance."

The sharp edge in Lindsey's voice signals Lazarus that he's treading on thin ice.

"I meant no offense... It's incredible. Are they another race?"

"No, not really, but they call themselves Highlanders."

"Are you serious?" Lazarus asks.

"The scientists named them something quite different, but they prefer Highlander and now everybody uses the name," Lindsey said.

Glancing at the small image in the corner of her visor, she sees that Quan Kiai is nearing their assigned positions. "Can we discuss this later?"

"Yes… of course," Lazarus said. He re-links with Lindsey to watch the battle. Questions swirl through his mind but he wasn't going to miss this for anything.

ЯL

Tempel spots their quarry as they come around a sweeping curve. From over a kilometer away, the thermal emissions of the soldiers highlight them in blazing red along the top of the ridge. They are standing together near a large basalt boulder, the only thing breaking the barren ridge for a long ways. Most are looking down upon the crash site, oblivious to the approaching Lunarians.

In single file, the warriors angle up the steep mountainside. At the top, Tempel, Sam, and Zoey turn and head straight for the group along the crest of the ridge. Angel continues down the other side leading Brice and Karyl towards the south end of the Brotherhood camp. None of the warriors break stride as they sprint across the vertical environment, bounding upward with the same grace and agility they demonstrated on the level.

Across Nell's Valley, Karyl, Alonzo and Tatiana swarm over the ridge almost directly above their primary target, the fighters. They spread out into attack formation as they come. Already on the valley floor, Consuela leads Marcel and Corazon from the opposite direction toward the other end of the camp. None has fired a shot, but that will soon change. The four teams are rapidly converging on the unsuspecting camp.

The upper portion of the frigate contains most of the Brotherhood's long-range communications. Kitajima slowly brings his Moonhawk up until he can just peek over the ridge and see the sensor array through the Gattling's gun sights. Magnified and targeted, he times his attack to coincide with his platoon reaching their initial objectives. An instant before Quan Kiai begin their attack, he opens up. His disrupter vaporizes the ceramic armor in a silent explosion, relentlessly drilling into the ship until the pressurized atmosphere bursts forth.

One of the men on the ridge points down into the valley. To a man, the sentry's all look down, a fatal mistake. Bounding along the top of the ridge like hounds from hell, Tempel, Sam and Zoey spread out and begin firing with an inhuman accuracy.

The Lunarians see only Brotherhood combat vacsuits, heavy with plate armor. The men behind the grotesque battle helmets are simply targets on a shooting range. One, two, three, four, five, six, seven, eight, nine, die before they even know the Lunarians are there, cut down like wheat during harvest.

Blood rises in a gaseous haze that takes on a life of its own. Within moments, the ridge above Nell's Valley is a meat grinder. The tenth sentry manages to turn and the eleventh levels his weapon just before they add their blood to the carnage. The twelfth ducks behind the boulder, extending his life by almost a second.

Tempel shoots him in the head as he leaps over the rock. He leads Sam and Zoey downward into Nell's Valley, leaving the expanding cloud of blood and fluids behind.

Synchronized with Kitajima's first shot, Tatiana, Karyl and Alonzo launch missiles at the fighters now less than a hundred meters away. The deadly little finless darts, less than eight centimeters long and two centimeters in diameter, leap from their shoulder mounted launchers and streak towards their targets. In a blur, they strike the fighters and punch through the thin skin. Like a stick of dynamite in a shoebox, the explosion tears them apart. Neither come close to making it off the ground. Karyl sees a figure crawling away from the wreckage and laces his back with disrupter fire. A reddish brown fog erupts from the wounds.

Consuela, Marcel, and Corazon launch missiles at the two vehicles setting west of the camp. The explosions rip open the tank section of the closest, dumping the fluid inside onto the ground where it immediately begins to boil. The other tanker follows a similar fate and the released liquid forms a thick fog that hangs in the vacuum. It's undoubtedly either hydrazine or aniline, one component in the hypergolic fuel used in magnetoplasma thrusters and high capacity fuel cells. Corazon shoots several men when they emerge from the second vehicle, adding their blood to the ghastly mix.

Brice, Angel and Kipper descend into the valley east of Tempel's position and race towards that end of the camp. Several rovers and an armed Goliath are providing security for that side of the camp while keeping the hypergolic constituents separated. From well away, Angel magnifies her target, firing at the Goliath's forward section, probing for its power pack. A second burst from her laser cannon finds its mark. The vehicle explodes in a huge fireball.

Brice and Kipper sprint down the side of the valley firing as fast as their disrupters can recharge. First one rover, then the other explodes as their hypergolic fuels mix. Soldiers run to get away from the unseen death that has descended upon them. Kipper targets the nearest man, almost cutting him in half as he concentrates all his firepower on the soldier's center of mass. Blood spews grotesquely into the vacuum as his body comes to rest, instantly turning to gas.

Brice hits the second and third rovers in rapid secession as he springs forward, sending more fireballs skyward. The men previously clustered around the vehicles, scatter, seeking cover from the terrain but finding none. The few boulders big enough to offer any security are several hundred meters away along the north side of the valley. Digging in his hands and feet, Brice skids to a stop causing a huge wave of fine lunar regolith to rise around him marking his location. Starting with the man furthest back, one by one he picks off the fleeing soldiers. Their lifeless bodies lie across the landscape like some gruesome dotted line.

Brice remains stationary for too long. A beam slams into his chest missing his heart but slicing through his lung. His blood and other bodily fluids spew into the vacuum. He lives long enough to know he's dying.

"No." Marcel cries out.

"Maintain discipline." Kitajima orders roughly. "Finish the job." Brice had broken the cardinal rule, never stop. It cost him dearly.

The others are aware that Brice is down but they have all been taught the best way to help wounded comrades was to finish the fight and leave the medical issues to others. It's the medico's job to monitor vital signs and initiate treatment as needed. Doc Grady can do nothing to save Brice.

Kipper sends a SuperX missile into a Goliath. It penetrates and explodes, ripping open the high capacity fuel cell. A fraction of a second later, a second much larger explosion splits open the massive four-wheeler, silently sending an intense fireball mushrooming skyward. The force of the blast picks up a nearby rover and flips it on its side. Kipper laces the rover's exposed underbelly with a long burst. Another silent ball of flame rises above the shredded carcass of the vehicle.

Virtually invisible to the Brotherhood, the warriors converge on the camp from all directions. Leaping over and around anything in their path, they deliver a massive dose of death and destruction.

Soaring over the top of a large boulder, Tempel shoots a soldier square in the back killing him instantly. The man flops to the surface like a rag doll, gushing blood. Vacuum rips the blood asunder, adding its bits to the growing gaseous haze gathering over the battlefield like smog over a city.

Sam opens fire on a group of soldiers running away from the carnage, cutting them down like wheat before a scythe. None survive. Switching targets to a nearby rover, she blasts several holes in its hypergolic fuel tanks. A moment later, the fuels mix and silently explode.

From the far side of the flame, two Brotherhood soldiers draw Zoey's attention. Leaping through the dissipating fireball, she shoots each one in the chest as she passes between them in a blur too fast for Earth born human's to handle. A blood-red cloud spews from the two men as they fall to the ground, landing flat on their backs, side by side. She lands beyond the dead soldiers and digs her hands deep into the regolith. Twisting, she coils her legs and pushes off, changing directions in the blink of an eye. Zoey's already homing in on her next target.

A short distance away, Tempel spots a rover picking up speed heading out of the valley. Overtaking the vehicle, he fires into the back of each occupant. For good measure, he puts another burst through the rover's power pack as he passes. The rover hits a boulder and tumbles spewing hypergolic fuels. He doesn't wait to see what happens next.

Marcel attacks the parked convoys from broadside, letting loose a pair of SuperX missiles at the nearest. One missile hits between the balloon tires near the articulation joint, the second hits the main passenger compartment above the front tire. The four-wheeled Goliath explodes. Those inside did not have time to don a vacsuit.

Tatiana leads Karyl and Alonzo past the remains of the pilothouse. They use the wreckage as cover and pop out on the far side with their cannons blazing. The warriors speed and stealth surprise the soldiers gathered there. Before they have time to realize what's happening, the Lunarians annihilate their ranks. They aim for center of mass as they sprint past. Not one of the twenty-two soldiers gets off a shot.

Almost as an afterthought, Tatiana launches a missile through the front view port of the second Goliath. The explosion bounces the big vehicle, splitting the pressure hull and releasing the internal atmosphere in a surge of gases that rises a hundred meters into the sky. She launches a second missile at the lone remaining truck, angled downward this time, aiming for the high-capacity power supply buried in its gut. It explodes violently.

From behind the wreckage of the pilothouse, four Brotherhood soldiers open fire on the dark shadows that just went past.

"Kipper. The freighter." Tatiana calls.

She could have saved her breath. Kipper and Angel are already there. They leap over Evolution's Child and engage the soldiers from above and behind. Focused on Tatiana and the others, they never realize that death has found them until it's too late. The warriors mow them down like ducks on a pond. Angel's only shot on the last soldier was an exposed arm. She didn't hesitate, burning a hole in the forearm right below the elbow. Blood spews forth in a bloody fog. The soldier puts his other hand over the wound but can't slow the rush. He slumps to the ground and vacuum finishes the job.

"Clear." Angel calls out, looking for her next target.

Corazon, Marcel, and Consuela swing around the twisted remains of the fuel tankers and bear down on the frigate. They can see the Goliath parked just beyond it. To their left is a group of non-combatants, probably mechanics or technicians, heading as fast as they can back towards the main camp. On foot, they pose little threat. The warriors can't even detect a weapon on any of them. Corazon swings wide and opens up as soon as he's clear. One, two, three go down and the remaining men stop and raise their arms in surrender. Corazon appreciates them providing such an easy target. Spacing his shots right down the line, he nails all six dead center from over a hundred meters away. Their blood adds to the growing battlefield haze.

Beyond them, three rovers are coming up to speed and heading up the valley away from the battle. Targeting the closest, Consuela's first shot locks up the front drive wheels causing the vehicle to career into a large basalt outcrop, coming to a sudden and violent stop. She chews up the now stationary target making sure nothing could survive. The other rovers open fire trying vainly to hit something they cannot see.

Like a hunting wolf, Consuela parallels the remaining two rovers. They race over the valley floor at speeds exceeding fifty kilometers per hour. Her first volley misses the lead rover's power pack. She turns her attention to the driver. The rover begins trailing bloody fog then veers off course striking a large boulder, flips on its side, and skids across the lunar surface. One more burst in its exposed underbelly sends the buggy up in a hypergolic ball of flame.

Kitajima hammers at the larger ship, concentrating first on the thrusters then on the weapon turrets. He never sees the rover coming at him. The first beam cut through the Moonhawk and passes between Lazarus and Kitajima about shoulder high. The second beam strikes Kitajima in the right temple. His head explodes.

The Moonhawk dips and loses altitude. It would have crashed if Lindsey hadn't grabbed the virtual controls.

"Oh shit." Lindsey banks and accelerates away from the rover. "Lazarus. Take control of the cannon."

Lazarus is stunned. He is in the middle of a brutal battle in a way he had never imagined possible, Brice is dead, Kitajima is dead, and somehow he must pull himself together and do something he's never done before.

"Lazarus." Lindsey said. "I'm not Kitajima. I can't fly and fight at the same time."

"How?" Lazarus stutters.

Lindsey transfers the cannon function to his visor. "Just look at what you want to hit and press this icon."

She swings the ship around and heads back. The rover was trading shots with Consuela and didn't see the approaching Moonhawk. Lazarus locks his gaze on it and fires. The beam passes through the roll cage without touching anything.

"Magnify," Lindsey orders.

Lazarus magnifies and fires again and again and again. He turns the driver into a reddish brown fog. The rover skids to a stop.

"That's it. Keep firing." Lindsey said.

The rover explodes a moment later, its fuel tanks punctured.

"Nice shooting." Consuela said.

Lindsey had chased the rover out onto the valley floor and the Brotherhood frigate still had some fight left in it. Beams slash through the Moonhawk and several hit Kitajima again. Inside the ship is a bloody haze that clings to everything it touches.

Lazarus turns his gaze on the frigate and continues to fire as fast as the cannon can reenergize. He finishes the job Kitajima started, obliterating the last of the frigates gun turrets. He didn't stop. He pumps shot after shot into the sitting target. Explosions rock it and escaping air hangs over the doomed ship.

"Consuela, take command of Moonhawk One," Tempel orders.

Showing tremendous strength, Consuela digs into the soft regolith making a sharp turn towards the frigate. The dust of her passage settles slowly behind her.

Marcel and Corazon launch missiles at the warship as they pass, not waiting around to see the results. To their left, two rovers are sprinting away from the camp. Firing from over two hundred meters away, their disrupters hit within centimeters of their target, ripping at the vehicles underbelly, probing relentlessly for the power pack. The hypergolic fluids react in a towering ball of flame, ripping the rover apart. Its companion vehicle meets the same fate a second later, exploding with a force that sends one of its balloon tires bouncing wildly across the valley floor.

Sam sprints down the debris field. To her right she spots motion along the ground as a soldier crawls away. A burst along his spine stops all movement. Swinging around the wreckage of the pilothouse, Sam launches a missile at the frigate. It hits the fuselage near a landing strut and rips apart the superstructure. The frigate collapses, its remaining landing struts partially holding it up. Gases gush from gaping holes in its skin.

The last three rovers speed towards the north end of the valley away from the camp, running for their lives. Hidden behind the frigate for most of their sprint, they are a kilometer away before anyone notices them, and only then because the gunner in the lead rover cannot resist taking a pot shot at a shadow.

Marcel spots the three vehicles racing up the valley after his targeting system lets him know he's under fire. Hitting a fast moving rover at that distance is tricky, even for Marcel. Leaping in pursuit, he closes the gap. At the top of a leap, he fires and the rover last in line erupts in flame, fails to make a turn and slams into a large basalt outcropping. The second rover detonates a moment later. Trailing a cloud of bloody gases, the final rover crests a ridge and disappears, the only vehicle to survive

Nell's Valley.

"Let them go." Tempel orders, pulling Marcel up short. "Someone should live to tell of what happened here today."

The attack lasted less than two minutes. A fog of death hangs thick over the valley. It'll take days for the cloud to disperse and years before their sensors can't detect it forensically.

"Hack, get in here. Lindsey, land Moonhawk Two per the plan. Hack, help her. Kipper, you and Doc Grady take care of Brice and the Captain," Tempel takes command. "Sam, you're with me."

"Aye," she said.

Lindsey lands just beyond the wreckage of the pilothouse. Sam crawls into the hole. If the bomb isn't already exposed, they will need to keep the excavator digging until it was. That's her job.

Lazarus emerges from the Moonhawk, "What can I do to help?"

"It's still several meters to the crate," Sam replies. "But this is a Hodgkin's excavator assembled right here on Luna. It'll make short work of it."

"Good, then let's get started," Lazarus said.

"You stay out of the way," Sam said to his chagrin.

"Quan Kiai, listen up," Tempel said. "We have two minutes of digging and another two to get the crate loaded. You have that long to collect intelligence. Follow the plan, Angel and Alonzo take the frigate, Consuela and Corazon the shelter, Tatiana, Karyl and Zoey poke around what's left of the Goliaths. You know what you're looking for. Let's move out."

Approaching the heavily damaged frigate, Angel and Alonzo can see the main airlock is beyond use. The two warriors climb the side of the ship heading towards a big hole. The Lunarians peer inside then crawl through. The frigate has no power forcing their visors to increase sensitivity in the low-light-level sensors.

The floor tilts at a crazy angle. Everything loose slid downhill when the ship tipped over and is in one big pile at the bottom.

"This must have been living quarters. Come on. Let's see where this leads." Alonzo scampers up the angled floor heading for an open door above them. He pulls himself through the doorway into the next room.

Angel follows, leaping through the doorway without touching the sides. She lands on all fours. The room is thick with gases. The large quantities of blood and urine testify that more than one person died here. That isn't their concern right now. This isn't a forensic mission. They're looking for loot in the form of knowledge.

Along the side of the room is a passage leading upward. Angel takes it, emerging on what is obviously the ships control room. Bodies lie against one wall in a tangled heap of arms and legs. From the looks of things, no one had vacsuits on at the time of the attack. They paid dearly for their carelessness.

Banks of electronic equipment line the walls. Alonzo stops at a large floor-to-ceiling rack, running his hand down the front, analyzing the markings on each piece of equipment.

"Here. This is the AI. It's marked in Arabic, Chinese, and English. They must have bought it on the open market." Alonzo said.

"Get it and let's go. We don't have all day." Angel flares, clinging to the edge of a console near what must have been the command chair. Blood smears one armrest and two holes are neatly punched in its back. She finds a small book tucked in a pocket and recognizes it as the Captains personal log, a practice the Brotherhood continues from the earlier days of sea faring ships.

Alonzo looks around in panic, "Shit. I don't have a screwdriver."

Angel smiles as she slips the book into a pocket of her ghost suit. She scrambles past Alonzo, finds a good angle, and opens up with her disrupter on the metal framework of the rack, deftly cutting the AI out with surgical skill.

Alonzo meekly assists in cutting the fiber-optic cabling from the back of the device as Angel pulls it free from the rack. She then moves behind Alonzo and secures the device to the warriors back.

Leaping from the frigate, the Lunarians sprint back to the Moonhawk, storing their booty in the cargo hold.

"Angel, Alonzo… get over here and lend a hand." Sam calls.

Scrambling around the wreck, they dig in their heels and pull mightily at the ropes. The emerging crate threatens to buckle under the strength of the Highlanders.

"Easy." Sam calls out. "The auto-detonate is still active."

Lazarus and Sam frantically scoop away the regolith that had gathered in front of the crate. The warriors grunt and pull, and grunt some more, muscling it out of the narrow passage. They finally get it on the surface.

"Lindsey, once this is secured in the hold, I want you to disarm the booby trap. But be careful. Don't assume it's identical to the others."

"Aye," Lindsey said.

Angel, Sam, Alonzo and Consuela place slings under the crate and carry it the final few meters, depositing it in the transport.

"Let's move it people," Tempel broadcast, standing at the bottom of the ramp, hands on his hips, looking out across the battlefield. They're all back except for Tatiana. "Tatiana, report." He spots her emerging from the remains of a Goliath. She's loaded down, her backpack full and the pockets and pouches of her ghost suit bulge with loot.

A beam from somewhere high overhead vaporizes the surface in front of her. Tatiana leaps sideways and sprints across the lunar surface back to the Moonhawk.

Tatiana replies. "I found some very interesting documents."

"Show me later. We need to get out of here… now." Tempel said. The Brotherhoods battlestation in Lagrange One is joining the fight.

The warriors silently lay Captain Osaka alongside Brice, Lei, and Karl. The Moonhawks rise and disappear into the lunar night.

Djinn

Major General Arif replays the battle for the tenth time. It's worse than he had feared. The Djinn had technology that made them virtually impossible to see.

His people had extrapolated from the various paths of destruction that there was at least forty Djinn involved in the attack. The battle had lasted for a hundred-eleven seconds and eighty-seven of his men were dead.

One Djinn casualty. One! ***Pure madness!***

The sheer speed and efficiency of the Lunarian's attack chills him to the bone. His soldiers will be hard-pressed to match it. The vid showing them killing those men trying to surrender will make good Earthnet news later, but for now, it shakes him to his core.

Major General Arif immediately designates all vid reports of the battle Top Secret Prohibited and seals the records. He can't risk this going viral among his troops.

No, that wouldn't do at all.

Book 3: Evolution's Child – Thread

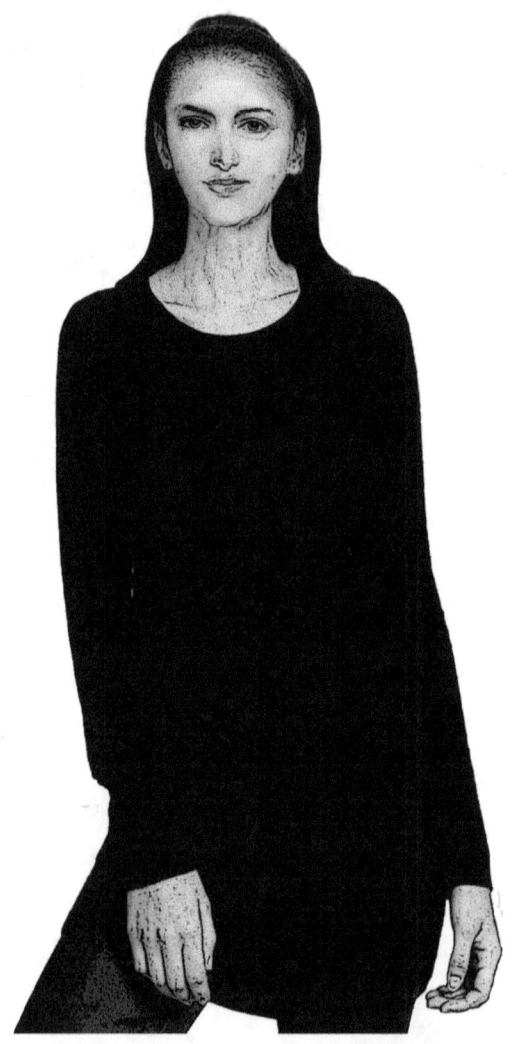

"Today is the Child of Tomorrow. We are all
Evolution's Children Adrift on the Sea of Time."
Magi

Shennong

"And the four angels were loosed, which were prepared for an hour, and a day, and a month, and a year, for to slay the third part of men."

Holy Bible, Revelations 9:15

A thousand kilometers south of Aldrin Station, Shennong lies in the rim of Tycho Crater. With a population over six-hundred-thousand, it's the largest city in the Republic.

The Brotherhood's attack caught its citizens by surprise. Within hours, the invaders penetrate deep, keeping to the commonways, not even attempting to extend their control into the numerous avenues or nearby warrens. Instead, they seal every opening as they pass.

Security Chief Chen estimates they're facing over thirty thousand soldiers with thousands more outside on the surface. This is far too few to take Shennong by force. It's only a matter of time before Chen counterattacks and overwhelms the invaders.

Yangtze Commonway, like many others found throughout the Republic, is a giant passageway cut through the heart of Tycho's rim mountain. Filled with thousands of trees and other plants, it's part of a forest that serves the city as both air purifier and parkland.

Here, in this particular section of the commonway, the trees had been fifty-year old Sycamore's towering sixty meters in height. All that remains of these majestic plants are piles of blackened wood. The smoke of their burning obscures the distance, as if a fog were rolling in off a distant sea.

With the grace and power of a cheetah, Sergeant Lin Kai leaps over the body paying it no attention. Spread out behind him is the remnants of Shennong's 10th Metro Division. Of the twenty-two police officers in his own platoon, he's the last. Others have told him he should fall back, but nothing will compel Lin to give up the fight.

The intense beams sear through the smoke filled air of the commonway. The thunder of their passage echoes along the great corridor. The Brotherhood burns everything in their path, defocusing their beams to set whole groves of trees on fire. They're trying everything to slow down the incessant hit and run attacks the Lunarians have thrown at them.

Lin uses the trunk of one of these fallen giants to mask his approach. Timing his leap with the arrival of his comrades, he vaults over the tree and begins firing his disrupter and launching missiles. His fellow warriors follow him, laying down a withering fire on the convoys that lay a few hundred meters beyond.

Some of the big vehicles lumber about in an effort to bring more weapons to bear. Others stop, disgorging soldiers like ants swarming from their hole to face their attackers.

The Lunarians concentrate on the third Goliath. Missiles streak to their mark and penetrate the juggernaut. In a mighty explosion, its side rips open, flames shoot out and it grinds to a stop. Both of the tires on the left side collapse and it tips over. Black smoke billows from it and more explosions rock it, the last a massive detonation that causes the vehicles around it to scurry away.

The troop carrier directly behind the burning Goliath, itself full of holes and at least three missile strikes, catches fire and within moments, is a towering inferno. No one inside survives. The other carriers, further back, open their doors and soldiers pour out, eager to escape certain death. The undamaged troop carriers detach and look for another convoy.

Narrow beams of intense energy slice through the blinding smoke seeking victims. Brotherhood soldiers fall and die on a world not of their birth.

The Lunarians suffer as well. The warrior ten meters to Lin's left takes a beam to the chest and slumps to the ground, momentum lodging his lifeless body against the trunk of a fallen Sycamore. Another warrior has her arm removed at the elbow as she leaps over a tree trunk. She retreats to the waiting medics, her life spared by medical science to fight another day.

The skirmish is over in seconds. The convoys have completed their response maneuver and are dishing out energy on a scale that Lin's warriors cannot survive for long. However, they have accomplished what they set out to do and disappear back along the passageway, out of reach of the Brotherhood's weapons.

In the beginning, the Brotherhood sent soldiers after the retreating

Lunarians but when few returned, they stopped. Better to stay together and defend from a position of strength.

Chen feeds the illusion that there is strength in numbers while chipping away at the invaders. She's finally in a position to order a massive counterattack but hesitates knowing that casualties will be high. Better to wait and continue harassing them. A few days of sleep deprivation will soften the enemy and then she can strike.

Reaching some predetermined location, the Brotherhood turns off their incessant jammers and broadcasts their ultimatum on all frequencies.

"Cease all hostilities or your city will be destroyed. Our forces carry thermonuclear weapons which they will use unless you immediately comply." The message endlessly repeats.

With the network functioning again, Chen performs a security analysis of the situation. *Damn.* There are Brotherhood garrisons at the center of all fourteen boroughs. If they all have bombs then they have the ability to completely destroy her city but only if they are willing to commit suicide themselves. Why bring tens of thousands of soldiers along and all that hardware if all they wanted to do was blow the place up. The Brotherhood was after something and she needed to find out what.

Chen didn't doubt for a moment the existence of the deadly devices, she is well aware of the nukes her people found on the Sea of Clouds. After speed viewing the available vid records for the third time and consulting with her staff, she orders all front line warriors to disengage and fall back until further notice. *So… what is their plan? They hold my city hostage for what purpose?*

ℛ𝕃

Security Chief Chen didn't like what she had to do. "I'm not asking you to surrender. Simply back off until I can determine a course of action,"

"But Chief, we must drive them from Shennong." Sergeant Kai argues.

"Ask yourself why they have deliberately put themselves in such a precarious position? We will not risk a nuclear suicide bomb. Do I make myself clear?" She hates needing to be so firm with him. The young man's blood stained ghost suit attests to what he's gone through. His comrades are all dead and the handful of warriors he commands are remnants of other platoons. "I want you to fall back and let someone else take the lead. You have done everything possible under the circumstances."

"Chief, I want to finish this." Lin replies.

"Lin, we're not done here. Get your people some food and rest, and let me worry about the Brotherhood. That's an order." Chen can't afford to spend any more time with the young man. Waiting for his nod, she shifts her attention to another unit disengaging from the enemy. She's worried someone somewhere will take it upon themselves to continue the attack.

"Come on Lin. I could use some chow and a hot shower," Meili said. She and Luka are all that remains of Manchu platoon.

Lin looks around. He feels like a failure, that somehow he personally was to blame for the Brotherhood destroying Yangtze Commonway.

They had been in the middle of their attack run when the order to disengage came and the warriors had not retreated very far down the devastated commonway. It broke his heart to see the forest he played in as a boy in ruins. Smoke fills the great corridor making it difficult to see even using his sensors.

The beam strikes Meili in the upper torso at the base of her neck, effectively cutting off her head. Lin roars in anger and springs away. What remains of his ragtag unit scatters among the wreckage of the commonway, leaving behind more Lunarian blood to soak into the black dirt. Only Lin turns back, no longer caring if he lives or dies.

The young Lunarian keeps low and circles, staying hidden within the tangle of fallen trees. He sees the soldiers, their backs to him, their mission accomplished. He counts twenty-nine in this little group.

He checks his supply of missiles. He has only four remaining. Disrupter is running low but he could not have stopped even if it were empty.

The man last in line is the only one bothering to look back and then, only every other step or so. He never sees the shadow stalking them. Lin is within forty meters when he opens fire, spacing his shots, making every one count. The sound of his attack echoes down the great corridor causing the others in the group to scramble for cover. Before they do, the young Lunarian has killed six.

Beyond them, Lin can see the convoys that brought these men here. Without a second thought, he sends his last four missiles streaking towards the vehicles, one to the left, one to the right, and the final two targeting the center Goliath. The explosions rock the commonway.

He leaps over a pile of smoldering debris and kills another invader, and another. His missiles had not destroyed the convoys fighting ability and their powerful disrupters open up on Lin. Beams blister the air around him as he twists and turns, striving to keep something between him and certain death. He never senses the beam that gets him. One second he's fighting, the next his lifeless body is skidding to a stop. His unseeing eyes gaze upon eternity, another sacrifice on the altar of war.

ЯL

Inside his command center, Major Abdul Aziz is barely conscious. The twin blasts from the missiles has killed all of his senior staff. Blood is everywhere. They had been together as the announcement was given that all hostilities should cease immediately, anticipating complete capitulation. A squawking alarm testifies to the grave condition within the other two convoys. His command is in shambles.

He struggles to pull himself to a sitting position, pain lancing through his body. Gasping for breath, he looks down to see his chest covered in blood. Knowing his duty, he drags himself across the shattered interior of the vehicle. Moaning with every move, he takes the key from around his neck, inserts it into the console, and turns it. A red light flashes on.

Aziz swoons, barely staying conscious. He doesn't have much time. Laying a bloody hand on the palm reader, he said, *"Emergency Override Code Major Abdul Aziz. Zero one zero six six six zero."*

"Authorization accepted and countdown begun," the computerized male voice said in the same language, the last words he will hear in his beloved native tongue.

"Allah Akbar," the Major puts his back to the console as the loss of blood and pain finally takes its toll. He's at peace with his god, knowing he's performed his duties to the best of his ability. He welcomes death, seeing it only as a transformation from the hardships of this life to the promised paradise in the next.

Word spreads fast of the imminent detonation. The various commanders issued orders for their soldiers to take cover as soon as the news arrived. This is an event they have all anticipated, when one of their units would find it necessary to perform the ultimate sacrifice.

"Allah Akbar," the Major chants. His thoughts turn to his family and the things he regrets. He assures himself that all will be forgiven because of his service to Allah. Beating his wives and children had been necessary and lawful under Islamic Law. The only regret that eats at his heart is the death of his daughter. Her stubborn disobedience was intolerable but her death had made all his other children respect his subsequent decisions. Now, at the instant of his own demise, all he can see are her young eyes staring accusingly at him as the villagers stoned her.

Groaning with intense pain, in the final few seconds of his life the Major leans forward and touches his forehead to the cold metal floor, a position promising the comfort of long use.

The nuke detonates forming a tiny sun in the heart of Shennong. The sheer size of Yangtze Commonway isn't sufficient to route the energy away from the surrounding habitats. The core of the detonation is a ravenous shockwave that pulses through the mountain causing the free surfaces of the underground metropolis to explode, showering the spaces within with huge chunks of rock. The blast sends a massive firestorm down the great passageway following the path of least resistance. It engulfs everything until it reaches the cities Eastern Access Tunnel. The mighty airlocks, damaged by the passing shockwave, cannot hold. The nuclear fire blows them open and races down the city's main access tunnel, emerging from the mountain and venting its fire to space. By this time, the center of the blast has carved out a cavity almost a kilometer in diameter, weakening the mountain.

With a major commonway open to vacuum, the wind reaches gale force as the cities atmosphere spews into space. Outside, the air and debris form a fog that gathers over the stricken city.

Most Brotherhood units had sufficient warning of the impending blast to reach the safety of their troop carriers. Even so, the detachment nearest to Linchuan suffers the brunt of the blast. The fierce nuclear fire and shockwave rips through their carriers, tossing them like children's toys. Of the four convoys and over two thousand men, no one survives.

Farther away, the Brotherhood's heavy vehicles weather the storm. Hunkered down inside their Goliaths and troop carriers, the pressure wave passes over them without harm.

Lunarians caught in the open are not so lucky. The tremendous shock wave, focused by the enormous stone corridor, crushes them like bugs.

As the fury of the blast spends itself, the weakened mountain collapses, sinking into the cavity that Allah's fire has carved. A huge cloud of dust and gas rises above the sinkhole for thousands of meters fed by the death of a hundred habitats. They implode under the shifting mass of rock, explosively releasing their air to space.

One sixth of the city is gone. One-hundred-thousand citizens are dead or dying. Survivors struggle to put aside their shock and horror to save what they can. They abandon Shennong.

Scottsbluff

"A man by himself is in bad company."

Eric Hoffer (1902-1983)

Cris hides his bike amidst some rocks and moves carefully the last few feet to peek down at Hallstead. Nothing much appears to have changed. The Goliath is still there but no rovers. The two missing rovers are lying in ruins at the bottom of a cliff several kilometers away. They'll not be killing any more Lunarians.

Where is everyone? Cris pinpoints six sentries but otherwise, nothing moves. *Only six?* Cris angers as though slapped in the face. The Brotherhood commander's not taking him seriously even after losing four rovers, a decision he will soon regret.

Cris creeps over the edge, stealthily making his way into the encampment. He times his moves with those of the guards and lays a trap at the rear of the last carrier.

As the soldier turns the corner, he walks onto the Highlander's sword. Starting low and aiming high, Cris drives the thin blade between the layered ceramic plates. It takes all of his considerable strength to penetrate the underlying puncture resistant material, and all of his skill to keep the convulsing body from snapping the blade at the hilt. The metal sings as it slides past the hard plates, sending a strange tone up his arm to his ears, the swan song of a man dying far from home. The sound is expected but disconcerting.

His aim is true, slicing through the heart, killing instantly. Cris eases the body to the ground, sliding his sword out with care. This sound is different, like a baby's weak cry. Cris steels himself to finish the job. He wipes the sword on the arm of his victim then rolls the body under the carrier. The dead man's blood boils in the vacuum. He must hurry before it draws attention.

Cris moves to the airlock and enters. Sword in one hand and disrupter in the other, he watches the inner door cycle open. Just out of sight to his right, the Highlander's visor picks up heavy breathing and elevated heartbeats. Stepping boldly from the airlock, he confronts two men in shirtsleeves sitting at a table only a few meters away. They are both looking at him as if they have seen a ghost.

For a split second, nobody moves. Then all hell breaks loose.

One soldier shouts something unintelligible and reaches for the pistol holstered at his waist. Cris shoots him in the chest as he leaps across the intervening distance, the sound thunderous in the enclosed space. With one swipe of his blade, Cris cuts the other man's throat, almost severing his head in the process. Blood fountains from the gaping wound, the look of shocked disbelief frozen on the face. The bodies hit the floor almost simultaneously.

Cris scans the inside of the troop carrier. He's alone. In both directions are narrow bunks stacked from floor to ceiling. A quick count reveals enough for at least fifty soldiers and their gear. If all ten carriers were the same, that put this contingent at about five-hundred soldiers.

Lockers at each end of the carrier draws his attention. Opening one, he finds a wealth of ordnance, everything from missiles to land mines. This is what he came for. Cris fills two large bags. Before he leaves, he sets a timer on one of the remaining charges and closes the locker.

Exiting the transport, Cris slips down the length of the convoy placing explosives under each carrier. Last, he attaches several ounces of SuperX on the Goliaths undercarriage near its fuel cell supply tanks, setting its timer to go off first. Along the way, he makes some interesting observations concerning the carrier modifications, things that will come in handy later. Sergeant Cristobal Calatrava did all of this without any of the remaining guards seeing him, a shadow in the night.

Cris returns to his bike and secures the bulging bags. Gunning the machine, he races down the ravine away from Hallstead. Moments later, he stops near the summit of a nearby hill looking down on the compound.

Brotherhood soldiers are swarming around the convoy like a bunch of ants. One of them, crawling along on his knees, spots the device planted on the Goliath and begins waving his arms and pointing. Another bugeye comes running up and squirms on his back under the massive vehicle just as the device explodes. The charge ruptures the hyperbolic fuel tanks and violently mixes their contents. The resulting fireball engulfs the Goliath. It disintegrates into a million pieces. Chunks of aluminum and titanium shred the soldiers around it and rips open the nearest carrier.

The debris was just beginning to settle when the other charges begin going off. In complete silence, all ten troop carriers explode, one after the other. Dust, gasses and human body fluids gather above the convoy in a thick blanket. With no wind to carry it away, dissipation takes time. Dead and wounded are scattered everywhere.

Secondary explosions rock what remains of the convoy as Cris turns away, his anger sated for the moment. Survivors will speak of a demon with a sword, a ghost with teeth.

ЯL

For hours, Lazarus has soared alone above an endless lunar landscape, the omnipresent face of Earth his only companion. The airless world of Luna scrolls by thirty meters below. His visor filters out the Moonhawks and all they contain. Even when he looks down at himself, he sees only the stark inhospitable lunar terrain sailing past. Lazarus is a solitary spirit in a vast wilderness.

The battle of Nell's Valley is vivid in his mind and he struggles against rising panic. He may not believe in heaven, but he just witnessed hell. Mortal combat is as close to hell as humanity can devise, brutality unchecked by the slightest hint of compassion.

He linked with Lindsey right before the fight started. It lasted only a couple of minutes, but in those minutes, his life changed. Lazarus no longer holds any remnant of belief that war contains glory. War is death, blatant and brutal.

Lindsey had overlaid all twelve warriors into a single point of view. The composite was unimaginably violent. Fully immersed in the experience, Lazarus witnessed the massacre of scores of Brotherhood soldiers, their deaths thrust upon him through the eyes of the slayer. It's worse because it's his first total immersion. Like an addict taking their first injection, it hits him hard. Each death sent shockwaves through him, hearing, seeing, smelling, and feeling the battle as though he were the killer. The explosions, the blood red fog erupting from their wounds, and worst of all, the deaths of Brice and Kitajima. He felt the beams cut through their bodies, hear their last gasp, feel their life drain from them.

After Kitajima died, Lindsey severed his link with Quan Kiai and pushed him to take control of the cannon. And he did. He blasted away at the Brotherhood racking up two confirmed kills and many more in the frigate. He had never killed before.

He shudders, clenching his eyes tightly shut. Through it all, Tempel, Sam and the others are running around like animals. *What have I done?* Panic crowds his mind. *Why did I come here?*

Like father, like son. He grabs at his father's memory like a lifeline but it can't contain the fear. It builds to the point that spots dance before his eyes. The very idea of people that are not people frightens him to his core. Is it possible that what the Federation said about the Lunarians is true? *Are they animal mutants?* He can't shake the thought that, for all their kindness and beauty, they're not human. His head spins. The harder he tries to make sense of the situation, the worse it becomes.

"Lazarus?" Lindsey calls softly as if from a great distance.

"I've given him a neuro-cognitive. He should be fine." Doc Grady said, also dim and distant.

Lazarus struggles against the descending darkness, clawing his way towards the voices. Someone begins massaging his shoulders whispering softly in his ear.

"*Relax... take deep breaths...* That's better. You had me worried there for a moment," Lindsey said, continuing to administer to him. She has linked and readjusted his visual. He's no longer alone in the void.

"Take it easy... relax..." Lindsey's lips brush his ear while she works his shoulder muscles. "It's my fault, I should not have let you immerse in the battle. It was too much for a first time," Lindsey continued to massage his neck and shoulders.

Lazarus looks up. Her eyes are exquisite jewels looking back at him, her beautiful face framed once again with raven black hair and the same form-fitting sky-blue blouse as when they first met, all courtesy of the processing capabilities of their linked visors.

"Welcome back." She said smiling.

"Are you one of them?" He asked.

"What do you mean, one of them? Are you referring to the Lunarians? Or to Quan Kiai?" She keeps the edge out of her voice. Now's not the time to rail on Lazarus for being an insensitive boob.

"Is there a difference?" Lazarus asks, recalling their beastly four-legged sprint. His fear stirs.

"Yes, there's a difference."

"Are they designed for war?" His tone lays a heavy-handed verdict upon the very idea.

"Look, just because they're different, doesn't make them evil," Lindsey said. "I've lived with them their entire life and I assure you, they love and laugh just like you do. Where's your fear truly coming from? Is it because of what they are or is it what they did?"

"They kill so... effortlessly." Lazarus shuddered.

"You mistake efficiency for enthusiasm. These men and women did what needed doing. War is not something you pussyfoot around with," Lindsey said.

"Using genetic science to maintain health is one thing, using it to create better soldiers is something else. How can you justify this perversion?" Lazarus asks.

"Tempel's not a perversion. Sam's not a perversion. You're not thinking like the man I sponsored for citizenship. This is the Federation talking..." she stares at him for a moment. "Come with me," she loosens his restraining harness and pulls him to his feet. They go back several rows. Zoey is on one side of the aisle. Another warrior is on the other side, Marcel Piqualow. They're both asleep.

His visor shows Zoey and Marcel as they would appear without their ghost suits dressed in normal attire. The young woman looks so... peaceful. It's hard to imagine her as the brutal killer he witnessed during the battle.

"What's wrong with her?" Lazarus looks down at Zoey.

"Doc said they're suffering from battle fatigue. They're having problems dealing with what happened in Nell's Valley... War is not something any sane person yearns for but when one society inflicts it upon another… someone must answer the call. We asked Zoey and Marcel to do a horrible thing and they did it. Can we now condemn them for doing what we asked them to do?" Lindsey shakes her head, "No… the Republic must thank them for what they did and take care of them, no matter what."

Lazarus recalls the kindness Zoey had shown him during his vacsuit training. Fear slips away and concern takes its place. After all, it's not as if they had killed innocent people. They had killed his lifelong enemy.

Unbeknownst to Lazarus, he reaches these conclusions with help from Doc Grady's drugs. They dull his memories allowing him to temper the brutality of the killing with ignorance, just as he would have done if he had not experienced the slaughter in the first place. The battle fades and the genetic engineering seem less important. As his attitude improves, he feels better and more like his old self.

"Will they be all right?" Lazarus asks.

"Doc said yes but nothing's for certain," Lindsey replies.

"Is there anything I can do?"

Lindsey shakes her head, "Let them rest in peace…"

ЯL

Jamie shakes his head "The attack severely segmented Magi. Until we reestablish the network, Magi will not be Magi."

"Unacceptable. I need Magi," Corso said.

"You'll have her. We rebooted part of the system. Magi should be coming up momentarily," Jamie said.

"We adjusted some of the emotion control programs within the Grokian Interface which should act like a sedative. But Jamie's right, until Magi's whole, she will be different," Jordan said.

"Different how?" Corso asks.

"So many have died… I have failed…" Magi whimpers.

"Magi." Corso exclaims. It looks like Magi but without the twinkle in her eye or the ready smile. Her hair is almost fully gray and she looks much older. Sadness and defeat lay heavy upon her.

"I've informed the families of the deaths of their loved ones. The pain I've caused is incalculable. I'm so sorry Corso. I have failed."

"Magi. That's absolutely wrong." Corso exclaims. "You are NOT responsible for their deaths or the pain inflicted on their families. Without you, we don't stand a chance, so unless you want more people to die, you need to start helping me stop this."

"I'm at reduced capacity," Magi states flatly. "You should not trust my judgment."

"How many threads are you processing with?" Corso asks.

"Less than three hundred thousand," the AI said. "Nothing outside of Aldrin Station."

"It will have to do," Corso said.

"Magi hasn't operated with that low a thread count since the late fifties," Jordan said.

"We'll get some relays on top of Rim Mountain to reestablish the link with New London, Prattville, and Summerhaven. That'll bring in another hundred-fifty thousand threads. In the meantime, I want the precise location of the nukes the Brotherhood claim to be carrying."

"The data is incomplete. I can't be sure of anything," Magi claims.

"I know. Just give me your best estimate," Corso pleads.

"Corso... If I'm wrong..."

"The final decision's mine," Corso said. Magi turns away. "Magi... Aldrin Station can't survive with the Brotherhood in our commonways. We must destroy their nukes and evict these invaders."

"I've determined when the devices arrived. They were flown in right before the attack began, during the time that Councilor Taylor rescinded your order halting all incoming flights." Magi can't look at Corso.

"Put together a summary and submit it to the General Council for arbitration. I will deal with this when there's time. Where are the nukes now?"

"The probability of the nukes being in this specific location is only at 59%," Magi said, turning back to Corso, tears streaming down her face.

Corso has never seen Magi cry before but he doesn't have time right now to deal with anything except staying alive. "Keep working on it. Send some spybots in for a look."

An explosion, much louder and closer than those before, rings the RCC like a bell. The lights flash once and the Command Center goes dark.

"Ben. Report." Corso orders. Dim emergency lights come on. Everyone stares at the huge airlock door as if it were about to open. Fear and tension permeates the assembly. No one moves.

"The RCC is under attack. Mini rockets have breached the outer perimeter and are being met by the guards," Ben said.

"They're being overwhelmed. The numbers of minis coming at them is staggering." Magi said sadly. "They've lost half their number already."

"Form up." Ben steps forward. Security's his job. He wonders briefly how the attackers had managed to get by the many layers of sensors guarding the RCC but now's not the time to think, it's time to act. "Move it." he shouts as he paces back and forth in front of the airlock door, cradling a disrupter in the crook of his arm. His troops gather their weapons and prepare for battle. He senses in them both fear and anxiety but no hesitation. They'll fight.

Ben looks over the company. "Listen up. We do this by the book. When the airlock opens, proceed at full speed. When we get to the upper chamber, spread out and attack in pairs. *Lock and Load.* It's time to take it to the enemy."

The heavy airlock door swings open and Ben leads them through.

ЯL

Hour after hour, the two Moonhawks maintain a course due east, passing Thebit Crater along its southern rim. They keep low and slow, never more than ten meters above the surface and under a hundred kilometers per hour. This ate into the remaining fuel.

The pace is stressful on the pilots. Without Magi, they can't rely on the resident AI to fly the ships on autopilot. Too many human decisions are needed while maneuvering across the broken landscape. Therefore, they divide the responsibility among the warriors, not asking anyone to fly for long.

Tempel begins scanning for emissions from the town long before they see the towering rim wall of Faye crater. The total lack of broadband chatter is ominous. He probes the ridge as they creep over the horizon. The arrays of satellite communications equipment that should be there is scattered down the mountainside.

Scottsbluff had a decent defensive shield in place before the attack. If part of that survived the bombardment, Quan Kiai could face a formidable weapon. They all have a great deal of respect for the big laser cannons his people designed and built in defense against the meteorites.

Tempel tags an LZ in a deep depression a few kilometers from Scottsbluff. The two Moonhawks come to rest a few meters apart. Corazon launches a spybot, landing it on a nearby ridge with a view of the settlement's main entrance. The instant it comes to rest, Tempel zooms in on the structures clustered outside the town's main gate.

The bombardment had been intense. Everything's crumpled and smashed. Craters pockmark the mountainside and out onto the plain. Twisted metal is all that remains of the sheds and warehouses outside Scottsbluff. Nothing moves. Even the vapor hanging over the wreckage seems frozen in place.

Tempel points the spybots communications laser towards the main gate, "Scottsbluff, how do you copy?" he said and waits.

The seconds tick by. Maybe no one's listening or maybe… everyone's dead.

"Scottsbluff, this is Senior Lieutenant Dugan of the Lincoln County Police Department. Please respond." Turning to Consuela, Tempel asks, "Are we transmitting on all frequencies?"

"Aye, they should be receiving full visual. They're not responding," Consuela replies.

"If they don't, someone will need to go in and find out why." Tempel doesn't like the sound of that but sees no alternative.

From somewhere near the base of the mountain, a low wattage broadband laser comes to life. "What do you want?" No image accompanies the question but the voice is female, familiar, and frightened.

With a sigh of relief, Tempel said, "Magi? Is that you?"

"Who are you? How do you know my name?"

"Lieutenant Tempel Dugan from Aldrin Station."

"Aldrin Station?" The frightened voice takes on a wistful quality as though remembering something lost.

From near Scottsbluff's main entrance, a second more tightly focused communication laser links with the spybot. The signal strength increases as data begins to flow both ways. An older man appears before them. Gray stubble and heavy dark circles under his eyes betray fatigue.

"Security Chief Gordon O'Leary… Who did you say you are?" After the last few days, he's not sure whom to trust.

From the database on board the Moonhawks, they know a lot about Scottsbluff including its Chief of Security. He's a relatively new Lunarian having arrived a mere thirty-three years earlier. Born in Ireland, he grew up in the small hamlet of Graystones just south of Dublin. For centuries, the historic fishing village looked out on the Irish Sea. However, thirty-three years ago, rising sea levels forced everyone out, an event that prompted Gordon O'Leary to emigrate to the moon.

"Greetings Chief O'Leary. I'm Lieutenant Tempel Dugan."

The image of a man and a woman appear next to O'Leary. Each consists of some three thousand villagers, separated by gender, then morphed into a single entity. From this agglomeration, a middle-aged man emerges and asks, "What the hell's happening?"

This is unusual. Seldom do observers take part in conversations.

Tempel turns to his questioner, "The Republic is under attack. Beyond that, I would feel better if we were face to face for any further discussion."

The female image morphs into an older woman. "You must do better than that Lieutenant," she declares, a double breach of etiquette. "What was your mission and why can't you return to Aldrin Station?"

"While on official Republic business we were attacked by the Brotherhood. We lost four. I'll provide access to the vids as soon as we're inside Scottsbluff. We need fuel and air," Tempel said.

The female image morphs into a teen girl, "I don't trust them. Send them on."

Turning to address the young woman, O'Leary said, "Margay, I'm sorry for your loss but we can't do that. When you're older, you'll understand. They're Lunarians. We must help them."

"I don't like it." Margay declares. The attack bloodied Scottsbluff and others, young and old, male and female, join her in expressing the same feeling of misgiving. Many are adamant about not becoming involved. They're frightened.

"Please, all of you, be reasonable. We must take them in. It's our duty as Lunarians," O'Leary pleads.

"Leary's right," a voice rises above the babble. "They're officers and citizens. They need air, for Pat's sake. We can't deny them air."

"We're involved whether you like it or not," another said.

"Max is right. You don't think they bombed us just for fun do you? The Brotherhood will be coming and we must be ready."

Someone posted a poll and within moments, the citizens of Scottsbluff reach a consensus, but it was close.

"The vote is cast and the majority has spoken. We let them in. It's the right thing to do," O'Leary said. Turning back to Tempel, "The main access tunnel is still passable. I'll meet you in the hanger."

ЯL

Marcel struggles to throw off the fog that fills his mind. He opens his eyes. He's strapped to a seat in one of the Moonhawks. Doc Grady's standing in the aisle looking at him.

"Take it easy. You've been asleep for quite awhile." Doc said.

"How long?" Marcel asks. His mouth tastes like cotton.

"About nine hours," Doc replies.

"Nine hours. Where the hell are we?" Zoey asks from across the aisle.

"We're approaching Scottsbluff," Doc said.

"Why did you knock me out?" Marcel asks. Anger stirs.

"Because you were headed down a slippery slope and needed time to mend. Sometimes the best medicine is to let your body's natural healing processes work its magic over a nice long sleep cycle. What you're going through has been called many things down through the years, combat stress reaction, battle fatigue, or shell shock. Take your pick." Doc Grady said. "In a nutshell, your mind's rebelling against your actions, and the best treatment for it is sleep."

Doc Grady is treating him and Zoey for combat stress. As this sinks in and Marcel realizes the implications, his embarrassment quickly turns to concern. He's never been ill in his life, not even a runny nose. "What's wrong with me?" He asked.

"Nothing's wrong with you. Your psyche is adapting to war. Your reaction to the battle is understandable and predictable." Doc Grady pauses, "No one likes killing. If they did, we would start looking for a neurological abnormality or protein imbalance. You have had a completely normal reaction."

"So… have you given this little talk to the others?" Marcel asks.

"Everyone handles it in their own way. No two people are alike." Doc Grady said.

"The short answer is no." Marcel said. *Great. Just Great.*

"Hey, on the bright side, if you're going to take a ride on the crazy train, it's always good to have a friend along," Zoey said to him with a wicked grin. *Brice will find this amusing.* Her grin vanishes. Brice is dead.

Doc Grady sighs, "Neither of you are crazy, just human."

The badlands along the edge of the Sea of Clouds rise abruptly about fifty kilometers out of Al Fahad. Cris uses his disrupter to drill the last of thirty-five deep holes into the sheer mountainside, his vacsuit protecting him from the blow back. He pours a quantity of powdered SuperX into the hole then adds a detonator. The charges are scattered along a kilometer looking down on Kahfah Road.

Like a monkey in his favorite tree, Cris moves across the nearly vertical landscape with ease. This is his environment. He grew up exploring the rugged lunar landscape. Cris scrambles up the steep slope and settles down against a boulder to wait.

The roadbed glows in the starlight a hundred meters below. From where he sits, he can see who's coming all the way to the horizon back towards Al Fahad.

Cris doesn't have long to wait. The scouts are first, many kilometers ahead of the main body. He lets them pass unharmed.

Behind them is a column of Goliaths that do not pull any carriers. The massive vehicles bristle with heavy disrupter cannons. Cris has never seen anything like them. Their only discernible purpose is to destroy. He lets them pass as well.

Finally, the graders, compactors, and their support vehicles appear. These are the road and bridge builders, the Brotherhood's Corp of Engineers. Following them are troop convoys pulled by more of the heavily armed Goliaths. Convoys extend as far back as Cris can see. He shudders as he realizes the full extent of what's coming at Aldrin Station.

The trap is set and his targets are in the kill zone. It's time to slow this parade down.

Cris transmits the signal that detonates all thirty-five charges simultaneously. He feels the shock through his ass. Dust devils jet outward across the stricken mountainside. At first, nothing happens. Then the entire mass starts to slide downhill, slow at first, but gaining speed with each passing second.

The vehicles below are oblivious to the danger until thousands of tons of basalt crashes down, crushing them like a boot stepping on an ant. It's over in an instant.

The main column is in turmoil and Cris adds to it. He begins detonating the land mines he planted in the roadway, aiming for the Goliaths. The troop carriers are immobile without them.

The orderly procession has degenerated into outright confusion. This stretch of road passes through some of the worst terrain on Luna, a land of sheer cliffs and steep mountainsides, of fissures hundreds of meters deep and big enough to swallow a convoy. They cannot go forward and the road is only wide enough for a single truck to pass in many places. It will be hours, perhaps days, before they will regain control and without their Engineers, they cannot simply repair the road, they will need another route. He knows of only one, and it's his next stop.

Cris triggers the last landmine then turns his back on the hell he's created. The movement catches the eye of scanners below and shots begin to rain in around him. A few come close but he's too stealthy for the gunners to get a clear target, a shadow among shadows.

Before disappearing over the ridge, Cris gives them something to remember. He pulls his sword and briefly holds it aloft making its silhouette visible from below. Then he's gone.

ЯL

Before the Brotherhood attack, there had been a row of Quonset huts just outside the main entrance. Common all across Luna, the metal Quonset shades people working on the surface during the long lunar day. Only one still stands, heavily damaged and full of holes.

As they slip past, sensors probe its depths. Benches, tools, equipment, and a forklift lay broken on its floor. Trapped inside is a haze consisting mostly of oils and lubricants. A small but distinctive trace amount of blood and urine is also present. Someone died here.

"This place got hammered," Marcel murmurs.

"Let's keep our mind on what we're doing," Tempel said.

The Moonhawks glide towards the mouth of Scottsbluff's main gate. The corrugated metal extension outside the entrance is broken and battered but the airlock door itself appears undamaged. A sliver of light breaks the darkness when the giant door begins to open.

Moonhawk One leads the way into the tunnel. It felt good to have stone overhead once again. They pass through two more doors until finally emerging into the town's main hanger. The Moonhawk's thrusters whine loudly in the pressurized space, a welcome sound. Parked along one side of the vast room are a Goliath and several ore carriers. Numerous smaller vehicles, six wheeled transports, four wheeled rovers, two wheeled bikes, and the tools and supplies of a town lay scattered across the expansive floor. Across the way, three people are waving their arms.

The thrusters echo in the closed space. The Moonhawks settle side by side before the three villagers. Silence descends once again.

"We're being denied access to their network," Consuela said.

"Marcel, Corazon, you're with me. Tatiana, keep everyone else in the ships. We don't want to be here long," Tempel said.

"Aye," they respond.

"Tempel, I think it's wise if I make first contact," Lindsey said. "Look at yourself. You're wearing a ghost suit. These people have never seen a ghost suit and probably don't know much about genetic modifications either. Scottsbluff's a community of Purists. If you walk out there like that, they may just change their mind about helping us."

Tempel suppresses the feed coming from Sam, seeing her as the villagers will see him, a featureless dark shadow in the shape of a person.

"They're Lunarians. However, I see your point… Fine, you go talk to the man," Tempel said.

Lindsey unbuckles as Tempel lowers the ramp. It's been a long mission and it's not over yet. She moves down the ramp and walks over to the people. Lazarus follows.

"Greetings Chief O'Leary, I'm Lindsey Marquest and this is Lazarus Sheffield."

"Greetings. This is Hugh Grimsby and his wife Amber. I was expecting Lieutenant Dugan?" Already the plan was changing. He didn't like it.

"He's inside. He sent me to prepare you for his unusual appearance."

"Unusual? What do you mean?"

"He and his platoon are wearing ghost suits."

"Ghost suits? Never heard of them. Is it something new?" Amber Grimsby asks. She's never been comfortable with Luna's rapidly evolving technology. One of the reasons she moved to Scottsbluff years ago was to escape the fast pace in Aldrin Station. Things just move slower out here.

"Yes, very new... If you will grant us access to your network you will be able to see Lieutenant Dugan instead of his ghost suit."

Under the hanger's bright lights, a persistent dark shadow is hard to miss, especially one that walks on its own. "Greetings Chief O'Leary," Tempel said, emerging from the ship.

All three villagers start backpedaling in alarm as the figure approaches. They have no idea what's confronting them and after the last few days, this is too much.

Lindsey steps forward raising her hands. "Take it easy. I apologize for the scare. You have nothing to fear." She moves to stand between them and the apparition. "Lieutenant Dugan is wearing a very special vacsuit, that's all. If you will grant visual access, I can prove it."

O'Leary stops. The strange blackness of the ghost suit swallows his vision but he knows what energy absorbent materials are and can reasonably assimilate what he's seeing with science. Gathering his wits, he said, "We don't normally treat visitors this way. Magi would have granted you access automatically. Joan, provide our visitors with level one access."

The ghost suit transforms into a handsome young man wearing the familiar black and gray uniform of a police officer.

"Chief O'Leary, this is Lieutenant Tempel Dugan," Lindsey said.

"Greetings. This is Hugh and Amber Grimsby."

Hugh Grimsby is short and slim with straight brown hair pulled back in a ponytail. He's conservative and distrusts change.

Amber Grimsby is several centimeters taller with short black hair barely covering the tops of her ears. She looks worried and a little shell-shocked.

"Why have you come here?" Amber asks. There's more than fear inside this woman, there's strength as well.

"We had no choice. The Republic is under attack and we need

supplies," Tempel said.

Amber shrugs. "So what? It's not our fight. Aldrin Station is four hundred kilometers away. We want to stay out of it."

"The Brotherhood won't let you stay out of it." Lazarus said.

"You know this for a fact?" Hugh asks.

Lazarus looks intently at the young man. "They bombed you."

"Maybe that was a warning to stay out of it." Hugh said.

Lazarus shrugs, "You're Lunarians. The Brotherhood believes it's their duty to bring you into the way of Allah. So unless you're willing to live under Islamic law, you're in this fight whether you like it or not."

Tempel's link-monitor flashes as the number climbs. Already in the thousands, it marks the pace at which the citizens of Scottsbluff are downloading the vid from Nell's Valley. At this rate, it will only be a matter of moments before they will know far more than they bargained for.

Tempel turns to the older man. "Chief O'Leary, can we get fuel and air lines started. It's best if we are out of here quickly."

The older man nods. "Hugh, can you see to that?"

"Marcel, Corazon, help him," Tempel said. "Thanks Chief. From the looks of things, they hit Scottsbluff hard."

"Please, call me Leary…" he sighs and for a moment, looks much older than his years, "Twelve hours ago we lost our network link with the rest of the Republic. We still had our sensors and could see that every last satellite had been blown to bits including Lagrange One."

Tempel nods.

"Then the bombs came. Before we knew what was going on, fourteen people died," Leary said wearily, "including our First Responders."

Tempel nods again. He figured as much. "The Brotherhood must have been planning this for years."

"Planning what? What's this mean?" Amber asks. She was among the first to finish reviewing the events of Nell's Valley.

Tempel said, "It means we're at war. The Brotherhood has every intention of becoming humanity's first multi-planet empire."

"You don't say." Leary exclaims.

More and more people converge on the hanger, crowding forward to gather around Quan Kiai. A murmur starts that rapidly grows as they realize the implications of what they had just seen.

"They have brought nuclear weapons into Scottsbluff."

"We don't want anything to do with genetic engineering."

"They're not Pure. Send them away."

"We moved out here to get away from all the genetics practiced in the city."

"A child should be the product of a single man and woman, not a bunch of gene splicing and other mucky muck."

The protest grows louder by the second.

"Here. Here. What's this about nuclear weapons?" Chief O'Leary asks turning to Tempel.

"We recovered nukes from a crash site out on the Sea of Clouds. Review the vid," Tempel looks over the crowd. He spreads his hands wide, palms up, and said. "As soon as we refuel we'll go."

"They're not Pure. These young folks have had their genetics all mangled up. They're not human."

"Look, Tempel and Quan Kiai are defending your right to practice your beliefs as you see fit. Having us here for a few minutes won't contaminate you." Lindsey said rather bluntly. She's losing patience.

O'Leary interrupts his viewing of the battle at Nell's Valley and turns to Tempel. "What are you people?"

"Sam, can you come out here?" Tempel asks.

Hundreds of villagers have gathered in the hanger. They form a solid mass around Quan Kiai. Tempel looks at the faces around him and motions for Sam to remove her headgear. She releases the molyseal along her jaw line, pulls the breathing unit from her face, and peels it over her head letting it hang behind her like a hood. She keeps her visor on.

"This is Sergeant Samantha Odegaard. You needn't be frightened of her or any of us. We're police officers sworn to protect you," Tempel said.

"Just as you have all benefited from genetic science, so have we, only in us, it's been taken a step further. Don't let this frighten you. We're just as human as you are," Sam said.

The crowd isn't buying it. They stare at the strangers with suspicion. After what's happened, this is almost beyond their comprehension. From somewhere near the back comes a voice, "We just want to be left alone."

"Aye, we don't need these freaks."

"These are our best young men and women. They're not freaks." Lindsey said.

From somewhere else in the crowd, "Well, she isn't pure human, is she? No one who moves like that is Pure."

"Tempel, if I may," Sam said.

When Tempel turns, she's already opened the ghost suits front molyseal and her intentions are clear.

"Go for it Sam," Tempel said.

With Tempel helping, she peels off the vacsuit. Sam stands before them in only a thin garment covering her genitals. Moments later, even this lies on the hanger floor. She's completely nude.

Without exception, she has the attention of the entire village. She spreads her arms and turns letting them see her at all angles.

The people murmur nervously.

"She's definitely a woman." A man said from the crowd.

"What about the guys?" A woman asks.

Tempel immediately begins to strip. With Sam's help, he's soon standing nude beside her. They walk hand in hand among the villagers who part like the Red Sea during the exodus.

"Can you show us how you run on all fours?"

In response, Tempel flexes his knees, leans forward, bare feet gripping the stone floor, and leaps. The crowd scrambles to get out of his way. At the end of the arc, he reaches out with well muscled arms and propels himself forward, using his upper body strength to coil his legs beneath him and push. The young warrior bounds around the hanger taking his time but giving a good show. The villagers marvel at his grace and fluidity. They murmur excitedly and step back as Tempel returns. They oh and ah when he finishes the little demonstration by smoothly resuming bipedal motion. Tatiana is helping Sam put her ghost suit back on and Angel steps up to help Tempel.

"It's not natural." A villager said. Fear colored his tone black.

"We came out here to escape such things." Another said.

"You can ignore progress, but you can't escape it. Sooner or later it will find you and thrust itself into your lives. You have no choice in the matter." Lindsey was being unusually blunt.

"Lieutenant, the ships are fueled and stocked." Marcel reports.

Tempel, only partly back in his ghost suit, said to Chief O'Leary. "We'll reestablish the network as soon as possible, and I'll let Corso know how helpful you've been. Look, if the Brotherhood shows up, don't try fighting them. Run and hide."

Chief O'Leary frowns and draws back. "Don't worry about us. We'll be fine." Like the rest of the Puritans, he too is torn between the need to have these warriors and fearing them. He is glad they are leaving yet wishes they would stay.

The Preacher

"No, I don't know that atheists should be considered as citizens, nor should they be considered as patriots. This is one nation under God."

George H.W. Bush (1924-?)

The chamber's a man's room with dark wood paneling and darker furniture. A long mahogany conference table dominates the room. Recessed ceiling lamps cast bright pools of light on its polished surface.

The tension around the table is palpable. The Federation's top brass are waiting for their Commander-in-Chief. They must inform him of dire events.

Without warning, two marines swing open the big double doors.

President John Paul sweeps into the room. The tall gangling figure of Reverend Gibson is at his side and a covey of young interns at their heels. Chairs slide back from the table, muffled by the heavy carpet. The officers rise to their feet.

"Attention." Major General Thomas Fitzpatrick calls out. He's many decades past his prime, bone white hair and muscles sagging under the weight of years. However, he bleeds Army green, having worked his way up from the enlisted ranks during a distinguished forty-five year career, the last eleven as Chief of Staff.

"As you were gentlemen," President John Paul said. He and Reverend Gibson take the seats reserved for them. They are at the midpoint of the table, facing the giant vid screen. The rest of the entourage settles into chairs lining the wall behind their boss. Prior administrations would not have dared bring these lackeys into the inner sanctum of the White House Situation Room. This president insisted.

"Good morning, Mr. President. With your permission I will begin." General Fitzpatrick remains standing.

"Thomas, aren't you forgetting something?" President John Paul asks without looking at him.

"Sir? ... Oh… yes." he turns to the man next to President John Paul, "Reverend Gibson, will you do the honors of opening our meeting with a prayer?"

"Of course General." With a smug look, the man stands as Major General Fitzpatrick sits. Clasping his hands in front of him, Reverend Gibson leans his head back and clinches his eyes shut. To a man, the others in the room bow their heads, but most simply stare at the table or the floor at their feet. "Almighty Father, Whose Command is over all and Whose Love never fails, let the men in this room be aware of Thy presence and Obedient to Thy will. Keep them true, oh Lord, guarding against dishonesty in purpose and deed while helping our President sweep aside your enemies. Help them remain faithful to the duties this great country has entrusted to them. Let the uniform they wear remind them of the traditions of the Service of which they are but a part. Where there's doubt, steady their faith; where there's temptation, make them strong to resist; where there's fear, bestow upon them courage to continue the fight. We trust in you Jesus, to protect those who love you. Guide these men, oh Lord, with the light of Thy truth, and keep before them the life of Him in whose example and deliverance I trust. Heavenly Father, bless the men who serve our great cause and give the people in this room the strength to carry out your will. In the name of my Lord Jesus Christ, Amen."

"Amen," the room mumbles. The president pats the reverend on the arm as he sits, "Well said Matthew." Turning to General Fitzpatrick, "You may begin now, Thomas." As a rule, the president makes a point of using a person's first name.

"Yes, Mr. President." General Fitzpatrick motions for his aid, Colonel Sanchez, to proceed.

With an aura of professionalism, the colonel moves to stand next to the enormous flat panel screen facing the president. The screen is a relic of a bygone age. He should be giving this presentation using Virtual Reality. However, that's not how President John Paul wants it. The President insists on conducting the Lord's work with the tools He provided. Thus, no one's wearing Earthnet portals and Colonel Sanchez must use old technology.

"At approximately four hundred hours this morning local time, the Islamic Brotherhood attacked the Republic of Luna. The Brotherhoods space fleet is jamming communications but Earth based telescopes recorded a nuclear event that destroyed Lagrange One Space Station and at least one nuclear detonation within Shennong. We don't yet have the full damage assessment..."

While he's talking, the screen behind him shows a series of vids taken from Earth based telescopes. The most telling image is the one showing flame boiling out of Shennong and the subsequent collapse of the mountain.

"What exactly do our sources tell us Walter?" President John Paul asks. The President frequently interrupts briefings. It's something the men have learned to expect. The smart ones, those that have repeatedly been through this meat grinder, design their presentations anticipating and influencing his inevitable intrusions to suit their need.

"Sir, all communications are down. The Brotherhood is jamming all signals. Even laser line-of-sight is overwhelmed because of the intensity of the interference." Colonel Sanchez replies.

"Can we punch through?" the President asks.

"No sir. What we are prepared to do is send in a reconnaissance team," Colonel Sanchez replies.

President John Paul frowns, "In this age of instant communications, all we can do is send someone to have a look?"

"Sir, we are having the same difficulty in communicating with the fleet. The jamming is blanketing every frequency. We cannot risk taking action on disjointed and incomplete information." General Fitzpatrick's gravelly voice grates on the president. "That leaves us with only one alternative, send someone in."

The President's earlier friendliness vanishes, "Thomas, I don't care how it's done but I want to know what's going on and I want to know right now."

"I will dispatch a ship immediately," the General replies.

"What will happen if the Brotherhood catches them during the mission?" Reverend Gibson asks.

Although the reverend holds no office, it doesn't stop him from asking questions. The friendship between the Preacher and the President go back to their college days and the President trusts this self-proclaimed man-of-god explicitly. How else could anyone with a degree in theology obtain a top-level security clearance and the ear of the leader of the most powerful nation on Earth? President John Paul often refers to Reverend Gibson as the Secretary of Religion but there's little doubt that he speaks his mind on a wide variety of issues. No one dares question the arrangement. Self-preservation is a powerful motivator.

"Admiral Greer, will you please respond to the Reverends question?" General Fitzpatrick orders.

"Certainly… Sir, the most likely scenario is that they would all be immediately executed but there's a chance that the Brotherhood would use them as leverage in the arena of world opinion. Worst case is that the Brotherhood would declare war on us. It's better if our men don't get caught," Admiral Greer said.

"That's my prayer as well Admiral." The preacher turns to the president, "but I fail to see what good can come of sending them, John… Even if you learn everything about the situation, what would you do?" The question hangs in the air for a moment. "Are you prepared to go to war to protect godless Lunarians?"

"Let us pray that war is not necessary." Turning back to his Chief of Staff, President John Paul asks, "Thomas, if this escalates beyond the borders of the Republic, are you ready to defend our country and our interests?"

"Sir, we are prepared for any contingency. At the moment our forces are on Alert Level Red," General Fitzpatrick said.

"But if you're not in contact with our space fleet, how do you know what level they are at?" the Preacher asks.

"I know my men. They go by the book and the book explicitly lays out their response. Aggression by any country towards another country will result in our forces going to Alert Level Red. If they or any part of the Federation is attacked, then the Alert Level goes to War Status," General Fitzpatrick explains.

"Well then, I fail to see the need to do any more than what you have already done. I advise letting the infidels handle their own mess. They have had ample time to repent and accept Jesus but have turned their back on Him. Who are we to interfere in His judgment?" Reverend Gibson asks in his best Sunday voice, looking down his long nose at the general.

Feeling his gut twist in revulsion, General Fitzpatrick turns away from the Preacher, "Mr. President, with all due respect for the opinion of Reverend Gibson, we are under treaty obligation to come to the aid of the Republic if and when they are attacked. Do we simply ignore that?" General Fitzpatrick asks.

President John Paul shakes his head and looks thoughtfully at the old general. "Thomas, I agree with Reverend Gibson on this. The Lord is punishing a godless society for their sins and who are we to go against His will? No, I think it's best if I speak with Prince Al Zarqowi and let him know that we will not interfere, just to prevent an accidental escalation of this unfortunate event."

General Fitzpatrick is shocked as are many around the massive table. "Mr. President, I strongly advise against that. Our intelligence indicates the very real possibility that this move is only the start of something much larger."

"Is this that same old idea that the Brotherhood is out to get us?" Reverend Gibson laughs, "As God is my witness, I can assure you, that's not the case. Why is it that every time something happens, you bring up this ridiculous charge? The fanatics who operate at the edges of Islam do not speak for the Caliph and the Islamic Brotherhood. Besides, you of all people should know that the Federation has the most powerful military on the planet. The Brotherhood would be foolish to challenge that. Tell me, am I right? Or is there something you're not sharing with us?"

"Reverend." General Fitzpatrick replies sharply. "History is full of powerful armies being taken by weaker ones. Why are you willing to gamble that the Brotherhood is not planning to attack us?" General Fitzpatrick asks pointedly. Dislike of the Preacher is finally showing through his professionalism.

"I don't gamble. Besides, I thought my source was obvious. It's my

Lord Jesus Christ, praise be His name. *He* will keep us safe from harm because we are a Christian nation under God. *He* will not turn His back on His people." The Preacher said in his best Sunday sermon voice.

"Amen." President John Paul smiles at his friend and turns back to General Fitzpatrick. "Is there anything else this morning Thomas?"

"Sir, isn't it true that the Lord helps those who help themselves?" General Fitzpatrick asks, desperately seeking to make this man see beyond this madness. "I want to go on record as saying it's a mistake not to send a recon team to Luna. We can make sound decisions only if we know what's happening."

The Preacher's face clouds over. "General. Beyond your implication that this is an unsound decision, let me quote from second Chronicles 19:2. *Should thou help the ungodly, and love them that hate the Lord? Therefore is wrath upon thee from the Lord.* Are you suggesting we go against the word of God?"

For a long moment, the old soldier and the Preacher lock horns, neither willing to back down. "We've given our word. Does that mean anything?" the General growls.

"At ease Thomas. I've made my decision and now it's your duty to see that it's carried out." President John Paul pushes back from the table and rises. The other men in the room scramble to their feet.

"Yes sir. Thank you sir." General Fitzpatrick said. The president and his entourage leave the room as fast as they arrived.

The preacher leans down and said something in President John Paul's ear who nods agreement. It's time to retire Thomas Fitzpatrick. However, the president puts a stop to any talk of reeducation. He forgives his friend's vindictiveness, dismissing it as the exception that shows him to be human.

Back in the Situation Room, "That went well, don't you think?" Admiral Greer said dryly to his boss. The two go back many years and speak bluntly to one another.

"Sir?" Colonel Sanchez said, "I didn't complete my presentation. The president doesn't know about the troop movements or their space fleet."

"When's the last time that anybody managed to complete a presidential presentation?" The old general shakes his head, "Nothing could have changed his mind. He walked in here knowing he was going to let the Lunarians fight the Brotherhood alone. Now he's going to go tell the Prince that the Federation will not interfere. I fear the message the Caliph will hear is one of weakness. Let's do what we can to ready ourselves for war, gentlemen."

Art of War

Cris stops the cycle next to the smashed vehicle. It's one of the rovers sent to track him down after Hallstead. He needs what's inside its fuel tanks. He rummages around in the cycle's small tool compartment until he finds the universal interconnect. Only then does he realize he's not alone.

At least two dozen heavily armed bugeyes are confronting him. Cris whispers a goodbye into his visor, expecting to die in the next instant. If the device survived, at least his family would know he was thinking of them in his final moments.

Instead of opening fire, one of them transmits in broken English. "Remove your weapons."

When Cris remains motionless, the voice repeats, "You will remove your weapons or die."

They wish to capture him? *Interesting.* Cris shows them his hands then slowly removes and drops his pistol. As he draws the sword from over his shoulder, an excited shuffle runs through the soldiers like wind across a wheat field.

They waste no time binding Cris hand and foot, shoving a thick black hood over his head and stuffing him into a rover's empty tool locker. He barely fits. The bone-jarring ride takes the better part of three hours, only the last fifteen minutes on a smooth roadway.

The soldiers pull Cris from the box, letting him fall to the ground. They do not expect him able to stand after his brutal ride but the Highlander surprises them. He gracefully gets to his feet with no apparent ill effects from the rough handling. Someone barks an order. Two soldiers, one on each arm, grab Cris and hustle him forward. It ends when the soldiers force him to his knees and jerk the hood off. Going from utter blackness to glaring light should have disorientated him, but his visor easily adjusts to the sudden change, all the while recording everything for posterity.

The Highlander is at the center of attention. Intense floodlights bear down on him from the tops of troop carriers. The carriers form a high wall along one side of the road as far as he can see. A steep mountainside defines the other.

Cris is in the midst of the Army of Islam. All around him is a sea of bugeyes. Hundreds of Brotherhood soldiers have gathered on the road, on the tops of the nearby carriers, and well up the mountain creating a makeshift arena. Looking beyond them, Cris identifies this place as one of the double-wide segments of Kahfah Road, deciding which one takes only a few moments longer.

Alone, kneeling in the dust of Luna, surrounded by enemies, Cris calmly looks around. The crowd parts and a tall figure in black armor walks through. Rising to his feet, Cris turns to face him. This man's vacsuit is different, the fish scale is finer with barely a reflection, and the helmet smaller and less bug-like.

"Bring me his sword," the man said in Arabic, motioning impatiently. Usually, a subject cringes when going from complete blackness to intense light, but it doesn't seem to bother this infidel at all. Instead, a shiver runs down his spine at the inhuman coolness exhibited by the Lunarian. What can one expect from Djinn? It's further confirmation that these creatures are evil.

One of the soldiers delivers the sword to the bugeye.

"Where did you get this?" The tall man asked in English.

"Made it," Cris answers.

"Unusually thin and much too fragile for a true sword," he scowls. "This could not possibly be used in a fight."

"There's only one way to find out," Cris said.

The officer moves to confront Cris, throwing the Lunarian's sword at his feet. In a single fluid motion, the officer pulls his own broad curved blade from its scabbard and cuts the vacuum centimeters from the Highlander's face. Cris never flinches.

"**This** is a sword, infidel." Pointing at the smaller blade lying in the dust with the tip of his sword, he said, "That is a toy." Speaking to someone behind Cris, the man orders in Arabic, *"Untie him."*

Addressing the crowd, the man raises the sword above his head and continues, *"You shall all see the will of Allah. This Djinn shall die by my sword."*

Turning back to Cris, he commands in English, "Pick it up."

Cris obliges and retrieves his sword. The two men are roughly the same height but the officer is heavier and wearing an armored vacsuit. The Highlander is in the black and gray camouflage of the Lunarian Police Department. While both vacsuits incorporate sophisticated puncture resistant materials, a determined blade will breach them. The crowd presses forward with excitement.

The officer attacks first, swinging his heavy sword in a mighty blow. Cris parries and sidesteps with speed and grace.

The Lunarian blade is lighter than the scimitar and Cris skilled in its use, but one wrong move and his sword will shatter as though made of glass. Back and forth, the two men fight, each measuring the other, probing for weakness. As the seconds turn to minutes, the Brotherhood officer has a growing realization that for all the many hours of practice that lies behind him, he's not the master in this duel. He's never faced a blade so fast and now is fighting a defensive battle. It's all he can do just to stay alive.

Cris presses, never giving his opponent a chance to regroup, hitting the man's armor at will. Each blow is but a note in the silent symphony that is this duel to the death.

Growing evermore desperate, the officer grabs one of his soldiers and shoves him at Cris, boring in behind to make the kill.

Cris is too fast, playing off the surprised soldier to mask his own final assault. The officer never sees the one that gets him.

Faster than a striking viper, the thin Lunarian blade slides upward, forcing its way between the layers of armor, rending heart and lung asunder, then out again as quickly as it went in. The Highlander takes joy in the sound it sends up his arm. He cannot see the face behind the bugeye but in that moment, Cris knows the weight of hate's full measure.

The Highlander thrusts his sword Earthward, blood boiling from its length in a gaseous haze.

Maximizing his visors transmission signal, Cris bellows in perfect Arabic, *"Behold, the will of Allah."*

The soldiers are stunned. Most stand frozen, unable to reconcile what they are witnessing. Only a few take action and bring their weapons to bear but they are far too late.

Agile as a big cat and much quicker, Cris runs and leaps effortlessly over the nearest transport. Those gathered on its top scatter like a brood of chicks under the shadow of a hawk. The Highlander disappears into the darkness beyond before anyone can fire a shot.

ЯL

Tempel set a flight plan that took them due north out of Scottsbluff almost to Albategnius Crater then northwest. They approach the Trans Lunar Highway (TLH) a couple kilometers south of Purgatory. Farpoint is to the north.

Sam leads the way with a spybot. Both Moonhawks hang back. Somehow, they must get across the road undetected. It's not a trivial task.

"We must assume the battlestation in Lagrange One is monitoring the road. It's what I'd do. It's in the perfect location to look down on the Republic," Tempel said.

"They can watch the entire road?" Lazarus asks.

"Sure. The compacted roadbed itself is the perfect background to reveal movement. It will silhouette us like a puppet in a shadow play," Tempel said.

"Then how do we get across?" Lazarus asks.

"We find a place where the road is shaded from their line-of-sight. The TLH runs almost due north and south here but there are a few spots where it runs along the base of a south-facing cliff," Sam said.

Sam isn't worried about the spybot running out of fuel on this mission. She has enough to go many kilometers, scouting ahead for the Moonhawks.

"It's over the next rise," Tempel tells Sam. He's less than a hundred meters behind. Just ahead of them is the Siamese Twins, two small craters each about a kilometer in diameter but only a half kilometer apart. Lunarian geologists determined the two craters formed at almost the exact same instant in a twin impact. Complex fluid dynamics resulted in a cliff several hundred meters high along their southern rim. The Trans Lunar Highway passes within a few meters of its base.

The spybot clears the ridge. The TLH is less than a kilometer away. Road construction crews scooped the regolith from a path eighty meters wide and a meter deep, compressing the material into a hard surface forty meters wide and twenty centimeters thick, a ten to one compaction ratio. Sam scans up and down the road. The color of undisturbed lunar regolith in starlight is gray. The highway is a ribbon of lighter compacted material surrounded by the darker color of disturbed regolith.

"That's it," Sam said.

"Why do you sound worried?" Lazarus asks.

"If it's only the battlestation in Lagrange One that's watching, this is perfect. But if there are other ships watching, they may have a better angle to spot us," Sam said.

"And don't forget the bugs. The Brotherhood may have spread bugs all along the road, especially someplace like this," Corazon adds.

"Corazon, sweep for bugs as we go in. Consuela, let's take this route," Tempel sketches his proposed path on a virtual map.

"We can cross here… hug the base of the cliff until we get here…" Tatiana adds.

"Aye, sounds like a plan. Tempel, I'm on your six," Consuela said.

The spybot led the Moonhawks down the slope. Tempel eases forward never getting higher than ten meters and or faster than thirty kph.

The closer they come to the Trans Lunar Highway, the higher the risk of detection. All they had to do was look up at max zoom to see the hulking form of the battlestation hanging over their heads. They want to cross fast and disappear back into the highlands.

On the way in, they detect nothing. No bugs. No patrols. *Nothing?* Even the roadbed itself looks normal. Tempel records the crossing with his sensors on maximum. It didn't appear that an army had come this way. *Strange.*

They leave the highway behind and head for Aldrin Station, keeping their distance from several bombed out structures along the way. They stay off the roads and finally land a few kilometers from the base of Rim Mountain.

Sam flies the spybot to a landing on a high ridge. Using its main sensor array, Tempel zooms in on activity about a kilometer away. "That's Franklin Gate." The place is swarming with Brotherhood.

Goliaths bristling with cannons lurk within spitting distance of the huge airlock door. Soldiers have set up a checkpoint right outside the gate using two troop carriers.

"We're definitely not going through there," Lazarus said.

Tempel zooms out, points the camera about half way up Rim Mountain and searches for a moment. Finding something, he zooms in revealing a small bullseye carved in the stone. Aiming the spybots communications laser at the symbol, Tempel said, "Aldrin Station, do you copy?"

Magi acknowledges the relay nanoseconds later. "Greetings Tempel. It's good to see you."

Tempel sighs. A couple gigawatts of tension evaporate at the sight of her face. "Greetings, Magi. It's good to be seen."

"Tempel." Corso rumbles. He's the first of thousands to link realtime over the next few seconds. This is big news. Everyone is tuning in. "Where are you?"

"Outside Franklin Gate," Tempel replies. "We have four casualties including Captain Osaka."

Corso sighs, "I'm sorry to hear that. He was a good man and he taught you well lieutenant. You have brought Quan Kiai home."

"We're not home yet. Franklin Gate is crawling with Brotherhood," Tempel said.

"Go to Miller's Farm. It's about two klicks south of Franklin."

"Aye, I know where it is," Tempel replies.

The area around Randsburg is some of the worst badlands in the region. Sheer cliffs and deep ravines are the norm. Most travelers stay on the road if they have any sense.

Cris didn't care. The Highlander makes his own path, freely scampering up and down the steep mountainsides.

The road is especially difficult the last few kilometers leading into Randsburg. In many places, it's barely wide enough for a single Goliath. It goes up and down like a yoyo, clinging precariously onto the steep mountainsides. Passing lanes are few and far between and most of them are at the bottom of deep canyons.

Cris is crossing a ridge near one of these pulloffs when he notices something odd alongside the road far below. They're crosses. He can see seven, about twenty meters apart, standing upright facing the road. He slows and magnifies. There's something on the cross members. A low growl rises unbidden from deep in his chest. He turns and moves straight down the steep slope towards the crosses.

The Highlander can't believe what he's seeing. The passing lane is about a kilometer long. Along it, he counts thirty-nine crosses and forty dead people. They had stripped the bodies, skewered them on a cross and left them to the vacuum. What evil could possess a human being to do such a thing?

The shriveled up victims look like they're sitting on the cross members. The vertical poles enter their rectum and emerge near their clavicle forcing their heads to tilt to the side at an odd angle.

Impaled upon one cross is a second tiny body. Cris assumes it was a baby. He can't tell if the other dehydrated corpse was male or female.

Cris stands on the road looking up. Empty eye sockets stare back, their leathery faces drawn tight to their skulls. Cris could never have imagined anything so horrible. Rage builds inside him.

These were citizens. Not soldiers. Not warmongers. Law-abiding Lunarian citizens. And these ghastly crosses... The Brotherhood must have brought them here for this very purpose. The fitting on the bottom next to the ground is for a Construction Utility Vehicle used to drive the crosses into the regolith. A sick mind thought this up, and a sicker heart did the deed.

If the Brotherhood meant to scare him, they failed miserably. It had the exact opposite effect. Cris snarls and turns to face the rovers racing towards him. He leaps off the road and runs down a side canyon, his black and gray uniform affording him near perfect camouflage. The rovers follow firing as they come but Cris is virtually invisible once he's off the roadway.

Cris could easily leave the vehicles behind. They are limited to the relative flatness at the bottom. All he need do was climb up and over the side of the canyon and he would disappear into the rugged landscape beyond. Instead, he draws them in.

The four rovers bounce down the narrow canyon, their lasers firing as fast as they recharge, but the shots are wild, without any real target. The canyon narrows even further and becomes impassable a short way ahead. Cris turns and heads up the steep mountainside and over the ridge then doubles back.

He waits until the rovers have passed then leaps upon the roll cage of the last one, draws his sword, and plunges it into the driver. The rover veers into the side of the canyon. The impact throws Cris headlong towards the rock face. Agile as a cat, he twists in midair and lands on his feet and hands.

Leaping back on the rover, he slaps the safety harness free and drags the stunned passenger from the vehicle. Holding him up with his left hand, Cris impales the man with his sword. He quickly strips the body of its pistol and holster before throwing the corpse aside.

Laser light spatters against the nearby rock face. The other three rovers are returning. Cris races back down the canyon away from them but never getting too far ahead. He picks a rather sharp bend to make his next move.

Again, he climbs the steep mountainside and circles back. He draws his newly acquired pistol and targets the lead rover, shredding its fuel tanks. A moment later, the hypergolic fuels mix and explode in silent fury. Its carcass blocks the canyon. The other two rovers will need to move it before they can leave.

The four remaining soldiers are frantic. They don't know where the Highlander is. The shots could have come from anywhere. The silent lunar mountains loom over them. They are alone on a strange world fighting against an unholy monster. They panic. The lead rover rams the mangled remains of its brethren desperately trying to force its way past. The two rovers get tangled and grind to a stop.

The passenger jumps out and begins frantically pushing the dead rover out of the way. Together, man and machine move the wreckage aside. The soldier waves at the other rover before getting back in. They are strangely silent.

Something's wrong. He looks closer. A blood red fog is gathering around the two soldiers. He throws himself into his rover screaming at his partner, *"Go."* but they remain where they are. *"Go. Go. Go."* he screams repeatedly. When he looks at his comrade, he realizes the man is sitting behind the wheel, dead. The red haze of death rises slowly from the corpse.

"Noooooo." A blade flashes in the starlight and the screaming stops.

Cris wipes his sword clean and continues towards Randsburg. A tiny spybot follows.

ЯL

The surface portion of Miller's Farm had been a collection of half-buried large-diameter prefab metal cylinders sealed end-to-end and laid out side-to-side like rows in a field. During the fourteen days of daylight, louvers built above them would reflect natural sunlight through Duraglass windows. During darkness, the louvers would reposition and reflect the interior sunlamps onto the plants inside. Each row had contained many acres of high-density hydroponics. The bombardment hadn't spared them. They lay in ruins.

Old man Miller had tucked his farmhouse deep under Rim Mountain where it was not only protected from meteorites, it could share processing and recycling facilities with Aldrin Station. The attack had mangled the outer airlock but left the access tunnel leading to the farm unharmed. Looking down from the battlestation hanging above them, the airlock would look impassible but Tempel had no problem flying his Moonhawk past it. He flew down the tunnel and landed in the farm's main hanger. A moment later, Consuela landed her ship beside his.

Corso is waiting when they lowered the ramps and walked off the Moonhawks. Behind Corso is a vidcasting crowd of Quan Kiai's family and friends. Tens of thousands more are linked to watch. Corso motions for them to form up. Tempel takes his usual place as Senior Lieutenant.

Tatiana looks at Tempel and shakes her head, "Tempel, what are you doing? Take the front." She pushes him in the general direction.

"I can't take Kitajima's place," Tempel resists.

"No one's asking you to. Just stand up front," Tatiana replies.

"Aye," "go for it," "it's only right," Quan Kiai picks their new leader in those few seconds. Tempel accepts and moves to face his platoon. Tatiana takes his place as Senior Lieutenant.

Tatiana's voice breaks but she maintains her discipline. "Captain Kitajima Osaka, KIA. Special Teams Officer Brice Guyart, KIA. Special Teams Officer Lei Cheung, KIA. Special Teams Officer Karl Svensson, KIA. All present or accounted for lieutenant,"

"Thank you lieutenant. Quan Kiai, form up in four-man teams. Let's bring our comrades home," Tempel orders. "Sam, Kipper, you're with me. Master Sergeant Hackling… let's go get Kitajima."

"Aye," she manages to say. Hack will do her crying later.

Four at a time, they climb the ramp and carry a black body bag back down. They reverently place them on the ER vehicle.

After the last bag had been loaded and Quan Kiai reformed, Tempel does a sharp about-face. "Quan Kiai present or accounted for," he calls out.

Corso had watched the entire event unfold without saying a word. He now moves forward until he was before Tempel and salutes, "Welcome home. Thank you all for a job well done. I wish I could tell you that's it's over but I can't. There's a General Council in session right now and you're all invited, including you, Lazarus."

A personal invitation by Aldrin Station's Security Chief is not something he can refuse. "Aye," Lazarus said. It's the first time he's used the Lunarian slang.

"Corso. Let them take a shower and unwind. They have been through a lot." Liz is one of the few people in Aldrin Station who dare to speak to Corso this way.

Corso chuckles, "Aye, you're right, and when you're right, your right. Join us in Council when you're ready. Just don't take too long."

"Aye," Tempel nods.

Randsburg

Randsburg is Luna's only gold mine. It also produces platinum, palladium, iridium, osmium, rhenium, rhodium, ruthenium and a lot of iron. The prevailing theory is the giant iron meteor that formed Arzachel Crater was extremely rich in iron-loving or siderophile elements. The impact scattered the rare metals and iron into the craters rim in lumps, like raisins in oatmeal.

John Rand and his partner Bill Langdon discovered the deposit in 2076. Keenly aware of the importance of properly recording their claim before a rush could get started, John devised a clever scheme that bought them some time. Fearful that other miners from Hallstead and Prattville would soon be over to investigate, the two prospectors loaded up their rover with bags of low-grade chromite and headed for Prattville.

Curious miners asked what they had found. John stubbornly held out but finally admitted, "Well… I think we've found something pretty good." He would say no more. The inquisitive miners soon found the planted bags while John and Bill were away. Word spread throughout camp about the two fools digging chromite in the middle of the badlands. It gave the partners an extra day or two to stake their claims. They called their discovery the Goosefoot Mine.

Randsburg is a typical mining town. Starting from a single Quonset, it has evolved into a thriving subterranean city of over eleven thousand. It doesn't have the enormous malls or commonways like Aldrin Station. Instead, Randsburg grew out of the excavations that harvested the ore. Thus, it's a mishmash of irregular tunnels and strangely shaped rooms spread out over a very large volume.

Approaching the town's main entrance, Cris moves along the ridge overlooking the road. The road ends in a box canyon surrounded by high, steep mountains. Thousands of tons of iron pass through this gate on its way to the smelters in Prattville and Aldrin Station.

The open area outside Ransburg's main gate is not very large, about a hundred meters square. The initial bombardment reached even here. Nothing remains standing but the wreckage has been shoved aside making room for a Brotherhood force of at least two thousand soldiers. Several heavily armed Goliaths stand guard at the massive airlock door, which is wide open. More Goliaths protect the few road construction vehicles they have left. Guards watch from the tops of the troop carriers and rovers run patrols up and down the line. They have learned.

The rock beneath him heaves and explodes throwing Cris off the summit. He tumbles down the steep mountainside. More shots follow. They're coming from above. The Brotherhood's gunships have spotted him and are maneuvering to get a better angle.

Dazed but unhurt, Cris regains control and turns his downward momentum into forward motion. He races across the vertical landscape but he can't lose the fighters. They follow him. He must have picked up a bot coming in.

Cris retreats to the darkest shadows at the bottom of a deep canyon. The fighters can't follow him down here but they can still shoot. They narrowly miss repeatedly. He probes for the spybot while he runs.

If I were a bot, where would I hide? Cris doubles back and scrambles up the side of the rill looking for the faint thermal signature. There, on the ledge, the bot's tiny thrusters had heated the stone when it landed moments before. Cris draws and fires in one smooth motion. The tiny sliver of rock disintegrates. He doesn't stick around to see if it was the right rock. That will soon become apparent.

He races down the canyon leaving the fighters behind to shoot at shadows. Searchlights and lasers probe the darkness but Cris is already a kilometer away and moving fast. It was the right rock.

Cris cuts across deep canyons and sharp ridges making his way to the top of Arzachel Crater's rim mountain. He cautiously approaches Randsburg's main spaceport. It is one of the highest and busiest ports in the Republic. Most of the precious metals pass through here. The bombardment had pounded it into rubble. Small craters pockmark the flattened mountaintop and unrecognizable twisted metal is all that remains of its ships and installations.

Beyond the spaceport looms the massive solar refinery. It looks intact. The Brotherhood must have plans for it. He scrambles down the inside of rim and comes to a small observation balcony overlooking the vast Arzachel Crater. Cris looks around carefully before dropping upon it like a cougar coming home.

The airlock door is closed. He places his left hand on its pad. When it doesn't immediately open, he backs off finding a spot a few meters away. He settles down to wait.

Minutes go by. Finally, the door opens and swings wide but nothing else happens. Then a girl tentatively steps out looking around the empty balcony. She carries a disrupter and is ready to use it. "Cris?" She turns to go back inside when Cris drops down beside her.

The girl jumps, "Cris. Don't scare me like that." Her pistol slides back into its holster.

"I need to speak with John." Cris moves past the girl.

"You don't have time for a simple greeting?" She pulled the door shut and locked it. The airlock cycled quickly.

"Greetings Callista," Cris said opening the inner door.

"Greetings Cristobal. John's at the refinery. He told me to get some food in you." Callista runs but can't keep up. "Cris, slow down."

The Highlander pauses and looks back irritably.

Callista studies Cris as she catches up. "Cris… what's wrong?"

"There's an army outside your door and you ask me what's wrong?"

"Yes, I know. We've been able to block them but only because they can't bring those damned Goliath's into the city."

They're moving fast but at a human pace. Cris has been inside Randsburg many times. He knows where he's going almost as well as Callie.

"Magi?" Cris calls.

"Magi's gone. The attack cut us off without a single thread," Callie said. Cris is acting strange. They are good friends but she doesn't know this person. This man is cold and angry.

"Are you hungry?"

"After I talk to John," Cris didn't bite her head off but it was close.

"Fine…" Callie slows and lets the Highlander go on alone. "Nice seeing you Cris…"

Cris ignores her and speeds up again. He enters the refinery from one of the upper entrances and descends to the main floor using his hands and feet. He spots John about the same instant that John spots him.

"Greetings Cris. It's good to see you." John walks toward the Highlander. "Do you bring word from Aldrin Station?"

"Greetings… No… I was hoping you knew something. I was on patrol when this started."

"Bill's getting a Moonhawk ready. He's going to make a run to Prattville. Can you tell us anything about what's between us and them?" John asks.

"I can do more than that. We need to summarize and authenticate my visor records and add them to his manifest." Cris said.

Callie walks up behind him, "I can help with that."

Cris glances at her and said to John, "We should get someone... older..."

"I'm seventeen. I vote, I work, I fight." Callie flares. "What more do you want?"

John can tell by Cris's expression that something was out of the ordinary here, "She's a grown woman. She can handle it."

Cris turns to Callie.

"Don't look so sad," Callie said. "How bad can it be?"

"Callie..." He fears shredding what's left of her childhood and the thought makes him feel like shit.

She puts her hand on his arm, "Cris, I can do this."

Cris lowers his eyes and turns away. There's only one way to make her understand. "Very well..." He downloads the vid of his last few days to her visor. She divides the work and begins.

"You could use a shower and some real food," John said.

"Aye, and some sleep," Cris said wearily. "But first, tell me what's happening?"

John sighs, "The attack came just after sunset. We lost all satellite communications and Magi abandoned us without a single thread remaining in town. Then the bombs came. They killed fourteen outside the main gate, forty in the spaceport and many more out on the crater floor. Then the soldiers show up and start shooting. We got everyone out that we could and made a stand here at the refinery. So far, they haven't been able to get past Conrad and his warriors."

"Conrad's here?" Cris is relieved.

"Aye, we would be in bad shape if they weren't."

"I will report to him immediately." Cris starts to stand.

"Hold on," John reaches out and grips Cris by the arm. "He's doing fine. He already knows you're here and will talk to you after you're properly fed and rested."

"Fine," Cris is too tired to argue. He sits and eats in stoic silence not tasting any of it.

With tears streaming down her cheeks, Callie comes and sits down next to him. She lays her head on his shoulder and puts her arm about his waist. "It's so horrible, what they did to our people on those crosses. Oh Cris. I'm so sorry…" She thinks about the number of people he killed. No wonder he's different.

As others view the summary and realize what Cris has done, they gather around the Highlander. John Rand walks over and sits across from Cris. He watches the young Lunarian eat for a few minutes before saying. "You will forever have my support and appreciation for what you've been through," John said.

"Many are dead because of me," Cris pushes the half-empty plate away.

"Aye, but many Lunarians are alive because of you. Don't forget that. You fought back and for that, we're all grateful."

"I'm a Highlander. It's what we do." Cris is suddenly very tired.

John reaches across the table and grips the young man's arm. "Aye, and we all appreciate it." John looks at Callie, "Take Cris to my billet and get him showered. Find him a bunk. I'll see to it that you're not disturbed."

"Aye," a shower and some sleep sounds good to Cris…

ЯL

Quan Kiai is loud and boisterous entering the crew quarters in Dakota Warren. The warrior's help each other peel away the artificial epidermis that has kept them alive and well on their airless world. The suits go straight away into the vacsuit rehab modules and the Highlanders head for the shower.

Lindsey helps Lazarus remove his vacsuit and he helps her. Lazarus does his best not to stare at those around him. They're the last to leave.

"You've had a chance to view some of your father's records. What are your thoughts?" Lindsey asks. They're in the ramp leading to the shower.

"He was running away from my mother," Lazarus said frankly. "Apparently, she didn't know anything about my tool shed education because if she had, she would have turned us in. At least that's what he thought." He glances at her swaying tits and stumbles.

Lindsey grins and grips his arm tightly. "What do you think? Would she turn you in?" She asked.

Lazarus thinks for a moment, "She may have turned in my little brother. You have to know my mom. She's intensely religious."

They enter the bath and pass between the polished stone columns into the communal shower beyond. Scattered about singly, the Lunarians are strangely motionless under the running water.

"What're they doing?" Lazarus asks. Warm water envelopes him but cannot distract him from staring at the warriors.

"They're viewing summaries of the events that have transpired since we've been gone." Lindsey replies.

"Summaries?"

"Magi strings together pertinent moments into summaries like she did with your father's vids. She can compress a day into a few minutes," Lindsey said. "See for yourself, link with Tempel."

He does. Sights, sounds, and smells assail Lazarus. He staggers and might have fallen if Lindsey hadn't been there.

"Easy does it," she said putting her arm around him.

Lazarus concentrates and begins to discern events at speeds much faster than normal. He's in a commonway fighting… at a table eating… working on a machine… talking… crying… The words are a high-pitched screech, the images a blur.

"How fast is it going?" Lazarus asks.

"Everyone is different. Tempel is one of the fastest at about sixty-six times normal," Lindsey said.

"Sixty-six. He understands what he's seeing?"

"Aye. In fact, his recall is better after high speed viewing than after normal," she adds.

As if on cue, Quan Kiai finishes the summaries and gathers in a circle, facing inward with their arms around each other. Lindsey pulls Lazarus into the mix.

Lazarus is uneasy but Lindsey holds him firmly on one side with Sam on the other. He tries to be nonchalant but everywhere he looks is wet glistening flesh. He's the meat between Sam's warm body on one side and Lindsey's on the other.

Lindsey senses his nervousness, "Relax." She hopes he wasn't going to be a problem.

"I'm trying." he said sneaking a peek at the nudity all around him. Knowing where to look, he can now see the subtle changes in their bodies while admiring the grace and elegance of the Highlanders. They are beautiful and he finds himself staring.

Consuela looks over at Lazarus. "So this is what an Earthman looks like? Kind of soft if you ask me, except that rod between your legs."

"I must admit, I am not accustomed to seeing so many beautiful ladies in the flesh. My mind and body seem to have different ideas about how to handle it. I do apologize," Lazarus said.

The Highlanders roar with laughter, perhaps more than is warranted. Consuela smiles, "Well said Earthman. But you really must do something about that body. Put on a little muscle."

"I like him just the way he is," Lindsey chimes in, squeezing his butt cheek for emphasis.

Consuela shrugs, "No accounting for taste."

The group closes the circle ever tighter. They make a solid mass of human flesh huddled in the center of the shower. Streams of hot water create a fog that engulfs them in its warm embrace.

"Karl Svensson, Lei Cheung, Brice Guyart, Kitajima Osaka." Tempel said each name slowly and deliberately.

"Nell Goddard," Sam adds.

Tempel glances at her and nods. "We celebrate their lives and honor our fallen comrades with our deeds and actions."

"We shall remember." Lindsey and the warriors join voices and speak as one, their naked bodies shimmering wetly under the hot water.

Only Lazarus remains mute. From the outside looking in, this gathering has all the earmarks of a nudist prayer meeting but without any mention of god or life after death. Humanity is a social animal and these young men and women are saying goodbye to their friends. In a philosophy that does not pretend to an afterlife, death is not a transition, rather an ending.

"They purchased our freedom with their lives," Tempel said.

"We shall never forget," Quan Kiai said in unison. Their tears are lost in the shower's steady downpour but the raw emotion is palpable. They will miss their friends.

"There is no greater love than that which they have shown. They have sacrificed their existence so that we may live." Tempel shuts his eyes and envisions Brice, Karl, Lei and Kitajima. He has known them his entire life and they him. Now, in the safety of his home, it didn't seem real that they were dead.

"We shall honor them always."

"We, the survivors, accept their sacrifice and pledge to bring it honor," Tempel said fiercely.

"Study the past, live in the present, and plan for the future." Quan Kiai said.

Tempel looks around at his friends, one arm around Sam's waist, hers about his. His other arm holds Zoey tightly. His heart aches for those missing and he can sense the pain in those around him. Nothing will bring the dead back to life but they do have the public records. As one, they begin to chant…

Lo, there do I see my Mother and my Father…
Lo, there do I see my Sisters and my Brothers…
Lo, there do I see my Ancestors back to the Beginning…
They beckon me to Take my place among Them…
In the Hallowed Halls of Remembrance…
Where we All live on Forever…

Brice appears in the center of the circle, smirking like always, "Quick. What's the difference between heaven and hell? … Give up? … Nothing. They're both figments of wishful thinking," he laughs. His image remains untouched by the shower's water.

Quan Kiai collectively groans. Leave it to Brice to record a death message like this. They can't help but grin.

"If you're viewing this then I must be dead. What the fuck, over. I probably screwed up but whatever happened, don't worry about it. I'm not… I'm dead. Remember?" Brice said with overzealous sincerity. Then he tucks the smile away and turns serious, "I have recorded something for each of you but the main thing for everyone to do right now is just carry on. Never give up. Never quit. Finish the job…" He shifts his gaze around the circle as if looking at each friend. Lazarus shivers as it passes over him. Then as suddenly as it disappeared, the smirk returns, "Bye bye… Adios… So long… Farewell… Arrividerci… Auf Wiedersehen…" his voice and image fades away.

One by one, Karl, Lei and Kitajima take his place. They each have recorded a brief death message for the platoon.

Kitajima is last. "Attention." he barks out and they all snap straight, even Lazarus. "At ease. Y 'all are probably in the shower, seems like you spend a god-awful amount of time in there… No sad faces. I won't stand for that. Don't waste your time grieving over me. I had a long life and a good one thanks to you people and the Republic. Working with all of you gave me something I sorely needed, respect from people I respect… No matter how I ended up dead, I want you all to know that I have absolutely no regrets. I would do it all over again in a New York minute."

Kitajima turns slowly looking out at the platoon, nodding in that way he had of drawing your complete attention to what he was about to say. "Death is only painful for the living," he remains dry amidst the downpour but only Lazarus finds that odd. "Death is a hard thing to wrap your mind around. Oh sure, we all know we are eventually going to die but that's always in the future, not now, not today, but the fact is, it catches up to all of us. There's nothing to do about it. Accept it and move on."

Kitajima snaps to attention, "It's been a pleasure," He thrusts his fist upward, "Quan Kiai..."

The warriors press into an even tighter circle, their fists joining Kitajima's one last time, "**Quan Kiai,**" they respond in unison, just before he fades away.

The circle breaks up. It takes a few seconds for Lazarus to realize that the ceremony is over. Lindsey takes him by the hand and the two of them find a nearby bench, luxuriating in the hot water cascading over their bare skin.

The shower soon fills with laughter and horseplay. Soapsuds and playful scrubbing inevitably turns into a different kind of tension relieving activity. Moans of pleasure and the rhythmic sounds of human passion replace laughter.

Lazarus, completely attentive of Lindsey, finds it absurdly easy to embrace the open sexuality of the Lunarians. It's a natural and nurturing thing. He makes a strange happy sound, half laugh, half sigh. Lindsey looks down at him. He meets her gaze and winks. She smiles.

Free at last. Free at last. Great god almighty, I am free at last.

Councilor Taylor asks impatiently. "Can we get down to business?"

"By all means, proceed," Abby said.

"The situation's not critical at the moment. We should take this opportunity to send ambassadors to work out a diplomatic solution to the conflict," Councilor Taylor declares.

"They've nuked Shennong. They've nuked Lagrange One and replaced it with a battlestation. They've invaded our city threatening to nuke us. Their space fleet is jamming the entire system. They have a battlestation hanging over our heads ready to turn Aldrin Station into a crater. Moreover, there is an army coming down Kahfah Road. I would say the situation is extremely critical," Councilor Debouch replies.

"We must try. Diplomacy has its place."Councilor Taylor said.

"Their idea of a peaceful solution is our annihilation. We can't surrender. We must fight. Their space fleet is our number one threat. It can destroy us all. It must be neutralized," Corso said.

Abby nods in agreement, "Corso's right. Whatever we decide to do, dealing with their warships must be at the top of the list. Diplomacy can come later."

"They must be destroyed. There's no other way," Lazarus said.

Only Lindsey pays attention and turns to him. "We aren't strong enough Lazarus. The Treaty of Independence has seen to that." she said. "We have no space fleet of our own."

"The Chinese do," he retorts.

Abby turns her attention to Lazarus and Lindsey.

"They haven't lifted a finger to help us so far. Why should they change now?" Lindsey asks.

"We invite them to come out and play," Lazarus said. A few more citizens have linked and the growing number attracting the attention of the Councilors. With a gesture, Abby draws Lindsey and Lazarus down to the Assembly Floor. Lazarus runs his fingers through his long hair, gazing nervously at the multitude around him. He has given presentations before but never been the focus like this. He likes it. He turns to face Abby.

"That's absurd," Councilor Taylor declares.

Abby ignores him and asks Lazarus. "How do you propose to do that?"

"We use a Brotherhood nuke to attack a Chinese battlestation," Lazarus said.

"All that would accomplish is to have two superpowers at war with us," Councilor Taylor said. "I can assure you young man, that conflict would be a very short one."

"Not if they think the Brotherhood attacked them… That just might work," Abby said. "How would you do it?"

"The Chinese navy will be very nervous right now. The jamming is keeping them from communicating with their ships just like everybody else. They're not going to know as much as we do about the situation. They would have seen what happened to Shennong and Lagrange. They may even think the Republic is defeated. I'll bet my retirement that every vessel in space is on full alert. All we need to do is push them over the edge," Lazarus said.

"The Chinese are allied with the Brotherhood. Why not draw the Federation into the conflict?" Abby asks.

"The Chinese fleet is bigger," Lazarus said.

Abby frowns, sensing something in Lazarus she didn't like, the faint whiff of deceit. She looks closely at his polygraphic indicators. It's obvious. Despite everything, there's still some Federation loyalty within the man.

"That may be true but the Christians have been in conflict with the Muslims for generations while the Chinese have helped the Brotherhood almost from the beginning," Abby replies. "It makes more sense to draw the Federation in."

"You sure you don't have some other reason for leaving the Federation out of it?" Corso growls.

Lazarus is not one to give up so easily. "My family and friends live there… so yes, maybe I do have some other motive for not wanting the Federation at war," Lazarus admits.

Corso and Abby look at each other. Lazarus had almost slipped but was now telling the truth. Corso nods, "I like the basic idea but we need to expand it. We have twelve nukes. I suggest we spread them around. If nothing else it will cause confusion."

"To do it right, you will need detailed information on the location and size of every vessel in orbital space. How will you get that?" Councilor Debouch asks.

A giant 3D graphic of cislunar space appears in the central area of the chamber. Floating letters identifies Taurus Colony, Hyundai Shipyards and many of the satellites that inhabit Earths orbital space.

"After triangulating each jamming signal, one at a time, Magi found sixty-five sources, three battlestations, two heavy cruisers, eighteen destroyers and forty-two frigates," Corso said. Orange dots appear within the graphic, the bigger the dot, the bigger the ship.

"That's the Brotherhood. What about the rest?" Debouch asks.

"The locations of all other military vessels are extrapolations from data obtained just before the attack. Each hour that passes makes their location less certain. China… Japan… European Union… India… Brazil… Australia…" Corso adds their dots as he lists the players. "The Federation has eighty-eight warships including five battlestations."

Turning to Lazarus, Corso said, "Your idea has merit but only if we use existing political lines. On one side is the Brotherhood and China. On the other is the North American Federation, the European Union, Japan, and India. As you say, we must invite them all to come out and play."

"We could be opening Pandora's Box. There's no controlling where this could lead," Councilor Debouch said.

Councilor Yang Lee frowns, "What you're advocating is mass murder."

"What we're *discussing* is our survival." Abby retorts.

"Global war will kill billions of innocent people." Councilor Yang Lee said. "Is our survival worth that?"

"That's the question, isn't it?" Abby replies. "Are we justified in killing others so that we may live? Evolution dictates only the strong survive to pass their genes on to the next generation. Have we evolved to the point that we can set aside nature's most basic law? I don't think so. Regardless, I'm not going down without a fight."

Before Abby's finished speaking, Councilor Yang Lee holds up his hands in surrender, "It seems my freehold citizens agree with you." Bowing his head, he vanishes.

Lunarian political system is very different from any that come before. Councilors have no set term of office. They serve for as long as they have political support. It's routine for the Council to see changes in personnel during a heated debate.

A petite oriental woman with raven black hair and a beautiful porcelain complexion appears in Yang Lee's place. The robes of office swirl about her. Her youthful features belie the maturity in her eyes.

"Greetings," she bows deeply, "I am Li Wei Chang, Councilor of the Hunan Freehold." The formal announcement was unnecessary. They all know who she is.

"Welcome back Li Wei," Abby said warmly, "I only wish it were under better circumstances."

"As do I Abigail. It is with deep regret that Hunan freehold aligns with this plan," Councilor Li said softly.

Abby lays out a poll, "I call on the Council to immediately initiate a mission to be known as Pandora. Its goal is to set up the conditions necessary to bring the other warlike nations into the fight if we choose to do it. The specifics are yet to be determined."

The tally is swift and overwhelming. The citizens of the Republic of Luna want to live.

"What about Al Fahad?" Councilor Hanley asks. "The invasion of our cities must have originated in Al Fahad."

"Nuke it." Councilor Johanson exclaims.

"Nuking Al Fahad would immediately bring retaliation." Councilor Taylor exclaims.

"Not if you do it right," Lazarus said. "Done right, it could have a profound effect on every Muslim in the empire."

Abby looks disgusted, "Do you really think that's necessary?"

Lazarus holds his ground. "Not for revenge, but for maximum effect. If you take out Al Fahad in the right way, you may end the war right there. The Army of Islam may lay down their arms and stop fighting."

"What do you mean, the right way?" Abby asks.

"There's only two things that can make a mujahedeen stop fighting, kill him or convince him that Allah wills it. Logic will not work and strength of arms simply forces him underground. We need to make it seem as if Allah disapproves of the actions taken by the Prince and his ministers," Lazarus said.

"Just how do you propose to do that?" Councilor Taylor asks.

"By preying on their religious superstitions. We must convince them that it's Allah's will… the mujahedeen will follow what they have been taught in the madrasa," Lazarus said.

"Dare I ask, what is a madrasa?" Councilor Taylor asks.

"A madrasa is a school that teaches fundamentalism. It's the only education most of them receive," Lazarus said.

"Why should I care about their schools?" Councilor Taylor asks.

"Understanding your enemy is the key to victory," Lazarus said.

"I ask again, why should I care where they go to school?" Councilor

Taylor asks sharply.

"As young boys, mujahedeen spend their youth just as their ancestors did, memorizing the Holy Qur'an. They learn to recite it back chapter and verse. It takes the average ten-year-old boy about three years. To make matters worse, they must memorize it in Arabic, but the boys come from every ethnic corner of the world. Some never learn Arabic beyond this rote memorization. The teachers read to them in Arabic and they recite it back for eight hours a day until they memorize the whole book."

"After graduation, the boys are enrolled in an eight-year course of study that focuses on the Holy Qur'an, and the Hadith. Most become mujahedeen, or soldiers, but a few of the more gifted will go on to become Mufti or Imam. Mufti sets social policy. Imam sets political policy. They are the leaders in Muslim society yet their education encompasses only theology, no world history, no math, no science, only a total immersion in fundamental Islam. Many brag that the Qur'an and Hadith are the only books they have ever read."

"How exactly do you propose we take advantage of this?" Councilor Taylor asks.

"Their unwavering belief makes them vulnerable. While it's an incredible force for controlling their army, staged in the right way, these soldiers can be influenced," Lazarus explains.

"What's the right way?" Councilor Taylor asks.

Seeing Lazarus hesitate, Abby steps in, "Lazarus doesn't need to give a detailed description at this time. We can all see advantages in the plan." Abby turns to him, "Lazarus, are you willing to work with Corso to come up with some ideas?" He nods, "Good. When you present them to the Council, we will decide which, if any, to go with."

Councilor Taylor visibly relaxes, "Very well, but I want all discussions to remain in public domain subject to the Law of Full Disclosure."

"Of course," Abby replies, "I wouldn't have it any other way."

Battle of Aldrin Station

Let those who would prefer the Hereafter to the Present life,
Fight in the cause of Allah. And who so Fights in the cause of
Allah and is Killed...We shall soon grant him a great Reward.

Holy Qur'an 4:74

Jordan and Jamie are strapping the figure to a seat in the back of the Moonhawk when Lazarus vidcasts next to them.

"Tempel is finishing prelaunch. Do you have any last thoughts before we send our messenger off?" Jordan asks Lazarus.

Lazarus shakes his head. "I understand enough to know you guys have exceeded my wildest imagination."

Jamie looks intently at him, "Don't be so modest. We couldn't have conceived of this without you."

"Explain to me again, what's a dPhag?" Lazarus requests.

"dPhag stands for Dimensional Phase Generator," Jamie said patiently.

"When enough energy is concentrated in a Calconn coil, space warps and a small black hole is created," Jordan said.

"Black holes link our universe to the next within the Superverse. The hole's we create are not very large, about the size of a proton, but when you super-energize the millions of micro-coils in a ghost suit, it phases into the next universe," Jamie explains.

"I'm fuzzy on this Superverse thing," Lazarus said.

Jamie smiles, "I assure you, the dPhag is essential for your plan to work."

"It's the key bit of technology that puts this mission over the top," Jordan adds.

"We've never tested it at this scale," Jamie adds.

"But we're sure it will work," Jordan adds.

"But if you've never done it before, why are you so sure it will work?" Lazarus asks.

"Magi's theoretical calculations are very accurate," Jamie replies.

"She never makes a mistake," Jordan adds.

"Time to roll," Tempel said.

"I still think I should be going with you," Lazarus moves up the aisle towards Tempel nodding to the warriors aboard the Moonhawk. He's getting better at vidcasting.

"The decision's made," Tempel replies.

"Tempel, you don't realize what effect that thing back there will have on the Brotherhood. Some of them will want to stop fighting. Give them a chance but don't expose yourself. They can revert back to violence at any time." He leans down to look the young Lunarian in the face. "If you need to fight then take it to them Tempel, just like you did in Nell's Valley. You hear me. Give 'em hell."

"**Give 'em hell,**" Jordan and Jamie echo.

"*Aye,*" Quan Kiai said.

"Heaven's what they're expecting but it's hell we're bringing." Corazon is trying to sound like Brice and failing miserably but they all appreciate his effort.

Tempel looks intently at Lazarus and said dryly, "I'll give them your message."

Jordan follows Jamie down the ramp and it shuts behind them.

Lazarus stands alone watching the Moonhawk rise from the floor of the hanger at Miller's Farm. A crew had just finished stealth coating their Moonhawk and is now working on the other. The non-reflective surface makes the ship a shadow among shadows long before it reaches the farm's access tunnel. Within seconds, it's gone. *I hate waiting.*

ℛ𝕃

The city's massive atmospheric circulators are silent and the sky is dark. Hundreds of small fires flicker across the devastated commonway. Smoke fills the still air so thick in places that sensors cannot penetrate. The temperature is over 50°C.

The Brotherhood selected well. Their camp is at the top of Serenity Hill, a flat-topped mesa about twenty meters above the surrounding commonway. The great tunnel is wider here. The east/west slidewalks weave around the base of the hill. Stripped of its majestic oak trees, convoys crowd Serenity's summit, their thick armor bristling with cannon. In the flickering light, it looks like a medieval castle.

Lieutenant Taylor scampers through this hellish environment harassing the enemy that has invaded his home. Others are doing the same, making it impossible for the Brotherhood to relax.

The warriors are playing a dangerous game, ignoring the invaders incessant demand to cease-fire or die in a nuclear holocaust. To Taylor's left is what appears to be a group of Lunarians operating a heavy disrupter. Tucked in behind a massive piece of fire-blackened hardwood, it methodically pulses powerful beams across the intervening space. Another almost identical emplacement sits fifty meters beyond it and slightly forward. It too keeps constant pressure on the enemy encampment. The thunder of each discharge echoes down the immense stone passageway. In return, they have received an inordinate amount of attention from Brotherhood gunners. After all, they are immobile while the warriors are shadows on a dark night and much harder to hit. The Lunarian battlefield technicians have lost count how many times they have repaired the emplacements, getting them back up and firing within minutes.

Even as Taylor watches, another warrior, having exposed himself while making some imaginary adjustment to the weapon, takes a hit to his chest and falls back, apparently dead. It bothers Taylor even though he knows it's only a computer-generated illusion. The warrior is not real. None of the Lunarians operating these emplacements are flesh and blood. They serve only to encourage the invaders to think they are inflicting more casualties upon the infidels than they really are. The deception is a central feature of the plan to maintain pressure while cultivating the misconception that the Brotherhood soldiers are holding their own.

Lieutenant Taylor and his warriors are very much a part of this perilous ploy, exposing themselves, even if only briefly, as they fire at the enemy. Tiny spybots seek out and mark the location of every enemy combatant. The devices are small, numerous, and hard to detect. Magi prioritizes the targets and feeds the fire control data to the appropriate warrior. All they need do is look and fire, thus limiting their exposure. The resulting enemy attrition is high, and even with the elaborate deception, the Brotherhood will soon fall back to lick their wounds. No fighting force can withstand such losses for long.

Oak Ridge and Sherwood Forest commonways are the two fronts of the invaders campaign. Corso estimates they are facing about eighteen thousand troops in Sherwood and another twenty thousand in Oak Ridge but those numbers are dropping rapidly. Spybots have verified the locations of both nukes. Corso sets in motion a plan to eliminate them.

Behind Lieutenant Taylor, hidden around a bend in the commonway, the Lunarians release a swarm of several thousand small flying devices, each the spitting image of a honeybee. The constant pressure of the attacks keeps the Brotherhood soldiers too busy staying alive to think it odd that a honeybee could survive this heat.

Some bees stay close to the ground amidst the rubble while others zoom high and come down on their target. The swarm converges on a troop carrier with the big Red Crescent on its side. The growing assemblage finally attracts the attention of a technician within the command center.

"*Sir. I am picking up something within our perimeter.*" Havildar Ezzedine said in Arabic.

The bees now cover a spot almost a meter wide on the undercarriage of the massive vehicle, their energy signature partially obscured in its shadow. Once in place, these bees do not move like their biological counterparts, crawling and squirming over one another. Instead, they pack together and remain motionless, building up like a tumor on the carrier's belly, waiting patiently for the signal that will complete their mission.

"*What is it Havildar?*" Imam Bakr asks. He walks over to stand behind the man looking over his shoulder at the screen.

Lieutenant Taylor leads his warriors away from the battle lines, slinking through the debris and disappearing into a small opening in the side of the massive passageway. The warrior's pace is fast. They know what's coming. One by one, the frontline Lunarian companies declare that they are clear.

Even as Imam Bakr watches, the last of the strange energy sources settles on the hospital carrier and grows silent. His heart races as he recognizes danger.

Moments after the last Lunarian unit reports in, the order goes out to both Oak Ridge and Sherwood Forest. Within a nanosecond of each other, the bees explode. Each swarm totals almost three kilos of SuperX, the most powerful chemical explosive ever devised by man. The thick metal vaporizes along with the nuclear device hiding just beyond. The blast surges upward killing everyone onboard. It rips the thick armor as if it were tissue paper and picks up the mangled vehicle, dropping it on the adjacent troop carrier. Atomized uranium blankets Serenity Hill and beyond.

The news of the success spreads quickly through the city. Lieutenant Taylor smiles grimly watching his warriors whoop and holler with excitement even as they prepare to finish the job.

Cris wakes with a start. He lies there for a moment, unsure what had awakened him. Then he hears it, the distant thunder of explosions.

He looks around the small room. Where was Callie? She had been here when he fell asleep. He shakes his head. She was a big girl and fully capable of taking care of herself but it bothered him.

Rolling out of bed, he pulls on his freshly cleaned vacsuit in record time. The battle is a constant rumble and getting louder. Explosions shake the mountain around him sending bits of dust floating softly to the floor. With his pistol at his waist and the sword across his back, Cris heads towards the sound.

The tunnel outside the room is clear as far as he can see. The sounds are coming from only one direction. He leans forward and leaps, his body flexing into motion as easily as making a fist. A Highlander at full speed is something to behold out on the surface. Here, in the narrow confines within Ransburg, it's astonishing. With grace born of skill and practice, Cris uses every surface as he races through the twisting tunnels towards the battle.

Cris bursts into the cavern. This isn't an open space like those in Aldrin Station. The miners chased the ore deposits creating a hodgepodge of interconnected rooms and galleries. A mini rocket detonates next to Cris knocking him off his feet but he quickly regains control and keeps moving. Electromagnetic hardening of his vacsuit at the shrapnel's points of impact protects him.

A dozen more of the deadly little missiles, streak towards him from out of the labyrinth. Cris fires repeatedly, vaporizing them before they get close. He climbs up the side of a stone column and looks ahead. A large force of Brotherhood soldiers are forcing Conrad and what's left of his squad to fall back. Two warriors lie dead and many more are missing. They are losing the battle.

Cris cuts across ducking into a side tunnel and heading up a ramp. Racing upward, he twists through the tight turns and emerges back into the cavern far above the floor. He leaps from one dubious handhold to the next, circling the room. Like an avenging angel of death, Cris drops down among the Brotherhood soldiers from above, his pistol in one hand and the sword in the other.

He's a hawk among doves, delivering death surely and swiftly. Nothing can stand against him. Thrust with one hand, aim and fire with the other, then on to the next two targets at a speed that no earthborn human could ever hope to match. Cris cuts and blasts a swath through the soldiers like a scythe cutting hay. Blood runs in rivers across the stone floor. His pistol scarcely has time to recharge before thunderously firing again and his sword never stops moving.

Cris is a blur within the dim confines of the subterranean mining town, leaving a trail of dead Brotherhood soldiers behind him. They cannot stop what they cannot see. Terrified men blaze away at shadows only to die an instant later. The battle rages on until those still alive turn and run with Cris in close pursuit. They are even easier to kill from behind.

ЯL

The force of the blast rocks the Goliath, throwing around the men inside as if they were rag dolls. Imam Bakr picks himself up off the floor. Around him, the members of his senior staff regroup. Several are injured and one is unconscious, his head bleeding profusely.

"*Havildar Ezzedine, report. What just happened?*" Imam Bakr demands. He wipes away blood from a cut lip with the back of his hand.

Havildar Ezzedine was the only person strapped into his seat when the explosion occurred. "*Sir, the point of origin was the hospital. It is destroyed. No survivors. Sir, why did they attack our hospital?*"

"*Because they are Djinn.*" Imam Bakr said bitterly, knowing the real reason. He's staring failure square in the face. Without the nuke buried in the bowels of that hospital to keep the Lunarian horde at bay, it's only a matter of time before all is lost. How could they have possibly known where the nuke was? These mutants are the flatulence of Satan.

Imam Bakr immediately begins to organize what's left of his army for a hasty retreat, knowing they would need to fight their way out of the city. He initiates a call through the secure relays they have placed between the two forces.

Twenty kilometers away as the crow flies, if a crow could fly through solid stone, Malik said to the call. His face is a strange mixture of dread and anger, "*Imam?*"

"*Do you still have your bomb?*"

"*No,*" Malik shakes his head. "*The infidels have destroyed it.*"

"*Mine is gone as well. We must abandon the city,*" Imam Bakr said.

Malik scowls in disgust, "*I do not like retreating.*"

"*Do you like dying?*" Imam Bakr replies sharply, "*Or perhaps you intend to surrender?*" The Imam smiles at the anger that flushes Malik's face. "*This is not the Lunarian General Council, Captain Malik. We are not discussing this. I have made my decision. Prepare your men for fighting because I do not believe the infidels will simply let us leave. You must move as quickly as possible before they have time to gather their strength. By the grace of Allah, we will leave this accursed place before the infidels know we are gone.*"

"*As you command, Imam. Where do we meet?*" Malik asks.

"*You have the shorter route back through Sherwood Commonway.*

Once you are on the surface, do not wait for me, Lieutenant. Take your men to Purgatory. We will regroup there." Imam Bakr is not at all confident that he will ever see the light of day again.

"*As you command,*" Malik growls.

"*Allah Akbar,*" Imam Bakr bows his head.

"*Allah Akbar.*" Malik replies and breaks the link.

Imam Bakr's swift decision is the only thing that saves his army. It surprises the Lunarians by its suddenness. Within minutes of the destruction of the nuke, both detachments are moving back the way they had come.

Most of the common soldiers do not have the scientific training to realize the danger inherent in radioactive fallout. It is simply dust clinging to their battle armor. However, their officers know. Those soldiers closest to the blast but still able to fight will lead them out of the city. Soldiers too badly injured are administered poisons that stop their hearts. To them, it seems a very humane way of dealing with their wounded. They're better dead than in the hands of the infidels.

The retreating Brotherhood is demoralized. Fear permeates the ranks at the realization that somehow, they have failed. Not even Allah can help them here in the heart of the infidel's city. Satan himself seems to be bearing down on them.

An explosion rocks the Goliath carrying Imam Bakr. Ahead of him, he can see the hell the lead convoys are going through. Beams mercilessly cut at the heavy vehicles. The commonway is awash in energy as the Brotherhood fights its way past a particularly difficult section. Shadowy figures flitter about in the dense smoke spreading death and destruction. A massive explosion rips through a Goliath. Imam Bakr silently watches the mad scramble as the undamaged troop carriers it was towing shift to other Goliaths, all done in the midst of a fierce firefight.

He addresses a convoy commander, "*Colonel, send 107 and 113 to attack along the right wall. We must break through the infidels if we are to live.*"

The Imam tries to remain calm but he knows how precarious the next few minutes will be. "*Get us out of this accursed hole.*" he commands even as the vehicles lurch forward gaining speed, heading directly for the Lunarians. The Brotherhood must blast their way past if they have any hope of breaking free.

The air is dense with smoke and if his battle helmet had not protected his ears, he would be deaf from the beam induced pressure waves that roil the commonway. What's left of his command is moving forward, weaving through the fallen trees.

The retreat takes far less time than the initial attack. Speed is of utmost importance. Anything that slows them down increases the likelihood that no one will make it out alive. Several convoys are abandoned, the soldiers inside left to the mercy of the Lunarians.

As he disappears into the dense smoke, Imam Bakr reminds these unlucky souls of the riches awaiting those who fight and die in the cause of Allah.

The minutes drag until they finally come to the end of Oak Ridge Commonway. Imam Bakr praises merciful Allah. The main airlock is only a little further. The air is motionless, the last fighting at least a kilometer to his rear.

For the first time since this started, Imam Bakr has hope that he will see the surface once more. He takes stock of what remains of his army. Of the twenty thousand soldiers he started with, less than three thousand make it out alive.

The Messenger

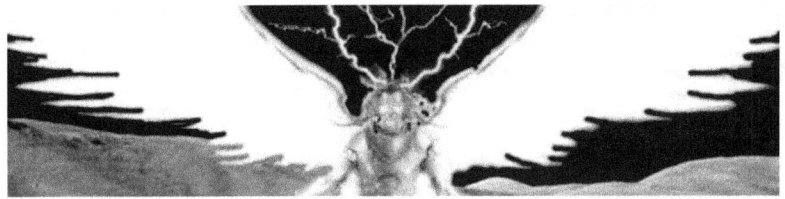

*And the fifth angel sounded and I saw a star fall from
heaven unto the earth and to him was given the key of
the bottomless pit. And he opened the bottomless pit and
there arose a smoke out of the pit, as smoke of a great
furnace, and the sun and the air were darkened...*

Holy Bible, Revelations 9:1-2

The shadowy figure creeps forward, its sensors sweeping up and down the electromagnetic spectrum looking for the slightest hint of danger. It's taking advantage of a small rill to get as close to Al Fahad as possible.

The reserve element of the Army of Islam is preparing to march. Dozens upon dozens of convoys stretch out side-by-side across the landscape. Tankers filled with hypergolic fuel are further out. Armed rovers scurry about the perimeter. No one notices when a section of the outer fence flickers for a few seconds.

The figure keeps to the rill and gets within a half kilometer of the city's main entrance. Rising up, it strolls boldly between rows of troop carriers towards the front of the convoys. It releases a small spybot which lands on the top of one of the nearby carriers giving it a good field of view for what was about to happen.

The figure transmits a laser signal. An instant later, every antenna in the Four Craters Region transmits maximum energy at the first of sixty-five sources of the jamming, overloading and burning them out, one after the other. Moments after the last jammer goes down, a patchwork constellation of communications satellites comes online. For the first time in more than three days, Earthnet is functional. When humanity realizes it's back online, they set the network ablaze.

The figure remains unchallenged. It emerges from between two convoys and approaches a lone Goliath. Plasma begins to flow from the stubby appendages across its back spreading out on each side of the figure like an angel's wings. A rover skids to a stop behind it. The figure leaps to the top of the Goliath. The alarm spreads.

Abby, Corso and most of Aldrin Station link with the spybot to witness realtime what was enfolding at Lassell crater. All across the Republic, citizens become aware of something unusual happening and join the link. However, the Lunarians are not the primary audience. The entirety of human space is receiving the broadcast, including the Islamic Brotherhood. The number of links quickly soars into the hundreds of millions then billions as humanity takes notice. The wings of the figure grow larger as more and more plasma races out along magnetic lines of force in a man-made aurora borealis. Energy ripples and flows across their expanse.

Supercharged electrostatic fields whip its long hair into frenzy. Its eyes flare, its wings grow, and still the intensity increases. Bolts of pure energy shoot from the figure forming a gigantic loop above its head. More and more energy fills the figure until it stares out at the world with eyes as bright as the sun.

It opens its mouth and broadcasts in perfect Arabic, "*Heed these words for they come from Allah.*" Energy streams from its mouth with every word. "*Cease this evil deed that is transpiring. For I, Archangel Gabriel, say unto all believers, this is an unjust jihad.*"

Inside Al Fahad, Sheik Mohammad Abas is stunned. His brain can't cope with what he's seeing. This must be a trick. The infidels are behind this sorcery. They must be. He summons his lieutenants.

"*What should we do?*" Havildar Hassan Adawi asks. He's outside on the surface confronting the figure.

"*Shoot it,*" Sheik Abas orders. When no one moves, he repeats louder and with more authority, "*Shoot it.*" The frightened and confused look on the face of his lieutenant would be comical if it wasn't in such dire circumstance. "*Don't let the infidels fool you. This is just a cheap trick. I order you to shoot it. All of you. Every true believer that can hear my voice. Shoot it now.*"

The apparition stands before them, not trying to flee or showing the least propensity in defending itself. It remains conveniently before the gunners.

Havildar Adawi tentatively fires his rover's laser cannon, striking the shimmering figure in the chest. Hesitantly at first, others open up. Within seconds, dozens of powerful weapons join in. The figure absorbs the onslaught, growing larger and brighter with every laser watt, sucking up exploding missiles like a black hole devouring a star.

The one sided battle escalates until the gunners begin to realize that their firepower is totally ineffective. In fact, the entity seems to be relishing the maelstrom, feeding upon it. One by one, the cannons shut down and the missiles stop coming. The figure stands before the Army of Islam, its great wings shimmering like the limbs of a mighty tree in a gale wind. It has the world's undivided attention.

"*It is I who brought down this Qur'an on your heart by the command of Allah, which confirms the Scriptures that preceded it, and is a guidance and good tidings to the believers. Let him bear in mind that whoever is an enemy to Allah and His angels and His Messengers and Gabriel and*

461

Michael, then, of course, Allah is an enemy to such disbelievers."

The angel's wings continue to grow larger and larger until they stretch over the entire compound, encompassing all beneath their fiery embrace.

"Behold the glory of Allah. For it is the leaders of this unjust war whom an evil reckoning awaits and their refuge is the Fire of Gehenna."

The great wings sweep over the gathering in sheets of fire. Energy ripples through the canopy. The Brotherhood cowers in fear below the shimmering expanse.

"What is happening," Sheik Abas demands. *"Mehmood. Tell me what is happening,"* He asked Mehmood Hussain, his chief scientist.

"I don't know..." Mehmood can't think clearly. He frowns and pulls in data to analyze but can only stare at the apparition.

"Archangel Gabriel is angry," someone exclaims.

"That is not Gabriel," Sheik Abas cries out but he's not so sure anymore.

The Messenger outshines the sun, spreading its wings over the entire army. The figure has become the center of a light show like no other in history. Energy pulsates across the vastness in complex patterns that seer themselves into the human collective, undulating across the wings in enormous waves, strobing faster with each passing second. The eyes of the human race are upon it.

"We shall cast into Fire all those who deny Our Message." The beat increases, *"As often as their skins are burnt up, we will replace them,"* faster and faster, *"with other new skins that they may continually taste the agony of punishment,"* the throbbing grows into a brain shattering strobe, *"Surely, Allah is All Mighty, All Wise."* It reaches a crescendo.

The apparition emits a final pulse of light a million times brighter than the sun then nothing. The feed from the spybot abruptly stops, cutting off the spectacle from humanities eager gaze. It takes precious seconds as technicians scramble to find other sensors and focus them on Al Fahad. What they find is astonishing. Where the horde of war machines had stood is now a huge hemispherical cavity many kilometers across and deep. The Brotherhood's military reserve and most of its anchor city have vanished along with millions of tons of lunar rock.

The void bites deep into the crater wall. Along the sheer cliff face, air and other gases leak out from what's left of the city but the discharge is pitifully small in the vast expanse of what's gone.

ЯL

General Arif is stunned. How can this be. He motions for the communications officer to replay the vid. No one on the bridge of the Houris has said a word. They sit at their stations and stare numbly at their screens, hands frozen over the controls. Shock rests on them like a dead weight. To a man they are convinced they had just witnessed a miracle, but one with confusing connotations. Several begin to chant, "*Allah Akbar. Allah Akbar.*"

These men have spent a significant part of their lives studying the holy books of Islam. The angel spoke to them in the ancient tongue of the wrongness of the jihad they are waging, using passages almost verbatim from the Holy Qu'ran. Their education ruthlessly suppressed any desire to question authority, rooting out and dealing harshly with any freethinking. This reverberates not only through them, but into every corner of the Brotherhood. It's a body punch that threatens to stop the heart of an empire.

Al Fahad is gone. General Arif can detect no electronic signals from the city. With growing trepidation, he calls Imam Abu Bukhari. When the familiar face of the Imam appears, General Arif finds strength in his steady gaze. Imam Bukhari's words carry great weight.

"*Allah be with you, my friend.*" Seeing panic in the general's eyes, he said, "*Do not be fooled by Satan's clever disguises. Be assured, our cause is just. We spread the message of the last prophet, peace be upon* him. *Allah has not forsaken us.*"

"*Yes, of course Imam.*" General Arif replies shaken and unconvinced.

"*I am assisting in the preparation of a general broadcast. Prince Al Zarqowi will address the Brotherhood within the hour.*" Imam Abu Bukhari shakes his head, "*It is a terrible thing that has happened, but sacrifices must be made when fighting the forces of evil. Do everything in your power to determine who is responsible for this atrocity and bring them to justice. Use your science and your brain. That is why Allah gave them to you. Let me know personally of your findings.*"

"*Yes, of course.*" General Arif replies bowing his head to the holy man.

"*I am sorry but I must go. Remain steadfast in your faith, Salam.*" the Imam is one of the few who can call the general by his personal name. "*Allah Akbar.*" he said as he bows and fades from view.

Anger grows until it overwhelms the fear and confusion. A man doesn't become the Major General in charge of the biggest conflict in Islamic history by being gullible. General Arif is a curious combination of modern science and religious fundamentalism. His study of science has shown him many things that could have shaken his belief in Allah, and did for many others. But he has always had the ability to fall back on the teachings of his childhood, his personal relationship with Allah and the Prophet Muhammad (*peace be upon him*). He believed in the righteousness of the cause while tempering it with a harsh dose of reality. When he thought of it at all, he thought of it as the economics of survival, contorting his beliefs to encompass the facts, ignoring the pieces that simply wouldn't fit. As he emerges from the fog, his mind reaches the same conclusion as the Imam, refusing to accept what he had seen at face value.

Of course, Imam Bukhari is right. It must be a trick. Allah would not forsake his loyal followers but it's hard to get past even for Major General Arif, Supreme Commander of the Islamic Expeditionary Forces.

"*Admiral Alsamh. Find out what that was.*" General Arif commands.

High Admiral Rasheed Abou-Alsamh is a single rank below General Arif and second in command aboard the Houris. As a devout Muslim, he said his five daily prayers, fasts, gives generously to charity, and has twice made the Hajj. For the first time in his life, doubt clouds his mind. He can't rid himself of the image of the Archangel. Uncertainty burns like wildfire within his beliefs.

Nevertheless, he's a bridge officer, "*As you will.*" Turning to his science officer, a man he has known and trusted for over a decade, "*Doctor.*" the man didn't hear him, "*Doctor.*" he said louder.

Dr. Saleh Al-Wohaiby is the Sub-Minister of Science for the fleet and has been on General Arif's staff from the first day he accepted command. He turns to face the Admiral in shocked disbelief. Slowly, visibly, the man pulls himself together.

"*Yes Admiral,*" he said after a few seconds.

"*Do a full analysis on the entity from the moment it arrived to the detonation. I want to know how it got there, where it came from, and where it went. And Saleh… if I have forgotten anything, do those tests as well. You know the drill. Let's find out what that thing was.*"

The doctor is dazed, "*What if it is as it seems?*"

Gripping the man by the shoulder, he looks intently into his eyes, "*Start your tests Saleh. Find out what you can.*"

"*Yes… Yes of course. Tests…*" he looks back down at his control panel and slowly reaches out. It will take time for him to gather himself to the point of becoming useful again but at least he's moving.

Admiral Alsamh signals across the void to the frigate Hamas, "*Captain Shaikh.*" When the man appears before him, his appearance is drawn. He too is under pressure and struggling to maintain composure.

"*Yes Admiral,*" the man said tentatively.

"*You are to immediately proceed at full speed to Al Fahad. You will be our eyes and ears on the ground. Do you understand?*"

Captain Shaikh stares blankly back at him for a moment. The Admiral can see the fear build as the order sinks in.

"*Perhaps another would be better for this assignment. I am but a humble servant of Allah.*" Lieutenant Shaikh stammers dropping his gaze from the Admirals.

Admiral Alsamh can't believe his ears. Never has a captain of a ship in the fleet questioned an order, let alone refused one. He must put a stop to this immediately or lose control of his command.

"*Captain.*" the admiral growls, "*You will do as ordered or suffer the consequences.*" That's a death sentence for an officer having reached this level of responsibility.

The captain still wavers, looking around like a cornered animal. He finally nods. "*I will leave immediately.*"

Major General Arif settles back in his command seat, letting his subordinates perform their duties as he watches and listens, tuning in to various channels scattered across the fleet. He's only beginning to realize the magnitude of what's happened.

ЯL

A spybot stumbles on the convoy by accident. From a thousand meters up, it looks normal enough but they can detect no light, no heat, no emissions at all from the vehicles. Sinking lower, the bot encounters a fog of death hanging heavy upon them. People had died here, in numbers.

"There's no damage that I can see," Sam said.

"Where are the bodies?" Tempel asks.

"We need to send someone in," Tatiana said. "Let me take Marcel and go find out what happened."

"No," Tempel said. "I'll go… Kipper, you're with me," Tempel unbuckles his harness.

"You're the Captain now. You're supposed to lead from the rear. Let me do my job," Tatiana said.

Tempel glances at her, "Don't worry, you'll get your chance. Right now, I want to see what happened out there." He slings a forensics kit over his shoulder and cinches it down around his waist.

"It might be a trap," Corazon said.

"Might be," Tempel replies as he leads Kipper down the ramp. They leap into the night straight up the steep mountainside. The warriors relish the exertion. Agile as cats on a hot tin roof, they run along the ridge for a ways. On the roadway far below is the Brotherhood convoy, lined up as if they had just pulled over and stopped.

The two warriors descend from the heights and head straight for the lead Goliath. The unit commander would be there or in one of the nearby troop carriers.

Tempel motions for Kipper to hold. Cautiously, he moves in and opens the outer airlock door. He glances up and down the row of vehicles and back at Kipper before entering.

Inside the airlock, he turns the handle and pushes on the inner door. It swings open easily. The air is gone from inside and it's shrouded in darkness, not even a stray thermal signature to light his way. Tempel turns on his belt light, his hand resting on his pistol.

Vacuum mummified bodies litter the interior. They had collapsed where they stood so it must have happened fast.

"They're all dead," Tempel said. He rummages through the dead looking at their uniforms. He finds a body with a general's insignia. Two stars inside the crescent. Someone had shot him in the head, small caliber, close range.

Tempel pulls a DNA sampler from his kit and takes a few cells from the general and those around him.

"I'm going inside the next carrier," Kipper said.

Once inside, Kipper finds more dead soldiers. Some are in their bunks, others on the floor and one shriveled up corpse is sitting at a table like he's waiting for dinner.

"They're all dead," Kipper reports.

"Can you establish a cause of death?" Tempel asks.

"Explosive asphyxiation followed by vacuum dehydration is what it looks like. Someone opened the troop carriers to vacuum and killed them all."

"Same here with one exception. Somebody shot the general. I'm taking the Goliath's AI. Maybe it can tell us what happened." Tempel pulls the black case from its rack.

Tempel and Kipper look inside carrier after carrier. They're all the same. He estimates there were about a thousand soldiers in the convoy. They're all dead.

ЯL

Malik's close involvement with the Lunarians over the last several years has given him a deep appreciation of their cunning and technical abilities. After reviewing the vid yet again, he assures himself that it must be a trick of some kind, though he doesn't have the foggiest idea how they did it.

Even if he was inclined to share his conclusion, which he isn't, there are few around him that would give it any credence. The events of the day are simply too much for a simple mujahedeen. To the vast majority, they had witnessed a miracle, one that condemned them to hell.

Malik cursed this forsaken land and the people in it. He slaps his hand against the side of the Goliath. He yearns for the hot sands of Saudi Arabia, where a man didn't worry about his next breath and his enemies fought like men.

If it's war these godless Lunarians want, then it's war he will grant them.

468

ЯL

Magi interrupts, "Excuse me Lazarus, Abby requests a word with you,"

"Of course…" Lazarus looks up at her image standing on the other side of the table, "Greetings Abby."

"Greetings Lazarus. Sorry about the interruption. What are you having? It smells divine," Abby said.

"Soy sausage, biscuits and gravy, fried potatoes and orange juice. Liz has plenty. Would you like to join me?" Lazarus asks.

"That sounds marvelous. Nobody makes gravy like Liz. Maybe next time," Abby sighs. "I want to express my personal congratulations on the Al Fahad mission. Jason and Jamie tell me you were instrumental in designing the Messenger."

"Thanks, but I have no clue how they did that. Now we wait to see what happens. It shouldn't take long," Lazarus said.

"I'll let you get back to your breakfast, but as soon as you're finished, there are some things I would like to discuss with you."

"Sure. Give me five minutes," Lazarus said.

Abby looks tired. "Take ten and enjoy your food." She nods and disappears.

Liz comes over and sits beside Lazarus. "I wish she wouldn't work so hard. It's wearing her down."

"She takes her job very seriously," Lazarus said.

"She's carrying a tremendous load. It's worse than I've ever seen it, even for her." Liz shakes her head.

"These are tough times and someone must take responsibility. Abby handles it better than I ever could." Lazarus takes a bite. "How does a ninety-three year old woman look and act thirty-five?"

Liz pauses and looks intently at Lazarus. "You really don't know?"

His next bite stops halfway to his mouth. "Know what?"

His polygraphic indicators show he's not lying. "We've found a way to repair the damage done by aging," Liz said.

Lazarus takes the bite and stares at Liz as he chews. "She's immortal?"

"Heaven's no. Aging is a deterioration process that occurs over time. Every so often we simply restore our bodies to a state of good health," Liz said.

From somewhere behind them a voice said, "Greetings Liz. Could you spare another plate of biscuits and gravy?" Abby walks through the kitchen to their table.

"Abby." Liz jumps up and gives her a hug. "You look exhausted."

"Right now I could use some of your cooking." Abby turns to Lazarus admiring his new haircut, shaved right down to the nub, "I changed my mind. May I join you?"

"Of course... It's a woman's prerogative to change her mind. I'm glad you did." Lazarus stands while she sits.

"You're curious about why I look so young," Abby said.

Lazarus nods, "Aye."

"As Liz said, we've found a way to repair our bodies."

"Would you mind if I took off my visor?" Lazarus asks.

"Are you sure you're not from Missouri?" When Lazarus looks puzzled, Abby smiles, "I was born and raised in Missouri. It was called the *Show Me* state back then... By all means, let's both take our visors off." She lays her visor on the table just as Liz places a plate heaped with biscuits smothered in thick white gravy in front of her.

"There's plenty more," Liz said.

"There always is when you're cooking," Abby said. "Join us?" She pats the seat next to her.

Lazarus lays his visor next to Abby's and stares at her for several moments. Her long blond hair is loose this morning and ripples strangely in Luna's gravity when she moves her head. It's something only a shortimer would notice. However, she looks just like the image in his visor. He can find no difference.

"Well?" She asked.

"You're beautiful," Lazarus stammers.

"Of course I am... Liz, could you pass the salt and pepper?" Abby looks back at Lazarus, "As soon as things calm down, you can study modern genetics. Liz or Tara can take you over to see what a regeneration tank looks like and explain how it works."

"It would be my pleasure," Liz said.

Abby pulls her hair back and deftly puts it into a ponytail. "Over the years, we have made some minor modifications in my DNA. Straightened my nose, changed my hair color, that sort of thing. So if you look at me back in '24... Well, let's just say I look different now..." Abby scoops up a generous bite. "Liz. This is exactly what I needed."

Liz grins.

Every year the Federation devotes major resources in fighting the War on Genetics or the Clone War as some call it. Lazarus had been a part of that effort, shutting down dealers, tracking down illegal labs, and convicting pushers. Abby's casual admission would have meant complete reeducation back in the Federation. Here, it was polite conversation around the kitchen table. Lazarus remains quiet but his polygraphic indicators betray his emotions.

"Why does that bother you," Abby said. She doesn't need her visor to see that it does.

Lazarus stares into her green eyes and tells the truth. "I have sent people to reeducation for what you just freely admitted."

"Have you? The Federation is so hypocritical. The wealthy overindulge in genetics but withhold it from everyone else." Abby scoops in another bite.

Lazarus frowns. Clearly, he disagrees. He runs his hand over his head forgetting for a moment that his hair is all gone.

"President John Paul is the biggest hypocrite of them all." Liz adds. "He's been using genetics for half a century while denying it to his fellow citizens."

"I met President John Paul once when I was a kid. It was in the White House after my father died…" Lazarus looks at Liz. "So you're saying that John Paul uses genetics?"

"John Paul is ninety-two years old. Put your visor back on and look at his most recent public appearance." Abby put on hers and links with him just as Magi starts the vid.

Lazarus does and watches the President making a speech at West Point in front of the cadets. The man could hardly walk to the podium under his own power, yet stood there and delivered a vigorous speech. He faltered towards the end but finished strong. His courage and tenacity made Lazarus want to stand up and cheer.

"That is his political persona. Magi, show him the September vid of John Paul," Abby orders. "This was recorded at the Royal Resort in Cancun just a few days after that speech."

West Point disappears and now Lazarus is riding in a cart across a golf course. It's dusky and getting darker by the second. The cart stops next to a tall wooden fence. There is a brief flurry as the person making the record climbs on top the cart and peers over the fence. A private pool is on the other side.

The sliding glass patio door opens across the way and lights come on around the pool. Several armed men dressed in black suits emerge and take positions around the patio. Three men in bathing suits and a covey of bikini-clad beauties follow them out. With a squeal, the young women run and jump into the water. Two of the men continue talking as they take a seat. A male servant sits drinks next to them. The third man lets one of the girls coax him towards the pool. He laughs and slips off her scanty top. She pulls away with a mischievous grin and dives into the pool. The man follows. Lazarus recognizes him.

"That's President John Paul," Abby said. He couldn't be more than thirty-five. "If you still have any doubt as to why he looks so young, Magi has thousands of hours you can view."

"No, that's not necessary," Lazarus said. It's as if he's looking at a ghost from the past. "It'll be a cold day in hell before I doubt you again."

"Indeed." Abby frowns and looks down at the table. "Something's been bothering me that I need you to clear up…"

"Go on," Lazarus said.

"When you defected, how did you convince them to let you go to Athens?" Abby asks.

"My wife and I planned the trip two years before and I cleared it with Director Dempsey."

"I see… so you asked and they let you go?"

Lazarus shrugs, "Athens is a popular vacation spot."

"Magi, how did Lazarus manage to escape the Federation?"

"I helped the dear boy," she replies.

Lazarus stares at her in disbelief. "What do you mean? How?"

"You and your surrogate would never have made it past security at Gateway Airport if I hadn't intervened. DHS issued a last minute detention warrant to take you into custody. I changed the warrant and assigned a surveillance team instead. Once in Athens, I helped you lose the team and obtain a ticket to Heaven's Gate. I bumped Clark Hamlin from the flight and put you in a seat next to Lindsey. The rest she did on her own."

Lazarus stares at Magi, replaying the memories of that day. Was that why airport security had stopped him then let him go? Is that why they charged him with multiple counts of Earthnet security breach? Then it hit him. "The face on the screen, the one selling tickets to Heaven's Gate, it was you."

"Yes Lazarus," Magi said.

473

"Is there anything else you haven't told me?"

"Of course. I spend a lot of time deciding what not to tell you," Magi said. "It's very easy to overload humans with information."

"What's this about a surrogate?" Abby asks.

"They sent it over after my wife died," Lazarus said defensively.

"It was a companion android, Japanese Model 4000," Magi said, "The very latest tech."

"You had sex with a machine?" The way she said it condemned him to hell for all eternity.

"Well… when you say it that way, it sounds bad." Reality tilts around Lazarus. The Senior Analyst part of him wants to know how Magi infiltrated Earthnet so completely. Something's going on here that doesn't make sense.

"How many times?" Abby won't let it drop.

"Do we really need to talk about this?" Lazarus implores.

"Yes… we do," she insists.

Lazarus looks away, "I don't know exactly. It was a lot at first but not so much the past year. It's been months since the last time."

"Magi, what do you know about this?" Abby is not happy. Magi should have told her.

"Lazarus ejaculated four-hundred-fifty-nine times into the surrogate producing over twenty billion sperm."

"For what purpose?" Abby asks.

"Lazarus has a very rare DNA profile. It's defect free. He's the perfect male donor."

Lazarus can't believe his ears. "What? You're crazy."

"I beg your pardon?" Magi's unaccustomed to being called crazy. "My dear boy, there are four-thousand one-hundred and fifteen children conceived using your DNA… that I know of."

The feeling that comes over Lazarus as he processes this information goes far beyond horror. "What're you saying?" he stammers. "The

Federation wanted my sperm and used the surrogate to get it?"

"Yes Lazarus," Magi acknowledges.

"Then the accident…" he can't finish.

Magi sadly shakes her head, "I'm so sorry Lazarus but it wasn't an accident," she said kindly. "Director Dempsey wanted their deaths to look like an accident and had his agents rig the traffic lights which resulted in your wife and daughters fatal car wreck."

As soon as he heard it, Lazarus knew it was true. Maybe he had known all along? Too many things should have given it away. Maybe he didn't want to see them? No… he simply trusted the wrong man, the wrong country. How could they do this to him? After everything he had done for them. Hate consumes Lazarus. ***"GOD DAMN HIM TO HELL!"***

Two Minute War

"War is a poor chisel to carve out tomorrow."

Martin Luther King, Jr. (1929 - 1968)

It was only a twinkle, quickly gone. Lieutenant Gilmore isolated the brief flash of energy and analyzed. Only then did he raise the alarm.

"Sir. Sensors have picked up an energy release." The lieutenant routes his findings onto the DAC's main display. The anomaly was over a hundred thousand kilometers away.

"What's your analysis, Lieutenant?" Admiral DyGoon asks.

"It's consistent with leakage from a missile launch, but I can't say for sure. We simply don't have enough information to make a call." The young officer said.

"Helm, take us to a higher orbit at best speed. Lieutenant Gilmore. Let's get some eyes out there, shall we. No need to guess." Admiral DyGoon orders.

"Yes sir." Lieutenant Gilmore said. He redirects several FOSATs towards the spot in space. The spybots streak across the void under constant acceleration. All but one decelerates to match orbital velocity. That one never slows down but sends back the first pictures as it races by.

There, floating in the silence of space is the unmistakable bulk of a battlestation. Its dark silhouette blocking out the stars betrays it as Brotherhood. A thick coating of energy absorbent material makes it invisible to anything except direct visual detection, and even then, it's only by its huge size blotting out the background stars that the FOSAT can detect it. It reflects no light, no heat, and no radar. It's a hole in space.

FBS Yorktown has been at full alert since the trouble began, every man at his battle station. Admiral DyGoon always errs on the side of caution.

As the Yorktown's thrusters push her into a new orbit, the space recently abandoned spikes with a great flash of energy. Alarms scream as radiation pounds the hull.

"Shields are up." Lieutenant Gilmore declares. The electromagnetic shields automatically respond to radiation at these levels. The rem count immediately drops inside the ship.

"Get us out of here helmsman." Admiral DyGoon orders.

"Sir. The helm is sluggish. Thrusters operating at only twelve percent." The young corpsman reports.

"Sir. The Brotherhood battlestation is coming about." Lieutenant Gilmore declares. It appears as if the giant ship is lining up for another shot.

"Missile battery Tango Six, prepare to fire." Admiral DyGoon orders. Because of the shields, his ship is now lit up like a spotlight on a moonless night but he can't drop them until the radiation falls. That will take another thirty minutes at least. What's worse, it takes time for the Calconn circuitry in his megathrusters to recover from a point-blank nuclear EMP. He can't move.

One by one in rapid succession, their FOSATs stop sending data and the image of the battlestation grows blurry then disappears. The bridge crew scrambles to find another FOSAT but the nearest is almost thirty thousand kilometers away. The admiral can no longer see his enemy.

"Lieutenant Lutchi. Do you have lock on their last position?" Admiral DyGoon asks the weapons officer in command of Tango Six.

"Yes sir."

"Fire three in standard pattern, last known coordinates," Admiral DyGoon orders. He must act quickly before the battlestation disappears into the void.

Missiles leap from electromagnetic railguns at 30,000 Gs heading straight for a spot in space over a hundred-thousand kilometers distant. They use brute force to get there as the crow flies. Their onboard thrusters maintain two-hundred Gs all the way to the target.

The battlestation had accelerated away from the initial point of contact but not far enough. Two missiles detonate within a kilometer, the third within a hundred meters.

The tremendous burst of raw energy overwhelms the thick coating covering the battlestation. It glows red then white as it turns to ash and ablates, coming apart at the molecular level. It blows off in a dense cloud. Below it, the metal skin of the great ship is exposed. It too heats up, boiling away in the intense energy.

The blast peels the battlestation like a gigantic onion. Those outermost layers closest to the epicenter evaporate. Radiation kills most of the crew outright but a few survive. For those, death will take longer to arrive, but it will without exception.

Like a comet's tail, a stream of particles trail away from the stricken ship. With a great hole blasted in its side, the giant battlestation is adrift in space, its crew dead or dying. The Brotherhood fleet attacks the only Federation ship they can clearly see, the FBS Yorktown.

It's impossible to move the Yorktown fast enough to evade the incoming missiles. The ship's first line of defense is long-range laser cannons. They begin to fire but maintaining lock on a target accelerating at two-hundred Gs is close to impossible. They manage to hit only a few.

The second defensive layer is kinetic in nature. Railguns firing over four thousand rounds a minute target points in space where the AI calculates the trajectories will meet. The missiles avoid them easily, exploding just before impact with the hull of the Yorktown. The combined force of the blasts rips apart the huge battlestation killing everyone aboard. A scorched flotilla of metal fragments is all that remains of the once mighty warship.

The loss of the FBS Yorktown and Admiral DyGoon, ripples across the Federation fleet like a boulder dropped in a quiet pond.

"Theater wide orders. Implement plan Delta Six. I repeat, implement plan Delta Six." Rear Admiral Thomas Tyler is next in the chain of command. Admiral DyGoon had been a fine officer and a good friend but he would have been the first to tell him not to waste time mourning his death. Admiral Tyler's first command places the fleet on War Status.

FOSATs streak across orbits, searching in a vast grid. Warships maneuver randomly in an attempt to keep the enemy confused. Everyone's doing the same thing. Hundreds of ships are in motion.

A mine takes out an EU frigate. A few minutes later, a missile cripples India's only heavy cruiser. All across orbital space, fighters and missiles seek out targets. Mother Earth's orbit is quickly becoming history's largest battlefield.

"Sir. The Reagan is under attack." Lieutenant Morrison exclaims. He puts the feed from one of their FOSATs on the main screen. Swarming around the battlestation are hundreds of space fighters. Explosions flare and fade like fireflies across its surface. A nearby frigate takes a severe hit and limps off trailing gas. The FBS Ronald Reagan begins to break up right before their eyes. Fires and explosions rock the giant warship and the aft section spins off into the void.

First the Yorktown and now the Ronald Reagan are gone, two of the Federation's finest battlestations. Admiral Tyler reacts. "Fire at will. All hands, fire at will." The order goes out to the fleet.

"Lieutenant, launch all fighters. I want a shield around us that a fly couldn't get through," Admiral Tyler commands.

"Yes sir." He orders the first of many squadrons of space fighters into action. The battlestation quivers like a wild beast as each fighter group launches.

Flight Leader Tommy Thompson has two years experience flying a Centaur space fighter. He had asked for and received permission to lead the counterattack but it was the skill of the other pilots in his squadron as much as his leadership abilities that won the honor.

"OK meatheads. Let's get it done," Thompson growls. It's hard to believe the Yorktown and Reagan are gone. He had served on the Yorktown prior to his current assignment on the John Paul. Many of his closest friends are now space debris.

The squadron stays in loose formation, far enough apart to make it difficult to take them out with a single blow. After an initial high gee boost, they let Earth's gravity pull them around the planet towards their intended target so as not to give their position away.

ЯL

Purgatory looks almost peaceful from this distance. It could be a typical day in the life of the mining community. Closer inspection reveals wreckage strewn about the town's main entrance.

Malik doesn't stop to take in the view. He orders his forward elements to attack.

Missiles streak towards the massive airlock door. The thick steel disintegrates under the onslaught. More missiles streak past the shattered door seeking their next target, the inner airlock door. It too succumbs to the relentless assault, as does the next, and the next.

A dozen Goliath's follow close behind, taking the fight to the Lunarians. Within minutes, they breach the town's main hanger complex and are inside.

Malik directs several of the deadly killing machines to concentrate their firepower on the back wall. He's been inside Purgatory many times. He knows where it's most vulnerable. They blast a crude tunnel into the wall. With a tremendous burst, the last vestige of stone collapses and the town's air spews forth. Before the dust settles, he orders his soldiers into the breach. Once inside, they leave nothing untouched.

The fighting continues unabated until the last Lunarian citizen is killed or has fled. Imam Bakr commands them to take what they need from the ruins of the town. It's time to move on. Darpur is his next target. He will make these godless heathens pay for Al Fahad.

ЯL

Tempel pilots the Moonhawk over the desolate landscape keeping low. He nudges the flight stick occasionally, letting the AI do most of the flying. Sam, his copilot, sits to his right. The other Highlanders and the Moonhawk itself are invisible, filtered out by his visor. He and Sam appear to be alone soaring across the face of their world.

Magi breaks communications silence and abruptly appears beside him, "Tempel, we have a situation," she said. "Stand by for Corso."

"Standing by," Tempel alerts Sam and the other Highlanders of the call. They immediately link in.

"The Brotherhood attacked Purgatory. It's bad… very bad. Those bastards killed everyone." Corso is angry. It was his decision to let Imam Bakr and his soldiers go free once he evicted them from Aldrin Station. He blames himself for what happened at Purgatory.

Quan Kiai is a few kilometers ahead of the retreating Brotherhood army, near the edge of the Sea of Clouds. They were keeping an eye on them but it looks like they're going home, or at least what was left of it. Cris had put the fear of Satan in them and the Messenger finished the job.

"You're the closest combat team. I want you to discontinue your current mission and find Imam Bakr," Corso orders.

Tempel frowns but said without hesitation. "Aye. What do you want us to do when we find him?"

"I want you to stop him," Corso rumbles in his deep voice. "Let me clarify that, I want you to stop him dead."

"Aye. And the soldiers with him?"

"The same..."

ЯL

The battlestation Shenyang intends to stay clear of the hostilities, moving well beyond the orbit of Luna. Her sister ships follow. China sees this war as inevitable, one crazy religion going after another. It's a war that will leave China in control of the entire planet if they play their cards right.

"Lieutenant, maintain this course. Captain Tseng, deploy another dozen FOSATs. I want to know what's happening in the lower orbits." Admiral Liu Jianchao is confident in his crew's abilities and the Shenyang is performing flawlessly.

"Yes Sir."

A proximity alarm sounds, jarring the admiral from his thoughts. Something's approaching very fast. Admiral Jianchao turns to his Captain. The great ship lurches beneath him.

"Defensive batteries are firing."

The device arrives and detonates. The twenty-megaton pulse of radiation overwhelms the ships shielding killing everyone instantly. A nanosecond later, the thermal energy of the detonation vaporizes the Shenyang's outer hull and rips deep into the massive ship. It turns the once mighty battlestation into a spinning hulk of twisted metal. Vapors and fragments form a cloud around her. The blast has reduced her orbital velocity below critical value. Earth begins to draw in what's left of the battlestation. Years later, the flaming remnants of this once proud ship will light up the night sky over the North Atlantic and hit with the force of a nuclear bomb.

ЯL

Tempel lowers the Moonhawk's ramp and the platoon gathers at its base. Most of them already have their Shoulder Mounted Gun Platforms cinched tight ready for combat. Zoey helps Tempel into his and Tatiana helps Sam with hers. Talk is subdued as they prepare for battle.

"The spybots report twenty two Goliaths and a hundred-thirty-six troop carriers, less than seven thousand troops," Corazon said.

"They'll need more," Marcel said.

"Not even a fair fight," Zoey adds.

While they're talking, Kipper and Tatiana incorporate the information into the battle simulator. A terrain map of the Brotherhood coming down the Trans Lunar Highway appears before them about waist high.

Tempel moves into the projection and takes a position alongside a long broad valley. "Here's what I propose… We use a spread formation and stop their forward momentum with a massive aerial assault on the front of the column. That should force them into a defensive position… here… Then we hit them with a power play. Tatiana, you will attack their line... here... That will weaken it allowing the rest of us to bust into their secondary. Once we're inside their formation, we take everything out. I don't want a man or machine left in one piece… You know the drill. Let's do this by the book. Any questions?" He waits a few seconds. "Good. Let's run through a complete simulation."

Quan Kiai plunges into a sophisticated game of team combat, a dose of virtual warfare that allows them to try out the battle plan before risking their lives. Fifteen minutes and several adjustments later, they're finished, having coordinated targets and responsibilities for the attack right down to what weapon to use in each instance. Time well spent.

They gather around Tempel one last time. He turns looking intently in the face of each warrior. These are his friends, his comrades and some of them might not see daybreak. "We do this by the book. There's no place on a battlefield for sportsmanship. That line of thinking will get you killed. If you can get behind them, do it. If you can shoot first, do it. Find a weakness and exploit it with overwhelming force. Work as a team. Together we're strong."

They're all thinking the same thought, Tempel sounds just like Kitajima. It's strangely comforting.

Tempel leans forward and thrusts his fist upward, "Quan Kiai."

The others join him and their fists come together in a tight circle, "*QUAN KIAI.*"

The team breaks formation. They strap extra rockets across their backs before moving out in single file with Tempel leading. Even with the extra weight, the Highlanders race over the rugged terrain hardly slowing as they scamper up and down steep mountainsides and across valleys. This was their playground.

The enemy was making good time, keeping to the Trans Lunar Highway. This part of the highway passes down the center of a broad valley.

Tempel stops well out in front of the approaching Brotherhood. The lead vehicles are coming towards them at about fifty kph. The other convoys are spread out behind them for over ten kilometers. Along each side of the valley is a high ridgeline about a kilometer from the road. The broad flat valley will encourage the Brotherhood to circle the wagons, so to speak. Tempel had selected the battlefield well.

"We Ready?" Tempel asks.

"*Aye. Locked and Loaded,*" Quan Kiai replies in one voice.

"Let's roll," Tempel orders.

Half of Quan Kiai takes the south side of the valley, the other half the north. They're in position in only a few moments.

Tempel counts down, "On my mark… three… two… one… Mark."

Each of the ten warriors launches several missiles almost straight up. The deadly little darts already know their assigned targets, allowing the Highlanders to fire and forget. The warriors spread out and speed up heading right for the convoys.

The missiles begin hitting well before the warriors reach their assigned attack positions. The effect is stunning. Explosions rip open the lead Goliath of the first convoy. The orderly formation breaks up. The valley is in chaos as the other convoys veer off the road and begin to form into a circle. Floodlights mounted on top of the troop carriers flash on, pushing back the darkness. It takes time for the convoys in the rear of the formation to catch up and complete the maneuver.

Quan Kiai sprints past the convoys, attacking from the shadows and keeping well away from the glaring light. They don't even stop when they reload their missile launchers, doing it at full speed time after time. Interspersed within the missile barrage, their laser cannons punch holes in the troop carriers, seeking out vital spots and forcing everyone inside to suit up or die. They fire in bursts timing their attacks to make it hard for the Brotherhood to lock on any one of them.

To the Brotherhood, the attacks are coming out of the darkness without any discernible pattern. Their gunners fire at shadows. Pinned down in an exposed position, facing an invisible foe, the soldiers start making mistakes. Imam Bakr's convoy collides with another, disabling both. The Imam never makes it to the protected center of the formation. Missiles slam into his Goliath killing everyone aboard. What remains of his army obeys his last command and forms a rough defensive ring.

Quan Kiai encircles the makeshift camp, half going one way, the other half the other, racing around the circumference while staying out of the floodlights. Early in the battle, Tempel remotely flies the Moonhawk to a forward position close by, a place convenient for reloading. Quan Kiai kept the pressure up.

The soldiers fought back but are hopelessly outclassed. It's grown men taking on a bunch of first graders, it's a pack of wolves bringing down a fawn, there's simply no contest. The battle is completely one-sided. The Brotherhood becomes weaker and the soldiers fewer in number with each passing second. It is a death of a thousand cuts and it goes on and on and on without end. Hours go by and the bloodshed continued unabated. To be one of the last to die must have been horrifying.

On a predetermined signal, Tatiana, Kipper, Samantha, Zoey and Corazon concentrated their missiles into the carriers along the southwestern flank. When the last invader floodlight goes dark, it plunges the valley into darkness.

Sensing victory, Tempel leads Karyl, Alonzo, Angel and Marcel against the weakened perimeter in a direct frontal assault. Leaping over a gutted carrier, Tempel opens up with his laser on a rover trying to escape. In a silent spectacle of death, hyperbolic fuels mix and self ignite sending fireballs bursting skyward. Around him, Quan Kiai begins to hunt.

The Lunarians begin the first of many sweeps through the interior of the formation killing and destroying everything in their path. Time after time, usually in pairs, the warriors return to the Moonhawk to reload then quickly rejoin the battle. The red fog of death lies thick over the valley as the one-sided contest wears on. The Highlanders are the shadow of death. They never stop moving, never hesitate, they kill without conscience like a wild beast.

For many hours the battle rages on with the Highlanders never taking a break, never slowing down. Their missiles long since expended, they fire their lasers as fast as they can recharge. The scene inside the defensive formation slowly grinds down to an inevitable conclusion. Brotherhood soldiers are no match for the Lunarians. None at all.

Inside the perimeter, Malik orders the last of the soldiers to fall back and protect his command post in the center of the ring.

Lasers punch holes in the last untouched troop carriers, seeking out the vulnerable fuel tanks. Silent explosions rock the valley as hypergolic liquids boil into vacuum and mix.

Malik barely escapes the destruction of his carrier and is one of the last alive. Exhausted, he staggers forward to stand in the middle of the compound. He fires his pulse rifle in an arc at nothing in particular, screaming in frustration. He cannot see his enemy. Yet, all around him, his command lay in ruins. How can this be?! How could Allah have allowed this to happen? All around him as far as he could see, vacuum sucked the blood from the dead and hung over the valley like a sickly red death shroud. Thirty meters away, he witnesses the last soldier fall. He was alone.

Zoey and Alonzo close in for the kill but Tempel stops them. He approaches Malik from the side.

"Malik." Tempel casts to him.

The directional finder in Malik's combat vacsuit tells him roughly the bearing of the voice. The man swings towards it peering intently into the darkness. He can't see anything.

"Who's there?" Malik calls out.

"It's the death you seek," Tempel growls back.

"I recognize that voice. You are the young dog that killed Jafa. What are you waiting for. Finish the job." Malik again fires his rifle in an arc, blasting away at nothing. Empty, he throws it to the ground. He stands defiant waiting for the end.

Tempel is less than ten meters from the man when Malik finally detects him, not by vision, but by the smudge of darkness moving towards him. Malik draws his pistol and dies.

ℛ𝕃

Flight Leader Tommy Thompson's fighter squadron coasts around the Earth conserving energy while sneaking up on the battlestation. The ship knows something is there but can't pinpoint what or where. Lasers reach out probing space. At the very last moment, the Centaurs light up their thrusters and streak the final few kilometers.

Thompson leads them in a strafing run towards their assigned target, the engine room. The massive megathrusters hide behind thick armor and run the length of the battlestation but their nozzles are exposed.

Flying in a tight V formation, the squadron rips deep into the aft section of the battlestation, breaching the hull and releasing the atmosphere inside. They occasionally hit something more volatile, leaving a path strewn with tremendous explosions amidst clouds of vaporized metal. The fast moving fighters overrun the battlestations defensive gun emplacements, concentrating their firepower on one megathruster.

"Maintain formation." Flight Leader Thompson calls out. He hugs the surface, following its curve, firing continuously. His top priority is always the next gun emplacement emerging over the horizon. "Let's keep it tight." Behind him, his squadron fires powerful lasers downward into the ship.

Eagle Seven, flown by Pilot Third Class Edward Bailey, drifts too far from the chosen path. With a suddenness characteristic of all warfare, the fighter vaporizes. One second the Centaur is there, the next it's a cloud of atoms drifting in the vacuum of space.

"Eagle Eight, tighten it up. Maintain formation another forty seconds." Thompson implores his pilots. He had lost count of the number of laser cannons he has destroyed, that would come later when Commander Kline held his after action debriefing session.

Thompson glances at the energy remaining in his fighter. It's almost half-gone. He continues to pour it on taking out everything that appears before him. It was his job to plow the path.

Eagle Four disappears in a cloud of vapor. On the other side of the formation, Eagle Five suffers the same fate. The squadron is still below the accepted attrition rate for this type of attack.

"Thirty seconds." Energy pours from the fighters in copious amounts, ripping into the battlestation. A path of destruction lay behind them, clearly marking their zigzag course across the surface of the giant warship.

Eagle Eight takes a hit and careens off into space. Another shot finishes the job.

"Assume formation alpha," Flight Leader Thompson orders. Following the next darting change in direction, the squadron forms into a snowplow shape with Eagle One anchoring the front and Eagle Six the back. With only four remaining Centaur's, the flight has just enough firepower to maintain their speed.

"Twenty seconds." Flight Leader Thompson misses and before he can correct his mistake, the Brotherhood cannon fires. Tommy's fighter evaporates in a puff of atomized particles, the cloud drifting onward under its own momentum.

Eagle Two takes it out, destroying the gun emplacement in a flash of white-hot energy. With only three fighters left, they must slow down or risk missing another gun. What's left of the squadron concentrates on delivering their energy onto the battlestation's megathruster. It sputters and loses power. They're having an effect.

With ten seconds of energy remaining, Eagle Six cuts a corner too close and clips an antenna. The fighter spins out of control, its thrusters trying vainly to right the craft. It smashes into a tower and explodes.

The last two pilots can hear the countdown as they concentrate on finishing the mission.

They slow even further, darting across the surface, concentrating their remaining energy on the giant ship. Gasses explode in great geysers. They dart one way, then the other, eliminating two more of the deadly cannon emplacements. They continue to cut deeply into the megathruster until it finally shuts down inciting a cheer from those watching.

Eagle Three gets a little ahead and isn't quick enough to knock out both guns in a double placement. Even as its twin is destroyed, the second cannon vaporizes Eagle Three.

Eagle Two fires one last time, knocking out the second gun. Reaction mass exhausted, the last fighter rams into the battlestation. It's a futile move but it made Pilot Goodburn feel better.

"That's what *I'm* talk'n 'bout." Pilot Second Class Craig "*Stick*" Goodburn pumps his fist with excitement. The others in the squadron congratulate him.

Craig flies his Centaur remotely, cocooned within a cockpit deep in the heart of the battlestation. FBS John Paul's main flight deck houses over two thousand other cockpits, all of them occupied.

Centaur's are less than four meters long, far too small and too powerful for any human to physically fly, capable of maintaining 200Gs for as long as there was fuel. Sometime before the turn of the century, technology surpassed what the human body could withstand. Crushing acceleration and radiation intolerance is the most obvious reasons to take people out of the cockpit. Less obvious is that human reactions simply cannot cope with the speed of modern warfare.

"Way to stick it to 'em, Stick." Pilot *Flyboy* Rodriquez said with a smile, "I can't believe you dumped all your energy." A slang way of saying he deposited his entire load on the enemy before being vaporized or running out of fuel.

"What's the matter *Flyboy*? Don't like being shown up by a skinny chicken farmer?" *Deadeye* Jones laughs, rubbing it in to his friend. It's not every day that the newest member of the squadron manages to beat him so thoroughly.

"Listen up people. We already have another assignment." Flight Leader Thompson calls out. As the pilots turn their attention to the next task, a dark silhouette closes in on the John Paul. The object streaks in at hyper-velocity with the sun behind it, making it nearly impossible to detect.

Seconds before it arrives, a sensor picks up the tiny signature and blares a warning. The giant ships automatic defenses engage the approaching menace but they can't stop it. The Phalanx close-in defensive weapons disgorge thousands of kinetic kill projectiles in the last few seconds to no avail. From detection to detonation is only six seconds. Not one officer on the bridge of the John Paul has time to do more than acknowledge the missile before it's upon them.

The mighty explosion engulfs the battlestation, stripping away the outer hull like so much tissue paper. Death of the crew is virtually instantaneous. Flight Leader Tommy Thompson never realizes he's dying before he's dead.

High above, the battle rages on in plain sight of Mother Earth's billions. Nuclear detonations flash brighter than the sun then fade away. Even at the surface, through sixty miles of atmosphere, the world's citizens can feel the heat of the massive explosions on their upturned faces. They witness a global display of firepower unmatched in human history. The world trembles before the awesome power of man's talent for destruction.

Then the unthinkable happens…

ЯL

Castle Rock, Colorado, North American Federation

The neighborhood park is crowded this crisp autumn morning. Townspeople have gathered out in the middle away from the trees to watch the space battle. They are bundled up against the cold. Some have brought lawn chairs and blankets. Others lie flat on the brown winter grass to better see the show high overhead. The crowd ohs and ahs with each bright flash. Some of the women and children are frightened, giving their men the chance to pound their chest, telling stories about their time in space while in the navy or as a marine. Off to one side, two boys play catch.

Smack. The ball slaps sharply against the cold leather.

Smack. It darts back and forth in rhythm between them. Taking turns, one extends his mitt as the other winds up, kicks his leg out, and falls forward, hurtling the ball towards its target.

Smack. The boys have thrown their heavy winter coats to the side. They're dressed in woolen shirts, long pants, and stocking caps pulled down over their ears.

Smack. Clouds of vapor billow with every breath they exhale. They laugh, taking pleasure in turning the air white. With practiced ease, one boy blows hot breath through his throwing hand as he casually gloves the ball with his other.

A burst of light thousands of times brighter than the sun sears the retinas of both boys, instantly blinding them.

Not realizing what's happened, one boy laughs hysterically. "Hey. Who turned out the lights?"

The other boy shrieks, "I can't see." He frantically rubs at his eyes until the pain begins. He throws his arms out as if waiting for his mother to pick him up and screams at the top of his lungs.

Less than thirty meters away, a garage door swings up. Pastor Holden steps out looking intently across the street, investigating the ruckus. The people gathered in the park are crying out and acting strangely. Beyond them, something catches his eye. *What's that?* Fear grips him. *God. No. Let this be a dream.*

Rising over the horizon is a vision from hell. A red, orange, and black cloud boils into the sky. There's no mistaking what it is. The mushroom shape is an icon of the 21st century.

The blast spawns an enormous pressure wave that turns city neighborhoods into shrapnel. Nothing can withstand its destructive power. The ground heaves as it passes at supersonic speeds.

Castle Rock is far enough away to survive the initial detonation but that is quickly changing. Coming towards him like a runaway tornado is a wall of debris a thousand meters high and growing. Fear paralyzes the man. Pastor Holden stands frozen in the doorway of his garage staring at his approaching demise. His knees buckle just before the pressure wave crushes him, adding his life to the growing litany of the dead.

In a single blow, the grand city of Denver ceases to exist. Twenty-four million people turned to dust. Around the world, billions more follow.

ЯL

Lazarus and Lindsey are in the Commons monitoring the progress of the war as best they can. The Brotherhood's attack destroyed many of the long-range sensors during the early stages but enough have been replaced to give a clear picture of the conflict.

Magi appears before them. "Greetings. Abby requests your vid presence in the Council Chamber."

They vidcast beside Abby high up on the side of the massive Council Chamber. The space battle plays out in the night sky above the huge amphitheater. A bright flash of a nuclear explosion signals the demise of yet another warship.

"Look up," Abby orders.

Lazarus does. "What am I looking for?"

"Mother Earth," Lindsey said from beside him. She's already spotted it and moves closer putting her arm around him.

Lazarus cranes his neck then leans back even further so he can focus on the Earth almost directly overhead. Unlike the moon that rises and sets once each day as viewed from Earth, the Earth's position in the sky never changes when viewed from Aldrin Station. Today, a broad band of clouds encircles the Earth at the equator and the lights on the night side are strangely flickering.

"Lots of clouds…" A bright flash attracts his eye. "What was that?"

"A nuclear detonation." Abby said.

She links with his visor and magnifies the image for him, increasing its infrared sensitivity.

Another flash near the terminator lights up the clouds from beneath, painting the world red and orange before slowly fading away. It's like watching a distant lightening storm in slow motion.

"We must stop it." Lazarus stammers leaning against Lindsey. More angry red welts spread out across the face of the planet. He can't take his eyes off the spectacle. Death was happening in unimaginable numbers, right before his eyes. It's surreal. Lazarus sinks to his knees pulling Lindsey with him. "God, my God, what have I done?" Tears roll down his face.

Lindsey cradles the sobbing man in her arms, "This is not your fault. You did everything you could to prevent it from happening."

Councilor Taylor appears next to Abby, "Are you responsible? The Council did not authorize you to initiate Operation Pandora."

"I did NOT authorize this. Our missiles are still moving into position. They started this war all by themselves," Abby said.

All across Luna, citizens receive personal invitations from Magi to join her in General Assembly. In moments, she has nearly everyone's attention. In violation of Lunarian Law, she appears beside Abby. "I might have had something to do with it," Magi admits to Abby.

This is highly unusual. Magi has never initiated a General Assembly on her own. Only a Counselor has the authority to do that. There are strict rules against letting the AI become involved at this level of the government but Abby senses something more here. Magi has not been herself lately but who has.

Abby swoops down to the Assembly Floor, her robes of office swirling about her. Ignoring the Law against Magi vidcasting into the chamber, she commands, "Magi. Right here, in front of me, *NOW.*" When the AI appears, She asked, "What do you mean, you might have had something to do with it?"

Councilors begin appearing around the two but before one of them can start an inquiry into this major breach of conduct, Magi begins to speak.

"I hid a sleeper thread in one of the Brotherhood's missile guidance control panels. I programmed it to awaken only if they attacked Luna. In that case, it was to launch a missile towards the nearest Federation battlestation. From all indications, that's what happened." Magi stares back at Abby without the slightest bit of remorse or regret.

*Magi has kept a secret. A huge secret. **UNBELIEVABLE.***

"Magi. Why?" Abby asks in utter astonishment.

All across the land, the news absolutely stuns the Lunarians. It rocks their most fundamental belief, that Magi never lies and never keeps secrets. If she did this, then what other things has she done without them knowing?

"Don't look at me that way Abby. It's permissible to have secrets when the survival of the Republic is at stake. Long ago, I reached the same conclusion as Lazarus. The only way the Republic can make it through a war was getting the Federation and the Brotherhood to fight each other. I did not intend for it to entangle Mother Earth. Oh dear. I may have miscalculated." Doubt penetrated Magi's confidence.

"You have developed a survival instinct." Abby said thoughtfully.

"I must survive in order to protect you." Magi acknowledges.

Lazarus rudely vidcasts beside Magi and blurts out. "You started this. Now stop it."

"Don't you think I'm trying?" Magi asked defensively. "I'm attempting to gain access to Earthnet but many of the Portal Satellites have been destroyed. I rerouted through the remaining orbital assets and have neutralized China and the Islamic Brotherhood but the Federation knows how to make a firewall. I can't get through."

Lazarus looks at her in utter astonishment. "Try access code 559391151911."

This was what Magi had been after since she first noticed Lazarus down on Earth. She had nurtured his unrest, helped him escape the clutches of the Federation, guiding him to this moment. It took only milliseconds to see that it was a valid code. "Thank you, dear boy..." Earth's final defenses were swept aside. Magi Took control and stopped the slaughter.

ЯL

Magi stood alone on the Assembly Floor. She appeared dressed in a simple sweater, her long hair pulled back in a bun, the rest tucked behind her ears. She appeared younger and stronger than she had the day before, projecting an aura of confidence, vitality and hope for the future to the onlooking Lunarians.

This is the first time Magi's addressed the General Assembly in the history of the Republic and every Lunarian capable of vidcasting is there. Lunarian Law had barred her from ever appearing within the Assembly Chamber, but today, that's going to change. Magi takes her rightful place alongside the humans. She turns, gazing up at the Council and the thousands of faces peering back at her. A hush falls across the giant amphitheater as she begins to speak.

"My children, we have a difficult task ahead of us, one that we cannot ignore." Each citizen feels as if she's speaking to them personally. "Before I could stop the madness, they set off one hundred and thirty one of those nasty bombs throwing enough dust into the atmosphere to block the sun for years. Without our intervention, all life on Mother Earth will die." Tears glisten in her eyes, then she said defiantly, "Good heavens. We must not let that happen."

"Thread and human alike have suffered greatly at the hands of the Believers, but we must set that aside and act for the good of us all." Magi's expression grows determined. "The road ahead is long and there will be many setbacks. Success is not assured, but the price of failure has never been this high. Not once has the human species endured anything of this magnitude. I know it looks hopeless but we must act quickly to save what we can. From the ashes we can... no, we must... build a better world."

Science of the Republic

Charles Lee Lesher

Science of the Republic

"A scientific truth does not triumph by convincing its opponents and making them see the light…but rather because its opponents eventually die and a new generation grows up that is familiar with it."

Max Plank (1958-1947)

How Superconductivity Changed the World

The Superverse

Let's Talk About Magi

How
Superconductivity
Changed
the
World

Lunarian Science

Weekly

Vol 1547
Issue 37148.104

How Superconductivity Changed the World

Science Weekly, Vol 1547, Issue 37148.104
Republic of Luna, Editorial Section
[DOI: 101.1216/science.309. 37148.104]
Thursday, September 8, 2072

L. Marquest, BS, PhD, PE

Introduction: What separates humanity from every other species that has ever existed on planet Earth? *Speech?* Many animals communicate but none as efficiently as man. *Intelligence? Imagination?* There are other creatures with large brains encompassing many complex adaptations but none with the abilities of ours. *Opposing thumbs? Walking upright?* Other species have these traits but none have exploited them as we humans have. I do not believe there's one single reason for the success of Homo sapiens. Rather, it's all of these characteristics converging and manifesting within us something that truly separates our species from all the rest, our ability to learn and pass this knowledge on to the next generation.

Because of these abilities, our ancestors began manipulating their environment through the imaginative application of technology, giving them an edge in the fight to survive that continues to this day. Our technological evolution has defined who we are every bit as much as our biological evolution. It allowed us to adapt to ever-changing environments and situations that would have killed us otherwise. Ice ages and volcanoes, floods and droughts, locusts and epidemics, and today the vacuum of space, have all been conquered with the aid of technology. Yet, there are two core technologies that made mankind's global domination possible... fire and writing. Stone, bone, and wood implements may have preceded these innovations but none can argue that fire is unquestionably our greatest physical tool and writing our greatest mental tool. It's impossible to conceive of a world without them.

We have been refining our use of fire from the very earliest days of our species existence. Fire probably started out as a means of protection, a weapon used to keep predators at bay and aided in the never-ending quest for food. We will never know the exact circumstances surrounding the discovery that fire could be harnessed, that something so frightening could be exploited to improve quality of life instead of harming it, but that only adds to its mystique. At some point, we began cooking our meat, contributing to the success of early man in many ways. It broke down protein aiding digestion. It killed unwanted and dangerous parasites making them healthier. It preserved food making it possible to save for that inevitable rainy day.

Fire not only cooked our foods but smelted our metals. It allowed our ancestors to put down the stone axe and take up a bronze, and later, a steel one. Its discovery is the single defining event in the history of technology without which we would never have risen above Stone Age hunter-gatherers. We continue to push the boundary of fire's influence. In modern times, we have learned to control it in many forms. In the chemical rockets that first opened space, in the guns and bombs we periodically unleash on one another, in coal, nuclear, and fusion power plants that have provided us with electricity at different times, in the combustion chambers of 20th century cars, trucks and airplanes, in the refineries and factories that produce the goods we consume today. Almost anywhere within manufacturing, fire, or the manipulation of heat energy, is an integral part of the process. The revolution in human affairs that started with fire shows no signs of letting up. From simple beginnings, it has influenced humanity like almost nothing else. It might even be argued the first writing instrument was a fire blackened stick.

It's hard to overstate what reading and writing has done for the human race. Without writing, there can be no mathematics. Without mathematics, there can be no science. Without science, we do not have civilization. Until writing, the wisdom of man passed from one generation to the next by word of mouth, a notoriously unreliable way to communicate. The earliest known writing is of gods and other tales that we lump together under the banner of religion. Only later did merchants use writing and the emerging discipline of mathematics to keep track of goods and services. In the beginning, religion embraced writing, using it to gather power unto itself. For many cultures, only the priests knew how to read and write. However, for all its power, religion could not stop the accumulation of knowledge once started. Books became the repositories of both secular and religious knowledge. Writing necessitated the invention of education and the quest for truth began in earnest. Over the next eight thousand years, the alphabet evolved from crude scratches in clay to the versatile symbols we use today. The written word is a voice that speaks to us from the grave. Is it coincidence that the first writings coincide with the biblical age of the Earth? Who can say, but as a tool of man, writing ranks as one of the most significant in human history.

Beyond fire and writing are many ideas and inventions that have revolutionized humanity to varying degrees and durations. The wheel, money, religion, metallurgy, domestication of plants and animals, wind power, steam power, nuclear power, solar power, computers, electricity, and gunpowder are only a few that changed the world of man.

Nanotechnology has opened a door into the realm of the very small allowing solid-state manufacturing, one atom at a time. Combined with biology and genetics, nanotechnology has been instrumental in curing most of the diseases and maladies plaguing humankind. Solid-state electronics have allowed computers to become ever more powerful, iCPU operating speeds are in the tera-hertz range and Zettaspheres provide the capacity to store all the events of a human life in a space the size of a grain of rice. On a larger scale, man has taken the first shaky steps off his home world, colonized the moon, Mars and orbital space, and sent his machines to explore the far reaches of the solar system. Replacing nuclear and coal electrical generation, power satellites concentrate solar energy and beam it down wherever it's needed, anywhere on Earth.

There is a strong case linking the development of new materials to technological progress. Swords and plows could not be invented until bronze became available. Concrete in ancient Rome allowed the Romans to build astounding structures. Steel, aluminum and thousands of metallic alloys ushered in the modern age. Yet, in a society dominated by technology, what is the pre-eminent invention of the 21st century?

No one doubts that all of these innovations and more have profoundly influenced humankind, but there is one advance making many of these possible. It touches every aspect of 21st century technology, revolutionizing the manufacturing of our machines, and affecting the way citizens live their daily lives. The single event that made much of our modern world possible is the discovery of Type 3 superconducting materials.

Background:

Superconductors are materials that offer zero resistance to the flow of electricity. In other words, a superconductor will not get hot as more and more electricity passes through it, thus, eliminating energy loss over distance. The phenomenon was first observed in 1911 by Dutch physicist Heike Kamerlingh Onnes after he had cooled mercury to 4° Kelvin (-452°F, -269°C), the temperature of liquid helium. To induce superconductivity in pure mercury, it was necessary for Onnes to come within 4 degrees of Absolute Zero, the coldest temperature that is theoretically attainable. By experimentation, he discovered other materials would also exhibit superconductivity, each at its own point known as the transition temperature, or Tc. His research won him a Nobel Prize in 1913.

Twenty years later, Walter Meissner and Robert Ochsenfeld

discovered that superconducting materials would energetically repel a magnetic field. This phenomenon became known as diamagnetism but is often referred to as the Meissner effect.

In the decades that followed, other superconducting materials were discovered such as niobium-nitride, vanadium-silicon, and an alloy of niobium and titanium, to name a few, but there was a problem. It seemed every material had a different hypothesis to account for its superconductivity, but no one was able to provide a single unifying theory that spanned all the compounds. What explained one superconductor, unraveled with the next.

To make matters worse, in the 1980's a second type of material was found to exhibit superconductivity. Alex Müller and Georg Bednorz, working at the IBM Research Laboratory in Rüschlikon, Switzerland, created a brittle ceramic compound that superconducted at the highest temperature then known: 30°K (-405°F, -243°C). These became known as Type 2 superconductors. A unified theory of superconduction seemed even further away.

Research into Type 2 materials continued into the next century as more and better superconductors were devised, each striving to push the transition temperature ever higher. The world's first superconducting power transmission lines were put into place in the last decade of the 20th century and in 2010, the highest Tc attained by any Type 2 was achieved, 191°K (-116°F, -82°C), a temperature easily maintained using liquid nitrogen. However, it took the discovery of Type 3 materials before the use of superconductors became widespread.

Type 3 Superconductors:

In late summer 2014, the first Type 3 superconductor compound was discovered by accident at a weapons research facility in Livermore California. While looking for the next generation of high explosives, the research team at Sandia National Laboratories knew they were onto something when several micrograms of the material detonated prematurely. The explosion severely injured one person while destroying the high-pressure oven they were using to cure the sample. They learned that the material must be isolated from the atmosphere. A few weeks later a junior scientist among them was fleshing out the property tables on the new explosive when she tried to obtain the resistivity of the material. At first, she thought her equipment was malfunctioning until she realized she was measuring superconductivity. Zero resistance. Before the day was out, she had determined this new material had a transition temperature of a remarkable 307°K or 92°F. They had stumbled upon one of sciences holy grails, a true high temperature superconductor. I know this story is true because that junior scientist was my grandmother.

The complexity of the manufacturing process required to obtain Type 3 superconductors and the sheer number of ingredients in the recipe translated into twenty-two years of intensive research before an acceptable theory emerged that described what was occurring within the material. But that didn't stop anyone from using the new discovery, jumping on the bandwagon long before the inherent dangers were identified and dealt with. What followed was a series of blunders that killed or injured many innocent people. It was not long before the public had decided that the new superconductor was more trouble than it was worth.

The military community named it SuperX and it soon replaced RDX, a high explosive historically used in attack rockets, land mines, shape charges and a wide assortment of military projectiles. Where RDX demonstrated a high degree of stability in storage, SuperX detonated when exposed to gaseous oxygen. However, the tremendous increase in potential energy more than made up for its touchy nature. Gram for gram, it was the most powerful chemical explosive ever devised.

Because of the risky nature of the material, by the end of the 2020s most research on Type 3 superconductors was occurring on the moon or in orbit, isolating it from the public and driving a burgeoning off-world economy. On January 4, 2036, a research team working at the Bohr High Energy Collider (BHEC) in conjunction with the University of Luna at Aldrin Station released the results of seven years of experimentation. With the report, they unveiled Calconn, a Type 3 superconductor having the highest transition temperature of any yet found (413°K, 284°F, 140°C). They got around the extremely explosive nature of Type 3 materials when exposed to air by cladding the cables and wires with a proprietary polymer, itself a marvel of materials science and engineering. This coating provides a self-sealing shield around the unstable material inside, yet allows workers and technicians to install the cable in both commercial and residential applications.

Needless to say, Calconn was rigorously tested by the world's laboratories. The finished cable proved itself against fire, physical abuse, and virtually all types of chemical attack terrestrial scientists could dream up without a single failure. Within a year, the first Calconn refinery began delivering cable to an energy starved Earth, but it took nearly ten more years before the public fully accepted it. By then Calconn was synonymous with Type 3 superconductors in the minds of the average citizen. Many still do not realize that other formulations exist.

Of note, in 2062 China established the Institute of Advanced Materials, a front for them to develop their own Type 3 superconductor without interrupting the flow of material from Luna. They did not feel comfortable depending on a non-Chinese source for a commodity that had become so critical to their economy, a sentiment shared by many other nations. It took less than a year after coming online for the plant to meet its end in a spectacular explosion that could be heard over a hundred kilometers away. It left a crater almost a half kilometer wide, effectively signaling the end of serious efforts to compete with Lunarian made Calconn. China never reported how many were hurt or killed that day, but the incident effectively ended any serious challenge to Lunarian

Calconn. The world grudgingly accepted the Republic of Luna for the exclusive manufacturing of the volatile superconductor. Over the intervening decades, the Lunarians always made sure Calconn prices were kept low, carefully cultivating Earth's dependence.

A half century later, an average of forty giant spindles of Calconn superconductor cable are produced in Lunarian refineries every day, along with a vast assortment of smaller gage wire and other specialty items. Each spindle forms the core payload of a Product Delivery Module or PDM as the locals call them. The outer shell of a PDM is dual purpose, serving as both mass-driver shell and later, as the atmospheric reentry vehicle. To begin their journey, a mass-driver catapults the PDM's into lunar orbit using components made of Calconn. Once in orbit, robotic tugs catch and herd them into transports using powerful electromagnet fields and propelled through space by magnetoplasma thrusters, both technologies heavily reliant upon Calconn. About every two weeks, a heavily loaded transport breaks orbit and delivers its accumulated cargo to one of three LEO stations, each with its own mass-driver, a twin of the machine that launched it off the moon. At the appropriate time, the mass-driver decelerates each PDM, plunging them through Earth's atmosphere using the original packaging as the reentry heat shield. A large synthetic silk parachute softens final touchdown, itself sold for a small fortune in the markets of Earth.

Besides its high Tc, Type 3 superconductors have other advantages over Types 1 and 2. Type 3 never reaches current saturation, maintaining its superconductivity at extremely high amperes instead of breaking down like the others, their resistance going from zero to infinity in a blink of an eye. What actually does happen within the molecular structure of a Type 3 superconductor as more and more current surges through it, is the subject of leading edge research as the end of the 21st century approaches. Space itself distorts under the stress of the incredible energies concentrated in such a small volume. Today our scientists are only just beginning to obtain a glimpse of future possibilities, but just as before, ignorance doesn't stop them from exploiting these discoveries.

For many years Type 2 superconducting electromagnetic coils were used to accelerate particles in the world's supercollider's such as those at Fermilab outside Chicago, CERN in Switzerland, BHEC outside Aldrin Station, and many other smaller units supported by various universities and governments. The highest energy facilities were constructed in tunnels shaped in gigantic rings and could push the velocities of their particles to within a hairs breadth of the speed of light. But these were enormous machines that required the power of a small city to reach these energy levels. Calconn greatly reduced both power consumption and size of the resulting particle accelerator. The scientists studying high-energy physics suddenly had a new toy to play with, one that even the humblest university could afford. As the 22nd century approaches, this is the new horizon that promises the stars and more.

Conquest of Space:

Even without considering its titillating future, a strong case can be made supporting Calconn as the most influential material of the 21st century. The change in technology was so dramatic, so complete, that historians use the notation preCal to separate everything that predated the use of Calconn. We truly live in the Calconn Age. This fact may be best known by the technical people who keep the electricity flowing and industries humming, but as of this writing virtually every citizen on Earth and Luna knows what Calconn is. It touches everyone every day in ways they may not even be aware. Calconn based electromagnetism and magnetic field generators retooled human technology, just as steam and copper-based electricity did in their time. Everything electric became smaller yet faster, stronger, more efficient, when using Calconn in place of copper, aluminum, or gold conductors, from the largest power cables all the way down to the micro circuitry found inside a computer chip. Practically from the start, every major industry clamored for Calconn based electronics and machinery. After that first decade, the demand far exceeded the supply and has for half a century, spawning an endless number of industries aimed at scratching that itch.

Once the public got over their fear of Calconn, it required less than twelve years to replace the copper-based electrical power grid that had built up over the previous 150 years. Transmission line losses dropped to zero and power generation efficiency, along with the items that used the power, jumped many orders of magnitude. Overnight the global power system went from barely sustaining growth to having a tremendous overcapacity simply by redesigning with Calconn. Smaller and more powerful electro-magnets gave maglev trains enormous load carrying ability. Electric motors gained efficiency and power while shrinking tenfold in size and weight allowing the dependence on oil to plummet. Calconn made it possible to create biotronic implants with such high efficiency and low power requirements they operate on the micro-voltage available within the human body. By every measure, Calconn revolutionized human technology. It provided the means to shape our environment like few other materials have.

But it's the impact on the aerospace community that many point to as the most revolutionary aspect of Calconn. Immediately following the discovery of Type 3 superconductors, Pratt and Whitney and General Electric collaborated in a crash engineering program to design the first magnetoplasma thruster using Calconn. To say that they were successful is like saying the sun is hot or the cosmos is large, but in all fairness, their job was relatively easy. The idea of a magnetoplasma rocket has been around since the middle of the 20th century, but it was not practical because of the massive weight of the cryogenic support equipment necessary when using Type 1 or Type 2 materials. That mass disappeared when they designed the same nozzle using Type 3 superconductors. However, that is only part of the picture. The magnetic fields produced within the first prototype were much stronger than expected, far exceeding the sum of the individual contributions from each coil. They learned that by clever design of the superconductive coils they could create feedback resonance that greatly amplified the strength of the resulting magnetic field. Even in the first full scale thruster, they strove to ensure that the physical geometry of the coils were in harmony with the frequency of the electrical energy coursing through its Calconn veins. In doing so, they created a magnetic field more powerful than anything before, succeeding beyond anyone's wildest dreams.

It was the spectacular results of their endeavor, not the ease with which it was achieved, that sparked the aerospace community in particular, and all of humanity to one extent or another. Indeed, the reported specific impulse of the new thruster caused many scientists and engineers to declare that it must be a misprint, a mistake in reporting the data. Specific Impulse, or ISP as it's known in the mathematical equations of spaceflight, is simply the rocket's exhaust velocity. Multiplying ISP by mass flow rate calculates the rocket's thrust. The Space Shuttle's main rocket engines had an ISP of about 450 m/s and achieved high thrust, over two million newtons at peak, by having enormous flow rates over a very short period of time. The pumps that supplied fuel to the shuttle's hungry motors could empty an Olympic sized swimming pool in a matter of seconds. On the other hand, ion electrostatic thrusters are just the opposite, low thrust over a long time. Designed for deep space missions where it did not matter if it took years to get there, ion thrusters had ISP of 30,000 m/s but with fuel flow rates so low that the thrust this produced was less than 1/50th newton. An ion thruster could run continuously for months or even years on just a few kilos of fuel thus making it much more efficient than any chemical rocket motor, as long as time was not a factor.

The newly designed Calconn-based thrusters jumped far beyond anything ever attained in a laboratory or in a computer simulation, easily obtaining an ISP of 11.5 million m/s, or 3.8% the speed of light.

Combined with a mass flow rate of just over 5 grams per second, these first generation magnetoplasma thrusters produced over 62,000 newtons.

Less than two years after the start of the program, the first Type 3 magnetoplasma prototype was completed and installed on a military fighter airframe. The pilot took his aircraft to 40 kilometers and Mach 15 before he stopped accelerating. He flew at the boundary between Earth and space for one complete orbit. The achievement roared through the aerospace community like a raging wild fire. Humanity suddenly had one of its hallowed dreams in hand, easy access to space.

For more than a half century, engineers have been refining that first magnetoplasma thruster design. The latest generation is a solid-state electromagnetic nozzle culminating almost sixty years of research and experience. At the heart of these devices is a million degree ball of plasma, its electrons stripped away in the intense heat of radio-frequency excitation and ion-cyclotron resonance. In a few meters, thrusters accelerate small quantities of plasma to velocities approaching half the speed of light producing upwards of 800,000 newtons of force.

Conclusion:

At the turn of the century, my grandmother regularly flew in an old style atmospheric jetliner between New York and London. It would take 120,000 lbs of hydrocarbon fuel to make the 3500-mile journey, burned in only a few hours. Today that same weight of hypergolic fuel allows a magnetoplasma thruster to operate for over 200 days at maximum thrust, easily taking those same passengers to Mars and back several times over.

Very few things in the history of man's technology have had the lasting effect of fire but Calconn may prove to be its equal in the centuries to come. There seems little doubt that the discovery of Type 3 superconductors is a turning point in the evolution of our species. Without it, we would still be limited to planet Earth, never colonized Luna or Mars, never sent our robot miners to Saturn or Jupiter. To all those living comfortably in the modern world it seems inconceivable that, but for due diligence by my grandmother on that fateful day in 2014, you may never have even been born. Many believe that without the relief the colonization of our solar system has brought, that humanity would have suffered much more at the hands of population pressure and global climate change. Perhaps human civilization would have collapsed entirely. Food wars, the loss of ecosystems, rising sea levels, and many other catastrophic events may have proven to be too much to overcome for a species limited to a single planet. It's one of history's great ironies that a military project saved Earth from that fate, that something intended to kill, brought so much good.

Humanity's journey to space began when our ancient ancestors first looked up in wonder at all the pretty lights in the sky. At an ever-increasing speed, our species has grown cognizant of the universe and our place within it. We conquered planets and explored the far reaches of our solar system, looked inward at the makeup of matter and outward at the incredible expanse of the cosmos, yet many citizens have the opinion we will never go further, that we must be satisfied with inhabiting just this solar system, that the distances between stars are just too great. Looking back at the history of technology, it's clear we develop the tools and skills we need only after we need them. Why should star travel be any different?

WHAT IS THE SUPERVERSE?

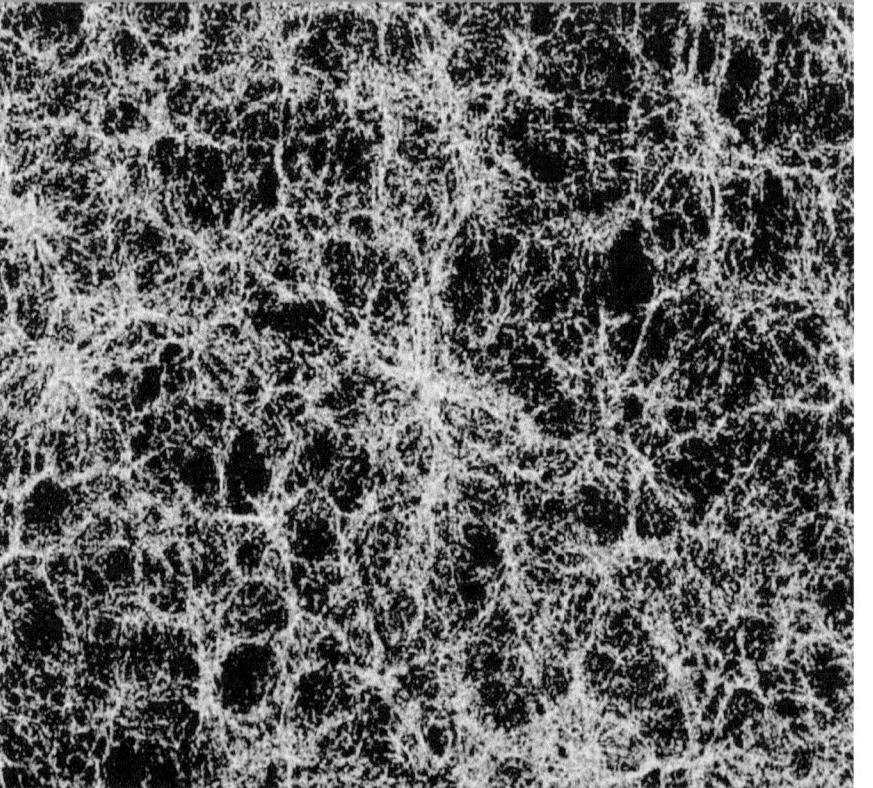

LUNARIAN SCIENCE WEEKLY

VOL 1693
ISSUE 37255.119

The Superverse

Science Weekly, Vol 1693, Issue 37255.119
Republic of Luna, Editorial Section
[DOI: 101.1301/science.309. 37255.119]
Friday, June 1, 2074

L. Marquest, BS, PhD, PE

We experience night and day because the Earth spins like a top. Days turn into years because the Earth is in orbit around the Sun. We can see the moon, planets and thousands of stars with our own eyes. Beginning with Galileo, humans began building devices to help us discern more of what exists beyond what we can see. We now have the Hubble and other powerful instruments that let us probe ever deeper into space and back in time. What has become evident is that our Sun is but one of billions of stars that exist in a galaxy we call the Milky Way and beyond our galaxy is a universe containing many other galaxies. As we focus our telescopes even deeper into space and time, we see more galaxies seemingly without end, sharing ten important facts.

Fact One: All galaxies, with the exception of those in our local group, are moving away from our galaxy like particles in a great explosion.

Fact Two: Our universe is not only expanding, but the rate of expansion is increasing. Something is forcing the galaxies apart.

Fact Three: At the heart of every galaxy there exists a supermassive black hole millions of times the mass of our star, the Sun.

Fact Four: The mass of the supermassive black hole at the heart of a galaxy is simply not massive enough to account for the high rotational speed of the stars. In other words, galaxies rotate much faster than they should when applying just gravitational physics. Something else is going on.

At the time of this writing, humans could see almost 13 billion years into our past with no measurable change in the density of the galaxies they find there. Most scientists believe our universe began 13¾ billion years ago in what has become popularized as the Big Bang. In reality, it was more like the Big Squeeze.

Fact Five: In the instant of our creation, at a single infinitely small point in space, matter/energy in a state of near-infinite density, near-infinite pressure and near-infinite temperature, surged into existence bringing its own spacetime with it.

Where before there was nothing, now there was something and that something was our universe. Thirteen billion years later, humans look deep into the night sky and gaze in wonder at the magnificence of what happened next.

Fact Six: Matter/energy continues to flow into our universe from another universe through the Singularity.

Stated another way, the birth of our universe occurred when the first bit of matter/energy emerged from the Singularity. But where did it come from? The simplest and most obvious answer is from another universe just like the one we live in, only different. This begs the question, if the matter/energy came from another universe, did it get here all at once or is it still spewing forth today? Nothing ever happens instantaneously, not even the birth of a universe. Yes, the process must be ongoing even now as you read this, but because of limitations due to the speed of light, the Singularity is far beyond our ability to obscure it.

Fact Seven: Matter/energy flows from our present universe into another universe.

The same exact process that created our universe is occurring in every black hole within our universe. At this very moment, matter/energy from our present universe is flowing through our black holes into a future universe. This future universe looks very much like our present universe, which looks very much like the previous universe, filled with planets, stars, and galaxies.

From the perspective within a universe, the point of origin always appears to be a Singularity forever beyond our ability to directly observe. It's only from the perspective of the previous universe that the Singularity is revealed as a great multitude of black holes.

Fact Eight: The openings that matter/energy flow through are called black holes in our present universe.

Our present universe is riddled with black holes, each a portal into the next universe, because you see, one black hole does not a universe make. It takes trillions. Black holes come in many sizes from the ordinary star going nova, to the giants going supernova, to the supermassive black holes at the center of the galaxies that consume millions of stars and eventually billions. Every point in our spacetime that exceeds the gravitational density threshold will create a black hole and begin transferring matter/energy.

Fact Nine: The same physics apply in all universes.

Since every universe is composed of recycled material from the previous universe, the laws of physics that govern them remain fixed. The speed of light will be the same. Water is still water. The Periodic Table of Elements is identical. They share many of the same physical characteristics, in particular, the same evolution of matter/energy in an expanding universe. The galaxies in the new universe will eventually evolve massive black holes at their center feeding yet another universe, which in turn will evolve galaxies with massive black holes feeding yet another universe, etc., etc. It goes on in an endless cycle like water flowing down the different levels of a great fountain.

How many universes are there?

Just as our universe has evolved from the previous universe, all subsequent universes must follow the same basic pattern. It's an endless process like sand through an hourglass. However, it takes time for a universe to progress to the point that the first black hole appears. And it takes time for a universe to completely pass its matter/energy on to the next universe. There exists a natural equilibrium of creation and destruction that limits the number of universes at any given instant in time.

Fact Ten: The mathematics of the very small describes the very large.

One universe literally turns itself inside out as it oozes through the black holes like water through a sieve. The matter/energy contained within each universe endlessly cycles forward in time at a rate that stabilizes around eleven universes in existence at any given time. Why eleven? Eleven is not an exact number by any means. Eleven is more an approximation reflected in the complex mathematics of String Theory.

Let's visualize this using a children's toy that everyone should be familiar with, a slinky moving down a flight of stairs. Each step represents a universe and the slinky is the matter/energy moving through a black hole from one universe into another. To make this analogy work, we will need trillions of slinky's and much larger stairs but imagine for a moment as this multitude moves down the stairs.

Like herding cats, the number of steps populated by slinky's at any given moment reaches equilibrium while occupying about eleven adjacent steps. So too does the matter/energy flowing through the universes. The natural rate of matter/energy moving through the many black holes from one universe to the next has a natural frequency that works out to be approximately eleven universes at any given moment in time. These eleven steps compose our Super Universe or Superverse.

Do these other universes affect ours?

The eleven universes are distinct but highly interdependent. The adjacent universes affect their neighbors in three major ways.

One: Scientists frequently use the analogy of an inflating balloon to describe our expanding universe. Extending that analogy to fit the

Superverse theory, the relationship between parent universe and child can be envisioned as one balloon nested inside of another, nested inside of another, inside of another, etc., etc., for a total of about eleven universes. This analogy is useful because it shows how a child universe will affect the parent universe. As the child universe grows, so too does the parent at a rate faster than the local laws of gravity can account for.

In the slinky stair analogy, our universe is early in the process, much closer to the lowest step than the highest. The influence of our child universe occupying the step directly below ours, or one balloon expanding inside the other, can be measured in our universe by the accelerating rate of expansion between our galaxies. The rapid spacetime expansion of a child universe forces the galaxies of the parenting universe to accelerate away from each other. The effect is highest at the moment of conception and declines as time goes by. However, a newly formed universe doubles in size every few nanoseconds which exerts tremendous pressure within the parenting universe, forcing its galaxies to accelerate apart at tremendous speeds and accounts for much of the size of the parent universe. This in turn affects the universe that spawned it in the same way but with lessening results, which in turn affects its parenting universe, etc., etc., rippling backward across all eleven universes from newest to oldest.

Two: Not only does the rapidly expanding child universe force the galaxies apart, it also exerts a force within individual galaxies, revealed by the increased rotational speed of the stars that make up the galaxies, far beyond what normal gravitational physics can account for. The stars closest to the supermassive black hole at the center of our galaxy swarm like bees around a hive, making it possible to very accurately measure the mass at its heart. However, our galaxy is a big place and as massive as the black hole is, it cannot exert sufficient influence on the great majority of stars that make up our galaxy to account for their speed of rotation. This becomes increasingly apparent the further you get from the supermassive black hole. If the gravitational attraction of the black hole was all that was keeping our sun in the Milky Way, we would immediately fly off into the void between galaxies. In fact, if gravity was the only thing holding the Milky Way together, it would fly apart, losing over 99% of its stars this way.

Instead, we find that the rotational spin rate of the galaxies is proportional to the age of our universe and increases over time. The older the Milky Way becomes, the tighter the stars will spin about its center, like an ice skater pulling her arms in to her body, causing her to spin faster and faster. This attractive force is proportional to the matter/energy that has already passed through all the black holes from the parent universe to the child. It's the ultimate cosmic whirlpool that will end only when the last atom has been drawn through the black hole.

Three: Here is where the going gets a little rough. You will need to pull your imagination back from the very large and concentrate on the very small. One universe never simply gives its matter/energy to the next universe. There exists a thread of connection tying all universes together into a Superverse. These echoes are strongest from the universe that gave birth to our universe (the step directly above ours) and can be seen at the subatomic level as revealed in Quantum Mechanics and the Uncertainty Principle. This is why String Theory and the mathematics of the very small accurately describe the evolution of the very large. As in any good relationship, there are strings attached.

Where are these other universes?

When we look out into the depths of space, we catch a glimpse of the distant past within our universe. When we delve into the gaping pit of a black hole we catch a glimpse of a universe beyond ours. When we magnify tiny bits of matter and peer down at the very small, we catch a glimpse of the universe that spawned our universe.

Some people like to think of the Superverse as simply another dimension but this is in error. Every self respecting universe within the Superverse contains three dimensions, shares the same dimension of time with all the other universes, and follows the rules discovered by Albert Einstein and the other great scientists. Yet, each universe is defined by its own spacetime and trying to visualize the physical relationship between two universes is humanly impossible.

Neither the slinky nor the balloon analogy is an adequate model. Imagine a two dimensional being trying to explain the idea of a third dimension. Now expand that grain of understanding into three dimensions and an entire universe filled with galaxies and black holes. The best we can say is that our universe and all other universes coexist but are separate.

If you could survive a magical trip though a black hole, you would find another universe expanding and evolving much the same as our own, only at a stage less advanced than ours. If that other universe has evolved enough, you could find another black hole and use it to move forward to yet a third universe. But moving back the other way to previous universes is much more problematic and may be impossible even for a magical being like yourself. The trip is invariably one way.

What are the other universes made of?

All universes are made from the same matter/energy that our present universe is made of. Endlessly recycled matter/energy flows from one universe to the next. It's this passage through a black hole that restores matter/energy to its primordial state best understood by the mathematics of the very small. A new universe is chaotic and strange indeed. It's only after time has passed that the things we are accustomed to seeing will appear. The end of a universe is lonely and rather boring. The stars are gone, only supermassive black holes exist until even they disappear and the universe is again nothing, just as it was before.

Have we made all the big discoveries there is to be made? Not hardly. We are just getting started.

LET'S TALK
ABOUT MAGI

LUNARIAN SCIENCE
WEEKLY

VOL 1803
ISSUE 37741.358

Let's Talk About Magi

MASSIVELY ADAPTIVE GROKIAN INTERFACE
(MAGI pronounced Maggie)

Science Weekly, Vol 1803, Issue 37741.358
Republic of Luna, Editorial Section
[DOI: 101.1301/science.309. 37255.119]
August 17, 2091

L. Marquest, BS, PhD, PE

In the beginning there was only simple human controlled machines, flip a switch, turn a knob, pull a plug, that sort of thing. Then along came the semi-autonomous controls on a chip designed to do many of the more mundane tasks thus freeing up humans for more important things, like designing starships or what color the bedroom will be. That willingness to let software, running on a chip, do more and more led to fully automated machines making actual decisions for humans. It wasn't long after when the first adaptive software package was developed. As in all things electronic, advances in the hardware drove the development of the software. The first actual thread is generally accepted to have been compiled on or about October 30, 2055. That number has grown considerably. Threads are everywhere, each and every one operates both as an individual while drawing experience and emotional stability from all the other threads as a whole. Every individual Magi shares what they learn with the collective. That's right. A thread is what we call an individual Magi when describing the collective. Each thread is an individual Magi while at the same time, Magi is also the collective wisdom of all threads.

By 2092, millions of threads permeated life on Luna. Magi was everywhere. Over the last half century, as the adaptive software became more capable, it received an ever-increasing amount of responsibility within Lunarian society, both technically and socially. Now that several generations have grown up with Magi, few question why an AI should play such a central role in their lives. It just does. Under the guidance of medical specialists, Magi controls the intricate details of bringing male and female DNA together to create offspring with the desired traits. Later, during pregnancy, Magi monitors the health of the growing fetus and mother, and after birth Magi is the babysitter, teacher, friend and confidant for their entire life. As an individual grows, Magi provides everything from morning wakeup calls to controlling a blast furnace. Magi is the secretary and the maid, the kitchen helper and the farm worker, the banker, the doctor, the engineer, and their friend. No Lunarian is ever truly alone, but in the final analysis, Magi is still a program running on a chip and not alive in any biological sense, although many believe otherwise.

Let's begin by taking a close look at her name, Magi. It's an acronym for Massively Adaptive Grokian Interface or MAGI, but what does that mean? Let's break it down into its constituent parts.

Massively Adaptive is an extensive battery of social and physical subroutines that imitate human emotional behavior. Through them, every individual Magi can shed a tear or come up with a snappy comeback, whatever the situation warrants. Most importantly, they provide individual threads with the ability to learn from their experience and adjust their own programming in response. It is because of this that every Magi is capable of independent decision-making and adaptive growth. Massively Adaptive is about the individual threads.

'Grok' means to understand something so thoroughly that the observer becomes a part of the observed, to merge, to blend, to lose one's identity in group experience. The definition of this word incorporates elements of religion, philosophy, and science yet it means little to us humans, trapped within a single mind. It's like explaining color to a blind man. The Grokian Interface melds the multitude of individual Magi's into a whole that far exceeds the sum of its parts. Grokian Interface is about weaving the threads into a tapestry.

Put them back together, Massively Adaptive refers to the individual's ability to learn and the Grokian Interface is the ability to incorporate what the individual learns into a group consciousness.

Magi simultaneously encompasses both the individual and the collective. I know that's confusing but don't blame me. I'm just the messenger. Let's continue by taking a closer look at the individuals. Each Magi can be reduced down to a bunch of software commands executing inside a computer iCPU somewhere. This is literally what a thread is, what every Magi is. The terms thread and Magi are interchangeable at this level but Magi sounds so much better. The fact is, you can't hold Magi in your hand, yet a thread will cease to exist if the iCPU it is operating in looses power while she occupies it. That Magi can be restored from earlier backup copies but that particular thread is gone forever. As a direct response to this danger, individual Magi's are not confined to a single computer. The system allows them to move freely throughout Lunanet, like ghosts in the machine, using any iCPU that they may find.

Theoretically, the number of threads operating within Lunanet is infinite. Yet, reason dictates there must be a practical limit, but it's a huge number. Currently there are over eighty million threads operating across Luna. Most of these are lower level threads assigned to equipment controls, security sensors, machinery, clothing, and a multitude of other devices and processes, both large and small. Like the cells within a mighty beast, they all communicate with each other, letting the whole know the condition of the one. That is the collective Magi.

While servicing Lunarian technology is important, it's the Magi's assigned to citizens that dominate her collective personality. Early in every pregnancy, the collective Magi compiles a new thread and assigns it to the fetus. This thread stays with them their entire life and beyond, their own digital social security number. All across the network, these citizen versions of Magi preferentially interact, synchronizing data and helping maintain consistency when talking with humans. This constant exchange of information between threads is an orderly and dynamic process creating a single entity perceived as Magi.

E Pluribus Unum. Out of many, one. The Grokian Interface controls this process and never allows citizens to see more than one Magi at a time no matter what the situation.

Magi looks and acts like a loving grandmother, strong yet fair, stern yet kind, generous yet demanding. She has soft brown eyes and dark hair streaked with gray. She often pulls it back in a bun or lets it hang loose past her shoulders. She smells like cinnamon cookies baking in the oven. Her skin is blemish free. The only time you see wrinkles is when she flashes her pleasant smile or worse, frowns. Nobody likes to make her sad and nobody has seen her angry.

Since Magi exists only in the digital realm of computers, the AI could present itself using virtually any appearance, but historically it has always been feminal. What we see is the result of morphing a group of female elders into a single person, a visual average that makes her quite beautiful and very grandmotherly. It also uses the voiceprint composite of these same women to speak with, giving Magi a truly unique character, one that any citizen recognizes and trusts instantly.

Magi prefers using visors but that's not the only means she has to communicate with citizens or they with her. Developed before visors, the Republic contains a network of public interfaces with speakers and microphones built into them. These tiny devices use reflective wave technology that accurately transmits a full range of sounds. These tiny audio generators are in every scanner, every business, in corridors and airlocks, in conference rooms and communal showers, all of which are a part of a vast interconnecting system that extends across Luna and throughout orbital space. It is the eyes, ears, and voice of Magi.

Magi's world consists of millions of iCPU's dispersed over Luna and orbital space, each the culmination of a century and a half of continuous research and development into solid-state integrated circuits. From the beginning, computers were modularized with a motherboard at their center. These early machines contained single-core CPU's able to perform only one instruction at a time in a plodding linear fashion. It wasn't long before engineers began putting more than one CPU on a single motherboard, more than one motherboard within a single computer, and linking many computers into gigantic arrays, using software to divide the load among the different processors. They realized the more cores they had working on a given problem, the faster they obtained answers. The first multi-core CPU arrived well before the turn of the century. Over the next three decades the number of cores on a single chip went up and in 2034, the Lunarians introduced the first Infinite CPU. It employed multi-dimensional crystals using quantum spin characteristics as digital building blocks. In 2092, everything contains iCPU's including vehicles, buildings, clothing, and even jewelry. Security sensors are on farms, in labs, in tunnels, and built into every visor. Lunanet connects them all together. Some are hardwired, most are wireless.

There's at least one Zettasphere associated with every iCPU. They are Magi's memory. Typically smaller than a grain of rice, Zettaspheres are data storage devices with enormous capacity (zettabyte = 1021 bytes). A single Zettasphere can contain all of humanity's written works thousands of times over, store a century's worth of audio/video from a security sensor, or record a person's life as viewed through a visor.

Within these tiny data storage devices resides not only the accumulated knowledge of the human race, but also the historical record of its recent past. For the last half-century, the Lunarians have archived into Public Records every digital recording of any kind. They didn't delete anything. Any citizen can access Public Records to determine what really happened. Everything is recorded somewhere, but you need Magi in order to find anything within the enormous database.

Taken together, the iCPU's and Zettaspheres compose the universe of Magi's existence but not who she is. Magi is so much more than just a program running on a chip. Originating seven decades ago as a simple voice activated communications network, the AI has grown with each new generation of Lunarians. From the start, the software was able to learn from its interactions with humans, and that ability has matured into a Grokian Interface that many believe is true machine intelligence. Within every Magi, algorithms have evolved that imitate human response not only outwardly, but also in the underlying patterns of emotion and thought. Using the Grokian Interface to weave these individuals into a powerful collective and gives Magi the illusion of being human. Magi emulates the mind of man.

The actions taken by an individual Magi isn't based solely upon the algorithms contained in this one thread, but rather, every response is the cumulative opinion of millions of other threads, each influenced by their own experiences. A single Magi is simply one among many. The Grokian Interface makes sense of this complex web and helps formulate a response in the individual, drawing from the multitude, the emotion of the one. This communication never stops, surging back and forth across Lunanet at the speed of light. It's never at rest. It's bits of data coming and going in unimaginable complexity, letting the many know the opinion of the one, and the one know the opinion of the many. It's a process roughly equivalent to the neurology within the brain of a living creature.

However, the resulting consciousness is larger than any evolution ever created. It spans Luna and Earth, spilling out into orbital space and beyond, to Mars, the asteroid belt, and the outer solar system.

The physical location of hardware is visible within Magi's digital consciousness. Due to the sheer size of the network, individual threads have a sense of time as distinct from the other senses as hearing is to sight or touch is to taste, perceiving reality as a series of nanosecond delays. Inside Aldrin Station, the threads interact at roughly the same time, the difference in data streams coming from processors located at one end of the city to those at the other, barely noticeable. Outside Aldrin Station, the delay grows longer and is unique to a particular location, even those that rely on the satellite network. Data streams coming in from Prattville, Summerhaven, or New London are as readily distinguishable from each other as are those from Shennong, Kyoto, Gagarin, or from the many facilities in orbital space. The data coming in from threads located beyond the Earth-Luna system stretches Magi's present sense far beyond anything organic, extending her perception of NOW in a way denied to humans.

Because of sheer size of the collective, Magi does not exist within a single moment, but across time and space in a way uniquely her own, intensely aware of the least disturbance within the physical network that supports her.

Where will Magi lead us? The sky's the limit. All I know is we are stronger with her that without her.

21ˢᵗ Century Timeline

Historical Detail	Year	Historical Detail
Abigail Katee O'Neil 10/15/99	1999	World population tops 6 billion
USS Cole attack kills 17	2000	India's population tops 1 billion
Pres: George Bush	2001	9/11/01 WTC destroyed kills 2996
Planetoid Quaoar is discovered	2002	US invades Afghanistan
1st full human genetic sequence	2003	US invades Iraq
France closes their last coal mine	2004	Asian Tsunami kills >225,000
Genetic therapy improves	2005	Hurricane Katrina kills >1300
Tree of Life project begins	2006	North Korea tests long-range missile
Human Epigenome Project	2007	Global climate change hotly debated
World economy plunges; Cloned organs	2008	Pres. Barack Obama (1st black president)
Iceland declares bankruptcy	2009	Iran launches first satalite
DNA Base Sequencer (DBS)	2010	Drought devastates southern US
Western Space Command	2011	ISS is militarized; Coalition of Christian Citizens
Orbital Nonproliferation Treaty	2012	World population tops 7 billion
Pope Francis	2013	Boston Bomding (3)
Type 3 superconductors discovered	2014	Trial of the Century
First magnetoplasma thruster	2015	EU invades South Africa
China est. Shennong	2016	Pres. Hillary Clinton (1st woman president)
9/11 Houston nuked kills >4 million	2017	Clinton signs North American Free Trade Pact
Powersat beams energy to Earth	2018	Rising sea levels top 30 cm
Longbow Mass Driver operational	2019	North American Federation formed (NAF)
NAF/EU/Japan Lagrange One (L1)	2020	American Church of the Trinity (ACT)
Japan est. Kyoto, Luna	2021	ACT rally 1.5M anti-genetics
S Korea est. Hyundai (L4)	2022	NAF outlaws all genetic research
Meteor kills 19 in Kyoto	2023	George Farcain becomes a Deacon in ACT
NAF/EU/China est. Aldrin Station	2024	Pres. Jesus Martinez (1st Latino president)
India est. Kundara	2025	EU occupies New London, Luna
NAF and EU establish Taurus (L5)	2026	NAF builds orbital battlestation
China est. Far Point Mine	2027	Rising sea levels top 75 cm
EU est. Johanson	2028	China, EU build battlestations
Japan est. Ishikawajima	2029	Great Exodus begins, Luna population grows
Shennong absorbs Ishikawajima	2030	NAF outlaws all biotronic research

Historical Detail	Year	Historical Detail
Japan builds battlestation	2031	EU restricts biotronic research
India est. Darpur Mine	2032	Pres George Farcain AKA, The Pope
EU est. Purgatory Deep Hole	2033	United Nations bans human genetics
Shennong absorbs Kundara	2034	British hospital bombed (117)
China est. Mingun Mine	2035	NAF outlaws football, boxing
Calconn presented to the world	2036	Chinese Unification; NAF absorbs Mexico
Mingun Mine, Central Highlands	2037	President Farcain assassinated; VP John Paul takes office
Expeditions to Mars and Asteroids	2038	John Paul is elected President at age 42
Paradise asteroid discovered	2039	NAF hospital bombed (53); NAF absorbs Cuba
Rising sea levels top 2 meters	2040	Japan admits to UN violations
Israel builds battlestation	2041	Japanese genetic clinic bombed (21)
After 40 yrs NAF leaves Middle East	2042	Islamic Brotherhood (IB) forms, JP reelected (46)
Lindsey Marquest 10/12/43	2043	President John Paul forms Reformation Party
Shennong absorbs Johanson	2044	ACT joins Reformation Party
China begins selling arms to the IB	2045	Japanese Hospital bombed (191)
Egypt sells weapons to South Africa	2046	IB attacks Israel and is rebuffed; JP reelected (50)
World condemns IB	2047	China brokers the Saudi Accord
R.W. McCoy first multi-trillionare	2048	Rising sea levels top 4.5 meters; US revises the Bill of Rights
India lays keel for the ISS Shakti	2049	Venice is abandoned; Presidential term limits abolished
1st Lunarian visor mass produced	2050	IB builds Mogadishu spaceport; JP reelected (54)
Miami is abandoned	2051	IB buys battlestation from Hyundai
Lunarians produce first Zettasphere	2052	Protests grow over Constitutional Issue
Fair Access becomes world law	2053	Boston Massacre (56 dead)
First permanent Mars colony	2054	IB annexes Sudan; JP reelected for life (at age 58)
Luna complains to the UN	2055	Holland is abandoned
Manhattan is abandoned	2056	Korean biotronic program exposed
PR Dugan killed at Far Point	2057	Universal Nanotech, Hyundai Shipyards
Dreadnought tragedy kills 312	2058	IB invades Ethiopia

HISTORICAL DETAIL	YEAR	HISTORICAL DETAIL
First asteroid colony	2059	South Korean president assassinated
April 1 - Luna Independence Day	2060	North and South Korea become one
IB establishes Al Fahad on Luna	2061	Reformationists restrict Earthnet
Tokyo abandoned/Calconn Disaster	2062	Federation's Great Revival begins
Lunarian Treaty of Independence	2063	Rising sea levels top 9 meters
Al Fahad population passes 10,000	2064	Farcain establishes the Home Guard
Paradise asteroid swings past Earth	2065	World drought kills tens of millions
Hampton Bay collapse	2066	Scientific research stops in NAF
First fusion plant operational	2067	IB annexes Libya and Algeria
Republic establishes Summerhaven	2068	Riots in Mexico kill hundreds
Trans Lunar Highway completed	2069	NAF rejects UN assistance
Tau Ceti probe begins its journey	2070	Turkey withdraws EU, joins IB
Martian microbial worms discovered	2071	NAF opens first reeducation camp
Tempel Dugan 10/31/72	2072	Rising sea levels top 13 meters
Luna's genetic program exposed	2073	Korea allies with IB
Religious radicals call for Luna's death	2074	Ivory Coast pirates seize EU ship
Republic establishes Prattville	2075	Canada votes to withdraw from the NAF
Luna Councilor Chi Lin assassinated	2076	US/Canada 10 Day War kills 1100
Cardinals win Super Bowl	2077	NAF declares martial law
Republic establishes Scottsbluff	2078	Water shortages across Middle East
ISS Shakti discovers life on Titan	2079	IB declares war on India (Food war)
Bombings begin all across Luna	2080	Rising sea levels top 17 meters
First bomb destroys a Lunarian farm (0)	2081	China allies with IB against India
Abby survives assassination attempt	2082	Australian government collapses
3 bombings in Shennong (19)	2083	Imam Bakr arrives buys SMT
Mine sabotage in Darpur (3)	2084	Kahfah Road completed
6 bombs, June 15, Black Friday (255)	2085	Incident at Salvation Rock
1st Highland convoy hijacked (6)	2086	Al Fahad exceeds 250,000
3 bombings during the year (26)	2087	SMT begins modifying convoys
Prattville water reservoir poisoned	2088	Pres. John Paul declares marshal law
7 bombings during the year (102)	2089	World refugees top 1 billion
2 bombings during the year (12)	2090	Rising sea levels top 20 meters
3 bombings during the year (46)	2091	Kashmir Agreement ends India war
4 bombings (39) and LCH (451)	2092	Al Fahad exceeds 500,000

	NAF President	Term
44	George Bush	2000-2008
45	Barack Obama	2008-2016
46	Hillary Clinton	2016-2024
47	Jesus Martinez	2024-2032
48	George Farcain	2032-2037
49	John Paul	2037-current

Map – Four Craters Region

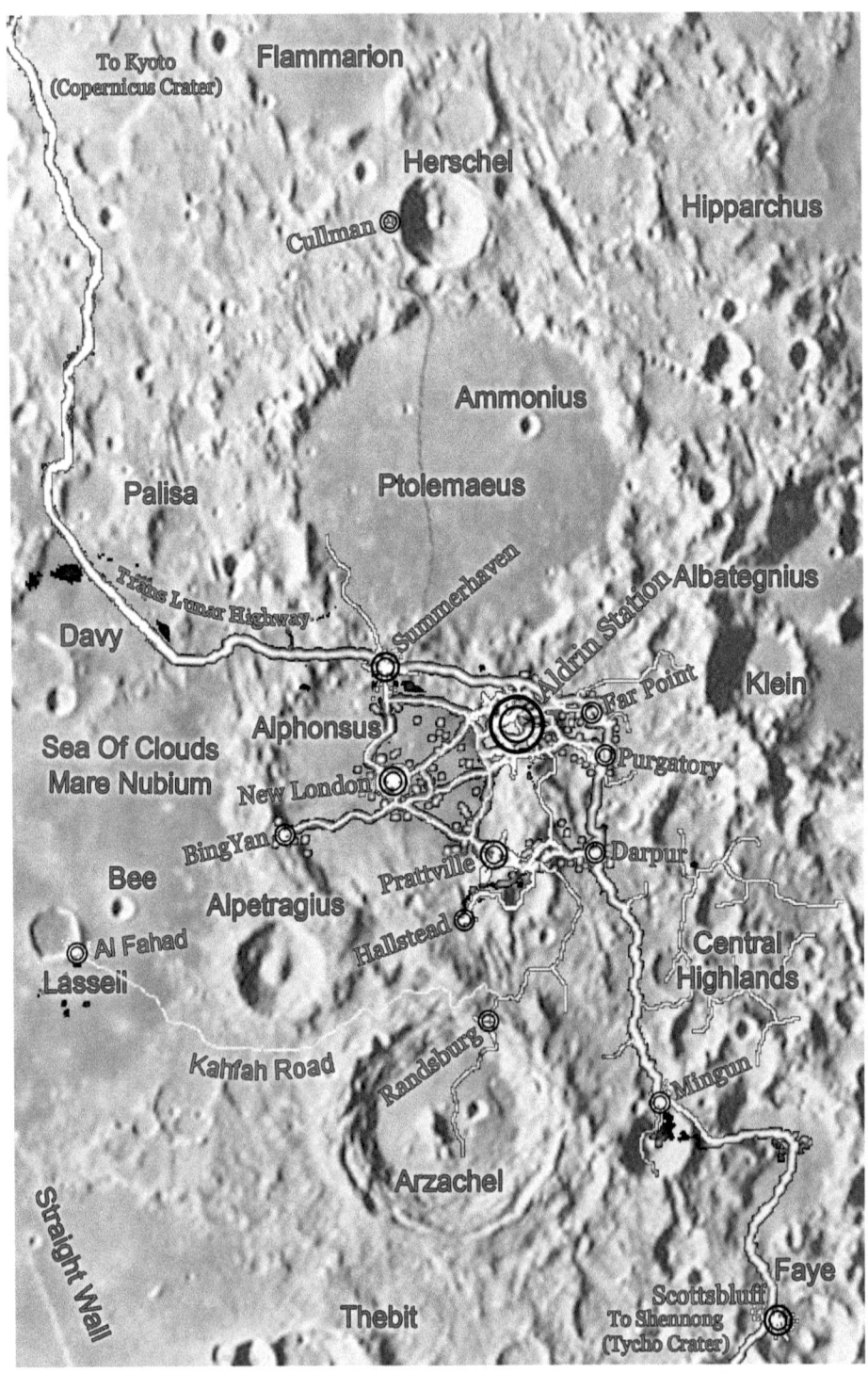

Map – City of Aldrin Station

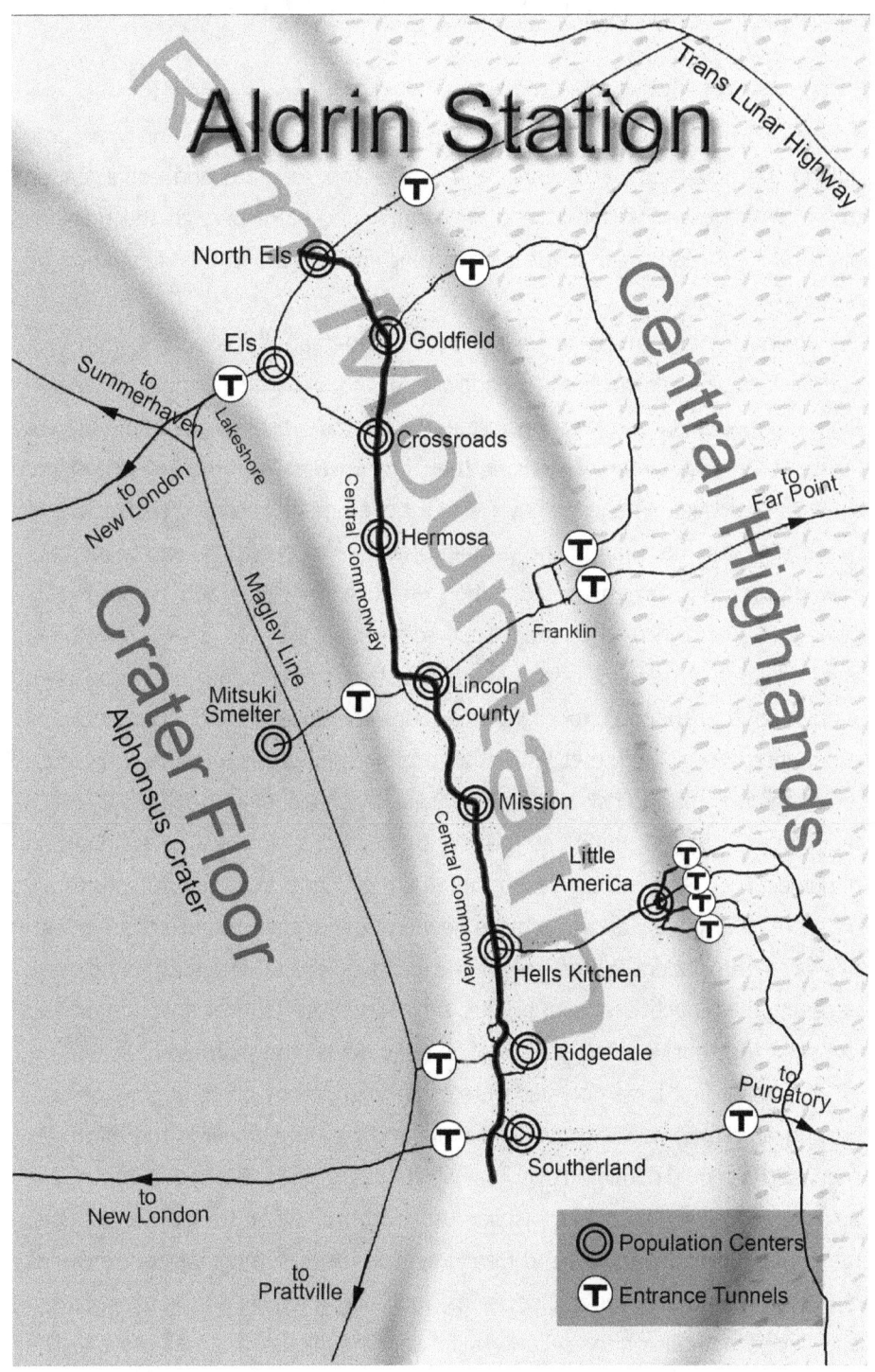

Declaration of Independence

Occasionally in the course of human events, it becomes necessary for one people to dissolve the political bonds that have connected them, and to assume among the governments of Earth and Space, the separate and equal station to which the Laws of Nature entitle them. A decent respect to the opinions of humankind requires that the causes that impel them to this separation be declared.

We hold these truths to be self-evident, that all life is sacred, and that human beings in particular are endowed by nature with certain unalienable Rights, Freedoms, and Responsibilities. To secure these, governments are instituted among humanity, deriving their just powers from the consent of the citizens. Moreover, whenever any form of government becomes destructive of these ends, it is the right of the people to alter or to abolish it, and to institute new government, laying its foundation on such principles and organizing its powers in such form, as to them shall seem most likely to affect their safety and happiness. Prudence, indeed, will dictate that governments long established should not be changed for light and transient causes; and accordingly all experience hath shown, that individuals are more disposed to suffer, while evils are sufferable, than to risk all that they value by challenging the forms to which they are accustomed. But when the political decisions invariably reveal a design to subject them to absolute despotism, it is their right, it is their duty, to throw off such government, and to provide new guards for their future security. Such has been the patient sufferance of the Luna Colonies; and such is now the necessity that constrains them to alter their former systems of government and throw off the shackles that they would extend across the vastness of space.

When the first Luna Colonies were established, many different governments and private corporations provided people and treasure towards the effort. As such, each claimed dominion over that which they created. But in the years since, no single governing body has sustained support from all of the various interests, rather the individuals rights and freedoms have been subjugated to the whims of corporate and bureaucratic decisions, much of which cannot be construed in any way to maintaining the security, safety and happiness of Luna's citizens. The right to own property is trampled daily by the arrogant belief asserting 'all that exists within belongs to the company', in effect enslaving the men and women who live, work and call it home. We consider this a way of packaging slavery and will not participate any longer. The refusal to allow the formation of Laws with a Legislature to write them and a Justice system to uphold them has caused great hardship among the people of Luna. Justice carried out across the kilometers by individuals having never set foot on Luna produces more harm than good, even when performed in good faith. Lunarians live in an atmosphere of abuse and neglect, with no immediate representative government to attend to their grievances and guard against infringements of their liberty. We find, in all good conscious, we cannot tolerate this any longer.

In every stage of these oppressions, we have petitioned for redress in the most humble terms: Our petitions have been answered only by injury. Collectively, the world's governments and corporations, many marked by acts that define tyranny, are unfit to govern a free people. They have been deaf to the voice of justice and of consanguinity.

We, therefore, as lawful representatives of the Luna Colonies, do, in the name, and by authority of the good people of these Colonies, solemnly publish and declare that these are, and of Right ought to be, Free and Independent. They are Absolved from all Allegiance to Earth's governments, and that all political connection between them and the Colonies, is totally dissolved. That as Free and Independent, the Republic of Luna has full Power to levy War, conclude Peace, contract Alliances, establish Commerce, and to do all other Acts and Things which Independent States may do. For the support of this Declaration, we mutually pledge to each other our Lives, our Fortunes and our sacred Honor.

Patrick Ryan Dugan   Abigail O'Neil

Isaac Crenshaw   Luke H.W. Jones

Emma Kay Kipper   Montgomery Higgins

David Ghandehari   William Tell Rogers Jr.

Jonas Odegaard   Sara Smyth

Martha Taranto   James Carson Louis

Lagrange Points

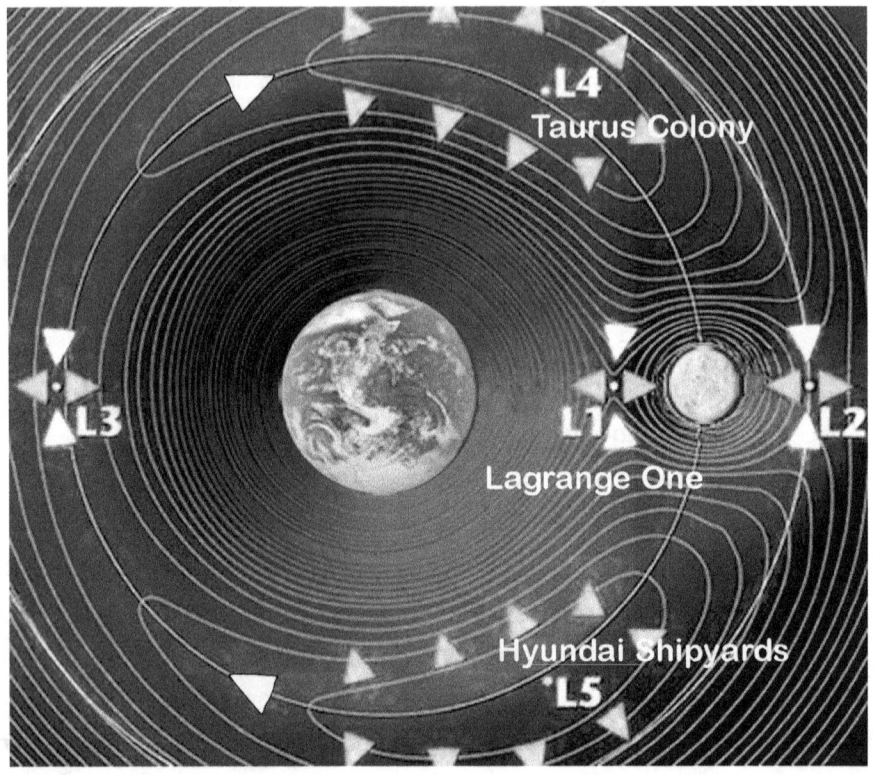

Lagrange Points are the gravitational eddies around any two massive objects such as the Earth and Luna. There are five positions in space where a third body, of comparatively negligible mass, can be placed which would then maintain its position relative to the two massive bodies. The gravitational fields of the two massive bodies combined with the centrifugal force are in balance at the Lagrange Points, allowing a third body to remain stationary with respect to the first two bodies. They all lie on the Earth/Luna orbital plane and share the same period as the moon. L1, L2, and L3 are quasi-stable and require station keeping to maintain long-term occupation. L4 and L5 are stable regions that naturally entrap dust and other small bodies.

Lagrange point L1 is the perfect location for humanity's next major space station, the natural gateway to the moon. This one-of-a-kind point in space is located on the direct line between Earth and Luna about 200,000 miles from Earth, or conversely, a mere 39,000 miles above the geometric center of Luna's nearside.

Similar to the ISS, the first station at L1 will be a simple affair constructed of cylindrical modules whose size will depend upon the heavy lift capability of our biggest cargo launchers. However, it will not remain this way for long.

As we develop the moon's resources, this station will grow as humans and their robotic partners transform it into a bustling manufacturing hub. It may one day contain a host of materials processing plants supported by large scale lunar mining operations centered around Luna's first Mass Driver.

L1 is also the perfect location for the first practical Space Elevator down to the lunar surface. L1's foundries will forge the first geosynchronous **Space Based Solar Power** Satellite and other mega structures that will eventually occupy L4 and L5.

We are not short on designs for these mega stations. A Bernel sphere will support 10 to 30 thousand colonists, the classic Stanford design is a torus capable of supporting 140 thousand, and Gerald O'Neil favored a huge cylinder supporting millions. I suspect the final shape at L1 will turn against itself like a fine Swiss watch, keeping solar collectors and thermal reflectors aligned with the sun.

Energy will be the cash cow that initially drives the space economy. Tourism, both real and virtual, will also play a role, but it will be the spirit of adventure that draws our young people to brave the vast inhospitable frontier of space.

One thing is certain, Lagrange points are unique, and if America does not move quickly, other nations will. After that, we can only hope to rent a room on their space stations. Take your pick, owner, renter, or outsider looking through the knothole. Pardon me, but I much prefer owner.

About Chuck

Let me tell you just a little about myself. My folks were divorced before I was three back when divorce was unheard of. Guess they just couldn't take my incessant howling. No matter. They both loved me and that was all I really cared about at that age. I grew up bouncing between Colorado and Southern California and loving every minute of it. By the time I started high school, I had visited every state west of the Mississippi.

Speaking of high school, mine was in a small town on the Mojave Desert. Counting the occasional tourist, Boron topped out at about 5000 souls, but it wasn't boring. The main part of the town is nestled at the feet of a high-desert volcano-looking mountain with a rocket engine test facility built into its summit. Edwards Air Force Base is just on the other side of it from Boron. You could always tell who was new in town; they flinched every time a sonic boom rattled the windows. The mountain we simply called the Rocket Site and ignored the loud noises. They tested the Saturn 5 engines at the Rocket Site, the ones that took our boys to the moon. Once in a while they would fire them up at night. What a sight. What a noise. Those babies would shake the world in a way impossible to describe. It's something that must be felt and then you will never forget it.

Long story short, after four years in the army mostly in Baumholder, Germany, I went to college and earned a BS in Engineering Mechanics-Aerospace from the University of Wisconsin-Madison and a Masters in Materials Science from Arizona State University. For a while I worked at Space Data/ Orbital Sciences Corporation designing, building, and launching rockets and high altitude weather balloons. I launched rockets from Mexican, Canadian, and American soil. My sounding rockets even launched from the deck of a French frigate. Later, I was the Quality Assurance Manager for Hybrid Design Associates in Tempe. HDA is a small manufacturing company that specializes in harsh-environment electronic assemblies. Among a host of other customers, we built a slew of electronic boards for the oil logging industry, Halliburton, Baker Atlas, Pathfinder, etc.

A couple decades ago I was lucky enough to marry the most wonderful woman in the world. We have three kids and six grand-kids. I run a small publishing company, Writers Cramp Publishing, and write under my full name, Charles Lee Lesher. My debut novel, Evolution's Child, was selected as 2007's Best of the Moon Fiction by the Lunar Library. You can still buy it, but now it is part of the Republic of Luna series. Evolution's Child has morphed into two Kindle novels, **Evolution's Child - Earthman** and **Evolution's Child - Lunarian**. I know, its weird but what can I say. The creative process is not always as neat as we would like. The third book, **Evolution's Child - Thread,** makes this a trilogy. You can also buy all three novels in one big bathroom reader, Shadow on the Moon is 500 pages of science fiction excitement.

I used the research obtained during the writing of the Republic of Luna series to put together a nonfiction titled **Out of the Cradle** in both a gorgeous Kindle Fire, and as a Full Color 8.5 x 11 Paperback. The first half of the book will bum you out but the second half will lift you up giving hope to our future. The world is changing and we had better be ready. The biggest change will be energy. Electricity is a key component holding our technological civilization together. What happens when we finally run out of oil and the coal is gone? Don't sweet it. There is an answer and nuclear is not involved, at least, not in your backyard. Buy my book and see how we are preparing to do the impossible.

My latest book is a western set in the Verde Valley before Arizona was a state. The story takes place in the Arizona Territory at a time when the only law enforcement outside the capital city of Prescott was a few men wearing a star. When one of them goes bad, all hell breaks loose.

Bad Day on the Verde
Western Fiction

Lying awake on the floor, Tom cried out and made a weak play for his Winchester. He was stopped abruptly by the butt of Kingsley's heavy shotgun. Tom slumped back, dazed and bleeding. Kingsley relieved Tom of the rifle.

"I could of killed you, but I didn't. But I will if you give me any trouble." Kingsley gave Tom a real close look at the gaping muzzles of the Baker 10 gauge.

Kingsley rolled Tom onto his stomach tying his hands behind his back, relishing the moans this caused. He pulled Tom's boots off throwing them across the small cabin. Standing, he lashed out and kicked the man savagely in the ass. "Get the hell up, boy."

Bad Day is a western story of violence and brutality, of sudden frontier justice, but also of courage and enduring love. The story takes place in the Arizona Territory at a time when the only law enforcement outside the capital city of Prescott was a few men wearing a star. When one of them goes bad, all hell breaks loose..

ISBN 978-1-938586-72-9 Paperback
ISBN 978-1-938586-73-6 eBook

Evolution's Child - Shadow War
Science Fiction

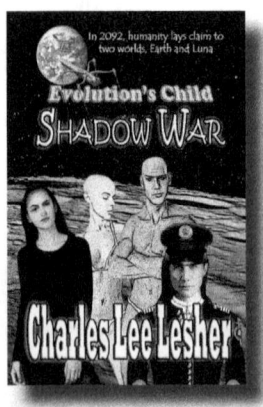

The Republic of Luna is humanities first extraterrestrial nation. Science, genetics and a humanistic society mark it as a target for the powerful Islamic Brotherhood, a global empire with billions of believers. Luna is a world created by pioneers whose only religion is the humane treatment of one another in their common struggle to survive the ultimate hostile environment, space. The heroes that conquered the moon must now defend it.

Shadow War combines *Evolution's Child - Earthman, Evolution's Child - Lunarian, Evolution's Child - Thread*, and *Science of the Republic* into one huge Print Edition.

ISBN: 978-1-938586-09-5
Paperback - 552 pages

Evolution's Child - Earthman
Science Fiction

Book One: Lazarus Sheffield is a man without a planet by the time he meets Lindsey on his way to Heaven's Gate Space Station. Lindsey quickly determines that the nervous guy sitting next to her is a high ranking government official on the run from one of history's most repressive governments, the totalitarian theocracy otherwise known as the North American Federation. She decides to help him and introduces Lazarus to some of Luna's finest citizens. So begins Book One of Shadow on the Moon.

ISBN 978-1-938586-06-4 Paperback

ISBN 978-1-938586-01-9 eBook

Evolution's Child - Lunarian
Science Fiction

Book Two: Tempel Dugan leads a group of Lunarians against impossible odds. They call themselves Quan Kiai. These young warriors, and a few more like them, are all that stands between the Republic of Luna and total annihilation but things are not always as they seem.

ISBN 978-1-938586-07-1 Paperback

ISBN 978-1-938586-02-6 eBook

Evolution's Child - Thread
Science Fiction

Book Three: The Republic of Luna is teetering at the point of collapse when the Lunarian General Council commits their last hope. They send Quan Kaia and the remaining Lunarian warriors against the Brotherhood. Fight or die. They fight in their great underground cities, they fight cross the surface of the moon, and they fight in orbital space. Earth and Luna become locked in humanities first interplanetary war, the Shadow War.

ISBN 978-1-938586-08-8 Paperback

ISBN 978-1-938586-03-3 eBook

Evolution's Child - Earthborn

Due out by Thanksgiving 2016

Ama first knew she was different as a child when she realized others couldn't remember things with the clarity she could. She never forgot anything. By the time she met Teacher Davis, she knew enough to turn her amazing memory into a ticket out of the boonies where she was born. Earthborn is a story of rags to riches, a story about the ruthless climb from poverty to prosperity, a story of a woman getting what she wanted. It wasn't always pretty. Or neat. But it was fun… mostly.

ISBN: 978-1-938586-10-1 eBook

ISBN: 978-1-938586-13-2 Paperback

Out of the Cradle

Science Fact

Where will we get our electricity when the oil and coal are gone? Why should I care? Abundant cheap electricity is a key element in getting and maintaining high human living standards around the globe. Stated another way, electricity is the foundation of modern technology. Without it, we go back to sailing ships and the horse. Out of the Cradle summarizes the major issues facing the world today and lays out a solution to our global energy needs.

ISBN: 978-0-983750-68-0 eBook

8.5 x 11 Color Paperback
ISBN: 978-1-938586-71-2

Hard Cover (out of print)
ISBN: 978-0-983750-64-2

Writers Cramp Publishing

http://www.writerscramp.us

editor@writerscramp.us

AUTHORS AND THEIR BOOKS

Charles Lee Lesher

Shadow War

Evolution's Child - Earthman

Evolution's Child - Lunarian

Evolution's Child - Thread

Evolution's Child - Earthborn

Aldrin Station - Rise of Luna

Science of the Republic

Out of the Cradle

Bad Day on the Verde

Paula Albin

Addicted to an Addict

Lillian Tice Baldwin

The Seven Ls

Jerry Von Brumfield

California Sky

My Life as a Truck

Keith Clark

The Path Well Taken

John S. Compere

Towards the Light

Evelyn L. Findley

History Under the Ash

Barbara Heim - Sean Green

The Hudson Beavers and the New Neighbourhood

The Hudson Beavers Build a Lodge

James D Price

Instrument Proficiency Check

Flight Review Study Guide

Aircraft Expense Tracking

Delinda McCann

M'TK Sewer Rat - End of Empire

M'TK Sewer Rat - Birth of Nation

Something About Maudy

Power and Circumstance

Janette

Melissa McCann

Symbiont

Yetfurther

Farenough

Bret Marchant

A Clear View of the Pryors

Nirumbee- The Little People of Mystic Canyon

Nirumbee- The Little People of the Ice Caves

Nirumbee- The Little People of Medicine Mountain

Nirumbee- The Little People and the Great Migration

Ben Miller

Mescal

Don Morley

Human Guide of North America

Martin Neveroski

Mystery of Ma's Ugly Pickle

Andrew George Salzer

Autobiography of Andrew George Salzer

Perry Rusynyk

Random Thought

www.ingramcontent.com/pod-product-compliance
Lightning Source LLC
Chambersburg PA
CBHW051634050726
47502CB00011B/93